The universe  with light that blasted in through the viewport, illuminating every nook and cranny of the *Sholto*'s interior in blinding bright crimson. Jamie covered his eyes and gritted his teeth, bracing himself for whatever else might happen. But nothing else did. *Not so bad this time,* he told himself. *Just a little light show.* As long as the light didn't leave them dazzled or blinded—and as long as there wasn't some other invisible, nastier sort of radiation along for the ride—they ought to be all right.

There was nothing left to do but wait it out. It was almost impossible to predict how much subjective time a transit-jump would take, but usually it was no more than a few seconds, or a minute.

It was only after about twenty seconds that Jamie sensed the vibration, the rhythmic shudder, that seemed to be coursing through the ship, fading out, and then reappearing, a little more powerful each time, each pulse coming faster and with greater intensity. The structure of the ship began to creak and moan. The interval between periods of vibration shrank until the shaking was nonstop. The noise was getting worse as well.

"Hannah!" Jamie called out.

"I have no idea!" Hannah yelled back, answering the question Jamie was about to ask.

They had gotten through the transit-jump. But the ship was out of control.

BSI STARSIDE

Death Sentence

A NOVEL BY

Roger MacBride Allen

BANTAM • SPECTRA

BSI: STARSIDE: DEATH SENTENCE
A Bantam Spectra Book / June 2007

Published by
Bantam Dell
A Division of Random House, Inc.
New York, New York

Bantam Books, the rooster colophon, Spectra, and the portrayal of a
boxed "s" are trademarks of Random House, Inc.

ISBN: 978-0-553-58727-2

Printed in the United States of America
Published simultaneously in Canada

www.bantamdell.com

OPM 10 9 8 7 6 5 4 3 2 1

To Eleanor Wood and Lucienne Diver, for generous aid and support above and beyond the call of duty—and then some.

ACKNOWLEDGMENTS

As always, I would like to thank my wife, Eleanore Fox. Her endless support, brutally honest editing, and infinite patience have made all the books I have written since I first met her far better than they otherwise would be.

Thanks as well to Eleanor Wood and Lucienne Diver, who have had to put up with a lot, and who have done so with grace and courtesy. This book is dedicated to them, and for whatever that small honor is worth, it is long overdue. I am as lucky in my professional relationships as I am in my domestic ones.

Speaking of domestic entanglements, thanks of a sort are also due to my sons, Matthew and James— if not for help with the book, then at least for their efforts to prevent it from being written, and thus for helping to keep me alert during the process. I learned long ago never to arrange the furniture in my office so that my back was to the door. Even so, they manage, somehow, to sneak up on me with alarming regularity. The word "alarming" is apropos; I think they like to see how high I jump.

I am, to put it mildly, ambivalent about Matthew's

habit of resting his chin on my shoulder and literally breathing down my neck, reading the book in the precise moment that I am writing it. If he ever changes his mind about being an inventor, that boy's got a great future as an editor.

Roger MacBride Allen
April, 2006
Takoma Park, Maryland

ONE
DEATH IN LIFE

The last of the alien boarding party struggled up the ladder, through the nose hatch into the air lock, and departed the *Irene Adler*. The hatch boomed shut, there was the whir and thud of the air lock, and a faint shudder went through the tiny vehicle as the far larger xeno ship undocked from the *Adler*. Trip Wilcox leaned back against an equipment locker and breathed a weary sigh of relief. The xenos hadn't found what they were looking for. He had won—this round, at least. But he had no desire to celebrate. He was too close to the end for that. The end of the mission, the end of the voyage—and the end of his life.

Better, though, to go out with a win—perhaps a very big win indeed. Bad as things were, facing his own end would be a thousand times more bitter if he had to die knowing that he had lost, knowing that his own personal end was a mere drop in the ocean of defeat, one death among countless billions, perhaps even the death of all humans everywhere.

He felt ridiculous, thinking of things in those terms, but Special Agent Trevor Wilcox III had been trained to focus on facts, not feelings. And as a matter of cold hard fact, he knew that threat was real. If his own death was some part of the cost of preventing *that* disaster, then he could have no regrets at all about the exchange.

He was going to die alone, on this ship. There could be no doubt of it. But that was of little consequence compared to the threat of universal death.

BSI Special Agent Trevor Wilcox III cut the ship's interior gravity field to seventy-five percent, waited for the artificial grav to fade, and moved slowly upward, hand over hand, to the *Adler*'s cramped and tiny flight deck. He eased himself down in the pilot's chair, strapped himself in, and watched as the alien craft backed away from the *Adler*. He stared at the other ship, marveling at her sheer size. It was a miracle that she had bothered to dock at all. That ship was a whale to the *Adler*'s guppy. It could have swallowed him whole.

He reminded himself of the good news: They had not found what they were looking for. Keeping *this* pack of xenos from finding the decrypt key was only part of the job.

He had to *keep* them from finding it if they came back for another try. He had to keep the key safe from any other xenos who might come looking for it. He had to make sure his ship got home, that the key *was* delivered, and that his fellow humans—preferably his fellow BSI agents—*would* be able to find the key after it had remained hidden from all other eyes.

He had to find a way to do all that, and to make all the arrangements, in the briefest possible amount of time. And he had to make it all work, reliably, after he was dead.

As best he could figure, he had about a week left.

Think, Trip told himself. *Think while your mind is still clear and you still have the strength left to carry out a plan. There's no hope left for you, but the only hope left for everyone else is that you can sit down, right now, and do the very best thinking of your life.*

He stared out the viewport at the gleaming expanse of cold and distant stars—and at the giant alien spacecraft that was already turning—either for home, or to bring her weapons to bear on the *Irene Adler.*

It was with a distinct sense of relief that he saw the big ship not merely turn, but depart, making no further attempt to interfere with him. It was likely only a temporary respite.

You've got a chance to come up with a plan, he told himself. *Now is the time to do it.*

Because it was the only time he had left.

TWO

FACTS IN RUMOR

Rumors weren't supposed to circulate in a place like BSI Orbital HQ, but they did. Even though the agents, technicians, and support personnel of the Bureau of Special Investigations were endlessly trained and indoctrinated to seek the cold, hard, verifiable facts and nothing but the facts, human nature was what it was.

Senior Special Agent Hannah Wolfson heard three different versions of the latest bit of instant folklore before she was even cleared through security. Another story was urged upon her before she could cross the Bullpen or check in with her partner, Jamie Mendez.

"Morning, Jamie," she said, ducking her head into his cubicle. "Heard the latest?"

Jamie swiveled around in his chair to face her and grinned. "Which latest?" He raised his hand and started counting on his fingers. "That they've pulled in a derelict ship, that they're about to, that there were three dead aboard, that it was mysteriously completely empty, that it's one of ours, that it's a Trojan Horse ship, a trap set by the Kendari, or that they spotted a ship and tracked it with every kind of scanner and detection system we've got—but that it vanished before a recovery ship could be launched?"

She was not surprised to learn that Jamie had already heard all four of her versions, plus two other variants. "Well, there's all that, of course—but I can shoot down about half of those already, unless I'm *really* off course. It was a real ship, it wasn't empty, and it didn't vanish—and it probably wasn't a Trojan."

"How do you get all that?"

"Because on my way in I saw Doc Vogel coming into the Bullpen from the direction of the medical labs, looking more annoyed than usual—and he just breezed straight into the Commandant's office."

Jamie nodded. "Gotcha. Commander Kelly wouldn't call in the chief medical officer to report on a ship that wasn't there or had no one on board. And if anyone thought the ship was a Kendari plant, it would be counterintell taking the lead, and not the med department."

"Which begs the question—exactly what sort of case is it where med *does* take the lead?"

Both of their commlinks went off simultaneously. Hannah managed to pull hers out and read the message a half heartbeat ahead of Jamie. "You just get called to Secure Conference Room Two?"

Jamie nodded. "I think we're about to get past the rumors."

* * *

Logically speaking, there should have been no need for secure conference rooms at all. BSI Orbital HQ was a secure location, isolated from all the other facilities aboard the massive Center Transit Station. Center Transit Station was in free orbit, and thus effectively isolated from the planet Center and the governmental offices there. And, of course, the whole point of the planet Center serving as UniGov's de facto capital was that it was out on the edge, so to speak, well away from Earth and the Solar System.

But that was the same sort of logic that dictated there should have been no rumors floating around BSI HQ. There were times when there was no sense in taking chances. So BSI had secure conference rooms, even if no one much liked them.

SCR-2 was cramped and stuffy. It was in essence a room inside a bank vault, barely large enough for a table with six chairs around it. It had to be kept fully isolated and shielded from the rest of BSI Orbital HQ and its ventilation and electrical systems were prone to misbehaving.

Jamie and Hannah went through the security scanners and into the room. At least the lights seemed to be working properly at the moment, though the ventilators were making their usual intermittent low grinding noises. They sat down at the back of the room. Jamie was not particularly surprised to see Commander Kelly and Dr. Vogel enter a moment or two later.

"Good morning to both of you," Commander Kelly said as she sat down. "Doctor, have a seat and let's get started."

Dr. Vogel set his datapad on the table as he sat down, peering distractedly at the screen. He frowned and reached for the power button. When the screen went dark, he looked around, as if he were only then fully aware of his surroundings. "Hmmph. This place. Do we have to be doing our talking in this damned tomb?"

Kelly looked at him with a half-amused, half-annoyed smile. "Yes," she said, and left it at that. She turned to the door controls, punched in a series of commands and clearance codes, then watched as the conference room's door swung inward and boomed shut.

Jamie swallowed as his ears popped. The ventilation system was up to its old tricks, forcing the air pressure in the conference room to rise the moment the door was sealed.

Kelly took her own seat with her back to the door and nodded to the two agents. "We've got an intriguing one for you," she said. "One you might take a personal interest in, Agent Mendez."

"How so, ma'am?"

"We finally found your predecessor. Trevor Wilcox. Or, more accurately, he found us."

"Too late to do him any good, unfortunately," Vogel added. "We've changed his status from 'missing and presumed dead' to plain ordinary 'dead.' "

Jamie felt his stomach do a backflip or two. It was one of the things that everybody thought about, but no one discussed, not if they could help it. An agent quit or retired or—more often than not—died. A new agent would be assigned, come into the Bullpen, and literally sit down at his or her predecessor's desk. Sometimes, as in Jamie's case, the new agent was assigned the dead agent's caseload, and even his living quarters and duty schedule.

Jamie had never met Trip Wilcox or known anything about him—but even so, he found himself, in effect, living Wilcox's life—sleeping in his bed, cooking in his kitchen, working in his cubicle, closing out the cases Wilcox had left unfinished. Sometimes it had been hard to tell if Wilcox were the ghost haunting him—or if he were the ghost haunting Wilcox, moving in the places he had been, doing the things he had done.

It had taken months before some people had stopped thinking of him as the kid in Wilcox's cubicle, before the work he did and the places he lived and worked had truly become *his.* Even so, it still happened that some busy, distracted agent would come bustling up to Jamie's cubicle, expecting to find Wilcox—and be plainly disconcerted to see Special Agent James Mendez there instead.

Would knowing Wilcox was well and truly dead put an end to all that—or merely remind everyone once again that Jamie was living in Wilcox's life?

"He was on this ship the rumor mill's been talking about?" Hannah asked.

Commander Kelly glanced at Vogel, grunted, and shook her head. "Word moves around fast, considering how security-conscious we're all supposed to be—but yes, Wilcox was aboard the BSI ship recovered in the outer reaches of Center's star system about a week ago. He'd plainly been dead for some time."

Kelly stared at her hands for a moment. "Wilcox was doing what we thought was a simple courier job. He was supposed to collect a document from the Metrannans that was to be handed directly over to the BSI Diplomatic Liaison Office. We have recovered the document from his ship's computer—at least we think we have. It's in the form of a highly encrypted data file—so encrypted we can't tell for sure if it's the file we want. The document is useless without the accompanying decryption key—and it might still be useless even so, without some sort of additional explanation that could provide a context."

"What is the document?" Jamie asked.

"We *think* it's some sort of complex technical report," said Kelly, "or else maybe some sort of political information pertaining to Metrannan relations with another species—and it is known that the Metrannans have been in talks with the Kendari on a few matters. BSI-DLO *claims* to know nothing more about the document, but they gave it the priority designation War-Starter—and, of course, we have to bear in mind that BSI-DLO doesn't always tell us everything."

"War-Starter?" Jamie asked. "I don't think I know that designation."

"Trust me—you don't *want* to know it," Kelly said bluntly. "It means what it sounds like. If the matter in question is handled badly, if things go the wrong way—the end result is on the scale of an interstellar, interspecies war. Not necessarily a war that directly involves humans, and maybe not a war at all—but something that could be just as violent and destabilizing. An uprising. A plague. Something that could do the same amount of damage as a major war."

"I read xeno-history a lot," Vogel said thoughtfully. "Often—not always, but often—in an interspecies war like that, at least one species is rendered extinct. Gone. Even if humanity wasn't directly involved in such a war, lots of humans could get hurt or killed, you bet."

"You're making us feel better and better," Hannah said.

"We're not planning to stop until you feel as good as we do," Kelly replied. "Let me back up and start over a little closer to the beginning. Plan A had been for Wilcox to be double-blind."

"Sounds like a sensible precaution for something designated War-Starter," said Jamie. Double-blind was BSI slang, the term borrowed from the scientific community, but with an entirely different meaning. A double-blind courier didn't know what he or she was carrying before *or* after the pickup.

"Very sensible," Kelly agreed. "But the BSI-DLO people didn't see it that way. They insisted on a single-blind pickup. They wanted Wilcox to get briefed at the other end so he'd know what he was carrying on the way back—and be able to tell them about it when he got home."

"Do you think he was killed because of that?" Hannah asked. "The man who knew too much?"

"We haven't even said that he was killed," Kelly said. "Just that he died."

"All right, then—*was* he killed?"

"It is a strange case," Vogel said sadly. "I believe so. No. That is not strong enough. I *know* so. It is a question of *proving* he was killed, demonstrating it. The cause of death is so, well, *peculiar*, that I cannot believe it was an accident or some strange 'natural' cause. It was murder—but we don't know how. Or why. But we will come to that, as well."

"In any event," Kelly went on, "we know for certain that Wilcox reached Metran, received the document and the decryption key, got his briefing, reboarded his ship, and headed for home. Judging from what we've learned so far of what was found aboard ship, he realized sometime after he was headed for home that he was slowly dying. He probably realized he wouldn't live long enough to get home. It also seems that his ship rendezvoused with another vessel while he was still alive and that outsiders came aboard his ship. Whether they were hostile or friendly, or why they came aboard, we don't know."

"Did these outsiders come aboard before or after he realized he was sick?" Jamie asked. "Could they have poisoned him or infected him in some way?"

"We don't know," Kelly replied, stony-faced.

"Wait a moment," Hannah said. "Wilcox went out before Agent Mendez was assigned to the Bullpen, something like six months ago. Mendez was assigned to replace him. When did all this happen?"

"You're right. Wilcox went out just over six months ago. The job should have taken about two or three weeks, all told. He arrived at Metran on schedule and departed three days later. We think he was boarded about three days out from Metran and died about two weeks after that—but that he was unconscious, or at least not fully competent, for some time before his death. We're basing this on very sketchy information and guesses, and dealing with some contradictions.

"He managed to configure the ship to do the jump from Metran's star system to the Center System before he died. He didn't rig any sort of beacon that would let us know to come get him. We don't know if that was deliberate or not. He might have figured that we'd find him sooner or later even with no beacon but that any bad guys wouldn't."

"Let me guess," said Hannah. "Since we don't

even know if there *were* any bad guys, you don't have much in the way of theories about who the theoretical bad guys might be. Right?"

"Got it in one," Kelly agreed. "Let me start at the beginning and go from there, and tell you what we know," Kelly said. "A rough sequence of events. Wilcox travels to Metran. Wilcox collects the document. Wilcox leaves Metran and heads for home. During his acceleration run out of the system, he realizes that he is sick, and even that he is dying. At about the same time—it might be before or after—his ship is boarded by someone. We don't know who, or why. That happens while he is still in the Metrannan star system."

Kelly looked around the table. "Some time after he is boarded, but while he is still in the Metrannan System, and well short of the coordinates of his calculated transit-jump—he throttles back his acceleration for half a day, then cuts his engines altogether for a day, then boosts intermittently, at low power, at various headings, for another two days. I'll skip the details, but the short form is that the way he did it came right out of the BSI playbook. He followed the procedures for making it difficult or maybe even impossible for anyone to track his vehicle. Random, low-power burns, in random directions."

"Reasonable enough," said Hannah. "He had been boarded once. He was trying to hide so he wouldn't be detected again."

"Right. But the *next* part of the doctrine is to go

back to continuous boost at as high a power as you dare risk, so as to get out of the search area as fast as you can. Normal acceleration to a transit-jump for the *Sherlock*-class ships is twenty to thirty gees. Wilcox boosted the *Adler* at one-quarter gee."

Kelly tapped her fingers on the table. "Now, there are some things we tend to forget about our normal operating procedure. There's no real *need* to boost at high gee-rates, or to get to as high a final speed as we do, in order to reach a transit-jump. Your velocity has to be taken into account for the jump computations, but it's a relatively trivial calculation and a minor adjustment. You could go through a transit-jump at five kilometers an hour, or five million. It wouldn't matter.

"It's physical position that matters during a jump. We boost our ships as hard as we do, and go as fast as we do, because the transit points tend to be so far out in space, and there's no particular penalty in technical terms for getting there faster, and besides, we tend to be in a hurry.

"But high-boost, high-velocity flight paths are madly inefficient in terms of energy expenditure. We boost to a very high speed, do the transit, and then immediately start decelerating. Do the math, and you'll see that doing it that way saves us time—but not very much time, because we spend very little time at that final high velocity.

"Mostly we do it that way because there isn't any reason *not* to do it that way. The ships we've got today have so much power it's ridiculous. But our ships would still go through a transit jump moving at near-zero velocity. Which is something that Wilcox proved. The *Adler* took two *months* to reach the transit point. He was almost certainly dead by then. But he had programmed the *Adler* to make the transit-jump on autopilot—and then to use maximum thrust, twenty-plus gees, to slow the *Adler* down to practically zero, a few billion kilometers out from Center. That's a lot of energy being released very quickly, in a way that's easily detectable. UniGov Military's space defense detectors *did* detect it—but they didn't investigate immediately because they projected that it would take the *Adler* six hundred years to reach the inner system. Not exactly an immediate threat."

"Let me guess," Hannah said. "The BSI waited a couple of weeks before we reported the *Adler* as overdue. We waited another couple of weeks or a month before listing her as lost, presumed destroyed. When she *did* show up, she was months late, and on a totally different flight path than what we expected, and it took a while for anyone to think of matching up Space Defense's blip with our missing ship."

"Right. And even then our people quite correctly concluded it was only a *possible* match, even a low-probability match. Odds were it was some other ship, nothing to do with us. Worth checking, but not worth tying up any of our people for the week or two it would take to fly to the outer system, locate the blip—then confirm that it was nothing. And, of course, there was a little bureaucratic gamesmanship to it as well. Space Defense *wanted* to say it might be our ship, so we'd be the ones who had to go out and do the recovery so they wouldn't have to spend their time or effort.

"By the same token, I *didn't* want to spend more time and effort than needed, because it probably had nothing to do with us. I figured we'd find a robot freighter with a defective propulsion system or something like that. So I ordered a BSI ship to go take a look, flying on automatic, no crew. It wasn't worth tying up a larger or more capable spacecraft than necessary, so I sent the *Bartholomew Sholto*, with a bunch of cameras and robotics and teleoperator systems on board. Once the *Sholto* got there, one of our techs back here could work the remote controls to investigate."

She frowned, leaned forward in her chair, and drummed her fingers on the table again for a moment. "Instead, we found the *Adler*. Dead. All power off, drifting. The *Sholto* docked to her, nose to nose, then used the *Sholto*'s engines to start boosting the docked-together ships back to base. The remote operators here at HQ managed to get the hatches open on both ships and sent a robotic camera into the *Adler* to look around. The first thing they found was Wilcox—dead. Very, very dead." She paused. "And that was pretty much the *last* thing they found. Or at least the last thing of any significance. But I'll come back to that.

"It took a while for the knowledge of what our team had found to percolate up from the techs flying the mission to the Bullpen, and to me. We notified BSI-DLO, and *they* notified the people who had been waiting for the document to arrive—and right now, today, I still don't know who that final 'customer' is. Things are being kept very quiet and compartmentalized. Whoever the customer is, it didn't take long for the word to come rocketing back down to us that the document *had* to be found, and found as quickly—and as quietly—as possible.

"The robotics on the *Sholto* scanned and searched every square centimeter of the *Adler*'s interior. We linked into all her data systems and searched them by remote as well. Nothing.

"As soon as we got her back here to base, and got Wilcox's remains off the ship—and did some decontamination—we sent search teams aboard as well. Nothing. And all the time, BSI-DLO has been jumping up and down, demanding we find what isn't there, and find it right away."

"We've searched the *Adler* twice, with BSI-DLO screaming at us to find the key immediately. Once via the remotes on the way in, and once here at base. We haven't found the decrypt key."

"Do you have any idea what it looks like?" Jamie asked. "Are you even sure it's there?"

"The short answers are no, and no," said Kelly. "Goes a long way to explain the problems we're having, doesn't it? Bear in mind that the key itself isn't a physical object. From everything we've been able to learn, it ought to be just a string of characters. Once it's recovered and handed over to BSI-DLO, some tech will key the characters into the appropriate computer program and the document will be magically decoded. Think of all the ways characters might be stored or written down or encoded or whatever, and then think of all the ways you might disguise or hide whatever it was that held that string of characters. It could be concealed just about anywhere, or disguised or embedded in just about anything."

"So what, exactly, do you want us to do?" asked Jamie.

"Really simple stuff," said Kelly. "Find the decryption key, find out what the document was about, find out who killed Wilcox, why they killed him—and *how* they killed him."

"I don't understand how that could be a mystery," Hannah said. "You recovered the body, right?"

"Yes, it was aboard ship."

"So you've examined it. How is it you can't tell the cause of death or whether or not it was murder?"

"Oh, yes, I can tell the cause of the death," Vogel growled. Jamie had noticed several times before that Vogel's syntax in English started to slide toward the grammar of his native German whenever he got upset. "My examination of the body told me that, and more. In fact, it was telling me far too much, more than makes sense. Wilcox had 25 years of age. He had perfect health at his last exam, ten days before he got this mission. No allergies, no bad teeth, good immune system. You name it, and that part of his body worked perfect."

He paused and glanced at his datapad. "If I wanted to be cute or didn't want to do my job the proper way, I could say he died of heart failure—but who *doesn't* die of that? Question is, what *caused* this man to have the heart failure? *Antwort*—I mean answer: BSI Special Agent Trevor Wilcox III, also known as Trev Wilcox or Trip Wilcox, male, age twenty-five, died of general systemic failure brought on by extreme old age."

"*What?*" Jamie asked.

Vogel went on, ignoring the interruption. "Old age. Everything worn out. Collapsed. All soft tissues were involved in failure. However, bones, teeth, hair, nails, that sort of thing, all showed as normal or with only slight alteration from normal state for person of his age and previous state of health. In other words, the soft tissues—skin, muscles, internal organs, and so on collapsed due to old age *before* the hard body parts had enough time to age."

The shocked silence hung there for a moment before Kelly drove it away. "However Wilcox was killed, he was killed on Metran—or at least as a result of something done to him in the Metrannan System. And we have to work on the assumption that he was killed for some reason related to his courier job—in other words, because of a document that might be a War-Starter. Dr. Vogel's full autopsy report has already been loaded aboard the data system of the *Bartholomew Sholto*, along with everything we've got on the Metrannans. You two will boost toward Metran aboard the *Sholto* this afternoon."

"But the *Sholto* is a *Sherlock*-class too, isn't it?" Jamie asked. "Aren't those single-person ships?"

Kelly looked at him with a bemused expression. "You've done your homework," she said. "You're right. The *Sherlock*-class are all single-ships."

"So why put two people in a single-seater?" Hannah asked.

"Because the *Sholto* won't be alone. She's already docked to the *Adler*, and we're going to keep them docked together. We're always short of ships, and scaring up another one would just waste time. But there are other reasons, which I'll get into in a moment," said Kelly. "Here are your orders. You'll fly the combined craft to Metran and investigate, searching for clues to where the decrypt key might be. Your cover story will be that you're trying to find out what happened to Wilcox. You'll leave the *Adler* in a distant and hidden orbit of Metran's orbit—a Pluto-class orbit ought to do it—and fly down to Metran aboard the *Sholto*. They're installing a second acceleration chair right now. It'll be a tight fit, but doable."

"Tight fit is scarcely the word for it," Hannah muttered.

"You will spend the transit time between Center and Metran searching the *Adler* and studying the data aboard her. We've searched her twice. You'll do it the third time. I think the key is aboard the *Adler*, but concealed in such a way that it is impossible to detect without an outside clue. I think that Wilcox left that clue behind on Metran. However, I could be wrong, so you'll search. If you do find anything of significance, you will abort the mission to Metran and head for home. But I'm not expecting that. We would have found anything aboard that could be found that way. I believe there will be some clue, some lead, in the Metran System, that will point you toward what we're looking for."

"What, for example?" Jamie asked.

"Tradecraft stuff," Hannah said. "If Wilcox knew or suspected that he was going to be in danger, he might have left behind some sort of lead or clue or message that would make sense to us but not to the locals."

"That's one class of possibilities," Kelly agreed. "There may be others. In any event, you'll have the *Adler* right there, near to hand, to check the leads out at once."

"Aren't we running a tremendous risk, taking the *Adler* along back to Metran when she's probably got vital data hidden on board?" Jamie asked. "She might be destroyed, or seized."

"Possibly. But if that information is there, two diligent searches did not find it. The key is, for all intents and purposes, lost already. Perhaps we could find it if we disassembled the *Adler* and had a hundred techs spend six months examining the pieces, one by one. But we don't have the hundred techs to spare, and BSI-DLO is making it very clear that they don't think we have the six months, either. If we take too long to find that key, that could be as bad as never finding it at all. We've lost months already, while the *Adler* was floating around in the outer edges of Center's stellar system. What if the crisis is just about to blow up in our faces? We don't even know what the crisis *is* yet. We need information, and we need it fast. You're taking the *Adler* with you. That's my decision—and my responsibility."

"And, bear in mind," said Vogel, "assuming the whatever-in-hell-it-is turns out to be on board the *Adler*, it's not just our people and our robots that have searched for it and not found it. The Metrannans—or whoever it was that boarded the *Adler*—have done the same. How likely is it they or we will find anything if they search again, without some sort of clue or guidance?"

Kelly nodded in agreement. "My hunch—or at least my hope—is that you'll learn something on Metran that will lead you to what is hidden—so I want you to have the *Adler* handy for reference. Time could be critical."

Kelly fell silent and stared hard at the wall over Hannah's head for a moment before looking at the agents again. "It's my further judgment that destroying whatever is aboard the *Adler* is preferable to risking the chance of its falling into the wrong hands—which very likely is the same thing as letting the Metrannans get it back—but maybe not. You are to escape to the *Sholto* and destroy the *Adler* if she is about to be captured or searched while you're aboard. We have a team aboard her right now rigging the ship to self-destruct if anyone tries to board her in your absence."

"What fun," said Hannah. "That sort of thing is always so relaxing when you're headed back to the ship and wondering if you remember the access codes correctly."

"So make sure you remember them," Kelly said. "The point is, the decrypt might still be there, on board the *Adler*. We have to find it." She looked at Hannah and Jamie. "Any questions?" she asked.

"Is the assignment physically possible for the ships?" Jamie asked. "Can the *Sholto* land and take off from Metran and do the boost back to where the *Adler* will be—and still be able to boost us back to here?" Jamie was getting the distinct impression that no one was worrying about the tactical and logistical angles enough—and it was going to be his skin and Hannah's out there.

"The short answer is no," Kelly said drily. "The long form is that we've had to do this sort of thing before. The techs on the flight deck are working on it now. We'll hang a booster off the *Sholto*. You'll use it on the boost out of Center System and dump the booster before you make your jump to Metran. You'll do a power-transfer from the *Adler* to the

Sholto, and then fly the *Sholto* in and land her—doing your best to make it look as if she flew there all the way on her own. And you'll most likely not have to ride her down to the surface. Apparently they have excellent orbital facilities.

"Your best-case scenario: The Metrannans are friendly enough—most of them, anyway—and you shouldn't have any problem refueling at that end. Worst case: You'll have to shift propulsion power between the *Adler* and the *Sholto*. If you have enough power to bring both ships home, fine. If not, you transfer every drop of propulsion power you've got back to the *Adler*, transfer to her, destroy the *Sholto*, and head for Center System. You *ought* to have enough power left to make it back to Center Station. If you don't, just get as far as the outer system, yell for help, sit tight, and we'll come get you."

"Another tight fit," said Hannah. "And one that could last a while. If it comes to that, just be sure not to take your time. We might be short of a few things besides propulsion power by then."

"There will be a fast ship on standby before you jump to Metran," Kelly promised.

"I see why we transfer from the *Sholto* to the *Adler* if we only have propulsion power enough for one ship," said Jamie. "We don't want to leave the *Adler* where the Metrannans might find her and have another crack at searching her. But why destroy the *Sholto*? It seems like a pretty high-handed way to treat government property."

"Because we do not, do not, do not want to get the Metrannans thinking about the *Adler* in any way at all," said Kelly. "We don't want them seeing two *Sherlock*-class ships at once. So far as they are concerned, the *Adler* never made it home and we know nothing about what might or might not be aboard her. We know nothing about how Wilcox died. They will see you arrive and depart on another ship. Your cover story—but it's not *just* a cover story, it's part of your assignment—is to find out who killed Wilcox, and why—and, if possible, how."

Jamie nodded. "Okay, I get it. That's why we're taking the *Sholto*—because she's the twin of the *Adler*. If they see us depart in the *Sholto*, and we're later forced to retreat to the *Adler* and destroy the *Sholto*, and they detect us flying a craft that shows exactly the same mass, size, configuration, and so on as the *Sholto*, they'll never know we've made the switch. So if comes to that, we're going to have to destroy the *Sholto* so completely that no one ever even finds the wreckage."

"Now you're getting the idea," Kelly said approvingly.

"If we can't admit to having any clues about how Wilcox died, that's going to make our investigation on Metran harder," Hannah objected.

"We all have our problems," Kelly said. "If the *Adler* has the key to a War-Starter on board, that *has* to take priority over the details of how an agent died in the line of duty—especially one who sacrificed his life in the act of *getting* that data *to* us."

"Have you made us feel as good as you do yet?" Hannah asked. "Or is there more?"

"No," said Kelly. "That's the whole brief. That's all."

"That's enough," said Jamie.

Kelly smiled. "Do you want to know the real reason the ventilation is so bad in these conference rooms? It's so we'll all have an excuse for sweating so hard in meetings like this one." She checked the time. "They'll have the *Sholto* and the *Adler* prepped for launch in three hours. Be ready by then."

THREE
HURRY AND WAIT

"Okay," said Hannah as she walked up to Jamie's cubicle. "Got your queries done?"

"Yeah, for what they're worth," said Jamie. "Sometimes a job gets easy because it's nearly impossible. We haven't the faintest idea what Wilcox was carrying, or anything else about the case. What was I supposed to ask?"

"Point taken. So what did you do?"

"I queried for all data on Metrannans and the planet Metran, a full bio and service record of Wilcox, a copy of his mission briefing, Vogel's autopsy of Wilcox, plans of the *Irene Adler*, and all logs and records of the ship."

Hannah grinned. "Great minds thinking alike, I guess. I went for all that as well—plus survey information on whatever conflicts the Metrannans have been involved with in the last thousand years or so."

"I should have thought of that one," Jamie said. Standard operating procedure dictated that once BSI Special Agents were summoned from the Bullpen and assigned to a case, they should expect to depart at once. Normally, the standard was an hour. Hannah and Jamie were catching a break; they had three whole hours to work with.

There was logic behind the one-hour standard. The minimum possible travel time between two planets in separate star systems was measured in days or even weeks. But practically every Bullpen case was time-critical—and the mere fact that Wilcox had been dead for months didn't change that in the least. If he had been killed trying to warn them of some danger that was months off back then, they might have mere days or hours left.

The solution to the problem, or at least the BSI doctrine meant to solve it, had been drummed into Jamie's head from the first day of training: Sit in your Bullpen cubicle and bombard the datastores with questions. Scoop up as much raw data as possible and pipe it to the ship you're going to boost out on. Then spend every waking moment available on the outbound trip digging through the gigabytes of data you had generated with your queries, trying to find the one-one-hundredth of a percent of it that would actually be of some use. It wasn't an elegant process, but it worked.

"Well, we've got what we're going to get," Hannah said. "Time to get moving. We've got some special equipment to draw for this mission."

"What kind of equipment?" Jamie asked suspiciously. There had been something in her tone of voice that warned him that the joke, whatever it was, was going to be on him.

"You'll find out soon enough."

"And you're having fun being mysterious, so it won't do me any good to ask 'soon enough' for what, will it?"

"No it won't. Come on, Special Agent Mendez. Quit your stalling and let's move."

Jamie sighed. Whatever it was, Hannah wasn't going to spill the beans until she was good and ready. "Do you ever get used to it?" he asked Hannah as he secured his cubicle, his tone of voice more serious. "Will *I* ever get used to it?"

"Get used to what?" she asked.

He opened up his locker and pulled out the duffel bag hanging there. "This, among other things," he said. "Being packed and ready to go at all times. An hour ago we were hanging around the office shuffling papers and trading rumors—and now we're scheduled to boost out of here in two hours and prevent a war—and we're not even sure who would be fighting whom, or over what. And we've got a few days between now and when we get to Metran to turn into experts on—on *whatever* it is, so we can deal with it all when we get there." He hoisted the duffel bag up, and stepped out of his cubicle, Hannah right beside him, hoisting her own duffel onto her shoulder.

"Look on the bright side," she said. "Our ride isn't quite ready, so today we have two extra hours."

"If that's your idea of a bright side, we're going to have to talk," said Jamie as they headed out of the Bullpen. "But seriously, you didn't answer my question. You've been at this longer than I have. Does it ever get less disorienting?"

Hannah thought it over for a minute. "No," she said. "Not exactly. But you get *used* to being disoriented. At least I have." Her voice went quiet. "Though I can think of a few senior agents that never have."

"Me too." There were a few lost souls among the population of the Bullpen. They did their jobs, and they were good agents—but something in their eyes hinted that they had seen too much, been exposed to a few more completely alien things than they should have. They made Jamie think of jigsaw puzzles that had been put back together with a few pieces missing, holes in the picture that could be guessed at but never known for certain. They coped as best they could—sometimes in ways that were not altogether wise. "Let's hope I don't get that way."

"Agreed," said Hannah. "I don't want to get partnered with Boris Kosolov—or someone twitchy enough to be doing an imitation of him."

BSI Special Agent Boris Kosolov did not so much speak a variety of languages as much as prove himself equally adept at mangling all of them. Somehow, despite work habits that were so haphazard as to be undetectable, he always closed his cases and completed his assignments. But it was far from the first time Jamie had gotten the message *don't wind up like him.*

They made their way through the labyrinth of corridors, entered an elevator, and headed down to the outer decks. Jamie punched at the button for the Main Docking Complex, but Hannah pushed the button for the floor above it, marked ARMORY, ADMIN & GENERAL SERVICES. "We've got that special equipment to collect," she said.

"And you're having so much fun not telling me what it is that there's no point in my asking again."

"You know me too well," said Hannah with a grin as the elevator door opened. "The thing is, I've dealt with the Metrannans before," she went on. "That's probably part of the reason Kelly dropped this particular case in our laps." She led him along a corridor full of glass doors with very official placards posted beside them. The first doors they passed were to larger rooms with signs that read ARMORY, ALTERNATE COMM GEAR, ENVIRONMENTAL GEAR, and SPECIALTY TRANSPORT.

"Go out on a case, and you learn a few things that aren't always emphasized enough in the datastores, or aren't even in them at all," Hannah said. "Details get overlooked. Like, maybe, yes, you can eat the local food—but it's normally odorless. If it smells good, it's gone bad. There's a high-gravity planet where you don't dare use an exoskel walker to get around because the walkers resemble a local species of giant carnivorous pseudoarthropod, and it's a deadly insult to the locals. But there's a low-gee planet where the local species *always* use the equivalent of exowalkers or lift chairs, even though they aren't needed. And you better use one too if you don't want to be arrested for devolutionary behavior—walking on your own two feet is considered animalistic and degenerate."

They turned a corner and kept walking. "And then there are the Metrannans," said Hannah. "*Very* concerned with appropriate behavior and appearance. You don't want to appear disrespectful by showing up dressed the wrong way. They don't expect you to wear Metrannan garb. You quite literally don't have the legs for it. Metrannans have four. However, they do expect the *equivalent* dress for your species. And the Metrannans *will* know if you show up in inappropriate clothes. They have a very elaborate database that covers just about every known race and the forms, styles, meanings, and rankings of any piece of clothing or decoration or body paint or whatever any being might use. They're well-versed in the dress of all sort of human cultures. In other words, Special Agent Mendez, you can't just wander around the landscape in your usual flight-suit and flak-jacket outfit. Not on this mission." She stopped in front of a door marked MEN'S TAILOR.

Jamie looked through the glass doors at a vast room in which every sort of costume, from kimonos to tuxedos to academic gowns, was hanging in the racks. "Wait a minute! I've got a business suit in my duffel bag. I'm not going to play dress-up just to keep—"

"Yes you are," she said, "because it's necessary for the case, and because I know for a fact that the suit you keep in that duffel bag has a missing button and a tear in the lining and it stopped being wrinkle-proof about five missions ago, and because there isn't time to argue. Now get in there for your fitting. They have your measurements on file, of course, but it's always best to double-check the fit. So go."

"What are they going to make me wear, exactly?"

"I don't know. The tailor shop has its *own* database of what you ought to wear when."

"So I have to wear whatever the tailors think the Metrannans think humans ought to wear? At whatever sort of occasion it happens to be? Suppose they've got their database wrong and they think I'm supposed to dress like an expatriated Zulu warrior?"

Hannah grinned. "Look on the bright side. The first time I dealt with a Metrannan, he was doing his best to dress like a human—not easy, considering he had four arms and four legs and eyes in the back of his head. But he tried. Believe me, you ought to be glad they don't expect us to dress like them. Anyway, I'll be next door in the women's tailor shop. I'll be as quick as I can. Have fun."

* * *

If there was in fact a male shopping aversion gene, forty-five minutes later, Jamie was sure he had it.

Not that he had done any actual shopping, in the sense of browsing or selecting or even looking. Instead the staff in the clothier's section had treated him like a poorly designed tailor's dummy, prying him in and out of check-fit garments, slipping shirts and jackets and shoes on and off him with a complete disregard for whether or not he was cooperating. They might not have been pleasant, but they were at least efficient, and they ushered him firmly out of the shop almost before he knew what was happening. He was still carrying nothing but his duffel bag, but the tailor shop manager assured him that everything that had been selected for him would be aboard ship by the time they boosted.

Hannah wasn't there when he came out. He checked the time. Roughly ninety-five minutes until they were cleared to boost—and Commander Kelly would not be much interested in the reason why if they were still on-station in ninety-six minutes. He decided to give Hannah five minutes, then head for the ship. But it only took two minutes of cooling his heels to realize why the time between briefing and boost was so short. It allowed less time for worrying.

By the start of the fourth minute, Jamie was twitchy enough to jump out of his skin. Hannah emerged, looking calm and self-possessed, moving at a pace that could only be described as leisurely. "So," she said, coolly glancing at her wrist display, "it looks like we've got a little time to kill. Let's go see how they're coming on the ship."

She walked away, without looking back to see if he was coming. Jamie stepped lively to catch up, not sure if he wanted to yell at Hannah for teasing him or laugh at himself for worrying too much. Probably Hannah had set the whole prank up to get his mind off larger worries. He *needed* to get the big problems out of his head, if only so he could concentrate on sweating the small stuff.

After all, it was the small stuff that was going to keep them alive—or kill them, if they got it wrong.

He hurried after her.

FOUR
DOWN IS UP

Hannah looked out the viewport of BSI HQ's Main Docking Complex and at the pair of fat cones, docked nose to nose, that hung there in the darkness. A system of bracing pylons held the two little ships firmly to the station, and an access tunnel led from the side air lock of the closer vehicle back toward the station. A tug was coming into view, carrying a booster unit that would add its thrust to the *Sholto*'s own propulsion system in order to compensate for the doubled weight of the combined vehicle. Without the booster, the time needed to reach their transit point out of the Center System would have been doubled—and a burn that long would have put dangerous strains on the little ship's own propulsion system.

Another tug was attaching six strain-relief cables between the two vehicles. *Sherlock*-class ships were fitted with a variety of hold-down points—recessed heavy-duty metal rings to which cables could be attached. The hold-downs were normally used to lock the little ships in place when they were being carried on or in larger vehicles. On this mission, they were seeing a different use. One set of six hold-downs was placed around the circumference of each of the cone-shaped ships about halfway up. Cables were being strung between the two ships, each cable strung from a hold-down on one ship to the corresponding hold-down on the other, then pulled taut.

The cabling was one of about a half dozen hastily improvised fixes being done on the ships. It was a lash-up, a crude sort of insurance policy against the fact that, while the *Sherlock*-class ships were designed to travel while docked nose-to-nose, or with a booster stage attached, there was no data that anyone could find in a hurry about whether it was such a good idea to fly them docked nose-to-nose *and* with a booster. The idea was to transfer as much of the load and dynamic stress away from the docking ports and onto the main structure of the *Sholto* and the *Adler*.

The engineers were all confident the cables would provide sufficient additional stiffening and strengthening to keep the combined vehicle safe. Hannah was glad to hear that—although she couldn't help thinking that the engineers weren't the ones who were going to be flying the monstrosity in question. What had her worried was how they were going to detach the cables when it was time to fly the *Sholto* on a solo run—and then how they were supposed to reattach them for the return flight.

Never mind. Those were worries for later. She

touched Jamie on the elbow and nodded toward a lock entrance a bit down the corridor. "Enough with the sightseeing," she said. "Time to move. That's where we're headed."

Jamie frowned and pointed out the port. "The single-ships are, ah, docked *sideways* to the station," he said. "That's going to make getting aboard a little tricky. Gravity's going to take a ninety-degree twist. Or do they just have the grav generators shut off in the ships so they're in zero gee?"

Hannah grinned. "That one they've managed to solve with the *Sherlock*-class ships. You'll see how. Come on."

She led him through the entrance and down a short passageway that ended in the access tunnel they had seen from the viewport. They walked down and came to a closed hatch that was plainly sideways, rotated ninety degrees clockwise from where they were standing. Right-way up, it would have been two meters high and a meter across. There were the usual red arrows labeled RESCUE pointing to the latch fixing, and a whole raft of yellow signs in any number of human and xeno languages explaining, in incomprehensible detail, how to open the door in an emergency.

In the center of the hatch, at eye level—or what would have been eye level if the hatch hadn't been on its side—painted in very official-looking black lettering, was a much larger notice. Hannah had to crane her neck to read it properly.

United Government Vessel
Bureau of Special Investigations
Vessel S/N UGV-BSI-3369-MTA6.167-JMAO.708

and, in elaborate red script under that,

BSI-3369
"Bartholomew Sholto"

"Okay," said Hannah, "so we've got the right ship."

"No we don't," said Jamie. "This is the *Irene Adler*."

Hannah looked at him oddly for a moment. "You having a little vision problem?"

"No," said Jamie. "But the paint on the signs is still fresh. Almost still wet. You can smell it a little. I assume they wouldn't just freshen up the paint job for the heck of it when the ground crews are under a lot of pressure to get us launched quickly. And pretending that the *Adler* is the *Sholto* is a big part of the plan. What sense would it make to play *that* game if the first xeno ship that got within range to read her hull markings would know she was the *Adler*?"

Hannah nodded. "So someone decided they'd have to re-mark the *Adler* if we're going to make it believable." One of the side effects of the brief-and-boost policy for Special Agents was that there was next to no time to discuss things, to decide things, to report decisions. Someone would realize something needed doing and just do it without telling anyone.

In the roughly one hundred minutes since the mission had been assigned, someone on the ground crew had shown enough initiative to repaint the hatch. There had no doubt been barely enough time to do the job itself—and there wouldn't have been a chance in the sky of getting it done if that someone had been required to get four approvals first. It was a system—if one could even call it a system—that required a good deal of common sense and initiative, and a great deal of trust among all the members of the team.

And it also required that the agents be ready to deal with any surprises that were thrown at them. "Your logic's good," Hannah said. "Let's see if it holds up." She consulted the access codes she had jotted down in the lockmaster's office, flipped open a panel in the hatch, and twisted her body around to punch in the key combination for the *Sholto*—only to be rewarded with a flashing red BAD CODE warning on the display panel and a harsh, low, error tone. "All right," she said, "we'll try it your way." She entered the *Adler*'s access code. There was a confirming beep, and a series of smooth clunks and thuds, and the hatch swung up and open. They had to step back a bit to get out of its way. "Right you are, Jamie," she said. "Let's see what other surprises there might be inside."

The two of them ducked to get under the hatch,

and entered the air lock chamber. The chamber was a cylinder on its side, about two meters high and eighty centimeters wide—a fairly snug fit for two people in flight suits, each carrying a duffel bag. If they had been in pressure suits, they wouldn't have fit in at the same time. The chamber's steel-mesh floor was level with the deck of the station's Docking Complex, so that it was offset from the inside and outside air lock hatches by a full ninety degrees.

"Why the heck did they put the air lock floor on its side?" Jamie asked.

"They didn't," Hannah said. "At least, not permanently." There were waist-high railings welded to the two sides of the mesh flooring. The one to the left had a small control panel bolted to it. Hannah pushed a button to close the lock's outer door. As soon as it was shut, the steel-mesh floor—and the direction of "down"—began to rotate slowly clockwise.

Jamie, startled, grabbed at the handrail and glared at Hannah, who was grinning ear to ear. "I take it that warning me wouldn't have been nearly as much fun, would it?" he growled.

"Nowhere near," Hannah said as the floor's rotation slowed to a smooth halt, level with the interior lock door. "The floor grating itself isn't even powered or anything. It's on rollers, so it will just naturally adjust itself to roll to where 'down' is. The air lock has its own independent grav generator that can redirect itself so 'down' is in any direction. Its standard setting is keyed to using the lock's doors. The grav field shifts by one degree or so at a time, about ten degrees a second, so as to match up with the local direction of 'down' inside or outside the ship."

"Cute," said Jamie, still plainly annoyed. "But if you've got any other clever pranks to play on me, save them for later, okay?"

Hannah grinned. "Let's see what we've got inside." She pushed another button on the lock's panel and the inner lock unlatched—to the sound of muffled curses from inside that became clearer and more distinct as the door swung open.

"What the—burning devils! Just when I was getting things squared away—oh, hello, ma'am. Sir." They saw a technician in blue, sweat-stained coveralls. He had obviously been crouching over, hooking something up, and been forced to scramble to get out of the way of the lock's swinging door.

Hannah recognized the man. Gunther Hendricks—one of the senior ground crew techs. Hannah never felt quite comfortable with the way Gunther called her "ma'am." He was too experienced, too skilled, to be showing her so much deference. She could only imagine how awkward Jamie felt about hearing himself called "sir" by a man old enough to be his grandfather. But Gunther Hendricks did everything by the book—and the book said that was how techs were supposed to address Special Agents.

"Sorry, Gunther," said Hannah. "We didn't know anyone was working in here. We didn't mean to barge in on you."

"No, it's all right," said Gunther. "I just get a little on edge when I'm installing one of these." He gestured toward a blue cylinder with rounded ends, about fifty centimeters long and twenty wide, on an equipment rack next to the air lock.

Hannah raised one eyebrow. "I don't blame you a bit for that," she said. The blue lozenge-shaped thing was a hellbomb, a self-destruct device that would destroy the ship so completely, vaporize it so thoroughly, that no trace of it would be left behind. "It'll put us a little on edge having it aboard."

"Good," said Gunther. "I don't care how many safeguards and lockouts and system checks you have on something like this. You know, and I know, as a matter of logic, that you could pound on that casing all day with a hammer, then fire a clip of heavy-caliber ammo at it, and it wouldn't even muss up the paintwork. That thing is *tough*.

"But if you're smart, you treat it like it was made of spun sugar. It won't go off. It *can't* go off without you doing about six very specific things first. But ma'am, sir—people make mistakes, and machines aren't perfect. It just *might* be that this thing was put together wrong, or got dropped in shipment in just the right way to bend a delicate part out of true. It *might* be that my bolting it to the equipment rack set up just the right stresses so that it's primed to go off the next time it gets jostled. It's not true, but it *might* be. It's a one-in-a-billion, one-in-a-trillion shot."

"We know," said Hannah. "We know." She couldn't help noticing that Gunther hadn't called the thing by its proper name. He could barely bring himself to call it a self-destruct device, let alone "bomb." It clearly had him a lot more on edge than perhaps he realized.

"And we know that there are ships that disappear for no known reason," said Jamie. "We'll be careful."

Gunther looked at Jamie with wry amusement but spoke with a note of sadness in his voice. "You do that, sir. Please be sure you do that. Because this ship here, the *Irene Adler*, is one of those ships. Or was." He gestured up toward the *Adler*'s tiny flight deck. "I was part of the crew that boarded her when she came in. He was up there, in the pilot's seat. I think he wanted to die looking at the stars." Gunther was silent for a moment. "Whatever it was that killed him was something he wasn't expecting, something we've never seen before. You'd call it a one-in-a-trillion chance," he said, "until it happens to *you*."

Gunther Hendricks looked at them with a fierce, almost angry intensity. "I don't wish to pull anyone else out of this ship. I don't *ever* want to draw that duty again. I don't want any more ships that vanish for no good reason. I don't need more reasons to lie awake nights. Don't just be careful on this mission. Be *careful*," he said, emphasizing the last word so hard that it was almost a shout.

The tiny ship filled with a suffocating silence. Gunther looked almost as startled by his outburst as Hannah felt. He spoke again, in a quieter tone, after a moment's pause. "Sorry," he said. "But—I knew Trevor Wilcox. Not well, but I knew him. And being part of the team that took him out of here, seeing what they had turned him into... well, that got to me."

"I believe it," Hannah said.

"You said 'they' turned him into what you found," Jamie said. "Who is 'they,' exactly?"

"The Metrannans, of course," Gunther said. "Who else would it be?"

"That's what we're going to find out," Jamie said. "Why do you blame them?"

Gunther frowned. "He went there young and healthy, and he died of old age on the way home. It must have been something there that did it to him, and it must have been the Metrannans that did it. Logic, that's all."

Hannah could see that Jamie was about to ask something more, to press the point harder. But Gunther wasn't a forensic pathologist. His logic was nothing more than a jump, a leap to conclusions inspired by fear. His answers on the subject would be useless—worse than useless, if they served to distract Jamie, lead him in the wrong direction. "That's enough, Jamie," she said, before he could speak.

And yet Jamie's instinctive urge to question Gunther was correct. Gunther was a first and unexpected witness. But better to talk to him about what he did know and had some expertise about. "Were you briefed on what this one is about, Gunther?" she asked.

He shrugged. "Some, not all," he said. "And I'm not feeling all that curious, I can tell you. There's something aboard this ship that you need to find. They've searched for it twice, and you're supposed to find it."

"So why are they having you install new equipment when we're supposed to treat this place like a murder investigation site?"

Gunther shook his head. "I don't know the why. I can guess that Kelly figures a max-power self-destruct means you can be sure of keeping the Metrannans from getting the document, and that's more important than *us* getting it. But on the how, I can tell you a lot more. We were ordered to do microscopic scans of the surfaces and subsurface density scans before we installed anything." He gestured to the spot where the self-destruct device was attached. "If there had been a microdot glued down on that piece of bulkhead, or a drilled-out and covered-over hollow big enough to *hide* a microdot, we'd have spotted it. Same thing with the section of deck where we attached the acceleration couch."

"I was about to ask about that," Hannah said,

gesturing toward their feet. There was a portable acceleration chair there, folded flat to the deck.

"Why not do that level of search on the whole ship?" Jamie asked.

"Lots of reasons," said Gunther. "Just setting up the gear and doing the scans of a square meter of bulkhead and a square meter of deck took hours—and that was on flat surfaces. It would be ten times slower to microscan complex surfaces. We'd have to search inside the control panels or inside a sealed tank. It might take years. We'll do scans of all the items we had to take off the ship— Wilcox's body, his clothes, decayed food, depleted air-regen units, that sort of thing. We'll be lucky to complete just *that* much before you get back."

"And probably it's not on a microdot," said Hannah. "I really doubt that's the way Wilcox would have hidden the item we're supposed to look for."

"Why not?" Jamie asked.

Hannah grinned. "That's a short question with a long answer, and we don't have much time before we boost. We'll go into it later," she said. But there was more to her reasons for keeping quiet than mere time-saving. They were already likely skating up to the edge of what the techs were cleared to hear about their assignment. It was a professional courtesy to keep Gunther from accidentally learning more than he'd want to know on a case like this. "Anything else we need to know from you, Gunther?" she asked, steering the conversation into safer areas.

"Just that we're installing the identical gear on the real *Sholto*," Gunther said, pointing upward toward the *Adler*'s nose hatch. "Two reasons for that, of course. You'll need two acceleration chairs if you're in just one of the ships during part of the mission, and of course we want the two ships to look as much like each other as possible, just in case."

"In case of what?" Jamie asked.

Gunther shrugged. "I don't know the plan, but it stands to reason, if you want the *Adler* to pretend it's the *Sholto*, it's probably smart if the two ships look the same, inside and out."

"Right you are," said Hannah. "And for what it's worth, we don't know the plan, either. We'll get out of your way so you can go ahead and finish up," she said. "I think we'd better get over to the *Sholto* and start prepping for our ride out of here."

"Very good, ma'am," he said. "Good luck out there. To both of you."

Hannah nodded unhappily. She had flown in them before, and she didn't much care for the *Sherlock*-class ships. They were supposed to be miracles of efficiency, the smallest all-mode ships ever built by humans, capable of landing on a planet's surface, boosting to orbit, crossing long interplanetary distances, and transiting between star systems. But there was a reason those jobs were usually divvied up between two or three kinds of ships. Shoehorning a reentry system and landing gear into the same hull as a stardrive and a long-duration life-support system meant a lot of design compromises, a lot of hardware that was expected to do two or three things reasonably well, instead of doing one job very well.

"This bucket doesn't look much bigger than the old *Orient Express*—back before we got her blown up," said Jamie. "And she was just a surface-to-orbit job. This thing is a *starship*?"

"She's a starship," Hannah confirmed, "and she's *exactly* the same size as the poor old *Express*. They're both modifications from the same hull design."

"Makes me appreciate the *Captain Hastings*," Jamie replied.

"You've been in the lap of luxury. Back before you and I partnered together, I practically *lived* in these tubs." The *Hastings* had been their star-to-star transport on a number of missions, and had carried the ill-fated and since-replaced *Orient Express* as a landing craft. Half of Hannah's career had been spent on riding ships like the *Adler* to and from missions—or at least it seemed that way to her. It was a bit of a jolt to realize that Jamie had never been aboard one before. He had been partnered with Hannah from his first day in the Bullpen, and therefore hadn't spent any time at all on single-ships.

The *Adler* was basically a rounded-off cone, and her interior reflected that. The lower deck, where they were standing, was a circle about five meters across, with much of the perimeter space taken up by the air lock, a small and uncomfortable refresher compartment with toilet and washing facilities, and various engineering and access panels. There was a fold-down bed, and a pull-down table, and a fold-out chair—but not room to have all three of them out at once. The galley was another series of pull-out modules, as was the miniature station intended for in-field forensic work. There was barely any room left for personal items or specialty equipment. Living in a *Sherlock*-class ship was an adventure in constantly stowing and unstowing gear. It was going to be doubly fun with two of them aboard, plus the luggage packed with fancy-dress clothes they had to to take along.

Hannah looked up toward the upper deck and the nose hatch. Of course, calling it an upper deck was a massive overstatement. It was all of three and a half meters above the level of the lower deck. At that level, the conical ship's diameter had narrowed to about three meters wide, at a generous estimate. The upper deck was really nothing more than a section of open steel-mesh flooring that took up only about half of the ship's interior diameter, with the rest left open to serve as a passageway between the nose hatch and the lower deck. Bolted to the steel-mesh floor was an acceleration chair that faced the ship's less-than-sophisticated control panel and three small viewports. The pilot's chair could be swiveled about to put the pilot's back to the deckplates so she was looking toward the ship's forward end for close-in maneuvering and docking with the nose hatch. There was a rope ladder rigged from the nose hatch down to the lower deck of the *Adler*. The steps of the ladder were heavy-duty plastic, and the ladder ropes ended in metal rings that slipped into snap-shut stanchions on the deck. The topside end of the ladder was secured the same way—and there was another set of snap-shuts that held the ladder in place at the level of the upper deck.

Hannah slung the strap of her duffel bag over her shoulder and started the climb up the ladder toward the nose hatch, and the *Sholto*. Jamie followed.

She paused at the upper deck, shifting to one side of the ladder to let Jamie come up alongside her. They both stared at the pilot's acceleration chair for a moment.

"Yeah," said Gunther, answering the unasked question. "That's where we found him. At his station, staring out at the stars. We, ah, had to remove and replace the pilot's chair. It wasn't in very good shape, after, ah, Special Agent Wilcox had been in it for all those months."

It seemed to Hannah that there wasn't any better response to that than a moment's silence. She let the moment pass, and then began climbing upward again. Jamie stayed behind a moment longer than he needed, staring at the empty pilot's seat.

Sometimes being a good partner meant pretending not to notice private moments seen from too close in. Hannah moved on to the top of the ship.

The rope ladder came to an end in two more snap-shut cleats just to one side of the open nose-hatch hatchway. The circular hatch was open, and the hatch cover was swung to one side and latched in place up against the inner hull, opposite to the pilot's station.

She peered up and through the open hatch. The *Adler* was joined nose to nose with the *Sholto*, and the interiors of the two hatches joined to form a tunnel about ninety centimeters wide and two meters long. Each ship's hatch had a tube-shaped section of cargo netting stretched taut around the length of its interior. The *Adler*'s netting was bright blue, while the *Sholto*'s was flaming orange.

"That's not all that identical," she said, pointing to the netting as Jamie came up behind her.

"Yeah, but it will help us tell which ship we're in," Jamie said. "And look there. We're covered." Jamie pointed to a carefully wrapped-up pack of orange netting tucked in between the *Adler*'s blue netting and the hatch tunnel's interior surface. Hannah peeked through the tunnel and saw a corresponding pack of blue netting tucked in behind the *Sholto*'s orange netting. They could swap one for the other in a minute or two, if the need arose.

Hannah grunted. She should have had more faith in Gunther and his team.

She pushed her duffel into the docking tunnel

and went in after it. She found herself suddenly in zero gee, all her reflexes scrambled as she floated rapidly upward toward the nose of the *Sholto* and the point where gravity would kick in again—with down in the opposite direction. She lunged for the netting to save herself and grabbed at her duffel just in time. Obviously, the engineers had rigged the gravity generators to provide zero gee inside the tunnel as a sort of transition zone between the two ships, since each had "down" in the opposite direction from the other. She took a moment to calm herself before turning around to see Jamie, grinning evilly back at her.

"I thought so," he said with a laugh. "That's why I let you go first."

She smiled ruefully. "Okay," she said, "I guess I had that coming. Let's go look around the real *Sholto*."

She pulled herself completely into the docking tunnel so that she floated in zero gee. It was a tight squeeze, but she managed to flip herself around so her feet were pointed in the opposite direction. She got the duffel strap around her shoulder again, then maneuvered herself around to the *Sholto*'s rope ladder. She eased herself downward into the full-gee interior of the ship. It was a decidedly odd experience to have her legs in full gravity and her head in zero gee.

Hannah quickly concluded that she didn't like it, and made her way rapidly down the ladder to the *Sholto*'s lower deck, dodging past two technicians crammed into the upper deck making some last-minute adjustment. Jamie followed behind her. They stood on the lower deck of the *Bartholomew Sholto* and looked straight back up the way they had come, toward the *Irene Adler*. Gunther was up there—or was it down there?—in the center of the *Adler*'s lower deck. He craned his neck up to look at them, waved, then turned back to his work, giving them a fine view of the top of his head as he walked out of view on what Hannah's hindbrain was quite certain was the ceiling.

"This is going to take some getting used to," she said to Jamie.

"You mean the way half of everything is upside down?" he asked with a laugh. "It's been that way since the first day I signed up with BSI. Come on, let's get squared away and ready for boost. We're on the clock."

FIVE
CONSTANT OF CHANGE

"Change is wrong," said the being on the low platform in the front of the room. The chamber was dimly lit, the rounded walls glowing faintly. A single shaft of light framed the glittering form of Bulwark of Constancy. The room's arrangements resembled something suitable for a place of worship.

Learned Searcher Taranarak of geneline Lucyrn resembled Bulwark of Constancy not at all, but her species and Constancy's had lived together in close quarters for millions of year. She could read Constancy's body language as perfectly as she could that of a Metrannan—and Taranarak knew that Constancy could interpret her own gestures just as well.

She bent her four knees in unison, a movement that, in her culture, was meant to express agreement more than submission. Taranarak's actual emotional state, however, might have been better described as weary toleration combined with frustration, though it would be unwise in the extreme to express anything like that to one of the Unseen.

"By all moral, philosophical, and cultural measures, you are no doubt correct, and I of course agree with you," Taranarak lied, "but right or wrong, change is forced upon us."

And change was not only absolutely essential for their mutual survival, not only a good thing, but an absolute moral imperative. However, one did not voice such opinions to the Unseen. "It infects, it spreads, like one of the illnesses in the Old Stories."

"The illnesses never touched *our* kind, but only yours—and they were stopped," replied Bulwark of Constancy. "And thanks to the unchanging determination of *my* people, they have never returned to harm *your* people." Bulwark of Constancy gestured with its upper-left and lower-right expressive mandibles, indicating dismissal of a poor analogy.

"I beg your pardon," Taranarak said. For a supposedly changeless being, Constancy was being— what was the delicious human word that Trevor of geneline Wilcox had used? *Crotchety!* That was it. Bulwark was being most unusually crotchety and fussy. But, of course, the mere existence of humans and Kendari, the fact that the Young Races must be dealt with at all, even if only as a mere trivial inconvenience, was a massive affront to the whole worldview of the Unseen Race. It was unfortunate that she had been forced to bring such matters to the attention of Bulwark of Constancy. "I did not wish to offend."

"Nor have you—yet. But it is desired that you proceed with your report and conclude with all deliberate dispatch."

"Very well," said Taranarak. "It is my opinion that the danger can only grow worse as the level of uncertainty grows. There is growing awareness, among many factions, that there is—or at least was—a treatment that can...alter matters." She dared not say anything more explicit than that for fear of offending Constancy.

"It is wrong to alter matters. As a matter of simple logic, it is plain that any change could only be for the worse, because circumstances and conditions remain optimal, as they have been for a significant part of a standard galactic rotation."

Not optimal for everyone, Taranarak thought. *For the Unseen, perhaps, but not for Metrannans.* "Wrong or right does not enter into it," she said. "The knowledge that there *is*—or even that there *might* be—a way to change matters is in and of itself destabilizing the situation." She hesitated. "Whatever we might think of change in general, or how *this* change might affect our society—our civilization—it is beyond any empirical dispute that this change might well have the potential to provide the deepest and most profound benefit to some individual Metrannans." *Practically all individual Metrannans.*

"That is of no importance, as the benefits would be short-term at best. The instabilities induced by societal change would more than cancel out any transient and individual benefit."

But if it benefits all individuals, how can it possibly be harmful to Metran society? But she knew the answer to that one. It was plain to see how a change so huge, so far-ranging, if left unmanaged, could upend things utterly and send Metran society spiraling into catastrophe and disaster. It was cursedly annoying to agree with Constancy, but Taranarak had to concede, even to herself, that *this* change might well be good for each individual, but wrong for society as a whole, dreadfully wrong—*if* it were not handled properly. "All your points are, of course, valid," she said. "But it would be a mistake to argue in absolutes, and a further mistake to believe that all circumstances are subject to our control."

Bulwark of Constancy set itself bolt upright and ceased all motion. It held itself frozen in an utterly neutral posture that indicated a complete absence of reaction or emotional response. But, of course, that was entirely deceptive, a mere first-level reading of Constancy's gestural signaling. What it really meant was that Constancy was so offended, so enraged, that it was refusing to signal its emotions at all.

Taranarak suppressed her own emotional signaling. The proper reaction to Constancy's not-actually-neutral posture would have been shock, dismay, fear, consternation, shame. It would do no good at all to let Constancy know that what she was really feeling was weary resignation.

It was plain that Bulwark of Constancy would have no more to say that day—and perhaps not for many more days. "I beg your forgiveness," she said, "and, unless you object, I shall now withdraw."

Bulwark of Constancy lived up to its name, and remained motionless with all the admirable constancy of a statue carved in stone. Taranarak made the obligatory gestures of respect and farewell, and withdrew from the chamber, careful that she never presented the back of her head or her rearward eyes to Constancy.

She got outside the structure and exhaled with relief. She had done her best. She had shown all due respect to Bulwark of Constancy, and, by extension, to all the Unseen Race. That ritual complete, she was free to move on to the next step in the process, without fear of accusation of disrespectful or inharmonious behavior toward the Unseen.

Bulwark of Constancy's quarters were very near the center of the Enclave. Taranarak set off walking toward the exit, and her own laboratory, just outside the western limit of the Enclave. She did not so much as glance at the low, graceful, rounded structures, or their subtle, muted, slowly shifting colors. Nor did she take much notice of the Metrannan city of bold spires and gleaming towers that surrounded the Unseen Enclave on all sides. Those were everyday sights, and of no immediate interest.

What went on in those ancient minds? she asked herself. *Why are the Unseen the way they are?* For far from the first time, and, no doubt, for far from the last, Taranarak wished that she could see, really *see,* the beings inside the exoskeletons, and not merely look on the perfect mechanical carapace that encased them.

Trevor of Wilcox had said that to human eyes, the carapaces of an Unseen Being resembled a clawless upright lobster that had been stuck on top of ostrich legs, then spray-painted in metallic colors. The imagery had made little sense to her until he showed her some pictures from his ship's very limited reference web, but the tone of what he said was instantly clear. To him, the carapaces of the Unseen were, somehow, simultaneously alarming and absurd. To Taranarak, and to all Metrannans, they were admirable, handsome, graceful, a pinnacle of good design and good taste, perfectly designed mobile life-support systems.

The problem was that the carapaces also *concealed* the being inside, not only from sight, but from all scientific inquiry. She had researched the point as far as she dared, but the literature said almost nothing about what was inside the carapaces.

She had found precisely seven accounts of Metrannans who had, by whatever means, seen something of the interior of a Unseen Being's carapace. Three contained no information other than the bald fact that someone had seen *something*, and the others contradicted each other in almost every detail.

It also seemed highly improbable to her that the seven occasions she had found referenced were the only sightings in all the endless years. No doubt many other accounts and reports of sightings had been expurgated from the records. But they were all she had to go on—and they provided so little data that speculation could be allowed to run all but unchecked.

There were four general classes of theory about what was inside the carapaces. One was that they were in fact superior artificial replacements for the natural carapaces evolved by the ancestor species of the Unseen.

Another was what Trevor of Wilcox had called the "hermit crab" theory—that the Unseen were actually smaller creatures that climbed in and out of the metallic casings, treating them more like vehicles to be operated rather than as integral parts of their own bodies. Or perhaps they stayed in them permanently, wearing a particular carapace continuously for years or decades at a time until it wore out.

A third was that the Unseen themselves were not in fact inside the carapaces, but were elsewhere, and operating the carapaces by some form of remote control.

The fourth was that the Unseen were formerly biological beings, but had gradually made the transition to being wholly robotic life-forms; the carapaces *were* the Unseen beings, and the Unseen were in fact there for all to see.

There were endless variations on all these ideas, and any number of theories as to *why* exactly the Unseen were determined to remain so—but it was unseemly, and unhelpful, to dwell on such matters.

Taranarak had dealt with the Unseen for all of her life, as had many Metrannans. She was used to such mysteries. They had remained unresolved for generations before she was born and would likely stay that way until long after her death. Usually, she was able to accept that fact—but somehow, this was not a usual day.

She reached the boundary of the Enclave, and crossed the unguarded border with the greater city outside. She turned and looked back the way she had come, really seeing the Enclave for the first time that day. Her own research had told her a lot—perhaps too much—about what it had once been like. The earliest records showed that there had been an Enclave here, even then—but in those early days, it was the city of the Unseen that had all but surrounded the tiny Metrannan village. Generation by generation, lifetime by lifetime, the Metrannan presence had grown, and that of the Unseen had shrunk.

One repair, one adjustment, one removal, one rebuilding at a time, at a pace too slow for any but the longest-lived beings to witness directly, the grand city of the Unseen People had shrunk, been slowly swallowed up by the burgeoning Metrannan metropolis. The very quiet, very cautious research done at Taranarak's request had demonstrated conclusively that the Unseen Enclave—and the planetwide population of the Unseen—had been shrinking at a steady if all-but-imperceptible rate for thousands of years. If the trend merely continued along the same curve, then the Unseen would be extinct on Metran, perhaps within the lifetime of Taranarak's great-great-grandchildren—perhaps even that of her great-grandchildren.

No wonder the Unseen feared change.

Taranarak was so entirely lost in thought that she was not even aware of the four officers from the Bureaucracy of Order standing in her path until she was almost on top of them. By the time she *did* see them, it was of course far too late to escape. The Bureaucracy of Order, after all, had a great deal of practice arresting radicals, dangerous dissidents, and anyone else who was a threat to the established system of stability and order. It was only in the moment that the other officers closed in behind her, sealing off any chance of escape, that she realized that those words were a precise and accurate list of what she had become without even trying.

Change, she suddenly realized, was even more infectious than she had thought.

SIX

ONE IS TWO

The technicians cleared out. Hannah strapped herself into the pilot's chair on the *Sholto*'s upper deck, while Jamie used the fold-down acceleration chair on the lower deck, and the combined vehicle that was the *Adler* and the *Sholto* undocked from the BSI HQ Docking Complex. The *Sholto*'s main engines and the booster stage came to life and launched the ships out toward the perimeter of CenterStar's planetary system at a constant ten gravities acceleration. The spec sheets for the *Sherlock*-class said fifteen gees would be safe with the ships docked nose to nose, but Hannah wanted a fat safety margin, and Jamie did not argue.

"So," Jamie asked as they secured the ship from initial boost, "which job do you want to avoid first? Researching the case or searching the *Adler*?"

"Well," Hannah replied, climbing down the rope ladder to the lower deck, "we're going to have to do both at once after a while. But maybe we can get some better idea of what, exactly, we're looking for if we study up on the case first." She pulled out a folding work chair from a compartment next to the air lock and sat down facing Jamie in his acceleration couch.

Jamie readjusted the acceleration chair, raising the back support so he sat upright. "Or else," he said, "we find the decrypt key five minutes after we start searching the *Adler* so we can abort the rest of the mission and head for the barn right away. We could get the key back to HQ, then go out and investigate what happened to Special Agent Wilcox without that job being a cover story."

"That's possible, I suppose," Hannah said. "We *might* find it in a hurry. But our people have done two searches of the ship's interior already. Short of going over every surface with a microscope and a scanner, I don't know what we can do that hasn't been done. And I don't believe the scanner and scope approach is the way to go."

"Yeah, that's pretty much what you said to Gunther," said Jamie. "Why not? A microdot is so easy to hide and so hard to find. Why *wouldn't* Special Agent Wilcox have gone that way?"

"For starters, because the equipment to make a microdot isn't usually carried aboard a *Sherlock*-class. Granted, that doesn't mean she didn't carry one. We can check the manifest for the *Adler*'s last trip, and see if one's listed—though of course things get aboard ship without being on the manifest. But if there were a microdot generator aboard when the ship was recovered, Gunther's team would have spotted it. Of course, Wilcox could have brought the dot generator aboard without manifesting it, or obtained it on Metrannan, made a microdot, and *then* jettisoned the generator to hide the fact that he was making microdots—but that seems unlikely."

"You haven't convinced me yet."

"Well, consider this: microdots are just one possibility. Wilcox might have used some *other* system to make the decrypt key very small. A strand of encoded DNA deliberately left behind on his toothbrush. Micro-etched dots and dashes burned onto one length of monofilament thread sewn into the padding on the pilot's chair. Techniques that would produce a message platform so small that a scan for a microdot might miss them altogether. So small that we couldn't prove absolutely prove he didn't go the micro-message route unless and until BSI HQ decides to disassemble the *Adler* and go over each piece by hand with every kind of scanner and microscope on the market. Which is why I very much doubt Wilcox would have done it that way."

"I don't quite see your point."

"It's trade craft and doctrine stuff. A microdot is a concealment technique you use only when you're confident that *you* will be the one to recover the message, or else if you're confident you'll be able to tell your people where to find it without the bad guys listening in. Wilcox couldn't be sure that he would survive long enough to recover the key, and knew he had no reliable way of telling us—telling BSI—anything privately.

"We haven't gone over the logs in fine-tooth-comb detail yet, but a few things jump out. It sure looks like Wilcox was boarded—and knew that he might be boarded before it happened. Maybe he figured that out an hour before, maybe a couple of days before he was visited. *And he knew that he was dying.* Dying of old age in his twenties. He would have no way of knowing how long he would live. Would his illness progress at a steady state? Would it slow, or accelerate? Was there one particular organ that would be more vulnerable to the effect and give out sooner?"

Jamie thought it over for a moment. "So you're saying he probably had to hide the key because of the boarding party, and he had to know he probably wouldn't make it back to base."

"Which is another way of saying he had to hide it where the boarding party wouldn't find it—but *we would.*" Hannah gestured up at the *Adler*, literally hanging over their heads. "If I have this figured right, whatever it is, whatever form it takes, however it is recorded, the decrypt key is concealed on that ship in such a way that humans *could* find it, but xenos *couldn't.*"

"Hmmm. I guess that all makes sense," said Jamie. "But where he had it hidden for the boarding party might not be where it is *now.* He could have been forced to stash it somewhere in a hurry before the boarding party came on board, then might have taken the time to conceal it more thoroughly once they were gone."

"That seems plausible," Hannah agreed. "And take it a step further. He couldn't know for sure the xenos wouldn't just wait for him to die, then reboard the ship to search at their leisure."

Jamie looked startled. "How do we know that isn't exactly what did happen?" he asked. "Maybe the Metrannans did wait for him to die, came aboard, found the decrypt key, and took it away. The reason Gunther and his team couldn't find the key was that it was already gone."

"You're not making me feel better," Hannah said. "But you have made up my mind about your first question. I say we hit the paperwork first, at least for a while. We should do a first pass that might at least help us whittle down the possibilities."

"Makes sense to me," said Jamie. "We might even find out something about what Special Agent Wilcox was supposed to be doing, what his mission was."

"I've got to admit I'm just a teeny bit curious about that War-Starter designation," said Hannah. "It'd be nice to know what that was about."

"What?" Jamie asked in mock horror. "And ruin the surprise?"

Hannah laughed. "Absolutely," she said, "even if it gets some xenos upset. Let's go to work."

METRANNANS—Native to the planet *Metran* (see reference). Physical description: There are eight limbs in all: four legs and four manipulating (e.g. nonlocomotive) arms. The legs are short, set close together, and arranged directly under the vertical torso. The typical upright stance of a Metrannan roughly resembles that of a standing human. Height is about one and a quarter to one and a half meters. The skin is covered by scales on all the body except for the hands, feet, and face. Scale coloration varies by individual, and ranges from light blue to pink, but seems to have no social or other significance.

The four arms are arranged with one "strongwork" pair positioned as with human arms, and a smaller "closework" set, better for fine manipulation, set at a position roughly analogous to the human rib cage. The hands consist of four mutually opposable fingers.

The head is large and rounded, and the neck so short the head seems to sit directly on the torso. There are four eyes—a primary pair facing forward and a rear-facing pair. The Metrannan head is generally, but not always, surrounded by a manelike ruff of hair.

Notable characteristics: The Metrannans are the shortest-lived of all the sentient species currently known to humanity. Metrannans typically live to the age of forty human years. Even that is a significant increase on their original life span.

Metrannans require a relatively high gravity field. A force much below the one-sixth-gee field of the Earth's Moon will eventually prove fatal. Metrannans lose consciousness after about thirty seconds in zero gee, and die if not returned to a strong gravity field within a few minutes.

METRAN—The human name given to the home world of the *Metrannans* (see reference), an intelligent species that was in turn named for the world. The Metrannans have their own names for themselves and their home world, but both are unpronounceable to most humans.

The world, and by extension the species and the culture, are named for the species' cultural habit of living exclusively in giant, highly planned and rigidly controlled cities— and only one city per planet.

The planet itself is somewhat larger than Earth, with a higher gravity and a denser atmosphere. Metran is unique among the human-cataloged home worlds of sentient species in that the species known to humans as the *Xenoatrics* (see reference) have had a colony established there so long that it predates the evolution of the Metrannans themselves. (The Xenoatric home world is not known to humans, but it is definitely not Metran.) The Xenoatric Enclave, estimated to be several million years old, still stands in the center of the Metrannan City. The Enclave is completely surrounded by . . .

Jamie blinked, jerked upward in his chair, and shook his head. It was far from the first time he had caught himself starting to drift off. He sighed, rubbed his eyes, and turned to stare out the viewport for a moment, if only to rest his eyes.

It wasn't that he wasn't interested in learning about Metran. It was just that he was so tired, so burned-out from reading, reading, reading the query results.

Working the file had never been the most exciting part of police work. Sifting through a pile of papers, or grinding through screen after screen of data, was just plain dull. Most of what was written in the average case file was set down in the most blindingly boring bureaucratese.

A report might spend pages and pages on the most trivial side issues and gloss over the key facts with no details at all. A file would have so many obvious sloppy errors and misstatements of fact that it became impossible to rely on anything in it.

And yet, examining the files was absolutely essential. They might contain—they *ought* to contain—that one golden nugget of information that could break the case wide open—or maybe just keep a certain James Mendez alive.

Of necessity, the query results covered not just the case in question—what little they had on it— but all the information BSI had about the culture, history, biology, and psychology of the species in question—a species that the assigned agent in question might never have so much as heard of before being tapped for the mission. Besides which, the files on a given xeno species were never complete and were often highly inaccurate.

It would be as if a xeno investigator had to come to Earth to solve a murder, and her sum total of information on the human race consisted of what she had time to learn en route from an old out-of-date encyclopedia with half the entries missing, plus some old newspapers and a stack of gossip magazines—with perhaps *The History of the Decline and Fall of the Roman Empire* and *The Diaries of Samuel Pepys* thrown into the mix on the off chance they might be of some use and because they were the only history books available.

"Getting on toward dinnertime, Jamie," Hannah called from the lower deck.

"Good," he said. "I'm too punchy to accomplish much of anything. Let me just tidy up my references, and I'll be down in a minute."

On previous cases, Hannah and Jamie had fallen into the habit of studying the query results individually, then meeting up at mealtimes to discuss what they had found. Having both of them shoehorned aboard the *Bartholomew Sholto*, a ship that was a tight fit for a single person, made both sides of that procedure difficult. Hannah was hunched over the one small fold-out table on the lower deck, struggling to keep her notes and materials from spreading out too far and falling to the deckplates or getting wedged in some bit of fold-out gadgetry. Jamie was in the pilot's station, which had the benefit—and distraction—of affording a spectacular view of the stars but also had even less to offer in the way of flat surfaces.

Jamie squared his data displays and notebooks up as much as he could, stood up, stretched, and made his way down the rope ladder to the lower deck. As he did, he glanced upward at the upside-down view of the *Irene Adler*'s interior, and felt a brief twinge of completely irrational guilt as he did so. So much effort had been taken, so many risks had been run, so that they could search that ship's interior as soon as possible—and yet neither of them had so much as gone aboard her since their launch from BSI HQ.

Hannah pretty much had dinner ready by the time he got down the ladder—but she hadn't had to do much. There was barely room enough to store food, let alone provide a real galley. Instead they had self-heating ready-to-eat meals in disposable containers. The BSI worked hard to make the meals palatable, and for the most part they succeeded, but mealtime aboard the *Sholto* was definitely not high cuisine. Hannah pulled the activation tab on a mealpack and handed it to Jamie.

"So," he asked. "Made any progress?"

"Some," said Hannah. "I think I've got a better handle on what Wilcox was supposed to be doing."

"I still don't get why Commander Kelly couldn't brief us on that."

"I'd assume it was because Kelly simply didn't know," Hannah said. "You haven't drawn any courier jobs like that yet, but they happen. The BSI Diplomatic Liaison Office will get in a request from the Diplomatic Service, or maybe even from some other agency that needs something moved quietly from here to there. It might be that no one in BSI-DLO would even know what, exactly, the message or item was, but if all they're doing is handing the task to us, they don't *need* to know—and neither do we. The argument is that it can be safer for the agent on the job *not* to know—and for it to be generally known that courier runs are double-blind. No one's going to hunt you down and torture you three months after you get back to find out what was in the envelope if everybody—good guys and bad guys—know that you didn't know yourself."

"I suppose," Jamie said, peeling back the top of his mealpack to reveal a reasonable facsimile of a piping-hot cordon bleu, "but somebody killed Wilcox for some reason, and being ignorant didn't save him. Maybe he could have protected himself if he had known the score."

"He started *out* ignorant," Hannah said, opening her own mealpack. She smiled, and Jamie knew why. French onion soup again, one of her favorites. "But we *don't* know whether or not he stayed that way. He could have been briefed in whole or in part while he was on Metran. And even if he wasn't briefed, he couldn't have helped but learn some things just by following his instructions."

"How so?" Jamie asked between bites.

"He was supposed to meet up with a certain Metrannan, Learned Searcher Hallaben, who worked at the City Geriatrics Research Center. Hallaben was supposed to hand him a document—no mention of any decryption key—and Wilcox was to bring it back to BSI-DLO for delivery to the ultimate customer. You spot anything wrong with that picture?" There was a faint smile at the corner of Hannah's mouth.

He thought for a moment but couldn't see any obvious red lights on the board. "The closest I can come is the bit about only one document. From what Kelly said to us, they recovered the document itself from the *Adler*'s computers—presumably from the onboard secure file system. But if this was a really secure operation, they would have used *two* couriers—one for the document and one for the decrypt key. Ideally, neither would know anything at all about the other, and they'd each travel by different routes at different times and so on. Maybe that's even what happened. Special Agent Wilcox got the encoded document and some other courier—maybe not a BSI agent, maybe not even a human—got the decrypt key. Gunther's team didn't find it because it was never there. It was sent by some other route."

"Possible, but not likely," Hannah said, poking at her soup. "If that had been the plan, an awful lot of things would have to go wrong for us to have gotten to this point. Someone at our end would *have* to know they were using two couriers. We knew about it when Wilcox failed to return. If there was a second courier, either he arrived and they know about it and they already have the key, or else he never showed up either. But they'd *still* know Wilcox didn't have the key. BSI-DLO wouldn't have asked for us to investigate if either of those things had happened.

"I *suppose* there might have been some night-mare bureaucratic foul-up, with everything so compartmentalized that no one even knew that they didn't know what was going on, but I doubt it. Commander Kelly might not have been author-ized to tell us everything about the case, but she wouldn't have sent us out unless there was very good reason to believe the decrypt key was aboard the *Adler*. And she wouldn't have risked sending agents on just guesses and hopeful theories. In other words, she wasn't allowed to *inform* us that there was only one courier, but she did know it."

"So at least we're not on a wild-goose chase—or at least not that *kind* of wild-goose chase," Jamie said. "But if someone who has more need-to-know than we have tagged this thing War-Starter, then it *should* have been a two-courier job. The fact that it wasn't—or at least our assumption that it wasn't—tells me that someone was making it up as they went along."

Hannah nodded thoughtfully as she blotted up the last of her soup with a crust of bread. "I'll go with all that. But you did flunk my what's-wrong-with-this-picture test."

"Fine," Jamie said. "You win. You're smart and I'm dumb. What is it?"

"Come on, think like a xeno, a proud member of an Elder Race species. Your civilization has been around for hundreds of thousands of years. Nothing ever changes and nothing is new."

"I still don't see it."

Hannah grinned again. "You ever hear the bit of urban folklore about the American patent office at the end of one century or another? The nineteenth, it must have been. Some old fogy suggests that they might as well save money and shut it down because everything worthwhile had already been invented. Turns out the story isn't true—a complete garble, a *reversal* of the truth, in fact, but that's not the point."

Then Jamie saw it. "Ah. I get it. A *research* lab. That would be a very undignified thing for an Elder Race to have around."

"Because they *have* closed their patent office," Hannah said. "They've been at it for hundreds of thousands of years. Some of the Elder Races have been around for *millions* of years. They *have* invented everything—or at least they believe they have. It's supposed to be close to an article of faith for a lot of races. Except someone has decided maybe they haven't gotten to everything. Which means this Learned Searcher Hallaben is committing heresy, or near enough. And wherever there's a heretic, there's bound to be a true believer nearby."

Jamie nodded eagerly. His mind had never been far from thoughts of their other mission—finding out who killed Special Agent Wilcox, and why. "Yeah," he said. "A true believer who just might have a motive for killing a courier."

SEVEN

SHORT AND LONG

Learned Searcher Taranarak stood placidly and listened to the bumping and thumping from the outside of her house as her jailers unbolted the door. Taranarak had had time to think things through. She had, thus far, been confined for thirty-two days—a barbarically long sentence by Metrannan standards—but she had found the solitude restful, even useful.

The door swung open. "Come! Now!" one of them shouted. But she was in no hurry. They had kept her under house arrest, with the doors sealed, the windows covered, and all communications cut off. If they were so disorganized as to be in a hurry when it came time for her to depart, that was not her problem. Nor was it her duty to put the Bureaucracy of Order in a good mood. She took her time, preparing herself carefully for departure, then stepping out of the house calmly and slowly, pleased to see that her state of calm was unnerving them even more than she had expected.

They urged her outside and toward the transport waiting on the landing pad by her house. It was her first time outside since her confinement had begun. They urged her forward, but, just as they reached the transport, the guards paused, as if by habit, as if every prisoner stopped at that point, and they had been trained to expect it.

No doubt most prisoners stopped to enjoy the feel of fresh air, the sense of a sky overhead, at least the momentary illusion of freedom. But Taranarak stopped to stare in horrified astonishment at the city vista spread out before her.

Her home was in the hills to the northwest of the city center, and it had a magnificent view of the whole grand sweep of the metropolis. But she had not seen that view for a long time, because they had been petty enough to board up her windows.

She saw towering plumes of smoke over the city and the marks of fire, disorder, destruction. She heard shouts, cries, the muffled, far-off *thud* of an explosion. Emergency vehicles of all sorts were rushing through the skies in every direction. She allowed herself to be guided into the aircar and stared numbly out the window as the aircar lifted off. It was bad enough to look down on the city torn by riot. But it was worse, far worse, to realize that it was possible, even likely, that she had *caused* those fires and riots.

* * *

The Order Patrol aircar swung south and east toward the center of the city, affording her a terrifying panorama of the city in chaos. The aircar began its descent toward the plaza in front of the

Bureaucracy's headquarters. The plaza was in utter turmoil. A burned-out aircar lay on its side, windows smashed, smoke still rising from its interior. Order Squad teams were struggling to hold back a crowd of angry, shouting protesters as workers rushed to assemble a heavy-duty barricade to surround the building.

It had been dozens of generations since an Order Squad had been forced to deal with violent protest, and it was plain they were woefully unprepared to handle the situation. Everything looked improvised, thrown together, poorly planned.

The aircar landed with a heavy bump, and she was being bundled out of the vehicle almost before it stopped moving. Just at that moment, the crowd surged forward, almost as if the landing were some sort of cue or signal. The Order Squad teams gave way, and suddenly she was swept up in a sea of angry, shouting Metrannans. She was knocked off her feet, but the crowd was so dense she could not fall down.

Suddenly, ungentle hands seized her by her right arms, and an Order Patrol officer was pulling her toward the Bureaucracy's main entrance. All of her disdain for the Order Service vanished in that moment, instantly transforming into pathetic, fearful gratitude for their protection.

As suddenly as the riot had engulfed her, she was pulled out of it and half-thrown through the heavily reinforced doors of the Bureaucracy's main entrance, stumbling through a lobby filled with worried Patrol officers, improvised care stations, command centers, and piles of ruined furniture shoved out of the way in corners or pressed into service as part of an interior barricade.

They got her into an elevator. They started it up and ushered her out onto an upper floor. It was a place of unexpected normalcy, up high enough that the shouts and cries of the mob outside were but dim murmurs. The smells of smoke, sweat, and fear so strong and pungent down below were here only the faintest hint, the merest whiff of disaster.

The officers guided her down a hallway. One of them swung open a massive ornamental door, and the others steered her through it.

She stepped inside, heard the door boom shut behind her—and found she was not before the Council of Determination she had expected, but rather a much different sort of meeting. They were not in the exalted, high-ceilinged, steely-grey confines of the Great Room, but in a smaller, more secluded, less formal chamber. A large window took up most of one wall, providing a very clear view of the city and the chaos that had engulfed it.

There was a table just inside the door, with a saddle-chair in front of it. Plainly that was meant for her. She took her place warily. Three beings sat behind the table, and a fourth stood.

This was no Council of Determination, but she could see at once she was on trial all the same. She sat before three high-ranking Operations Managers from the Bureaucracy of Order, all of them known to her. Also there, for some reason, was Bulwark of Constancy. The Unseen People were not supposed to have any formal role in strictly Metrannan affairs. This was a remarkably overt intrusion into an extremely delicate area. Taranarak could think of a half dozen reasons why Constancy might have been allowed in. None of them were good. All of them suggested that this meeting was to be secret. And secrecy might not be the best thing for Tananarak's health.

"Let us begin. The riots started two days ago," Operations Manager Yalananav said wearily, barely looking up at her. "That is to say, shortly after the rumors reached the general population. Prior to that, the stories had been confined to the scientific and administrative communities. Over the objections of Bulwark of Constancy," he went on, "we of the General Operations group felt that, despite the antisocial behavior that led to your confinement, you might have some insights that would be helpful in this circumstance."

Taranarak was silent for a full fifty heartbeats before she could bring herself to speak. "I very much regret that the second half of your statement is as unfounded as the first. I committed no antisocial act—but likewise I do not have the least idea how to curb the riots. I know nothing about them. I only learned of them from what I saw on the trip here. I have no skill or background in security matters."

"Your behavior was indeed antisocial," said

Bulwark of Constancy, using tone and gesture to indicate the statement of indisputable fact, not mere opinion.

"That is not what is at issue here," said Manager Yalananav. "We have far more urgent matters to consider."

"I disagree most strongly," Constancy replied.

"In this matter, at least, I must agree with Bulwark of Constancy," said Taranarak, "though my reasons are quite different. You must have the complete facts before deciding how to proceed— not only in regard to the riots, but to longer-range and larger-scale issues. If there is any information you need, you need it now."

"While the city burns, she wishes to discuss— and rewrite history!" Bulwark of Constancy protested.

"Granted, Unseen colleague," said Operations Manager Fallogon, "but if she talks, it will not delay the security forces, and perhaps she can tell us *why* the city burns—and I wish to hear her."

"I must speak frankly then," Taranarak said, "and that might cause me to speak with less discretion and courtesy than would normally be the case. I ask your forgiveness for that in advance." *After all, what are you going to do to punish me for rudeness?* she asked to herself. *Lock me up?*

She gestured toward Bulwark of Constancy, then nodded toward her other inquisitors. "Why does the city burn? I suspect it is because both the Unseen People and our own people have lived in such quiet and stable times for so long that we have forgotten change, and we do not truly understand that change cannot be undone. Our lives are so ordered, so patterned, so sheltered, and have been for so long, that we fail to understand change to be an unalterable fact rather than some sort of nuisance that can be pushed away if it becomes too troubling."

"But nothing has changed," protested Manager Yalananav. "Yes, there was the threat of a huge shift in how we live our lives, but it did not come to pass."

"Manager Yalananav, have you noticed that everyone, including myself, speaks of the new thing, the change, in such generalities that we never identify it at all? I believe that is because we fear its power, and half hope it will not be quite so powerful if we do not speak of it openly."

"We are not superstitious savages, frightened that this thing is some monster from the Old Stories," Yalananav replied peevishly.

"No? Then why have you still not dared to speak the monster's name? Why haven't I? And why do we try to wish away the great changes by saying they did not happen? For there were *two* great changes, and you have just described them. A factor in our lives that all of us, for unnumbered generations, have firmly believed to be set, established, inalterable, was found to be none of those things. And the *knowledge* that things might change escaped from the land of bureaucrats and specialists and into the general population."

She set her four legs square on either side of her saddle-seat, laid both her pairs of arms at her side, took a deep breath, and spoke again. "I have had much time to think during my confinement. Bulwark of Constancy told me, in no uncertain term, moments before I was arrested, that 'Change is wrong.' She said we have—or had at that time— an optimum situation, and therefore any change could only be for the worse. But I have to think that the thing that ails us is absolute and rigid resistance to change.

"If two geologic zones move past each other along a fault line at a slow and steady rate, there is the occasional slight tremor, but nothing more. It is when a fault line is locked up, frozen, held rigidly in place for a long time, that stresses build up, accumulate, amplify, until the forces of movement are simply more powerful than the forces holding things in check, and everything breaks loose with unimaginable violence." She gestured out the window. "*Then* comes the massive earthquake, the tidal wave—the chaos. For how many endless, weary years have our people known all the other starfaring races live twice, three, five, twelve times as long as us? How long has the frustration of our short, short lives been simmering?"

"From before the time our history books record," Yalananav said testily. "What is your point?"

"That it is time to call things by their proper names, and to face the facts. The Metrannan race has the shortest life span of any known intelligent species. Our maximum life span is roughly half the average life span of even humans—and they are the shorter-lived of the two currently known Younger Races. *All* of the Elder Races live far, far longer. Historic records show that, in pretechnological times, our lives were a third shorter than they are now. The common and received wisdom is that everything that *could* be done to extend our life spans *had* been done. Were we even to attempt further life extension, we would at best fail, but would, more likely, kill or seriously harm those who received such treatments."

"You speak harshly of unhappy subjects, but all this is known to all of us here," said Yalananav, sounding uncomfortable.

"But it needs to be said, and accepted as the true state of affairs before we face the next and darker truth," Taranarak replied.

"Which would be what?"

"*That nearly all of it is false.* Before his death several dozen twelve-days ago, my predecessor, Learned Searcher Hallaben, did new work—I emphasize, *new* work—in the field of geriatrics that established beyond any doubt—not just reasonable doubt, *but any doubt at all*—that significant extension of life span was possible using treatments that were safe and inexpensive, and that the treatments would be beneficial even for older

Metrannans, even those who had reached three-quarters of their expected life span—though not as dramatically effective as if the treatments were provided at a younger age."

"That cannot be!" Yalananav protested.

"It can be, and is true," Taranarak said. "And, I might add, since our basic technology reached its current state of maturity thousands of twelve-years ago, there was nothing preventing this discovery other than our own belief that it could not be done." Even as she spoke, she wondered if that was strictly true. It was hard, even for her, to accept the idea that even Hallaben had needed outside help in order to find the way forward. "And there is more," she went on. "Early versions of the treatment might be more complex, but it seemed likely that, in final form, in order to receive the full benefit, an individual would require only a once-only dosage that could be eaten, drunk, or even inhaled. Repeated doses would have no additional effect."

"Shock and glory," said Yalananav in astonishment. "You could simply add it to the water supply and treat the entire population of the city at one time."

"In theory, I suppose," said Taranarak, "but it would be foolhardy in the extreme to do it that way without massive planning and testing. I should add that it even seemed possible—though far less certain—that the results of the treatment could, with further careful and cautious research, be made heritable. Parents would be able to pass down the genetic trait of long life to their children."

There was a moment of strain, of silence, as the managers took in the new knowledge. All of them had heard rumors and stories, of course. But she had given them *facts*. Cold, hard facts. She glanced toward Bulwark of Constancy, but the Unseen was motionless, frozen in an utterly neutral pose.

"How—how long?" Tigmin asked. "How much longer a life might I—might a person—expect?"

"That is far from certain, as it was not possible to run extensive tests. After all, it has only been a few months since the new process was discovered. But our experts in geriatrics estimate that it could provide a doubling of life span if treatment was provided before the midpoint of life. An older person in good health, who had not reached the point of sudden senescence, the onset of rapid final aging syndrome, might expect something like an extension of an eighth to a twelfth of his or her life span. Two to four years, perhaps."

"That is not possible," Fallogon objected. "Our scientists proved thousands of years ago that no such dramatic extensions of life were possible."

"They *are* possible," Taranarak said. "I can show you the test results." *And it was not, strictly speaking,* our *scientists who found that out.* But there was no point in dragging that humiliation into the conversation. There was enough shock, fear, and bewilderment in the room already—to say nothing of the fact that each of the Metrannans facing her was suddenly distracted by calculation of how much longer each of them might live, and what he might be able to do with the years.

"If what you say is true," said Yalananav, "then it is no rumor that sparks the riots outside."

"Or, rather, the rumors have a strong basis," said Tigmin. "There are claims that some high-ranking persons have already obtained the treatment and are keeping it to themselves, or that the discovery has been suppressed."

"That last item is far from a rumor," Taranarak said. "Why have I been detained for my antisocial behavior if not to keep the work quiet?"

"Because of your lies!" Bulwark of Constancy half shouted, in tones so violent that everyone else in the room jerked back in surprise. The others had almost forgotten that Constancy was there.

"I have told no lies," said Taranarak. "I have spoken truths that are unexpected, unsettling, and new—but no lies of any sort."

"The things you speak of cannot be! They must not be!"

The things I speak of might lead to the extinction of the Unseen Race on this planet, Taranarak thought. *Already your Enclave grows a trifle smaller every year. How would your people cope with a doubling of the Metrannan population?* Of course, that question was at the core of ·other problems as well. *How well would we Metrannans cope? What would we have to give up? How would families change? What traditions would al-*

*ter? What patterns of life would no longer make
sense, or even be possible? How would long life affect our culture, our art, our relations with others
of the Elder Races?* Metrannans had always had
something close to a racial inferiority complex that
had doubtless shaped—and even warped—their
relations with other sentient species. What would
change there?

"The things I speak of *can* be," said Taranarak.
"At least, they could be. If the lost work is recovered."

" 'Lost work'?" Yalananav echoed. "Do you
mean to say that mob out there is rioting for a cure
for old age that we no longer have?"

Taranarak forced herself to speak calmly. "That
is the case," she said.

"I thought you said you had proof."

"We do," she said. "Full and convincing results
that demonstrate, on the cellular and biochemical
level, the suppression of premature senescence,
along with other data from our standard geriatric
modeling systems that confirm the effect is real,
and transferable to real living tissues, organs, and
individuals. The treatment will—would—work."

"Then what is missing?"

"Nothing!" Bulwark of Constancy said.
"Taranarak's predecessor wisely and deliberately
sent away the data concerning the formulae and
manufacturing process and other details of the
treatment."

"Whether it was wise, I do not know, but yes, he

sent it away—at your urging," Taranarak replied accusingly. "And even that was a compromise. *You* wished to see the work destroyed altogether."

"I do not deny it," said Bulwark of Constancy. It gestured toward the window and the disturbances in the city. "Change is wrong. Even the idea of change, the *threat* of change, is enough to set off upheavals. What will happen if the treatment does not work perfectly? Or if it works on some individuals, some gene groups, better than others? Even if it is flawless—consider! The duration of childhood and adolescence are unaffected by this life-extension treatment. This means that if you double the life span, you *more* than double the *adult* life span, the productive working life of every person. Will there be enough work for all? And at the same moment, when it will be necessary to *curtail* reproduction or face a ruinous population explosion, the period of fertility for adults will likewise more than double! What of the costs of new dwellings, new infrastructure—in effect, a whole new city to support the increased population?"

"Every other sentient race manages with a longer life span," Tigmin said. "Some live far longer than we will—we would—even with this new treatment."

Tigmin had said more than he intended, but in a sense it didn't matter. It was impossible *not* to guess the thoughts of the others in the room—the fantasies of long life racing through the minds of the Metrannans.

And the Unseen Being had revealed far more than Tigmin. Moments before it had been denying the existence and effectiveness of the longlife treatment. But it was plain from what she had said about the details of the process that Bulwark of Constancy was intimately familiar with the science behind the treatment.

"At present," Taranarak said, "no one can expect to live any longer at all. Yes, we have the proof that the treatment will work—but we no longer have the treatment itself, or the data needed to re-create it."

"Where in the dark skies is it? Has it been destroyed?" Tigmin asked.

"In the dark skies indeed. We do not know it has been destroyed. According to what I have been able to learn, Bulwark of Constancy of the Unseen People, after long and careful and quiet negotiation, convinced my predecessor, Searcher Hallaben, to arrange for a courier from the human world known as Center to collect the main data files and remove them to the safekeeping of the humans. All other copies would be destroyed. Hallaben hoped to gather together a group of planners, economists, philosophers, and various experts to consider the consequences of massive life extension. It was hoped that, with enough time and reflection, a proper and prudent way could be found to make use of the—his—discovery.

Unfortunately, he died before that process could begin."

"But why humans? What possible reason could there be for involving ourselves with a pack of Younger Race upstarts?" Tigmin demanded.

Taranarak still saw no need to add humiliation to all the other powerful emotions in the room. Better to deflect the question and answer it only in part rather than let the whole galling truth come out. "My predecessor, Hallaben, apparently believed that no Metrannan could be trusted with the formula, for what should be obvious reasons."

"Obvious enough to our rioting compatriots," Tigmin said wryly. "But that tells me why not Metrannans. But why humans?"

Taranarak shifted her four feet for a moment, devoutly wishing Tigmin had not asked that question quite so directly. But perhaps she could still get by with a partial answer. Certainly Constancy would not wish to endure the damage to its pride that a full answer would produce. "We have always had good relations with humans—and, after all, they are the younger of the two Younger Races—weak, with few alliances, eager to establish themselves, wanting to make friends and curry favor. And, because they are not powerful, they are safe. They are far too weak to threaten us."

"Wrong," said Yalananav. "Most wrong indeed. For Hallaben gave them a weapon—one that can only be used against us."

"What?" Tigmin said sharply. "How?"

"In two ways," said Yalananav. "One, Tigmin, you yourself described. All they would need to do would be to introduce the treatment into the city water supply, here and on all the other worlds settled by our people, then sit back and watch our civilization unravel under the pressure of unplanned, unexpected, uncontrolled change."

"To what purpose?" Taranarak demanded.

"I have not the faintest idea," said Yalananav. "I am thinking of capability, not intent. Perhaps some species that is our enemy would put them up to it. The other weapon would be even more insidious: simply to *threaten* to unleash the treatment in an uncontrolled manner. What better form of blackmail could you imagine?"

"All of this is paranoid fantasy!" Taranarak shot back. "You imagine a species that is not our enemy could attack us—and therefore *will* attack us simply because they *can*." She calmed herself and spoke again. "In any event, the entire issue is moot. The courier never reached Center. We have made repeated and careful inquiries."

She paused for six heartbeats and spoke once more. "While I do believe your fears of attack and blackmail are vastly overstated, I concede that the situation does expose us to certain vulnerabilities. For good or ill, there is one other vital point: As best we have been able to learn, no human besides the courier was ever made aware of what, exactly, was in the document that the courier carried, though plainly the humans knew it was of great importance."

"So, this knowledge has existed since before Hallaben's death but was first suppressed, and then lost altogether?" Tigmin asked.

"Lost, but not lost altogether," Taranarak said eagerly. She gestured toward the window and the plumes of smoke over the city. "I did not expect this day to come so soon, but I did expect it to come. Sooner or later, secrets will come out. It was inevitable that *someone*—probably several someones—among the dozens who worked in our laboratories would talk. Dribs and drabs of fact would come out. Rumors would pop up. All this has happened. We have a city full of people angry that we cannot or will not produce the magic potion that we have thrown away.

"Furthermore, knowledge cannot be suppressed. Not forever. Since I took over the laboratory and gradually learned of Hallaben's discoveries and the manner in which they were lost, I have been working to reconstruct them. We have much of the original research data he had, along with the results data, and various other pieces of information—as well as the knowledge that he succeeded. I hoped to reconstruct his work in time, to be able to provide you, our leadership, with the treatment."

"So that we could release it to the hordes outside and save ourselves?" Fallogon asked. "Bribe them to stop the madness?"

"No," she answered. "So that you would have options, the ability to choose rather than being forced to do nothing but sit back and watch the city burn."

"How close are you to success?" Yalananav asked, making no attempt to conceal his eagerness.

Taranarak longed to make a triumphant declaration, to tell them she was merely three twelve-days, only one twelve-day, just a single day, a mere heartbeat from the solution. But this was no time for idle boasts. "At first, progress seemed rapid. But I have bogged down and spent far too much time tracking down leads that have not worked out. I have made no progress to speak of in the last three twelve-days."

"But how could that be?"

"Because Hallaben was a genius and I am merely very smart," Taranarak snapped back. "I could offer a great many other far more complicated explanations, but that is what they would all come down to." She paused. "No. That is not a fair or accurate summing up. Hallaben's genius is undoubted, and its loss is a large part of the problem. But we have not recovered all of the underlying data." She looked over at Bulwark of Constancy, who had resumed its previous motionless state, then looked back at the trio of Metrannans. "It would appear," she said very stiffly, "that a great deal of the material was deliberately erased, deleted, and destroyed."

"So we are left with the worst of all cases," said

Yalananav. "We have a population utterly convinced that there is a cure for their short lives, convinced that we have deliberately denied it to them—which is in fact what Hallaben and Bulwark of Constancy did—and we now have no treatment, and no prospect of a treatment." An annunciator chirruped, and Yalananav consulted his pocket dataviewer. "The commander of the Order Patrols reports that maybe—maybe—the riots are subsiding," he said. "He believes we may have a period of quiet setting in."

"At least until the next rumor breaks loose," Tigmin said.

"I no longer fear rumors, Colleague Tigmin," Yalananav said as he put away his dataviewer. "But after what I have just heard, I tremble at the very thought of the *truth* breaking loose."

EIGHT
THERE AND GONE

Jamie squirmed in the *Sholto*'s pilot seat and flexed his fingers a few times before placing them on the controls. They had topped off the *Sholto*'s thruster power as much as possible, transferring energy from the booster stage. It was time to cut loose from the booster and head out on their own. Jamie had drawn the piloting duty. He wasn't yet fully qualified, and wasn't supposed to fly a ship except under direct supervision of a certified pilot like Hannah.

"Okay," said Hannah, "take it easy. No need to rush."

"And no need to breathe down my neck quite so hard," Jamie grumbled. He did a mental check of his planned procedures and sequences, took a deep breath, and keyed in the first command. He watched the displays as first the *Sholto*'s engines, then the auxiliary booster's thrusters, throttled down to zero. He could almost imagine that he felt a flickering shift in weight as the thrust zeroed out, but he knew it was an illusion. The *Sholto*'s acceleration compensators were far too powerful, precise, and sensitive to allow any such variations.

Otherwise, Hannah and he would have been mashed flat into jelly at the start of the flight. The gravity field in the *Sholto* was a steady one gee and was going to stay that way.

Jamie checked his displays again. There was no great rush to complete this maneuver, and he was much more interested in getting it right rather than doing it fast.

"All right," he said. "All ship thrusters and auxiliary booster throttles are at zero. Main and aux booster propulsion systems to safe mode. Prepping for undock from aux booster."

"I'm right here, Jamie," Hannah said, plainly amused. "I can see the displays as well as you can."

"Just trying to do it right," Jamie said, trying to sound calmer than he felt. "Call-outs are part of the official procedure."

Hannah gestured out the viewport toward the lonely stars. "No one else around for about a billion kilometers or so. I won't tell if you won't."

"So sue me. I'm trying to develop good habits here, okay?" He checked everything over one more time and moved to the next step. "Confirming prep for undock," he said.

"And then you can confirm the confirmation," Hannah said.

"All right, all right, all right." Jamie was inescapably reminded of his first driving lessons. He had tried to convince his father that manual operation of a ground vehicle was a totally archaic skill, as dead as blacksmithing or archery. But his father had insisted, and reminded him that automatic systems can break down, or impose needless limits in emergencies, or simply not be available in out-of-the-way places. The same arguments could be applied to flying a BSI starship. The BSI ships were *supposed* to be totally automated, but if an agent trained to fly was aboard, that pilot-agent could serve as a backup or deal with unexpected situations.

No one had ever bothered configuring an autopilot system to deal with the case of two *Sherlock*-class ships docked nose-to-nose that needed to be *un*docked from an auxiliary booster strapped on underneath. This one needed a pilot.

"All systems in green. Initiating strap-down release command." He pressed the appropriate button and heard the massive latches letting go with a series of echoing booms. "All strap-down latches showing good release. Initiating safe distancing maneuver." Jamie took the joystick and used it to tap the forward attitude thrusters just ever so slightly, pushing the *Sholto* and the *Adler* away from the aux booster. "Clean separation," he announced, indulging himself far enough to allow a note of smugness to shine through.

"All right, very good," said Hannah, giving him a pat on the shoulder. "You get a gold star. You acted just like a real pilot, and you'll get the proper notation in your file. Get us a safe distance from the booster, send it back to the barn, get our candle lit again, and let's be on our way."

Jamie had all the appropriate sequences programmed in already and was just about to execute the first one when he hesitated. "Wait a second," he said. "Just for a minute, let me think like a ship's commander and not a pilot."

"Okay, Captain Mendez. Or aye, aye, sir, I suppose. What have you got?"

"Come on, I'm being serious. We're supposed to order the booster to decelerate itself, then boost itself back to BSI HQ to be picked up, refurbed, and reused, right?"

"And we're supposed to eat all our vegetables at dinner and brush our teeth before we go to bed," Hannah said. "So we follow the rules. *That's* command thinking?"

"My point is that it seems to me we've got a lot of possible scenarios where we come back short of propulsion power," Jamie replied. "You and Kelly talked about it at the briefing. We might have so little juice left that we could be stranded, waiting for pickup—maybe long enough for food or air or water to start running short. The booster's supposed to use much lower thrust—only about two gees—to get itself back, since they aren't in a hurry to have it returned and there's no point in running it at full tilt and wearing it out. As of right now, the aux booster still has lots of power stored on board.

"Suppose instead we just left the booster on its current heading and brought it to near-zero velocity relative to CenterStar. Rig it so we could find it again on the way back in. If we had a high-precision lock on its trajectory, and we *did* get back to CenterStar System with our tanks just about dry, we could order it to home back in on us, redock, use the booster's propulsion, and boost home under our own power, get back a lot sooner, and return the booster not much later than we would have otherwise."

Hannah frowned, then nodded. "Okay, Cap'n Mendez. That makes a lot of sense. See if you can set it up. I like anything that gives us more options. Just don't spend so much time on it that we arrive late at our transit-jump point and have to recalculate. Meantime, I'm going to get back to reading the files before we get to the fun part and start searching the *Adler*."

"All right," he said. "It shouldn't take me long." But somehow he found himself wishing it would. It was wholly irrational, of course, but the longer they put off searching the *Adler*, the longer they delayed going back aboard her, the more he dreaded doing so.

You starting to be scared of ghosts? No, that wasn't it. But it came close. Aside from studying up on Metran and Metrannans, he had also read over the personnel file of Special Agent Trevor Wilcox III as closely as he could.

There was often an odd one-way intimacy between a murder victim and the investigator on the case. Jamie knew things about Special Agent Trip Wilcox that Wilcox's own mother likely didn't know. There was every evidence in the file that

Agent Wilcox had been a fine and admirable person—but even a saint commits minor sins on occasion.

It was a violation of Trevor Wilcox's privacy for Jamie to know all about the mistakes on his income tax, his repeated requests for advances on his pay, the small fortune in QuickBeam messages sent back and forth to the fiancée on Earth, the two mental-health days he had been granted when he received the news that she had married the boy next door instead, even a brief report on the ruckus his mother had caused when the former fiancée had refused to return the ring that had belonged to Trevor's grandmother. The file was silent as to how or whether that crisis had been resolved. When he had read that, Jamie had felt torn between desperately hoping the ring had been returned, and a deep sense of something close to shame for knowing such an intimate detail.

In a normal murder investigation, there might have been some purpose in knowing such things. The fiancée might have been a suspect. The financial problems might have served as a warning flag, pointing toward some other difficulty that might in turn point toward motives or suspects. The transcripts of the QuickBeam messages might have had some reference to a time, a place, a person, an event that might be a lead.

But Trevor Wilcox III was found in the depths of space months after dying of old age, alone, billions of kilometers from any human being, and the only reasonable explanation for how that could have happened was that he had been killed by a xeno using some weapon utterly unknown to humanity or, far less likely, by some previously unknown illness. Nothing in Trevor's personnel record could possibly offer any sort of clue as to how that had happened.

Jamie looked up toward the *Adler*. Except maybe, just maybe, knowing every single thing there was to know about Trev Wilcox was going to be absolutely vital. Maybe he used his ex-fiancée's name on a password. Maybe knowing that Wilcox had consistently misspelled the same word over and over in his love letters would tell them that a log entry supposedly written by Wilcox was a plant, a forgery, because the misspelling wasn't there.

After all, Wilcox must have known he was going to die. He must also have known that Jamie and Hannah, or someone like them, would be sent to investigate—and he would have known how the BSI worked. He would have *known* that someone like Special Agent Jamie Mendez would study his personnel file, check his bank records, study his love life, read the notation on his mother's weakness for drink. Wilcox might well have factored that into whatever plans he made, whatever means he chose to conceal the decrypt where xenos would never find it, where, perhaps, most humans would never find it, but where two BSI agents who studied the murder victim *would* find it.

Did that make the intrusion even worse—or did it, somehow, make Trev Wilcox into Jamie and Hannah's silent coinvestigator, working with them from beyond the grave?

Or are you just trying to come up with excuses for snooping around in his private affairs to make yourself feel better?

Jamie turned back to his piloting problems with a heavy heart. If he had been trying to make himself feel better about the case—or about searching the *Adler*—he was definitely not doing a very good job.

* * *

A more practiced pilot might have been able to do it sooner, but after a few false starts, Jamie had the booster programmed to slow itself down to a crawl and then wait for their return on a very precisely designated trajectory, and also managed to get the combined craft of the *Sholto* and the *Adler* back under boost, relying solely on the *Sholto*'s main propulsion.

"Ready to get moving?" Hannah asked. They stood on the *Sholto*'s lower deck, looking up the rope ladder toward the *Adler*'s waiting interior. Both of them were in hooded white isolation suits, with gloves on their hands and pullover booties covering their shoes. They looked like a pair of high-tech ghosts preparing to haunt the ship where Trevor Wilcox had died.

"No," said Jamie. "I'm not ready. I feel as if I'm

getting ready to spend the night in a haunted house because someone dared me. Or that we're about to clear out a family home after a relative has died."

"Now I know why the whole idea of this search has been giving me a case of the creeps. Come on. The sooner we start, the sooner it's over with."

Hannah led the way up the ladder past the upper deck and the open hatch cover. She paused for a moment, and then moved carefully into the zero-gee confines of the docking tunnel. She grabbed on to the netting, flipped herself over, and aimed her feet at the *Adler*'s ladder. She started moving down into the other ship. Jamie followed her up the ladder and felt his stomach do a few flip-flops as he went into the zero-gee zone. He grabbed hold of the netting, flipped himself around—and then had to pause for a moment as his stomach nearly rebelled altogether. He swallowed hard, took a deep breath, maneuvered around to the *Adler*'s rope ladder, and made his way down into the ship in which Trevor Wilcox had died.

Both agents made their way down to the lower deck of the *Adler* and stood there, looking around uncertainly. Hannah shook her head. "Weird. Really weird. These two ships are supposed to be exactly the same. They *look* exactly the same. But somehow this one just screams out *different* to me."

"I know what you mean," Jamie said. It wasn't any one thing that signaled the differences to him—in fact, at first, he wasn't even sure what the differences were. No doubt most of them were due to the fact that the *Sholto* had just come off a refit and refurbishment. There were no scuff marks on her control panels, no scratches in the paint, no dents and dings in the bulkheads. The interior of the *Adler* had any number of such small signs of wear.

But that wasn't all of it. There were subtle differences in the rhythm of the *Adler*'s interior noises and vibration, the way the air circulated, perhaps even the color of the light. "The two ships might be twins, but they aren't identical," he said. "Not by a long shot. It's all subtle stuff, yeah, but you couldn't trick any human who had spent time aboard any sort of spacecraft that the *Adler* was the *Sholto*. I'm guessing that xenos wouldn't be any easier to fool. It would be a good idea if we could avoid boarding parties."

"That's exactly what I was going to say," Hannah said.

"Okay, let's get to the business at hand," said Jamie. "You're the senior agent. What's your carefully thought-out, rigidly logical plan for managing the search?"

Hannah shrugged, rustling the fabric of her isosuit. "I never know how to do a search until I'm there and about to do it. I don't want to get all mystical or anything like that, but I always try to listen to what the search area, the crime scene, is telling me." She paused for a minute. "And this one is trying its hardest to lie to us."

"What are you talking about?"

She gestured to indicate the whole of the *Adler*. "This ship is saying *empty*. *Untouched*. *Unused*. Climb back through the docking tunnel to the *Sholto*, and her interior sure doesn't look that way. We've taped research notes to the wall, stowed our luggage less than perfectly—by the way, you left your socks on the deck again—eaten meals, and done any number of other things that leave traces. Signs of habitation."

"So what?"

"So there's *none* of that here. Even allowing for the fact that Gunther and his crew had to do a very nasty cleanup job—removing the body and the pilot's chair and any, ah, decay products and so on—the place is too clean." She looked around, and shook her head. There were two small lockers off to one side of the air lock, meant for stowing personal effects. Hannah stepped over to them and opened them up. "Empty," she said. "It should have jumped out at both of us when we first came through the ship," she said. "Where is it all?"

"All what?" Jamie asked.

"His personal items," she said, gesturing at the empty lockers. "Courier runs aren't brief-and-go jobs, the way a criminal case usually is. They're scheduled in advance. I checked the records. He had more than forty-eight hours' notice that he was headed out on this run, and he had been on *Sherlock*-class ships before. He knew how Spartan they are, and his planned mission would have him cooped up on this thing for eight days outbound and eight inbound, with only about a day off-ship in between. And he wouldn't need to do the usual panic-stricken study-in-transit job either. He must have known he was going to have time on his hands. So what did he do to keep from getting bored out of his mind? Where are his books? His movies to watch? Every agent in BSI is nuts for crossword puzzles. *I* keep four or five books of them in the Ready-To-Go duffel in my cubicle back in the Bullpen, plus books, movies, that sort of thing. They're in the *Sholto* right now."

"For that matter," Jamie said, "where are his clothes?" There was a larger locker on the opposite side of the air lock intended for hanging up shirts, jackets, and trousers. Jamie opened that as well. "Nothing," he said. "Nothing at all to meet with the very, very clothes-conscious Metrannans. What did he do, live in one set of shipboard coveralls for the whole mission?"

"Not unless he wanted to be beheaded for insulting his hosts," Hannah said. She pulled a datapad out of her iso-suit's outer pocket and worked the controls. "Lemme just check the manifest for his mission."

"That wouldn't have a detailed inventory of personal effects," Jamie objected. "Just a report that the agent had carried his standard Ready-To-Go duffel or whatever other luggage he had."

"I know," said Hannah. "But it *does* report his RTG duffel and one other 'suitcase containing personal items for use in transit.' " She looked at Jamie. "So where are they? Where are the suitcase and the duffel? And where is *his* suitcase full of fancy-dress clothes for Metran?"

"Gunther and his crew must have taken all that stuff off," said Jamie.

"No," said Hannah, checking the datapad again. "They didn't. They did a detailed inventory of removed items—and *none* of his clothes or personal items—or the luggage itself—the RTG duffel bag or the other suitcase—were listed."

"They *must* have taken them off," Jamie said. "Books and clothes and luggage would all give you lots of places to conceal the decrypt key. Stick it inside the binding of a paper-page book. Sew it into the lining of the duffel, or razor open a seam in your jacket lining and stuff it in there. Plus they wouldn't have gone through all that stuff here on board. They'd have been able to do a much better job searching through all that stuff back in the BSI HQ forensics lab."

"I agree. You're absolutely right," said Hannah. "They would have taken all the personal effects out of the ship and searched through them with scanners and probes and opened up all the seams and bindings and fasteners and so on. Except they didn't."

She handed him the datapad, a grim look her face. "You've seen them already, but look again. Evidence photos taken just after they came aboard, before Wilcox or anything else was removed. A couple of shots of Wilcox are taken from over-head, and you can see the lower deck pretty clearly below and behind. The lockers are empty—and you can tell because the locker doors are open. *Latched* open, so they couldn't swing shut."

"This doesn't make any sense," Jamie protested.

"Food containers," said Hannah. She pulled open the trash compactor and checked the bin. "Empty." She checked the datapad again. "There was a small bag full of trash sitting on the upper deck, next to the pilot's station. You can see it in the crime scene shots. They removed it and examined it. No decrypt key found. Just the remains of eight opened mealpacks, three empty, five partially empty, with the remaining food still there 'in an advanced state of decomposition,' plus three empty water bottles. Four unopened mealpacks and two full water bottles were also found strapped to hold-down netting by the pilot's chair." She glanced up at the pilot's station. "Those are still there. No other reports of trash or unopened food containers found."

"Why are we the first ones to notice this?" Jamie asked. "Why wasn't it in any of the reports?"

"Because everyone's always doing everything at once when they're prepping for a mission at crash speed. There isn't time to sit down and have a staff meeting about every decision. They trust—what was that slogan? It's on some motivational poster in Gunther's office. 'Trust Initiative over Coordination.' That was it. No one told anyone to re-mark the hull of the *Adler* to pretend it was the *Sholto*. Someone just realized it needed doing and went and did it. There were probably four or five crews—forensics, Gunther's crew, launch prep and replenishment, tech data recovery—that went in and out of this ship. Probably Gunther's team was too busy with the corpse to deal with anything else, and all the other teams assumed that one of the others had done the clean-out."

"The *forensics team* missed the clean-out?" Jamie objected. "The launch prep team I can see, but forensics should have screamed bloody murder."

Hannah checked her datapad one more time. "What the—how in blazes did *this* not jump out at me? They didn't protest because they were never on board."

"*What?*"

"Don't look at me like it was my fault. I'm standing in an iso-suit squinting at a datapad billions of kilometers from where it happened."

"What happened?"

"The log files show what teams with what personnel came on board. There was a forensics tech assigned to Gunther's team—but just to help with the body, and she was a medical forensics specialist, not an evidence tech. They remove the body. Then there's some sort of lock-down declared, and everyone ordered out of the ship. That was about twelve hours before we got our briefing." Hannah thought for a moment. "Sometime right about then, I'd guess, is when they got word back from BSI-DLO and the whole business about the War-Starter designation and so on. Next thing in the case log narrative is Kelly ordering a rush search of the ship for the decryption key, to be done at the same time as the ship was being prepped for launch—refueled, replenished, and so on."

"It must have been about then that Commander Kelly decided to send us out with the *Sholto* and *Adler* docked together. That's where the break comes," Jamie said, who had pulled up the same data on his datapad. "The prime focus up to then had been figuring out how Special Agent Wilcox died. That was what the medical forensics specialist was doing there. But then that gets shoved on the back burner when they hear about the decrypt key and the War-Starter warning."

"I think you're right. And up until that point, forensics was there for the medical-pathology angle of understanding why Wilcox died," Hannah said. "That part of their assignment is canceled, suddenly everything is rushed—and so their time in the ship is canceled. And the ship is searched by Gunther's people, who are just looking for the decrypt key, rather than the ship being examined by the forensics people who would be trying to determine what happened on board."

"And in the rush and the shuffle, it doesn't really register with anyone that the ship is completely empty. So no one stops to realize, gee, *that's* kind of strange."

"Until we notice it billions of kilometers from base with our transit-jump to the Metran system eight hours away." Hannah sat down on the edge of the pilot's chair and looked around. "So what the hell happened to all his personal gear? Did the Metrannan search party take it all? Just leave him enough food and water to get home, but take everything else so *they* could search it?"

"That doesn't make much sense either," said Jamie. "They'd have the clothes and other stuff, but they would have left behind the ship, with all of its hiding places. They'd be volunteering to leave the *Adler* itself unsearched, or at least not as thoroughly searched. If they were going to search his clothing and personal effects in such detail that they needed to seize them to do microscans, then they'd *have* to be prepared to search the whole ship the same way. They should have just impounded the whole ship, thrown Agent Wilcox in the brig on their ship, hauled the *Adler* back to base, scanned her from stem to stern, and then started taking her apart down to the molecular level."

"I think you're right—if we're assuming their behavior is always rational. Otherwise, of course, we can have them saying or doing anything we like, no matter how silly or illogical, because we can't possibly fathom what motivates the strange and mysterious Elder Races. Let's leave out that sort of logic." She thought for a minute. "Maybe the Metrannans stripped his ship *before* he left for some reason."

Jamie shook his head. "No," he said. "It's another way of saying what you just said. If we can't think of a reason for them to do X, I don't think we can spin theories that *rely* on their doing X. Besides, I think I have an answer."

"What?"

"Trevor did it," Jamie said. "For us. For you and me. To help us on the case, the search."

"I—I don't understand," Hannah said.

"Remember all your arguments about how the decrypt key isn't going to be in a microdot or anything like that? You convinced me. We're working on the theory that the decrypt key is going to be someplace we can find it, but the xenos can't—or at least won't. But Trevor knows—knew—that time might be short. Maybe he doesn't know that BSI-DLO had designated the case a possible War-Starter, but he's been briefed by someone on Metran, and he knows it's serious.

"He's left the planet, he's headed back, he's been boarded once already, and he might be boarded again. Maybe he knows that however he hid the key, he might not be able to stay lucky on the next search. He hid it someplace *safe,* somewhere the xenos wouldn't look. But he knew *we'd* be in a hurry, and he didn't want us to waste our time checking the seams on his coveralls or peeling back the lining of his duffel. Once he was clear of the boarding party, and while he still had the strength to do it, *he* put all his personal gear into the air lock, closed the inner door, and opened the outer door while it was still under pressure. He jettisoned the stuff for *us*—to help *us* on the investigation. He's the third agent, the silent partner, on this case. He knows he's under a death sentence, but he's still doing his job."

"Jamie, you're making the hairs on the back of my neck stand up. That's spooky. Really, really spooky."

"It fits the facts. It's not only possible—it makes sense. Trevor had a motive for doing it. And it's testable. We can check to see if it happened."

"The ship's auto-event log," said Hannah. "It would show when the air lock was used."

"Come on," said Jamie. "I think we're onto something." He turned and began climbing the ladder to the upper deck.

NINE

LOST WHILE SEARCHING

Jamie stepped off the ladder, Hannah right behind him. The two of them practically filled the tiny flight deck.

"The auto-event log. Would it show if the outer door was opened with pressure in the lock?" Jamie asked.

"I don't know," said Hannah, "but we can check." She started to sit down in the pilot's chair but caught the look in Jamie's eye. "You do it," she said. "This one is yours."

Jamie hesitated a moment, nodded, and then sat down in the pilot's chair. It was not the chair in which Trevor Wilcox had died. That one had been removed and replaced. But this chair occupied the same place, put Jamie's body where Trevor's had been, positioned his head, his eyes, where he could see what the dead man had seen, placed his hands on the controls the dead man had used. What he was seeing—the control panel, the viewport, the cold and lonely darkness, the remote and distant stars—were the last things Trevor Wilcox III had ever seen.

He allowed himself a moment to acknowledge

that fact, to get past it, and even to offer a silent apology to Trevor's spirit for the intrusion, before he forced all such irrational thoughts from his mind and focused on the job. He brought up the log display system and made his selection.

"Hey, that's the personal log, not the auto-event log," Hannah protested.

"I know," said Jamie. "But there's something else I want to see first. I want to reread a few log entries from around the time he would have done the jettison, if he did it at all."

Quick entry. Craft has docked with *Adler*. I am invited to permit visitors aboard. Visitors wish to view and admire the interior and contents of my fine spacecraft. I of course gladly accept this invitation to allow their visit.

"Obviously, he wrote that assuming that he was already being monitored," said Hannah.

"Agreed," Jamie said. The *Sherlock*-class ships were not large enough to be well shielded, and many of the Elder Races had astonishingly good detection systems that could easily monitor the electric impulses produced by typing at a keyboard or using a microphone connected to a dictation system. He read on to the next entry.

My visitors have up and gone, departing after an extended visit. They took a strong interest in all I had aboard and did not wish to miss any chance to learn more about my ship and my work. It may be that they will wish to return and learn more in future. It is likely they have arranged to know more about me even when they are not here. I of course wish to be generous with my time and to inform them as much as possible, but my other duties might prevent this.

It was the final entry in the personal log. It wasn't hard to interpret those words. *The boarding party has left at last. They searched everywhere, and questioned me extensively. They might decide to come back and search again.* And they wouldn't need to do that if they had found what they were looking for, Jamie reminded himself. *They have probably installed listening or monitoring devices on the ship. I'll cooperate with them and tell them anything that won't do any harm, but I won't let them find what they shouldn't get.*

"That part about how the Metrannans might *arrange to know more about me even when they are not here* is pretty clear. Did Gunther's people find any listening devices or tracking units in the *Adler*? We don't want to fly back into the Metran system with the ship we're trying to hide booming out some beacon signal telling our friends where we are."

"A little late to worry about that," said Hannah, checking her datapad. "I'm sure they checked—yeah, they did. Devices found in and on the *Adler*," Hannah said. "A small listening unit attached to the base of the pilot's seat, a signal monitor near a comm conduit, where it could read all the incoming and outgoing traffic, and a combination beacon and data transmitter stuck to the hull. The notation is that it is 'possible but highly unlikely' that there were others that they missed. If there are others, we're probably going to find out the hard way. By the way, though, you're assuming that it was the Metrannans who boarded. Wilcox doesn't say any such thing. We don't know who it might be—and it does take at least two sides to start a war."

"Point taken," said Jamie. "But why was *he* so cagey about it?"

"Maybe he was worried that they'd blow him out of the sky if he said anything they didn't like or said more than they wanted to be heard. That's probably why he stopped making personal log entries."

"That makes sense."

"Come on. Let's check the auto-event log."

Jamie paused a moment before he closed the personal log. He had been half-hoping that there would be something more, something beyond the log entries that he had already examined on his datapad. Some last word from the ghost in the machine that he had not seen already. But there was nothing—not in the personal log, anyway.

He switched over to the auto-event reporter log.

The autologger monitored all the electromechanical systems on the ship and recorded every action they took.

Neither Hannah or Jamie had much experience with the recorder used on the *Adler*, and it took them a while to figure out how to bring up detailed displays of air lock activity while filtering out everything else. Once that was accomplished, it was simple enough to examine air lock activity for the period between the departure of the boarding party and the recovery of the *Adler* in the outer reaches of the CenterStar System.

What it showed was exactly what they had expected to find: The inner hatch had been opened, then closed and sealed about an hour later—long enough for Trevor to load all of his effects into the lock chamber. Then the manual override system was used to bring the lock chamber down to one-quarter of standard pressure, rather than to zero. The manual override was also used to disengage the safety systems and hydraulic door controls and send the rapid-open command to the outer hatch, releasing the pressure latches in an instant, so that explosive decompression would force the hatch door open and blow the lock's contents into space. The air lock was designed to be used that way, down to shock absorbers on the hatch hinges to keep it from slamming into the outer hull.

The autolog showed that the hydraulics were then reengaged, the outer hatch swung shut and resealed, and the lock interior repressurized.

"So that ought to prove it," said Jamie. "A perfectly standard junk-jettison job, from start to finish. It must have been Trevor that did the clearout. And if he did do it, can you think of any reason for it besides his helping *us*?"

"No, but that doesn't mean there *isn't* another reason. Still, you've convinced me, at least provisionally. Except all you've *really* proven is that he deliberately cycled the lock with pressure between the doors. It probably was to dump unwanted gear, but we don't *know*. And there's one detail that doesn't quite fit with your theory."

"What's that?"

"Look at the time indicator on when he opened the lock: less than a day after he was boarded and more than two days before the *Irene Adler* made her transit-jump back to the Center System. The Metrannans, or whoever it was that boarded him, might still have been close enough to detect the jettison. Why would he want to attract their attention again by doing something suspicious? And if the whole idea was to clear the decks and make our search easier, then he'd want to do the reverse of that as well and make *their* search harder if they came back. He'd want as much junk as possible on board, so they'd be forced to paw through more stuff. He'd have wanted to do the jettison as late as possible. Why do it so early?"

"I can give you two plausible theories," said Jamie. "One, he *wanted* to jettison the stuff where the xenos would see it. Maybe he wanted to confuse them. Maybe he was hoping the xenos would have some reason to think the decrypt code would be in with the junk he was jettisoning. Maybe they did think that. Maybe the gag worked, and they went off after the junk instead of reboarding the *Adler*.

"Or two, and I think this is the better but grimmer explanation: Trevor knew he was *dying*. He could see that his strength was failing and figured he'd better do the jettison procedure while he still could." Jamie studied the log display, and scanned the major event reports. "That fits," he said. "Unless I'm missing something, closing the air locks was just about the last event recorded that required Trevor to perform any physical act, like carrying things or moving equipment. Everything else from there on in was pretty much done on automatic, or else was something he could do from right here at the pilot's station by working the controls."

"That is pretty grim," said Hannah. "But it does fit." She leaned in over the main data display. "Look, as long you're confirming theories, let's go back to the time period when his personal log reports the boarding party. I want to see what it says about air lock use."

"Why do you need to confirm *that*?"

"The personal logs are pretty sketchy," she said. "The autolog's reports on air lock activity will tell us how long the xenos were docked to the *Adler*. It might give us an idea how thorough the search was."

Jamie punched up the right commands, then frowned. "That can't be right," he said. "No use of the main air lock at all during that time period."

"*What?* Check again."

"I'm checking, I'm checking," said Jamie distractedly. "Date codes right, time codes, air lock activity report active—everything correct." He turned and looked at Hannah. "No air lock use," he said. "So how could there have been a boarding party?"

"The times must be wrong. Maybe your junk-jettison air lock use was really the boarding party."

"With the lock pressure cut to one-quarter and then a quick-release explosive-decompression outer-hatch opening? If there was breathable pressure on the other side, the hatch wouldn't have opened. He *couldn't* have opened the hatch—there would be higher outside pressure, tons of it, holding the hatch shut."

"Okay, okay. I take your point. But that means there wasn't a boarding party, and about two-thirds of our assumptions are out the window—and it means Wilcox was lying or delusional when he made those log entries."

"Wait a second. *We* just came aboard the *Irene Adler*, and we didn't use the air lock."

Hannah frowned. "You mean Wilcox had the other ship dock to the *Adler* through the nose hatch?"

Jamie worked the auto-event log again. "Bingo," he said. "About thirty minutes after that first personal log entry, the nose-hatch docking system was activated and made a hard dock with—whatever it was. This is just an engineering log. It doesn't identify the other ship. The interior pressure in the *Adler* didn't change, which probably means the other ship had an air lock system and used that to match pressure. I don't know if that tells us anything, but there it is. The hatch stayed open for just about four and a half hours, and once it was closed, the docking system released from the other ship. Half an hour after that, we get the second log entry. It all matches up."

"But why would he use the nose hatch?" Hannah asked. "I can tell you that the Metrannans wouldn't like it. They aren't exactly built to move gracefully on rope ladders. They have four arms and four legs, a morbid fear of exposed heights, and no arboreal ancestors to provide them with climbing instincts."

"Maybe that was exactly the point," Jamie said. "The Metrannans *wouldn't* like it. We're assuming that Trevor knew he was dying by that time, and he might well know—or at least assume—that it was the Metrannans who had done it to him. Why would he do them any favors? And what were they going to do to him if he wasn't nice? Kill him?"

"Well, maybe. But tweaking their noses as revenge for their murdering him doesn't seem quite in character for Wilcox, somehow."

"Too petty for a man brave enough to do everything we know he did?"

"Something like that," Hannah said.

"Who knows?" Jamie said. "Maybe the pilot of the Metrannan spacecraft picked the nose hatch, and Trevor just didn't feel like correcting his dumb mistake. Besides, we still don't know for sure that it *was* the Metrannans. It could have been some other species that's comfortable with ladders and heights."

"Hmmph. True enough. We'd know that and a hell of a lot more if the *Adler* had been recording the feed from her interior cameras."

"Yeah, but Trevor deliberately disabled the cams for the same reason we did. You don't record yourself on a mission designated 'War-Starter.' The bad guys could have just played back the recording and watched where he hid the decrypt."

Cutting out all the auto-record cameras and microphones was standard operating procedure for most BSI missions. Far safer to keep the system turned off at all times instead of running the risk of forgetting to turn it off while performing some crucial and secret part of the job.

"I know *why* nothing was recorded," Hannah said with some irritation in her voice. "That doesn't stop me from wishing we had the recordings. I suppose we're lucky to have the engineering logs." She thought for a second. "Any change in the gravity system while the boarding party was present?"

Jamie checked and looked toward Hannah with surprise. "Yeah," he said. "Interior grav got cranked *up* to one-point-two-one gees—Metran surface gravity."

"Huh?" Hannah leaned in and checked the display herself. "I was figuring that if Wilcox was trying to annoy them, he would have dialed gravity *down* a ways. Metrannans *hate* low gravity—and with good reason. Even a brief exposure to zero gee can kill them."

Jamie checked further along in the log. "It gets weirder. After the boarding party is gone, interior gravity was reset to three-quarters of a standard gee for several days. It was cut to zero for a couple of hours, then returned to three-quarters and left there."

"I don't get it," said Hannah. "The second part makes sense. Dialing gravity down to three-quarters is a pretty smart move if you're dying of a degenerative disease. That's enough of a reduction to ease the stress on your system, but not so much that your reflexes would get messed up, that sort of thing. But if he's going to do that for himself, why crank *up* the interior gravity to make his guests comfortable—especially when he's just docked using the nose hatch to irritate them, and when higher gravity has got to put a strain on him—maybe a big enough strain to kill him?"

"I've got all the same questions and none of the answers," Jamie said. "But at least setting the system to exactly one-point-two-one gees signals that he was boarded by Metrannans."

"Maybe *that's* why he did it," said Hannah.

"It's for our benefit, just like clearing out all of his personal effects. It's a deliberate signal to us that it was beings who liked that gravity field who boarded him."

"It could be," Jamie said. "But somehow it's not all that convincing. Would he really risk a heart attack just to send us such a subtle and easy-to-miss message? *Especially* when he had so much to do after they left. Yeah, later on, he went to a lot of effort jettisoning his gear for our benefit—but it wasn't at the risk of *dying* before he could complete his preparations. Cranking up the gravity system while he was aging by, say, a year every hour would increase the odds of his dying before he'd done his job. He would only do it because it was absolutely necessary, not to let us confirm a very obvious theory about who boarded his ship."

"It almost seems like poor sportsmanship for you to punch such big sensible holes in a flimsy little theory," Hannah said.

"Yeah, right," Jamie said, smiling. "You're always so kind and gentle about blowing my theories out of the water."

"Touché," said Hannah, staring thoughtfully at the display. "But still, finding all this out makes me feel better," she said. "It's very obvious that Wilcox was working very purposefully and carefully, thinking through everything as best as he could—and everything we've learned so far suggests that he was *very* good at that kind of thinking. I don't think my odds of beating him at chess would have been all that good. I'd be willing to bet a year's pay that his using the nose hatch and increasing the gravity during the search were necessary to accomplish clear and specific goals."

"I'll go further," said Jamie. "My guess is that his using the nose hatch and cranking up the gravity were all of a piece with his clearing out the gear. They're part of a whole we're not seeing yet, but they're all very clean, well-made puzzle pieces. There's going to be a way to fit them all together. And if we find *a* way for them *all* to fit, it's going to be the *only* way. When we have an answer, we'll know it's *the* answer."

"I bet you're right," said Hannah. "Unless senile dementia had already kicked in before the boarding party arrived and there isn't any sense to *anything* he did after that."

"That's why I like partnering with you," said Jamie. "Your cheerful attitude and irrepressible optimism. Come on, let's get started with the physical search."

TEN
SAVED TO BURN

Three numbingly dull hours later, Hannah felt certain that there was nothing remotely cheerful left in her attitude. A spacecraft, even a small one, had a remarkably large number of places where an object could be hidden—especially when Jamie and she had only the vaguest idea about what they were looking for. If—*if* their assumptions were right, and if the logic underlying those assumptions was even close to right, then they were looking for an object large enough to be visible to the naked eye onto which the decrypt key could have been recorded using the equipment normally carried aboard a *Sherlock*-class ship, or with the personal gear Wilcox had carried aboard.

Unfortunately, that description covered everything from a note written on a piece of paper and taped to the inside of an access panel to a standard miniature memory chip hidden inside a hollowed-out key cap on the pilot's station main keyboard.

They had quickly worked out a series of rules for the first-pass search, mostly based on making a further series of not entirely reliable assumptions about what Wilcox would and would not have done—and also what he physically could and could not have done.

He wouldn't have risked damaging the ship or making it harder to operate, or dared take any step that might require a repair he might not be able to do once he got much weaker—which made the idea that he had fiddled with the main control panel seem less likely.

They quickly established that Wilcox couldn't have hidden the key on the *exterior* of the *Adler*, or anywhere inside the ship accessible only from an exterior access port—a fuel door or a maintenance hatch. There was an emergency pressure suit on board, but it was still unused and in its sealed shipping container. Nor was there any record of either hatch being used between the time of his departure from Metran and the arrival of the boarding party. Besides, a man dying of a rapidly progressing degenerative disease wouldn't have risked the rigors and dangers of a space walk. It was possible that the *Adler* might have been docked or landed in some facility with breathable air while in the Metran system, and Wilcox could have gotten at the ship's exterior then—but the risks of being observed would have been far too high.

All that gave them at least some reasonably logical guidelines for their initial search. They were also paying at least some attention to the idea that Wilcox *could* have hidden it in some place that a xeno couldn't or wouldn't find it, but that a human—more specifically a BSI agent—*would* think of looking.

The only trouble with that idea was there weren't all that many ways to hide things that would utterly confound a nonhuman. Jamie had suggested that they concentrate on the upper deck, given the Metrannans' dislike of heights. A flimsy bit of reasoning, granted, but there was something to it. However, there was barely enough room on the upper deck for two people, even when they *weren't* crawling around peering into things. Jamie could concentrate his attention up there as much as he wanted, so far as Hannah was concerned. She was perfectly happy to work on the lower deck, where there was more room to turn around.

Jamie had another bright idea that seemed to have some promise, at least at first. As a general rule of thumb, xeno food was literally indigestible to humans: The differences in biochemistry were large enough that, unless the foods were specially processed or treated, the human digestive tract could draw no nutritive value from Kendari fare or Pavlat cooking. Because human and Metrannan biochemistry had some features in common, some Metrannan foods were edible to humans—but most of their foods were deadly poison, while others could induce violent allergic reactions. The reverse was likewise true—many human foods were actively dangerous to Metrannans.

Fortunately for the health of both sides, each also found most of the other species' meals utterly nauseating. The average Metrannan dish was about as palatable to a human as a plate of rotten eggs served in light lubricating oil. Metrannans were no more fond of most human foods. Perhaps, Jamie speculated, Special Agent Wilcox had taken advantage of that and hidden the key inside an unopened mealpack, on the theory that a Metrannan wouldn't be very eager to open it in the first place, let alone search it too thoroughly.

There were four unopened mealpacks left aboard the *Adler*. Jamie and Hannah spent an unpleasant half hour dissecting every morsel in every one of them on the off chance the key had been concealed inside a meatball or the like. They likewise carefully examined the interior and exterior of each container. But there had been no sign of any memory chips floating in the gravy, or suspiciously long strings of characters inserted into the expiration dates.

But worse than searching the food was the fact that they had to preserve it all, just in case their assumptions were wrong, and they later discovered that Wilcox had somehow concealed the decrypt key inside a strand of DNA in the cabbage used to make the kimchi or the like. They sealed it all up as best they could and stuffed it in a corner of the *Adler*'s air lock.

But merely setting foot in the air lock had given Jamie another inspiration, and he set to work taking apart the air lock's self-adjusting floor mechanism. If Trevor had concealed the decrypt key on the underside of the floor panel, that would have given him a reason to use the nose hatch for docking, simply to keep the xenos from spending more time than necessary in the main air lock. That theory had come up dry, too, with no better result than a set of scraped knuckles for Jamie and a series of large grease stains on his iso-suit.

Even Jamie had run out of bright ideas at that point, and the search had devolved into the dullest possible grunt work, crouching over in every possible awkward and uncomfortable position, peering and poking and prodding into every nook and cranny of the *Adler*'s interior, popping every access panel, checking every bit of equipment that might have served as a place to conceal the decrypt key. The grease marks and dirty smudges and sweat stains on Hannah's iso-suit multiplied as her mood darkened.

What made the job even duller was the absolute necessity of documenting all of it. They had to photograph everything they searched and keep up a running monologue of description, in preparation for the all-but-inevitable time when they would have to go back through it all again.

If, as seemed increasingly likely, they didn't find the key on this pass, they would have to try again, and again, and again after that. Without documentation, it would be almost impossible to remember what had and had not been searched, or how thoroughly each item had been checked. And, after all, it was just possible that they would come across a clue later on that would suddenly make sense of something they had found long before. It would be extremely useful to have a record of everything accessible from their datapads, with all the commentary transcribed and cross-indexed.

Time seemed to flow past Hannah, as if she existed outside it and was not there at all, but was being forced to watch from the outside as two white-suited figures hunched over display screens, control panels, trash containers, storage lockers, fold-out furniture, both of them constantly muttering into their throat mikes, each of them pausing every now and again to get another careful, detailed close-up of another perfectly ordinary item that might, just might, conceal the decrypt key that some faceless bureaucrat in BSI-DLO had decreed might start—or prevent—a war. It was hard to avoid thinking they were following a meaningless ritual for no better reason than that it was what they were expected to do.

Hannah had promised herself that she would plod grimly on, searching for a decrypt key that could be anywhere, any size, and disguised as almost anything and hidden almost any place, until one hour before the transit-jump. She found herself checking the time almost compulsively, every few minutes, sometimes every few seconds, as if some part of her subconscious refused to believe that time could possibly be passing so slowly, and required constant confirmation that it was so.

Hannah began searching through the next storage locker. Part of her mind was on the job, part of it straining against the temptation to check once again how much time was left, but most of her attention was focused on the sharp stabbing pain between her shoulder blades and the dull soreness in her knees. Check the time. Ten minutes to go. A can of blue-grey spray-on touch-up paint, matching the ship's interior, nearly full. A can of flat black paint, and one of red, both full. A small toolkit containing screwdrivers, wrenches, a small hammer, a measuring tape, a factory-sealed tube of flexible patching material, and a battery-powered drill.

Check the time. *Still* ten minutes—no, now nine minutes—to go. No visible changes to the tools or the plastic box that held them. No indications of hollowed-out volumes in any of the items. A plastic box subdivided into small drawers about eight-by-eight centimeters, each drawer containing a different type of screw, nut, bolt, strap, or other small fastener. Empty each drawer and examine each small part to confirm that nothing had been concealed in among them. Each small drawer has a label with the item name and item count for the contents. Examine each emptied drawer. The counts all matched. Nothing appeared to have been concealed in any of them. Five minutes left until she could stop.

Confirm inventory of each item so as to establish none had been used. *That* was sure to soak up some time. Counts match stated inventory. No fasteners have been used. One roll of heavy adhesive-backed strapping tape, partly used. One roll of light-duty adhesive-backed tape, partly used. One half-full box of large trash disposal bags. One nearly empty box of small trash disposal bags. There wasn't any way of knowing when, where, or by whom the partially used items had been consumed. It might have been on the *Adler*'s last voyage, or on some other mission six months or a year before. Probably some combination of all those. Check the time. The time *must* be up, or nearly up, by now.

And, praise the stars, it was! Time was up, and then some. There was a mere fifty-six minutes to transit-jump.

She put the boxes of trash bags away, closed the storage locker, shut down her camera, mike, and datapad, and stood up slowly, painfully, all her muscles cramped and sore from sitting in awkward and uncomfortable poses.

"Jamie!" she called out. "Quitting time!"

"Huh? What? Oh, yeah, okay," he said, his voice distracted. "Come up here, will you?" he asked.

"You haven't *found* something, have you?" she asked as she stretched, and then climbed the ladder to the upper deck.

"I've found *something*," Jamie said. "But I don't think it's anything we can use." He stood up and stretched, then moved over to one side of the tiny pilot's station and gestured for Hannah to take the pilot's seat. "Grab the chair," he said. "It feels good to stand up properly."

"Glad to," she said. "It feels good to sit *down* properly." She sat down and turned to Jamie. "So, what have you got?"

"I decided to save the most obvious for last," said Jamie. "Notebooks. The standard investigator's notebooks."

"Yeah," said Hannah. "That is a little too obvious." There were BSI Special Agents who sneered in contempt at anything as old-fashioned as a paper notebook. They used nothing but datapads, scanners, cameras, and digital recorders to record information in the field.

Hannah and Jamie were in the other, pro-paper, camp. The electronic tools were all quite useful, obviously, but paper most definitely had its place. The pro-paper Special Agents argued that there were many tasks for which pen and paper were the best choice. An agent using a notepad and pen never worried about running out of power—though, granted, the agent could run out of ink, or paper. A notepad couldn't be electronically jammed, and no electronic eavesdropping gadget would ever be able to read its contents if you kept the cover closed.

And paper was easy to get rid of. It could be shredded, burned, pulped, simply torn up and scattered over a wide area, or, in a pinch, chewed and eaten.

And, of course, there was the advantage that

paper was so hopelessly old-fashioned that many xenos never even thought of notepads as a way to store information, and they certainly had no expertise in recovering data from destroyed paper pages.

Those inside the pro-paper camp were almost obsessive about the *type* of paper notebook to be used—what size and weight of paper, whether or not the pages could be easily torn out, what sort of cover. Some agents even had their notebooks custom-made, at ruinous expense. Hannah and Jamie, at least, stayed out of that trap—though Hannah had to admit she was tempted at times.

Both of them normally worked with the sort of standard-issue BSI investigator's notebook Jamie had just handed to Hannah. It was a flip-top spiral-bound notebook, about thirteen centimeters wide and twenty-four centimeters tall. Inside were three sections, with stiff cardboard dividers between the sections. The front section was horizontally ruled paper for general note-taking. The middle was graph paper, with vertical and horizontal lines breaking up the page into one-centimeter boxes for making rough scale drawings in the field. The third section was unlined paper for freehand drawing. The front cover was emblazoned with the BSI badge-star design, and under it

FOR OFFICIAL BSI USE ONLY
60 sheets 20 lined/20 graph/20 blank
Form 401920/2482

Under that were blanks for the user to fill in.

AGENT NAME:_____
CASE NUMBER REFERENCE:_____
DATE USE STARTED:_____
DATE USE ENDED:_____

and a series of other boxes that no one ever bothered to fill in. The inside front cover, and the fronts
and backs of the section dividers and the back
cover displayed a series of supposedly helpful
look-up charts. One set converted metric measures
to the various Galactic systems, and, for the real
throwbacks, even to feet, miles, ounces, and
pounds. Another was a list of "Useful Phrases" in
Lesser Trade Speech, the language of commerce
and diplomacy used by many xeno species. The
guides and charts were all well-intentioned, but
Hannah had never heard of anyone using any of
them.

There was something oddly comforting about
seeing the familiar, old-fashioned charts. She had
used a notebook exactly identical to the one in her
hand on her first case—and she had kept it as a
memento, even if that violated five or six security
regulations. No doubt because she herself had
such a sentimental attachment to them, examining
Wilcox's notebooks seemed a particularly personal, almost intimate, thing to do.

Except, suddenly, it dawned on her that they
hadn't been personal, or special, or intimate to

him. "Wait a second," she said. "Wilcox isn't a paper guy."

"Right," said Jamie. "At least we don't have any proof that he is. Everything we've seen suggests he's a digital guy."

"Have we seen a single example of his handwriting?" Hannah asked. "Or *anything* on paper? Printouts? Sketches?"

"Not that I've spotted."

"Does that mean he never used paper, or just that he scooped up every scrap of paper in his general clear-out?"

"Well, if he cleared everything else out, he missed the notebooks," said Jamie.

"But they're blank. Empty."

"Not the one you're holding," Jamie replied. "Not all the way. Flip to the back of the graph-paper section."

Hannah did so—and frowned in puzzlement at what she saw there.

In the center of the page was an elaborately drawn and decorated design, a sort of logo, of the initials BSI. The *B* and the *S* were fully drawn and filled in with flourishes and backgrounds and curlicues, but the *I* was merely sketched in, as if the artist hadn't quite gotten around to finishing it. Centered directly under it was a two-line slogan, written in very careful script.

Where we protect our treasures
unless we must destroy them

Hannah laughed. "This is from a little before your time," she said. "It's an old in-joke. Ask anyone in the Bureau's Internal Investigations Unit, and they'll tell you that *BSI* stands for *BURN STASH IMMEDIATELY.* According to them, every time they ask for an agent's work notes, wouldn't you know it, bad luck has struck again and he's tossed the papers they want into the destruct oven, just five minutes before. The regs say that everyone's supposed to 'destroy unneeded insecure notes on a regular basis,' but most agents tend to hold on to their old notes, just in case. But as soon anyone hears a rumor that IIU might come looking around, everyone starts following the regs to the letter."

"Well, Wilcox seems to have followed *that* rule."

Hannah tapped the design with her finger. "We don't even know that this is Wilcox's doing," she said. "We can't even be sure he was the one who drew the logo or wrote the words. This could have been left behind by the last agent to fly the *Adler* prior to Wilcox's mission, or the one before that, or the one before that."

"But only if Trevor missed this notebook while he was doing the clear-out. We haven't caught him making too many mistakes so far."

"The mistake being that he left these notebooks behind when he was clearing the place out to make our search easier?"

"Right."

"I'm not sure I can count it as a mistake not to

check carefully every single page of every single notebook to make sure they're all blank when you're clearing out an entire spacecraft."

"No. But think about it. Trevor is sitting where you are right now whenever he pilots the ship. The notebooks were held to the bulkhead with that elastic restraint loop there, like this." Jamie took the other notebooks, pulled back the loop, slipped them into it, and let the loop go. It made a loud snapping noise as it slapped into the notebooks. "Right in his line of sight whenever he turns his head."

"And if he's not a paper guy, why does he put a stack of spare notebooks right there?" Hannah asked. "Unless they were put there by the agent before or the agent before that, and were just left there."

"Even so—he's cleaning out everything else on board the ship. It would take him five seconds to grab the notebooks and toss them into whatever trash bag he was using."

"So you're saying if he left them behind, he did it on purpose."

"Right."

"And if so, he did it for a reason."

"Right."

"And, unless we go over the books with a scanning electron microscope looking for DNA-encoded microstrands and such like, the only thing in any of the notebooks is this design and the words underneath, so what we have on this page has to *be* the reason."

"Right. Unless I'm wrong."

"Yeah, but *you* don't make many mistakes, either," said Hannah. She stared thoughtfully at the design and the words underneath it. " '*Where we protect our treasures unless we must destroy them.*' The way that's placed under the BSI design, it looks like it's supposed to be a joke, that it's the Bureau's motto. But there's more than one way to read it. Instead of referring to the organization, it could also refer to a physical place. A place that's on this ship—and every BSI ship."

"The destruct oven if you rig it for Mode Two!" Jamie said. "The search team didn't look there, did they?"

"Not that we have any record of," said Hannah.

"And *we* haven't looked there either," said Jamie. "How could we all miss that?"

"Rush and panic and trying to do everything at once," said Hannah. "And no one would think of it because no one ever uses the oven in Mode Two. You don't use them that way until things are in very bad shape."

"Well, things got pretty bad for Trevor," said Jamie. "Plenty bad enough if he had a boarding party to deal with. That sounds like a Mode Two situation if I've ever heard of one."

There was a concealed and camouflaged destruct oven aboard every BSI ship. It consisted of a sealable chamber that could be heated to extreme temperatures, combined with an oxygen feed system and a sophisticated venting system, all of it designed to promote rapid and thorough burning. Every piece of portable BSI data-storage equipment from the paper notebooks to the highest-end datapads and computers was designed to fit into a destruct oven, and was specifically made so it could not survive a destruct oven burn cycle.

In Mode One, an agent simply shoved whatever needed destroying into the oven, sealed it, and turned it on. It was intended for the routine and precautionary destruction of potentially sensitive material.

Mode Two was for when things got much hairier. If an agent thought he or she might be caught or killed, or his ship captured, and if the agent was carrying high-value materials, data important enough to protect that was also data that couldn't be allowed to fall into the wrong hands, the standard operating procedure was to store all sensitive documents in the destruct oven and leave them there. The usual protocol was to rig it so that it would start a destructive burn cycle if anyone tried to open it without entering the proper pass codes. The oven could also be triggered by more or less any sort of remote control or panic button or timer or deadman switch the agent might choose.

"So let's look now."

"Forty-five minutes until transit-jump," Hannah said. "We need to make sure we've got time to get ready for it. We'll have to move fast."

"I don't even know where the oven is hidden on this class of ship," Jamie admitted.

"I do," Hannah said grimly. "It's concealed in the bathroom, the head. It's under the deck—right in front of the chemical toilet."

* * *

"Take the powerdriver and hand me that prybar, will you?" Hannah asked as the last of the screws holding in the deckplate came loose. She swapped tools with Jamie and wedged the prybar under the lip of the deckplate.

It lifted up easily, and Jamie grabbed the edge of the plate and lifted it clear. A sprinkling of smoky-smelling dust swirled in the cramped compartment as he swung the plate out of the way and leaned it against the wall. They looked into the space it had covered and saw what resembled a small but highly complex safe, complete with combination lock and reinforced door and armored hinges. "So," he said, "what are we going to find here?"

"Well, with any luck at all, the decrypt key, of course," said Hannah, reaching for her datapad to pull up the codes to unlock and disarm the system.

"But if it's stashed here, *when* did he stash it?" Jamie asked. "It couldn't have been *before* the boarding party arrived, because he did the gear-jettison *after* that, and we haven't come up with any explanation for the gear-jettison, unless it was to help us search the ship and not be distracted by searching through his personal effects. Why go through all *that* if he already had the key hidden in the destruct oven and the boarding party had missed it? And if he hid it in there *after* the boarding party—again, why do the gear-jettison? He'd have to know that sooner or later someone would think of looking in the oven—and probably assume that they'd think of it sooner than anyone actually did."

"He could have stashed the destruct key in the oven the second he was back on board after leaving Metran," said Hannah, "before he knew anything at all about the chances of his being boarded. He might figure the oven was the safest place on board. It functions as a hidden wall safe. It would just be a sensible precaution."

"Let me ask you this," said Jamie. "I didn't know where the destruct oven was, since I've never flown one of these tubs—but I knew there was one. What do you want to bet that every Kendari Inquiries Service agent in the field knows all about BSI destruct ovens?"

"No one's talked about the Kendari being part of all this," Hannah objected.

"No, but information can be bought and sold," said Jamie. "Besides, the data wouldn't need to come from the Kendari. The logs show that Trevor docked—or more like landed—his ship at the Metran's Grand Elevator and then rode down to the surface. I'm sure he left the ship locked and sealed and so on—but that wouldn't stop the locals from scanning it fifteen different ways. The

Metrannans are a well-connected Elder race. They must have a lot of tech we can't even dream of. Trevor would have to have assumed that whoever boarded him would know where the oven was, and maybe even how to get past the ship's security and the oven's."

"Okay, so maybe he didn't stash it there then," Hannah said. "Or else your argument is very logical and convincing—but it's just plain wrong—and he *did* stash it there, before or after the boarding party, and what does it matter if he did it before or after?"

Jamie scowled. "I'm not sure. But I think we owe it to Trevor to try and understand everything he did as best we can."

Hannah looked at him hard. "Listen up, Special Agent Mendez, and get it straight. Trevor Wilcox III was *my* colleague, too—but this case got War-Starter slapped on it, and investigating his death is a secondary mission—something close to a cover story. Your trying to be his posthumous best friend doesn't do him any good, and I'm starting to worry it's going to get in the way of us doing our job. We're supposed to find the decrypt key, first and foremost. We're *not* supposed to be building a monument to Trevor Wilcox. Got it?"

Jamie wanted to argue—but he knew she was right. If desperately wanting to know and understand everything about Trevor in his final days was interfering with the job, well, then, Trevor wouldn't want that either. He had sacrificed every-thing for the sake of the mission. It would be pay-ing him no respect for Jamie to be distracted from it. "I've got it," he said.

Hannah's face softened. "Believe me," she said. "I understand. I've felt the same way. Maybe I'm feeling more of it than you realize, right now. But it can't get in the way of the job. Now let's get this thing open. It's going to be one of three things. Either the decrypt key is in it and the key is intact, and we can abort the mission, bring the key back to Center, *then* investigate how Wilcox died. Or else the key is there, but destroyed, in which case we have to abort, report *that* news to Center HQ, and see what they want to do about their War-Starter being missing. Or else the oven chamber will be stone empty—and we go on to Metran. So let's get to it. Okay?"

"Okay."

"Good. Hang on a second while I key in the se-curity codes." Hannah consulted her datapad, en-tered the codes, and set the lock dials. Then she pressed down a control stud while twisting the handle.

The oven unlocked. Hannah swung the door up and open—and a choking cloud of dust and ash plumed up and into the compartment, setting Jamie and Hannah to coughing and wheezing. They retreated from the refresher compartment and Hannah slammed the door shut. "Emergency kit," Hannah managed to splutter out. "There on the wall behind you. Breathing masks."

Jamie wiped the grit from his eyes and his mouth and nodded. He crossed to the kit hanging on the wall and opened it. It was intended for use in case of a meteor strike or other air leak problem. Jamie pulled out a can of sealing foam, and an open pack of hull patches, and then found the masks. Fortunately, there were no fewer than three breather masks in it. Jamie handed Hannah a mask, wiped his eyes and mouth again, and put on his own.

"We've only got a little more than half an hour until our transit-jump," Hannah said, her voice made faint and muffled by the mask. "No time to do more than take another quick peek in there. Let's go."

Jamie grabbed a handlight from the emergency kit and switched it on. Hannah pulled the door to the head back open. The dust had settled a bit, though the air was still hazy. Hannah stepped inside and shifted over to make room for Jamie. He went in and shined the handlight down into the still-open door of the destruct oven.

The interior of the oven was jammed full of the ashes of burned paper and roasted, melted electronics, and other ruined debris that couldn't even be identified that generally. "So maybe he was a paper guy after all," said Jamie.

"And maybe, in there, is whatever is left of the

decrypt key," said Hannah. "If so, there's nothing left of it now." She shook her head. "Not any of the three cases we expected, is it? So much for logic."

"But what do we do?" Jamie asked. "If the decrypt key was in there, it was fried. It's gone. That's game over, isn't it? We abort and go home?"

"We don't *know* that the decrypt key was in there, so we don't know if it was fried," said Hannah. "If there was *one* destroyed object in there, we could assume with a high degree of confidence it was the decryption key. But the key could be on or in anything. A chip, a piece of paper, a datapad, a photo. There's too much ash and melted junk in there for us to have any hope of identifying one bit of it as the missing key—so we have to assume that *none* of it is. Maybe Wilcox filled up the destruct oven with junk as a decoy for the boarding party. But if there's one place we won't find the key, it's in the middle of *that* mess." She bent down, swung the oven hatch shut, and relocked it.

"So what do we do?"

"So we go on with the mission," she said. "Let's get that cover plate secured before the transit-jump." The two of them wrestled the deckplate back into position, and Hannah used the power-driver to screw the hold-down bolts back in. She stood up and looked down at her work. Somehow the moment felt like standing at a freshly filled grave of someone who had not been gone very long. "This doesn't change anything about the job," she said. "It just makes it harder."

She checked the time and cursed. "Twenty-two minutes to transit-jump," she said. "Let's go."

ELEVEN

JUMP TO TUMBLE

It was an axiom, a truism, a cliché: No two transit-jumps were alike. The jump in and out of other dimensions to move from one star system to another required incredible delicacy, accuracy, and power. The slightest error in navigation could produce huge errors at the arrival end—and some wholly remarkable visual and physical effects during the jump itself.

On the best-calibrated runs, with the distances and masses of the departure and target stars known with great precision, the jump effects were minimal, or even undetectably small. But BSI ships didn't always fly on the best-charted, best-calibrated routes—and the jump effects were often most decidedly detectable.

Colors, lights, vibrations, distortions would flicker in and out of being. The effects were not illusions, but all too real, ripples and shifts and twists and turns imposed on space-time itself. Mostly the effects stayed outside the ship, and acted on the vehicle as a whole. Sometimes, however, the distortions were sufficiently fine-grained, sufficiently complex, to reach *inside* a ship, so that what happened in the stern was different than what happened in the bow. Sometimes two people sitting next to each other would witness totally different effects.

Usually, the distortions were harmless and vanished in the moment the transit-jump was completed. Usually.

What worried Jamie about this run was not so much the navigation as the ship-handling—and that was no knock on Hannah's admittedly limited skills as a pilot. The *Sherlock*-class ships might be constructed in such a way that the ships could be docked together nose to nose and flown that way, but that didn't mean they were *intended* to be flown that way. If they had been designed from the ground up to fly in tandem, Gunther's people wouldn't have felt the need to rig six reinforcing cables between the ships.

But it went further than making the ships strong enough. The *Sholto*'s jump generator was designed to transit one ship from star system to star system. It was asking a lot of the generator to handle an off-center mass twice that size. One thing they had going for them, oddly enough, was that the *Sherlock*-class ships were just about the smallest starships ever built by humans. Several of their components, including their jump generators, had originally been designed for much larger vehicles. Various other components were also more robust than might be expected, for similar reasons. But that didn't mean the integrated system was tuned, optimized, or fully rated for flying two ships instead of one. In theory, nothing ought to go wrong. But they weren't flying inside a theory.

Hannah and Jamie rushed through the last-minute prep for the transit-jump, powering down every possible system on both ships and closing the hatches between them.

Hannah had judged, and Jamie had agreed with her, that during the cruise phase of their flight, either the acceleration compensators would hold or they wouldn't. If they failed, and the interior of one or both ships were suddenly exposed to double-digit gees, it really wasn't going to matter if the hatches were open or shut—and keeping them shut and sealed would have slowed down their searches and investigations.

But they weren't going to be doing any searching or investigating during the transit-jump, and the jump would be, by far, the part of the journey that put the greatest stress on the ships.

Jamie drew the hatch-closing duty—and almost immediately ran into trouble. In order to pull shut the *Adler*'s nose hatch, he had to brace his legs in the netting in the zero-gee section of tunnel between the two ships, then stick his body out into the topside end of the *Adler*'s cabin, undog the hatch from the hold-open clamps that anchored it to the wall of the *Adler*'s cabin, then retreat back into the tunnel, holding on to a handgrip on the hatch and pulling it along with him.

The first time he tried the maneuver, the hatch

refused to swing to, and instead bounced out of his hand. The hatch had caught on something hard. He let the hatch go and checked for obstructions. It was only then that he discovered that the stanchions holding the top of the rope ladder were on a set of short rails, about half a meter long, allowing them to slide back and forth between two positions.

When slid to the end of the rails closest to the hatch, it was an easy straight-line climb up the ladder and into the hatch tunnel—but the ladder obstructed the outside edge of the hatch. When the stanchion holding the ladder was slid to the end of the rails closest to the wall of the cabin, there was plenty of clearance to close the hatch—but to get from the top of the ladder to the lip of the hatch would require an extremely awkward and dangerous backward lunge.

Two knobs held the stanchion in place. Jamie loosened them, slid the stanchion into the outer stowed position, tightened them back down, closed and sealed the hatch manually and checked it carefully, then retreated down the tunnel, back into the *Sholto*. He had to perform some further gymnastics to reposition the stanchion of the *Sholto*'s ladder, undog her topside hatch, and then close and seal it as well.

Hannah, seated in the pilot's chair in the upper deck of the *Sholto* and busy with her own part of the prep for transit-jump, didn't notice Jamie's minor struggles until he was almost done. "Would that be any easier if I cut the internal gravity?" she asked, raising her voice so he could hear her. "I'm going to have to do it anyway."

"Thanks, no," Jamie said as he wrestled with the hatch latches. "I don't do all that well in zero gee."

"You *still* get a queasy stomach?" she asked, the amusement plain to hear in her voice.

"No, I don't," Jamie said, stretching the truth just a trifle. "But I'm just more comfortable doing this kind of work with some weight under my feet. I can brace myself better."

"Okay, fine."

"Anyway," said Jamie as he pulled the hatch to, "that's just about got it. Closing up now."

"Check that seal," Hannah said absently as she checked the status displays on the pilot's control panel.

"Thanks, Mom," Jamie said as he checked the seal. "Don't know how I'd make it through the day without you reminding me to keep breathing."

"Ha-ha," said Hannah. "Just for that, you can double-check them, and make sure we will keep breathing."

"Okay, okay. Double-checking—and seal confirmed. We're good."

"Then get down below and strap yourself in," said Hannah. "We're getting close to time—and the sequencer's going to be cutting lights and gravity in about three minutes."

"That's making it a little *too* exciting," Jamie

said. He triple-checked the seal and hurried down the ladder. He paused at the upper deck and reached out to the pilot's chair to give Hannah a quick pat on the arm. "Good luck," he said, then climbed the rest of the way down the ladder to the lower deck.

"See you on the other side," Hannah said. "Hurry up now and get strapped into that flight chair."

Jamie didn't need any more urging. He got off the ladder and into the acceleration couch that Gunther's crew had installed so hurriedly. He couldn't keep himself from glancing at the brightly colored self-destruct bomb they had installed at the same time—but it wasn't always best to dwell on such things. He strapped himself in, double-checked his belts, and let out his breath with a whoosh. "Here we go," he muttered to himself, before raising his voice and calling out to Hannah. "Secure and ready for transit-jump."

"Stop kidding yourself," she called back. "No one's ever *ready* for a transit-jump. Stand by for ninety more seconds—mark—and we'll see what happens this time."

Jamie, fidgeting in his acceleration chair, looked up toward Hannah on the flight deck. She had rotated the pilot's chair around so that she was in effect lying flat on her back, her spine parallel to the deck, her feet elevated and pointed toward the nose and the centerline of the ship, and her head right in and under the viewports. The position gave her the best forward view possible from the pilot's chair.

From his angle, Jamie couldn't see much more than the back of her head, a bit of her chair, a small slice of the control panel, and a sliver of the view out the pilot's viewport. He could only see a small patch of stars and sky in the corner of the viewport. With the two ships docked together nose to nose, mostly what he could see was a section of the *Adler*'s hull and one of the six reinforcing cables strung between the two ships.

He felt as if he were in the bottom of a pit looking up. Hannah had done nearly all of the piloting on their previous missions, but they had flown on ships designed to carry two people. He had flown the transit-jumps in the copilot's seat on the flight deck, where he could see out the viewport, see the status displays and controls, and lend a hand if anything went wrong. Strapped into a jury-rigged acceleration couch on the lower deck, he was blind and helpless.

Well, it wasn't as if Hannah was much more in the know, or even the least bit in control. The *Bartholomew Sholto*'s automatic sequencer was running everything at this point anyway. Hannah wouldn't even want to risk a manual abort this deep into the jump sequence.

"Throttle-down complete," Hannah announced. "Zero acceleration. Stand by for internal gravity system shutdown—now."

Jamie felt his stomach do a sudden flip-flop. It

wasn't zero gee itself that bothered him. It was the sudden shifts back and forth that scrambled his insides.

"Life support shutdown—now. Interior lighting shutdown—now."

The ventilation system sighed to a halt and the inside of Jamie's barrel suddenly turned black. The only light left was a faint glow from a few essential displays that would remain powered-up during the transit-jump and the ghostly pale image of part of the *Adler*'s hull, now lit only by the distant stars. Hannah moved her head a bit to check one of the displays, and he saw her head as a jet-black silhouette in front of the viewport. "All nonessential systems now safely powered down," Hannah announced. "Transit-jump in twenty seconds. Fifteen. Ten. Five. Four. Three. Two. One. Jump!"

The universe turned flaring bloodred with light that blasted in through the viewport, illuminating every nook and cranny of the *Sholto*'s interior in blinding bright crimson. Jamie covered his eyes and gritted his teeth, bracing himself for whatever else might happen. But nothing else did. *Not so bad this time,* he told himself. *Just a little light show.* As long as the light didn't leave them dazzled or blinded—and as long as there wasn't some other invisible, nastier sort of radiation along for the ride—they ought to be all right.

There was nothing left to do but wait it out. It was almost impossible to predict how much subjective time a transit-jump would take, but usually it was no more than a few seconds, or a minute.

It was only after about twenty seconds that Jamie sensed the vibration, the rhythmic shudder, that seemed to be coursing through the ship, fading out, and then reappearing, a little more powerful each time, each pulse coming faster and with greater intensity. What had begun as a barely perceptible background sensation built rapidly into something that seemed certain to shake the ship apart. The structure of the ship began to creak and moan. The interval between periods of vibration shrank until the shaking was nonstop. The noise was getting worse as well.

"Hannah!" Jamie called out.

"I have no idea!" Hannah yelled back, answering the question Jamie was about to ask.

"Can you do anything?"

"I don't dare try!" she shouted back. "Any change right now would probably just make it worse. All we can do is hang on!"

Jamie resisted the temptation to ask how much longer. Hannah could have no better idea of that than he did.

Then, as abruptly as it had appeared, the lurid glare of bloodred light vanished, dropping him back into darkness, and the shaking ceased so suddenly and completely that it was as if a switch had been thrown.

Jamie was just about to breathe a sigh of relief when the whole world abruptly lurched hard to the left and dropped into a violent spin. Jamie could see the stars streaking and whirling past that one little patch of black sky. Suddenly he was being spun and tumbled about violently enough to pull him half-out of his acceleration chair, held in place only by his restraint harness.

They had gotten through the transit-jump. But the ship was out of control.

TWELVE

VACUUM UNDER
PRESSURE

The sky and the stars were whirling past them, spinning and gyrating wildly. Hannah blinked hard and tried to concentrate, forcing herself not to be affected by the mad tumbling whirl that was scrambling her inner ears.

"What happened?" Jamie shouted from below and behind her.

"Stand by!" Hannah called back in a tone that she sincerely hoped relayed the message *shut up and let me work the problem.* She was forced to wait and watch as the automatic sequencer brought the ship's systems back online. If the maneuvering system didn't get back online quickly, she wasn't sure she was going to be sufficiently alert and conscious enough to deal with the problem.

Just as the controls powered up, Hannah found something else to worry about. The reinforcing cables she could see out the pilot's viewport were *flexing,* bouncing and twisting, stretching and recoiling.

"Dammit!" Hannah cried out. "The cables are going! Hang on while I try to damp out this tumble. Attitude thrusters on!" The *Sholto* had no

sophisticated automated tumble recovery system—
and certainly not one that was up to autorecovery
with the deadweight of the *Adler* strapped to the
nose of the ship. Hannah was going to have to do
it on manual. Somehow. One axis at a time. Kill
the end-over-end pitch-down tumble first. She fired
her stern Y-axis thrusters hard, at full force—and
saw the number three cable snap in two right in
front of her eyes, sending an echoing *bang* re-
sounding through the hull—and, more disturb-
ingly, she saw a plume of gas jetting out from
somewhere beyond her field of vision. Whatever
that was would have to wait. She had to get the
ship out of its tumble before it tore itself apart.

She gritted her teeth and kept the thrusters
burning, even as she heard another almighty *bang*
from somewhere belowdecks, and then, a half moment later, a terrifying loud thump and a prolonged scraping noise. Something had just broken
loose and slammed into the *Sholto*'s hull. She
glanced at the strain meters and saw that cable six
had dropped from off-scale high to zero. Too late
now. She checked her rates and saw that the tumble was slowing, though not fast enough to suit
her. She brought the tumble through pitch down to
a rough first approximation of zero, then worked
to kill the smaller Z-axis spin through yaw. It
wasn't as bad as the tumble had been, but it was
still a fast rotation. It took some time for the
Z-axis thrusters to bring the rates down enough so
that they weren't scary.

That left her with the X-axis spin along the long axis of the combined ships. She didn't kill it at once. She had another job to do first.

She had two broken cables out there, and both ends of each were no doubt flailing about wildly, likely to swing around and smash into the hulls of the ships or do other mischief in unpleasant and unpredictable ways the moment Hannah relit the engines. For the moment, the barrel roll might keep the broken cables safely at bay, thanks to the centripetal effect—unless there was some weird harmonic resonance in play that would keep them swinging and oscillating unless or until they smashed into something. She didn't dare take the time to power up the external cameras and do a visual inspection—precisely because a broken cable could smash into either ship at any moment.

Furthermore, she couldn't keep even the uncertain protection of the spin going forever, and the broken cables would be a menace as long as they were attached to the ship. She had to get rid of them. And the cables were an all-or-nothing deal. She would have to jettison the two broken sets and the four unbroken cables all at the same time.

A quick glance at the strain gauges convinced her that wouldn't be a bad idea. At least two of the surviving cables looked ready to snap themselves. There would be consequences—real and serious consequences—to dumping the cables, but Hannah saw that she had no other choice.

She set up the jettison-cables command. She

wanted to activate it the moment the command was ready, before she could have second thoughts. "Cable jettison!" she shouted, as if Jamie was going to be able do anything about it. No time for any chitchat. A display lit up, announcing COMMAND SEQUENCE READY, and she slammed her palm down on the button.

Bang bang thud Bang bang thud and the four whole cables and two broken ones were cut loose from the *Sholto* and the *Adler* simultaneously.

No need for the barrel roll anymore. After all the rest of it, killing their long-axis spin and their residual pitch and yaw seemed almost too easy. Hannah let out a deep sigh of relief and slumped backwards against her pilot's chair and called back to Jamie. "All right," she said. "We're secure. I think."

There wasn't any answer for a moment, and she popped open enough of her restraint harness to let her twist around and look down at him. The auto-sequencer hadn't brought the main cabin lighting back on yet, and the lower deck was little more than murk and shadows. "Jamie?" she called out. "You still with me? Jamie?"

"Oh, yeah," said a muffled voice. "Just about. I didn't want to answer before my stomach decided whether to hit the eject button. Ah, you'll be— mmphhm—glad to know it decided against. But it was a close vote."

Hannah grinned and twisted back around to face her control panel and the half dozen warning lights that were blinking for her attention. "Special Agent Mendez, my friend—you don't know a thing in the world about *how* close things can get."

She remembered the venting she had seen just after the cable snapped. They were going to have to check that next, before anything else happened. She released her harness the rest of the way so she could get up close to the viewport and see more of her ship's exterior, and the *Adler*.

What she saw proved that *she* hadn't known how close things could get, either. She immediately shut down the autosequencer before it restarted the environmental systems or the ship's internal gravity. They didn't need any more variables at the moment.

The spaceside end of a broken cable was floating motionless outside the ship, about ten meters away from her face.

The other end had smashed clean through the *Adler*'s starboard viewport.

* * *

Ten minutes later, with Jamie at her side, she had every external camera available pointed at the problem, but none of them told her much that she didn't already know. She had very carefully brought the *Sholto*'s ventilation system back on-line while leaving the *Adler* in vacuum and left the grav systems on both ships shut down. The artificial-gravity fields were supposed to stay inside the hull, leaving the exterior of the ships unaffected, but the induced gee effect could leak outward at times, and both ships had been knocked around enough to detune any grav system. Until that hunk of cable was clear of both ships, she didn't want to try any experiments.

"It's the *Adler* end of cable number six," she said quietly. "When the cable snapped, that half of it whipsawed somehow, and smashed right through the starboard panel of the *Adler*'s viewport. A hole that size must have vented every millibar of pressure out of her cabin in twenty seconds. And no, there's no reason besides dumb luck that it wasn't the other end of the cable, or that it didn't smash through *our* viewport instead and leave us breathing vacuum."

"The venting didn't cause that violent a tumble, did it?"

"What? Oh, no, not at all. I'm sure all that atmosphere blowing out added to the tumble, but not by all that much. This"—she gestured at the cable smashed through the viewport—"was pretty much the *last* domino to fall. Nowhere near the first. The only noticeable transit-jump effect we got was a very mild red-lighting. Perfectly harmless. But what I can read from the autolog, we also ran up against a very slight pseudogravity field during the jump—not enough for us to feel, but enough to cause trouble. Not all that rare, but not common, either. The *Sholto*'s jump generator could handle the jump effect pseudogee field, *or* the off-balance mass of the *Adler*, but not both at once. The interaction between the two induced just enough of a gravity flux to induce a tumble that built up during the jump, but that had no effect on us until we were dumped back into the normal universe. Probably the techs back home will be able to read our event logs, figure exactly what went wrong, and tweak and twiddle and tweedle the jump generators so it won't happen next time—but that doesn't do *us* much good. But, anyway, I figure we were already spinning in three directions inside the jump—but we just didn't feel it until we popped back out here."

"Where *is* here?" Jamie asked.

Hannah checked her nav displays. "Good news there," she said. "Right on the money, in the Metran System, and on a clean initial course for Metran itself. Except of course that we have to start our braking maneuvers pretty soon or we'll just shoot past the planet and head right back out the other side of the star system."

"But now that the reinforcing cables have failed, can we put on the brakes?"

"The cables *didn't* fail," Hannah said. "If they hadn't been there to take the strain, it would have been the docking rings that would have had to take it on—and probably torn themselves to shreds."

"Okay, I take your point," said Jamie. "But I'd suggest that having a cable snap, then bury itself in a viewport wasn't exactly what Gunther's team had in *mind* when they attached them."

"I won't argue—but we're alive right now because those cables snapped instead of the docking rings shredding. As to whether we can fire up the *Sholto*'s engines and brake the combined vehicle— we'll have to inspect things as best we can. My guess is that yes, we can, if we don't crank the thrust up too high. But—I think it's obvious that we shouldn't attempt another docked transit- jump. We've lost the cables; and both ships have damage to the hulls caused by cable strikes—plus the smashed-in viewport window. Space knows what hidden damage there might be. We'll have to jump the ships back individually—or else abandon one of them here and fly both of us back in one of them. *That's* going to complicate matters."

"Yeah," said Jamie. He was quiet for a moment before he spoke again. "This is one hell of a mess," he announced.

"Yes it is," Hannah agreed. "But at least we have some time to work on sorting it out." She ran some numbers through her nav plot. "Even if we keep the thrust down to say, five gees, we have about—let's see—eighteen, nineteen hours before we have to start the burn. We can hold off a lot longer than that if we decide we can use a higher thrust."

"But the other minor issue is that we brought the *Adler* along for a reason. We need to get aboard to continue searching her as long as we can. And we can't fly her down to Metran."

"I know, I know."

"But can we do anything else? The basic flight

plan was for both ships to ride in together, riding on the *Sholto*'s engines until we were most of the way slowed down, then to cut loose the *Adler* and have her light her own engines and park herself in a Pluto-class orbit while the *Sholto* flew on to Metran. And then there's the trip back. The *Sholto* doesn't have enough power to do all the work by herself. The *Adler* will have to accelerate herself and match course with the *Sholto*. We need both ships at least reasonably healthy to do all that."

Hannah nodded. "Even if we weren't planning to search her, we still have to get back aboard the *Adler* to program her for autonomous flight and configure her to receive external flight commands."

"It was a mistake to bring her along," Jamie said.

"It's starting to look that way, at least for the moment," Hannah agreed. "But it was Kelly's call—and mistake—not ours. But what if, right now, we're five days away from whatever will touch off this war, and we save three days by having the *Adler* along for the ride? Even if it turns out that we both die and we lose both ships, but we stop a war—well, you and I won't enjoy it much, but could you really say Kelly made the wrong decision?"

Jamie didn't answer directly. "Okay, let's forget about the big picture just for the moment," he said. "The main thing is that we have to get aboard the *Adler*, repair her, continue searching her, and then program her for autoflight and external control and cut her loose. Right?"

"Right."

"Okay then. A good solid mechanical hard dock connection is one thing, but airtight is another. After what it's been through, the flexing and twisting and who knows what other forces, would you trust the docking tunnel to serve as an air lock?"

Hannah checked her instruments. "The tunnel was pressure-matched with the *Sholto*'s cabin when we closed the hatches ninety minutes ago. It still is."

"That's something," Jamie said. "In fact, it's quite a lot. But *do* you want to trust it as an air lock?"

"No," Hannah said. "Not after what it's just been through. I think it's even possible that we won't be able to undock the two ships. The whole mechanism might be fouled up. We'll worry about that when it happens. In the meantime, I don't want to stress the system any more than we have already."

"And using the lower-deck air lock on our ship, doing a space walk right past that loose cable and the smashed window, then opening the *Adler*'s lower-deck lock manually and cycling through it seems awfully risky, too. A lot could go wrong. I think we have to depressurize the *Sholto* so both ships are in vacuum, open the nose hatch, and then open the *Adler*'s nose hatch and cross to the *Adler* that way."

"Agreed," said Hannah. "But there's one slight problem. Let me check something." She pushed back from the control panel and started taking advantage of zero gee. She spun herself around, grabbed the rope ladder, and pulled herself down toward the lower deck headfirst. She propelled herself across the lower deck toward one of the equipment lockers and opened it. She sighed wearily. "We're really going to have to talk to Gunther about improvising more brilliantly and making sure all the bases are covered when they're doing what no one has ever done before on the rush and without anyone in overall charge. His people didn't hang an extra suit here."

"What?" Jamie called down.

"Suit. Pressure suit. There's only one emergency pressure suit on this ship. There's another on the *Adler*, but that's not going to do us much good right now." She looked up at Jamie as he stared down at her from the upper deck. "Any suggestions?"

* * *

"I was the one who worked out what to do," said Jamie as he entered the lower-deck air lock, hauling in a stack of gear. "I still think I should be the one who goes over."

"This from the guy who almost lost his lunch when the ships starting tumbling and who is looking a little green after doing nothing more than floating from one deck to another in zero gee," said Hannah as she set down the stack of air-scrubber canisters in the corner of the lock chamber. "Okay, air scrubbers, spare oxy, food, water. Comm system up, running, and patched into the loop with the suit radio."

"Check, check, check, check, and check on the supplies, and yes, the comm system is online. If I never get any practice in zero-gee operations, I'll never have a chance to adapt."

"Agreed," said Hannah. "But this isn't the time to practice—or the time to start acting like the big brave hairy man who has to do all the dangerous stuff. What if your stomach hits the eject button when you're in the suit, you've got the helmet on, and you're in vacuum?"

Jamie shrugged. "Then we probably both die," he conceded.

"Look, if we live through this, we can leave the grav system shut off for the whole ride back, and you can do all the practicing you want."

Jamie grinned. "I don't know if that's such a good idea. I'm not sure I want to have to spend the whole trip back cleaning up after myself."

"Well, don't expect *me* to do it," Hannah said with a laugh. "Look, I know it's not exactly an ego rush, but this is the way we *have* to do it if we want the best chances of both of us staying alive. You hunker down in the lower-deck air lock, while I use the suit and do the repair. For what it's worth,

I wouldn't want to do what *you* have to do. I'm not that crazy about getting crammed in a box."

"Thanks for putting it that way." Jamie glanced around the inside of the *Sholto*'s lower-deck air lock. "I feel a whole lot better about it now."

"Sorry," Hannah said. "I shouldn't have said it like that."

"It's okay," said Jamie. "But look me in the eye and tell me that you really think getting stuffed in the lower-deck air lock, because it's the only place that we can keep pressurized, seems heroic to you."

"No," said Hannah, without any attempt at joking or banter. "No, it doesn't."

"But being dead wouldn't feel much better," Jamie said ruefully. "So lock me in and go do your job."

"You get in there, and do yours, Mr. Tactical Planning Genius," she said. "We're going to need lots of options for maneuver-masking and rendezvous flight plans."

"Yes, Mom. I promise to stay in and do my homework."

"I'm not kidding, Jamie. We're going to need those options, and we aren't going to be able to work them out from scratch on the fly before we cut the *Adler* loose. The time when you're locked in here might be the only chance you'll have to work them out."

"And I will. I know. I know."

Hannah rubbed her eyes and sighed. "Well, if

we both weren't on edge by now, there would be something wrong with us." She glanced around the tiny chamber. "Sorry it's so cold in here," she said. "But you'll be glad we cranked down the temp soon enough. Sooner or later, the lock chamber's going to start getting warm."

"I know," he said. "Believe me, I know. Good luck out there."

"And good luck in here," Hannah said. "I'll keep you posted over the suit radio."

Neither of them was eager for what came next, but both of them knew it had to happen. Hannah pulled herself forward, they shook hands awkwardly, and Hannah gave Jamie an affectionate cuff on the shoulder. Then she grabbed at handholds and pulled herself out of the air lock and into the *Sholto*'s lower deck. She braced her feet on the deck and closed the air lock hatch while Jamie stayed where he was, silently watching her. Jamie knew beyond all doubt that the same thought was going through both their minds.

This could be the last time we see each other alive.

* * *

Things always took longer than planned. It was a half hour later before Hannah was sealed into her suit and the main cabin of the *Sholto* was in vacuum. She hauled her improvised pack of cobbled-together equipment and supplies behind her and made her way toward the nose hatch. She worked the controls to drop the pressure inside the hatch tunnel and waited while the scavenger pumps ran. For about the hundredth time in the last ten minutes, she resisted the temptation to give Jamie a status report on every trivial step of her progress. *Okay, I've pushed the depressurize tunnel button. Okay, the tunnel is depressurizing. Okay, the panel is showing vacuum in the tunnel. Okay, I'm opening the hatch. I've got the hatch open....*

It might make her feel better to keep up the chatter, but she knew it would drive Jamie to distraction—and probably she'd start getting on her *own* nerves before too much time had passed. He could hear her breathing through the comm loop. That would be enough to let him know she was still more or less all right. Far better simply to keep him posted on the big items and otherwise leave him be.

The panel showed the tunnel in vacuum—and once again she resisted the temptation to report that thrilling news. She popped the hatch and moved on into the tunnel, hauling the gear behind her.

She paused in the tunnel to examine the join between the docking rings of the two ships, but she could spot no obvious flaws or damage. But, of course, the most crucial and complex parts of the docking system were hidden from view inside the tunnel walls. They wouldn't know for sure until they tried to undock the ships, and even then they wouldn't be absolutely sure they would be able to *re*dock without giving it a try. But that was so many problems down the pike that it wasn't even worth worrying about.

Time to open the hatch to the *Adler*. Hannah moved forward down the tunnel, worked the controls, and pushed the hatch open. She latched it open, but didn't bother sliding the stanchions that held the rope ladder back into place. In zero gee, it didn't much matter if there was an overhang between the top of the ladder and the lip of the hatch.

The power was still out on the *Adler*, and she planned to keep it that way until she had checked out as many systems as possible. She powered up her helmet lights and peered into the shafts of light and ever-shifting and looming shadows they revealed.

It was amazing how utterly foreign and mysterious, how *menacing* a perfectly familiar place could look, merely because it was in darkness. Except this place *was* menacing, in fact downright dangerous, after that cable had come smashing through the viewport. There could very easily be razor-sharp shards of viewport or other debris floating around—and her suit was a lightweight one-size-fits-nearly-all emergency job, not an armored hostile-environment unit.

She scanned for debris as best she could with the helmet lights but didn't spot anything. She used an oversized eyelet attached to her gear bag to secure it to a handhold, then opened the bag up. The first things she pulled out of it were two empty utility bags.

First things first. She made her way carefully down to the *Adler*'s lower deck and starting going through the equipment lockers. She pulled out the *Adler*'s emergency pressure suit and the breather masks and any other sort of gear that they might conceivably need two of in the next emergency. Better late than never. That equipment went into one bag. The other she filled with the *Adler*'s patch kit and leak-repair supplies. They were going to need just about every bit of patching material from both ships if they were going to have a prayer of sealing the hole where the viewport panel used to be.

She zipped both bags shut, then moved carefully back up to the nose hatch. She lined up the bag with the pressure suit and the survival gear in it, aimed it down the tunnel, and gave it a gentle shove. She felt mildly pleased with herself when she saw it sail smoothly down the centerline and clear into the *Sholto*.

In theory, she was at the point where she could return to the *Sholto*, repressurize the cabin, get Jamie out of the air lock and into the second suit, then depressurize again and have both of them go aboard the *Adler*. But Hannah doubted the time burned up in all that would be saved by having two people on the repair job. Besides, given what the docking systems and the hatches and associated equipment had been through already, she didn't want to cycle any of it more times than necessary. Every time she sealed a hatch might be the last time it would seal properly.

And though she wouldn't admit it unless pressed, she genuinely didn't like the idea of Jamie's slightly spacesick self working in a space suit in the dark in zero gee. Someday there would be enough time between missions to get him on a zero-gee acclimatization course. Until then, she didn't want to risk his pride, let alone his life, or the mission, if it wasn't utterly necessary.

Which left her to get on with the job. Still unsure whether there was sharp-edged debris floating in the darkness, she pulled worklights from the gear bag, clipped them to convenient handholds, and pointed them at the pilot's station and the viewports. The result was a vast improvement on the lighting provided by her helmet lights alone.

"Jamie, you there?" she called over the suit comm.

"Where else would I be, and how would I get there?"

"Yeah, you're there all right. I'm in the *Adler* without any problems. It's a mess in here, but it could be worse. Whatever they make those viewports out of is mighty tough stuff. The cable smashed into the starboard viewport and punched the whole thing, viewport, edging, and all, clear out of the frame. The cable end hit it more or less end on, somehow, and simply lodged in the transparent viewport material. The whole show slammed right into the headrest of the pilot's seat. If I'd been sitting there, I would have gotten my head sliced clean off before I even knew the cable had struck the viewport."

"Aren't you full of cheery thoughts," said Jamie.

"I am, actually. I was imagining the *Adler*'s cabin full of shards of glass and the cable snaking and twisting everywhere. Instead, I've got one solid chunk of viewport and the cable just hanging there peacefully, sticking straight out the hole where the viewport used to be. It doesn't seem to have struck anything else or damaged the control panels or any of the electronic systems. All I have to do is rig some way to hold the cable motionless while I bring up the cutting laser, slice through it, shove it very carefully out the window—and I've got a nice clean hole to patch that shouldn't be too big for the patching equipment we jury-rigged."

She and Jamie had removed a couple of deck-plates from the *Sholto*'s lower deck and then used the *Sholto*'s viewports as a sort of template to guide them in cutting the pieces into the right size and shape to give a rough fit over the viewport. They had cut two such patches in case Hannah needed more than one try to get it right, but at the moment the job looked a lot more straightforward than they had assumed. By combining the cut-down deckplating with all the patching material from both ships, they ought to be able to seal the hole. Hannah was very decidedly not all that happy about using all the patches on both ships. They'd be in big trouble if another leak developed. But they didn't have much choice. They'd need every square centimeter of patch they had for this job.

"Great," said Jamie. "So, what? I'll see you back over here in, say, five minutes?"

"It *might* take just a bit longer than that," she said. "But I'll keep you posted."

"No more than you have to," Jamie said. "I'm trying to catch up on my sleep."

"I'll bet you are," she said. "Wolfson out."

* * *

Jamie hoped his kidding around was enough to keep Hannah from worrying about him. She hadn't been joking about how hot it would get in the lock chamber. The air lock didn't really have an environmental system to speak of. No reason why it should have one. It had been designed as a way in and out of the ship, not as a place anyone would need to stay for hours on end. That was why they had had to bring in the air scrubber canisters to remove carbon dioxide from the air, and the breather mask and oxygen tanks.

By running the scrubber and keeping the breather mask on, he was able to keep the carbon dioxide level within safe ranges and also get enough oxy to breathe. But there was no way to get rid of the heat generated by his body, or the sweat that had nowhere to go in zero gee, or the water vapor he was exhaling. He had plenty of water to drink, if need be, but the climate in the lock was getting to be something close to a steam bath. He wasn't in much danger of drying out.

He was as physically miserable as he could remember being in a long time, enough so that he was glad to have the navigation problems to distract him. Not that he was doing the nav work on his own. It was more a question of setting up problems for the nav computer to solve and approving or rejecting the proposed solutions. The challenge was not in planning an efficient trajectory for the *Sholto* toward Metran. The trick was in setting up a flight plan that would put the energy plume of the *Sholto* directly between the planet Metran and the *Adler*, so that the *Adler* could perform her independent braking maneuver without being spotted by whatever high-powered detectors were on-planet.

Jamie was asking the computer to find flight plans that would allow the *Adler* to hide behind the *Sholto*'s energy plume not only while they were inbound, but also during their exit from the Metran system. The further challenge was to avoid its *looking* like they were doing it. That meant that the *Sholto* had to fly as smooth and steady a flight path as possible while leaving the *Adler* to do the fancy maneuvers.

It was the sort of thing Jamie was good at, and he worked the system quickly, developing a dozen basic scenarios for both their inbound and outbound flights. When the time came, they would be able to pull up the scenario that was the closest fit to the real-life situation and tweak it a little, rather than being forced to develop the flight plan from scratch in the middle of whatever emergency might develop.

After a while Jamie recognized that he was reaching the point of diminishing returns, having developed so many variations that there was barely anything to pick between them. He shut down the system. All that was left would be to upload his work to the *Adler*'s nav system once they had the other ship patched up and put back together.

Patched up. The phrase reminded him of something that had been niggling at the corner of his mind. When they had been planning the repairs to the *Adler*'s viewport, Hannah had mentioned that the hull patch kit aboard the *Adler* had only three of the circular twenty-centimeter patches left, instead of the four that should have been in the package. There certainly wasn't any chance they had overlooked a bright orange patch the size of a dinner plate slapped on the inside hull of the ship.

It didn't necessarily mean anything. Maybe some agent on a previous mission had had a big evidence bag split open and simply reached for whatever could seal it up fast. Maybe one of the patches had gone bad, the adhesive dried out or whatever, and been discarded. It should have been logged or reported, of course. A hull patch was an important piece of safety equipment. But not everything that *should* have been reported *was* reported.

But thoughts of the missing patch brought him back to the reason he was sealed inside an air lock, in zero gee, and floating in a film of his own sweat. He keyed on the comm loop. "What's the state of play, Hannah?" he asked.

"Well, I've got the cable cut, and I only nearly sliced through my own suit twice. I've managed to push the cable end back out of the hole where the viewport was. It was a little exciting when the broken cable started to tumble. It sort of scraped against the hull, but nowhere near fast enough to do any damage. It's drifted well clear of both ships now and shouldn't be hard for us to miss when we start maneuvering. I'm just starting to squeeze a line of sealant around the edge of our slice of deckplate. I did a test fit already, and it ought to go into place just fine. Then I can slap the four *Sholto* patches and the three *Adler* patches around the edges of the deckplate and hose the foam-up sealant over the whole mess."

"Good," Jamie said. "Report unto me when thy seventh seal is setteth in place."

"Don't go all biblical on me."

"Do you realize how long I've been waiting to use that line?"

"Yes, because I've been waiting just as long but you beat me to it. And besides, I don't think 'setteth' is a word. Wolfson out."

THIRTEEN
LOTS OF NOTHING

Hannah checked the pressure in the *Sholto*'s main cabin, then wearily opened her suit helmet and felt her ears pop as the slight residual pressure differential adjusted itself. She pushed herself over to the air lock hatch and punched up the automatic controls. She was just too tired to open the hatch on manual.

The door swung open—and the blast of locker-room air that struck her in the face made her wish she had kept her helmet sealed just a bit longer. Jamie propelled himself out of the lock chamber and peeled off the breathing mask. All of his clothes were soaked through with sweat. The inside of the hatch and the interior walls of the air lock were coated with condensed moisture. A faint misty cloud appeared for a moment as the hot wet air of the lock chamber came in contact with the cooler, drier air in the cabin.

"I think I sweated off two kilos in there," he gasped.

"You ought to measure it in liters, not kilos," Hannah said. "I was going to say I get to use the shower first, but you take the prize."

"I'm not going to argue. So how's it look?"

"Better than we have any right to expect," Hannah said. "No significant damage to the *Adler* besides the viewport and the pilot's chair nearly getting sliced in half. I left the viewport wedged into the chair and the stub of the cable still lodged in the viewport transparency. Our patch is ugly as the devil, but seems to be holding pressure without problems. But we're going to play it very, very safe. We'll keep both ships on reduced pressure to lessen the strain on the patch, and we'll wear pressure suits with the helmets on and open whenever we're aboard the *Adler*. We're going to keep both nose hatches shut when we're in the *Sholto* in case the patch fails. And we're going to keep both hatches *open* whenever we're aboard the *Adler*, just in case the patch fails and we need to be able to get back into the *Sholto* fast."

"That's just about the rules that I was going to suggest," Jamie said. "What about the grav systems? Do we stay in zero gee or back to one gee on both ships, or what?"

"I haven't decided," Hannah admitted. "I don't think that it's going to make any difference to the patch over the missing viewport. The ships were designed to operate under gravity."

"Then if it's all the same to you, let's go with standard grav on both ships. Sitting still in zero gee was bad enough for my inner ears. I don't think I'd like to try moving around in a large space for hours on end. And besides, it's a *lot* easier to take a shower in gravity."

"Okay, you sold me right there. Gravity it is," said Hannah. "Now get yourself freshened up fast. I'm itching for my turn—and that's no figure of speech."

Twelve hours later, both of them were cleaned up and had managed to get at least some rest, if not much in the way of proper sleep, and they were back at it, searching the *Adler*.

The job was harder than it had been at first. Working in open pressure suits, however necessary, was awkward and uncomfortable. The ruined pilot's chair still had the smashed viewport panel and the stub of cable was still lodged in place. There was no sense wasting time or risking injury trying to repair the chair or remove the debris from it. But there were enough broken and sharp edges that they didn't want it around, either. They wound up removing it from the upper deck and stuffing it in the *Adler*'s lower-deck air lock just to get it out of the way. It was a necessary job, but it cost them nearly an hour of time that neither of them much liked losing.

The other problem was that they weren't just *searching* the *Adler*. They had to inspect her as well, checking and double-checking to make sure that she had not suffered any other, hidden damage. That, of course, went beyond examining the accessible parts of the ship's interior. They went through the process of powering up the *Adler*'s systems in the slowest, most careful and painstaking way they could manage, checking every subsystem and status display before going on to the next step.

They lost more time checking the outsides of the ships. Hannah used the external cameras to inspect as much of both ship's exteriors as she could. Both had suffered scrapes, dents, and dings from cable strikes. Nothing bad enough to threaten the hull structure, but certainly bad enough to foul up both vehicles' aerodynamics. It was just as well they weren't expecting to fly either ship in an atmosphere. While it was entirely possible that there was severe damage just out of sight of the cameras, Hannah ruled and Jamie agreed that the dangers of doing an inspection space walk were far greater than the chance of discovering significant damage that they could actually repair.

But even with all those distractions out of the way, Jamie was far from enthused about continuing the search. He felt himself to be every bit as intent a hunter as Hannah, every bit as eager and determined to track down a clue, a lead. But part of that talent consisted of listening to one's own instincts—and Jamie's instincts said they were on the wrong track. They had missed something. Somewhere, somehow, all their logic and searching had taken them off course. He was finishing up searching under one deckplate when he finally decided he had to say something. "Hannah?"

"Yeah?"

"Whatever it is we're looking for—this isn't the way we're going to find it."

Hannah sighed and looked up from her own searches inside a breaker panel. "No, we're not. This isn't working. Unless it does work, and we do find it. But I agree. The odds are against us. The trouble is I don't know what *else* to do. Do you have any ideas?"

"No," he said. "But what worries me is that under the flight plan we've chosen, we light the candle on the *Sholto* in eighteen hours, and we have to cut the *Adler* loose ten hours after that, and let her do her independent burn. And we have to eat and sleep, and get the *Adler* configured for auto and external control and probably about half a dozen other things as well. Even if this search was worth doing, we don't have time to finish it."

"I agree with all of that," said Hannah. "This is probably a complete waste of time. Unless you find the decrypt code under the next deckplate. We just don't know enough to do anything else—and we won't learn anything more until we get on-planet. So until we have to cut the *Adler* loose, or until one of us comes up with a brilliant solution, we're going to keep on searching through this haystack for the needle that's probably not here." And with that, she turned back to the interior of the breaker panel, slowly and carefully studying each section of it before moving on.

Jamie shut his eyes and allowed the sense of weary frustration that he had been holding back to wash over him, just for a moment. *Slogging is part of the job,* he told himself. *It's the only lead we've got, so it's the lead we're going to follow.* That sounded like the sort of thing Commander Kelly would say. And if there was anyone who was right more often than Hannah Wolfson, that person was Commander Wilhelmina Kelly.

Jamie opened his eyes, shook his head to clear it, and moved on to the next deckplate.

* * *

Everything went according to plan. Unfortunately. They searched until they were flat out of time for searching, did all the preps on the *Adler,* retreated to the *Sholto,* and lit her engines to start the initial braking maneuver to start trimming their ferocious velocity as they entered the Metran star system.

Hannah insisted on running at five gees for a full four hours, watching every sensor and strain gauge all the time, before she grudgingly agreed to throttle up—very slowly and carefully, over a period of two hours—to twelve gees, but she flatly refused to risk their much-abused spacecraft at anything higher than that, even though all the boards showed solid green. There had been enough surprises.

Hannah brought the main navigation plot up on the largest of the screens on the *Sholto*'s control panel. On the left of the screen, slowly creeping toward the right, was the double dot that represented the current position of the *Sholto* and *Adler*. Along the right side of the screen was the bright reddish-gold circle representing the local sun, and, much closer to it than to the incoming ships, the present position of Metran itself.

Hannah didn't bother to display any of the other planets or satellites or other bodies in the Metran system. None of them were going to enter into their problem, and she didn't want to be distracted by them. However, there were two other elements visible in the display: a blue and a red arc, both centered on Metran. They represented the approximate maximum range of ship-detection equipment watching from the planet for a ship under high-gee reactionless thrust. The blue one was far closer to the planet.

It showed what human equipment could do. The red represented the best current estimate for what Elder Race detection systems could do. It was about three and half times farther out from the planet. Anything they wanted to conceal was going to have to be accomplished well outside that range. Inside that radius, they would have to rely on the much trickier task of maneuver-masking, of constantly keeping the *Sholto* between the planet and the *Adler*. On the plus side, spotting a ship with its engines off was a far more difficult task. Once the *Adler* was in her concealment orbit and had shut her engines down, she would be essentially undetectable to anyone's sensors.

"The thing I don't understand," said Jamie,

leaning over the pilot's chair and staring at the display, "is why are they only three or four times better than us?"

"Hmmm?" Hannah asked absently as she checked her status boards again.

"The detection range for the Elder Races. Why isn't it a lot better than it is? They've had thousands or millions of years' more time for technical development."

Hannah grinned and raised a conspiratorial finger to her lips. "Shhh," she said. "UniGov doesn't want people asking that question. It could lead to trouble."

"What are you talking about?"

"Actually it's not just the United Human Government. It's *all* the human governments, and *all* the spy agencies. That question gets them nervous. People are starting to notice that the Elder Race xenos are just way, way, ahead of us, instead of way, way, way, *way* ahead. Some people even think *we're* ahead of *them* in some fields. Remember how the Reqwar Pavlat had to call in human genetics experts?"

"Hard to forget," said Jamie. "But what's so bad about us not being so far behind?"

"Because it might make people start to tell themselves that human civilization isn't as weak or vulnerable or insignificant as the Elder Races keep telling us. The trouble is that, even if their detection systems and data systems and star drives are 'only' twice or three or ten times better than ours, when you'd assume that a million years of technology would make them a hundred or a thousand or a million times better—they still *are* three times better than our stuff. And there are a lot more of them than there are of us. If we humans started feeling our oats too much, and started to make nuisances of ourselves, it might just make a few of the old races—like the Xenoatrics on Metran— wake up from their nice long naps and decide to do something about it. And if they wanted to take the trouble, they could render the human race extinct inside of a week. So better not to rock the boat when you don't need to."

"Yeah, I guess," he said doubtfully. "But why *aren't* they a million times better than we are?"

"Pick your theory. Maybe there is some sort of inevitable plateau. Maybe there is some mental block that is innate to all intelligent life—a wall inside the mind that no race can get past. The Elder Races reached it long ago, but we just haven't gotten to it yet.

"Or else there are explicit, objective limits to possible technical achievement, the way they used to assume there was no way to exceed the speed of light. Maybe there *are* limits to what can be done with electronics, computers, chemistry, and so on. The Elder Races have bumped up against them, and rightly assume that sooner or later, we'll hit them too. Or maybe it's all about attitude. Maybe the spirit grows tired. Why go to huge effort to get something that's utterly amazing when you already have something that's splendid? They don't need better than what they have, so why bother?

"They're always so condescending and amused about how hard humans and the Kendari are trying to catch up, trying to buy or steal or create or surpass all the inventions they've had since we were duking it out with the Neanderthals. They pat us on the head and roll their eyes because they know we'll grow out of it, and maybe catch up with them sooner or later—but never, never go beyond.

"Or else you could listen to the people who do technical projections for UniGov. *They* say that if current trends continue, in another century or two, humans *and* Kendari will blow right past what the Elder Races can do." Hannah stared silently at her displays before she spoke again. "And if the tech projection people are right—then you'd better pray that humans and Kendari learn to get along with each other before then—or there's going to be nothing but smoking ruins left where the Galaxy used to be." She drummed her fingers on the control panel and glanced up at Jamie. "But catching up with the Elder Races is a dream—or maybe a nightmare—to worry about later. Right now all we have to do is keep them from spotting the *Irene Adler*. Let's get started."

* * *

"Okay, engine stop," Hannah announced. "Confirming hatches sealed on both ships. Closed hatches confirmed."

"Now who's doing call-outs?" Jamie asked, raising his voice to be heard from his seat on the lower deck.

"Hey, you're a bad influence. Now let's see if the docking system really did come through unscathed."

"What do we do if the docking rings *are* jammed together and we can't undock the two ships?" Jamie asked.

"I have no idea," Hannah said. "Let's just hope that thirty seconds from now, we won't have to worry about it." She flipped a switch. "Undocking commenced."

There was a comforting series of rattling *bang*s as the capture latches released. "Okay, that's a good sign," Hannah said. "I'm showing all latches fully released. We're at soft dock now. Disengaging soft seal connections. Stand by for the champagne cork."

There was a loud cartoonish *pop* as the air in the tunnel formed by the two docking hatches suddenly escaped into space, gently pushing the two ships apart. Hannah gave the smallest of taps to the attitude jets and pushed the *Sholto* clear of the *Adler*.

"Okay, we're clear," said Hannah. "You can unstrap."

Jamie did so and scrambled up the ladder to the upper deck to get a better look at the *Irene Adler* as the *Bartholomew Sholto* backed away from her. "Well," he said. "So much for the idea of taking advantage of all that extra search time because we brought her with us. We looked everywhere. It wasn't there. But it *has* to be there."

"Agreed on all counts," said Hannah. "For all the time we spent, all we bought was a whole lot of nothing. And I'm starting to worry that we're going to get another dose of the same down on Metran. What could anyone down *there* tell us that would help us find where Trevor hid it?"

"That's the first time you've called him by his first name."

"Hmmmph. You're right. It is. I *knew* you were a bad influence. Come on, we've got an hour to kill before it's time to relight our engines. Let's grab some dinner."

FOURTEEN
NEW IS OLD

Learned Searcher Taranarak rose from her sleeping pad and prepared to start the next day of her endless house arrest. "Preventive detention" had shifted smoothly into "Protective detention" without any intervening step. What difference was there between being locked up because she might harm others and because others might harm her—especially since both claims were little more than implausible excuses?

She no longer bothered to count the days, or check if the security shutters had been removed from her doors and windows overnight. She no longer had any illusions that her jailers would suddenly come to realize that confining her made no sense, accomplished nothing, and likely was counterproductive to their goal of keeping the situation quiet. After all, the armed guards around her house and the sealing of all its entrances were a plainly visible sign to all that not only was something seriously wrong, but that it involved Taranarak; it was but a simple jump from there to guess that it involved geriatrics. Under the circumstances, even the Order Bureaucrats should not have been surprised to see the crowds that gathered outside.

Taranarak shuffled through what had become her new normal morning routine, scarcely noticing the jarring incongruities anymore. She washed, she dressed, she knocked at the steel shutter at the rear door, waited for it to open, and exchanged yesterday's empty receptacles and her other trash for a parcel containing her food and other necessities for the day. She exchanged a few pleasantries with the guard who made the delivery, put the food away, prepared and ate her morning meal, cleared up afterward, then went to sit in her great room and resume her work: her searches into what Hallaben had learned.

Other than the fact that she had rearranged her furniture so that she did not face the massive featureless grey shutter covering her view window, nothing had changed about the room where she spent most of her days, and that, in a strange way, was comforting. Almost daily, she actually caught herself fretting that something would happen to alter the routine, to change what she had now grown used to.

Those moments told her a great deal about herself, and about her people, and the truths she learned were not comfortable to face. Bulwark of Constancy and the Unseen Race were not the only ones who feared change.

Taranarak looked down at her study materials and came to herself with a start. She realized that she had moved through her entire morning routine not merely on automatic but almost unconsciously. She had to think, really *think,* in order to recall what she had said to the guard who delivered her food that morning, and for the life of her she could not remember what sort of meal she had prepared, eaten, and then cleared away.

What *could* she remember? She shut her forward and rearward eyes and asked herself, what, exactly, she had been studying—what document, what data. It was a major effort of will and mind to recall.

She remembered what she had learned, what she had accomplished, what she wished to do. All that was clear and sharp in her mind. But remembering the actions themselves was another matter. And it was not merely the utter sameness of each day that made it hard to recall what this day was like. It was, she knew, a compulsion deep inside her, inside all of her people to *make* each day the same, to keep things unchanged, to tell themselves that things were best as they were, that anything new was unsuitable, wrong, dangerous.

There were cases of Metrannans successfully running businesses for years on end, of Metrannans operating space facilities, who later were found to have no conscious memory of doing the job in question.

When taken to excess, it was even a recognized psychiatric syndrome—"the normal desire for everyday life to be predictable, taken to an extreme." To

Taranarak's thinking, the half-approving way the illness was described in and of itself demonstrated just how deeply the illness was embedded in Metrannan culture.

Taranarak stood up and resolutely faced the great grey slab of blank nothingness that hid the view of the city from her. What she saw was not any sort of "new" normal. It was not acceptable. She might be required to endure house arrest, but she dared not get used to it, grow comfortable with it, even come to enjoy it. There was a point beyond which she must not cooperate with it or with those who imposed it.

There was a familiar banging and clanking at the main door of her home. Taranarak knew what that meant. The back door was for delivery of provisions. The front door was for comings and goings. The distinction was already absolute, unquestioned. And there was only one place to which she was ever taken. The Order Council had summoned her again. Once again, no doubt, she would face the same weary questioning. Always, it was the same. *Have you succeeded?* No. *Have you made meaningful additional progress?* No. *Do you believe it is worth continuing the effort?* Yes.

Perhaps they found that repetitive ritual comforting as well. All was well so long as the answers were always the same.

Taranarak walked to the hallway and glared at the still-sealed door. The Order Bureaucracy hadn't exactly installed a sophisticated security system. It would still take them several minutes to get the shutter clear and the door open. She went to put on appropriate dress, collect her things, and be ready when they were.

* * *

Taranarak stared out the viewport. The same flight path over the same city. No fires were burning at the moment, but there were a few new broken windows, and a few more repairs under way, a few more signs of ruin, a few more of renewal. Strange how even civil disorder had somehow been transformed into something normal, accepted, made routine, institutionalized. She would almost be prepared to believe the small and murky rebel group negotiated the upcoming schedule of attacks with the Order Bureaucracy. Neither side would be able to abide making the chaos *too* chaotic.

Or perhaps she was merely projecting her own experience onto what she was seeing out the window, indulging in another familiar Metrannan psychological impulse, the desire to make things all the same, to fit all into one pattern. The Order Council was temporizing, playing both sides against the middle with her, and therefore she was assuming it would do the same with the rebels—if "rebels" was not too grand a term for what was merely a frustrated mob. That, too, was part of the pattern. Reifying things, sticking understandable labels on mysteries, then assuming that the label was all one needed to know.

Taranarak knew few of the details other than what the officers who held her would tell her, or what the Order Council let slip during their interviews with her, and what she could see through the windows of the aircars as she was flown back and forth. From what she could gather, nothing had yet reached the level of those first riots; but there had been repeated disturbances, and even the periods of relative calm were unsettled and anxious.

It was as if the long-suppressed desire for extended life spans had broken free—and dragged something else out of the shell with it: an anger that had been held in check for so many generations that no one had even known it was there.

Taranarak had been astonished to learn from casual side comments in the Order Council that there had been several assaults on visitors from other worlds—and even one incident wherein one of the Unseen People had been threatened in a public place. If, even in their state of fear and denial, they had to admit to such things, what worse things had happened? What else were they still unwilling to face?

Am I watching myself go mad, or my society, or both? They flew past the Enclave of the Unseen, and she gazed sympathetically down at its empty streets. If the Metrannans were failing so miserably to deal with change, how must it be for the Unseen?

But she had to focus her thoughts on the Order Council. They wanted her to continue her efforts to recover Hallaben's work and had provided her with the study materials she needed.

At the same time, she could see a trend of conversation in her last few visits. They were looking for reasons that meant they could not, should not, would not release the treatment. They seemed almost relieved every time they brought her in and she had to report that she had made no further progress. Even the promise of long life for themselves was not enough to tempt them to turn their world upside down.

The aircar landed in the same spot in the courtyard as the first time she had been summoned. The courtyard, however, was a very different place. All the temporary improvised barricades and protections had been replaced by grim permanent barriers. All the wreckage had been cleared away and a wider perimeter established, turning what had once been a lively public plaza in the center of the city into a sealed-off and controlled military staging area, as orderly, lifeless, and soulless as the grey security shutters bolted to Taranarak's house.

The guards led her along the familiar way, past the quietly bustling semipermanent command post in the ground floor, up the elevator, and back to the same room in which she had met the same three Order Bureaucrats as before—and there, once again, fulfilling whatever unexplained function, was Bulwark of Constancy, standing silent and motionless as a devotional statue. The only indication that it was alive was a slight swiveling of its eyestalks toward Taranarak.

But not all was the same. Taranarak realized that the great window that dominated the room had been set to full opaque, to the same lifeless grey as the shutters on her house. They were voluntarily blocking out the same view they did not wish her to see. She could understand why they would wish to hide the view and be hidden from it. For what they would have seen was a city wracked by repeated waves of upheaval—upheaval they had been unable to prevent, control, or end.

But the three Bureaucrats before her seemed, if anything, busy and content—alert, rested, even happy. They had found their new routine, their way to make disaster a normal part of the everyday world, a way to pretend that everything was the way it had always been and always would be. Change was wrong, and bad. Pretend hard enough that nothing had changed, and all will be well. Pretend that this is how it has always been, that we have always done things this way, and there will be no need to fear. Pretend the world is ordered and rational, that all is as it should be, and none need admit they have gone insane.

Taranarak stared at the three Order Bureaucrats, Yalananav, Fallogon, and Tigmin, and felt certain she saw madness in all their faces.

"Greetings, Learned Searcher," said Tigmin.

Interesting, thought Taranarak. *It used to be Yalananav who spoke first, who served as first*

*among equals for this triumvirate, Tigmin who fol-
lowed him, and Fallogon who sat in silence. But
now perhaps the weakest of them holds sway.*

"Greetings to you, Bureaucrat Tigmin, and to
your associates," she replied. It was a perfectly respectful way to address them, at least in principle.
But the slightly fretful looks on the faces of
Yalananav and Fallogon told her, every bit as
much as Tigmin's pleased expression, that she had
scored a point. "Why am I summoned to your
presence today? I have no further progress to report at this time."

"Nor did we expect you to have made progress," said Tigmin, a new and wry edge to his
voice. "And while we thank you for your report,
we did not invite you here for the purpose of delivering it. There has been a—development."

"A development of what kind?"

Tigmin looked unhappy, and shifted his posture.
"One of an unexpected nature. One that will require you to—shall we say, *assist* us—in a different
manner. It will require you to indulge in a form of
deception for the common good."

"What—what sort of deception?"

"Quite simple. We will pretend to set you free,
and you will pretend to be free, for the duration."

"Excuse me, but for the duration of what?"

"Of a visit we are expecting." Yalananav pre-
tended to consult a document in front of him.
"There is a small and primitive spacecraft—hardly
large enough to be dignified by the term

'starship'—currently inbound for Metran from its jump arrival point. It's from that Younger Race species—humans, I believe they are called—with which Hallaben and Bulwark of Constancy had some dealings."

Taranarak felt the fists of her strongwork hands clench up, and her rearward eyes snapped open of their own accord. She fought for a moment until she had her danger reflex under control, and then spoke in as calm a voice as she could. "Humans have come to Metran many times," she said. "It is not the most common of events, but nor is it wildly rare."

"Oh, yes, quite, quite," Yalananav said. "But the interesting thing here is that a signal from the ship identifies it as from the, ah—'Bureau of Special Investigations' that provided the courier during the incident sometime back."

"Yes, yes, I remember," Taranarak said. All their careful and indirect inquiries to the humans had led to the same conclusion: The courier was long overdue and must be presumed lost. Whatever documents he was carrying must be considered lost as well. What had changed to bring the BSI here? But Yalananav seemed to be expecting a further reply. "I grant the contact from that organization is of interest," she said, "but it does not follow that their arrival concerns us in any way. They are likely here on an entirely different matter."

"Ah. That is where you are incorrect," said Yalananav. "Perhaps dangerously so. I hope for your sake that it was not a deliberate error. But the plain fact of the matter is that these humans have specifically asked for you. Or rather, for Hallaben, your predecessor."

Yalananav looked up at Taranarak with a baleful expression. "He's dead, of course, so the duty is yours. See that you don't end up the way he did."

FIFTEEN
UP IS DOWN

Whoever had done the general intelligence report on Metran hadn't wasted any time trying to learn the local names for buildings, structures, and so on. That was, perhaps, understandable, given the difficulties that human tongues had with the Metrannan language, but it did take the poetry out of things. It seemed especially true of the Grand Elevator. The terms for its various components were accurate enough, but not quite in keeping with the heroic scale of a Space Elevator. It was as if the *Mona Lisa* had been labeled "Portrait of Unknown Female Subject" or the Coliseum in Rome were called "Ruin of Obsolete Mass-Entertainment Structure."

But, as Hannah pointed out to Jamie, gen-intell reports weren't supposed to be poetry. They were supposed to tell you what you needed to stay alive.

The *Bartholomew Sholto* cut her engines and came to a dead stop relative to what the intell reports called the Free Orbit Level Station of the Grand Elevator, five kilometers ahead of it in orbit. Hannah sat in the pilot's seat, Jamie standing behind her left shoulder. Even at five kilometers' distance, the massive structure that was Free Orbit Level Station took up nearly the entire field of view—and it was merely *part* of the Grand Elevator.

Free Orbit Level Station resembled a giant rimless plate, roughly three kilometers in diameter, with the concave side facing the planet's surface. Gravity generators provided normal gravity over as much of the inner surface as was convenient at any given moment. At the center of the Main Field was Free Orbit Level Station Nexus itself, in effect a small domed city, with the cable clusters running through it.

The orbit-side end of the Elevator was parked over the equator of Metran, in an exact stationary orbit. The shaft of the Elevator dove straight down to the far-distant surface of the planet, a massive pillar of impossible length and impossible strength, seemingly supporting the weight of the Free Orbit Station Level, and, thousands of kilometers farther out, Counterweight Level Station as well.

That was illusion, of course. The connection to the ground was not a tower or any kind of rigid structure. It was a tether, a cluster of cables, and the Free Orbit Station Level was in fact in orbit, with no more need to be supported than the Moon needed to be held on a string to keep it in place around the Earth. The cable cluster merely provided a physical connection with the ground, a path along which the Grand Elevator's cars could travel back and forth to the surface of the planet.

The cable cluster leading to Counterweight Station served a similar purpose to the cable to groundside. Counterweight Level Station mainly consisted of a small asteroid tethered to the Grand Elevator in order to balance the weight of the groundside cable, thus lifting the center of gravity of the Elevator as a whole up to Free Orbit Level's altitude.

Far below, at the equator of Metran and invisibly far away, stood Groundside Station, atop an artificial mountain built for the specific purpose of supporting the Station high enough to get clear of the thickest part of the sensible atmosphere.

The huge structure moved passengers and cargo back and forth between space and the planet's surface with the greatest possible efficiency. An Elevator car would leave the planet's surface, riding its cable, moving through the lower and upper atmosphere at relatively low velocities of no more than a few hundred kilometers an hour, and then accelerate to a speed of several thousand kilometers an hour once it reached space. It would race up the tens of thousands of kilometers to Free Orbit Station, riding on super-high-efficiency electric motors, with no need for pilots or navigation or orbital computation or course corrections or fuel tanks. The cars could even recover a large fraction of the energy used to lift them by regenerative braking on the return trip.

Each part of the Grand Elevator was massive in size and hugely impressive. Taken as a whole, it was daunting, gigantic, overwhelming.

"Still want to talk about how we've almost caught up with them?" Hannah asked Jamie quietly.

"No," said Jamie, and left it at that.

"They're *starting* to think about an Elevator for Earth," Hannah went on. "It's probably been tried about a dozen times, but it never comes to anything. But this—this is ten times, a *hundred* times, more ambitious than what they have in mind for Earth. And this is for what is really a pretty minor world. The Metrannan population on-planet is only about twelve million or so, and essentially all of that is in one city. This structure is there for the benefit of something like the current population of Los Angeles plus London. There are Vixa worlds that have *multiple* Elevators, five or six of them strung around the equator, and all the orbit-side levels connected by a ring structure that goes clear around the planet."

"Okay," said Jamie. "If you wanted to make sure I was even more intimidated, you've done your job."

"Good," said Hannah. "We don't have the least reason in the universe to feel sure of ourselves."

"This I understand," said Jamie. As he looked out at the Grand Elevator, it seemed impossible that their clever little cover story about looking for a missing agent could ever stand up against the beings who built *that*.

A green light illuminated on the control board, and a cheerful beep tone went off. A message on the display screen confirmed that the Grand Elevator's Traffic Control Center had managed to lock in on their ship's nav systems, primitive though it might be compared to local designs. "The *Sholto* has received and accepted a final approach flight plan and will fly it on automatic," Hannah announced, reading the display. "Suits me. I wouldn't want to try flying through artificial grav bubbles and risk dinging their nice shiny giant dinner platter." She keyed in the approval code, and the *Sholto* immediately came about to a new attitude and began moving smartly toward their designated landing spot.

They flew over the edge of the inner side of the Main Landing Field about twenty meters up, the *Sholto*'s landing gear extending and locking into place as they approached. The *Sholto* pointed her nose directly at the planet and her base at the field, sliding sideways over the featureless white expanse. They passed by three or four different ships as they went in, all of them far larger, far sleeker-looking, and far more beautiful than the stubby little *Sholto*. It was impossible not to feel like the ugly duckling in among the graceful swans, the grubby little child in rumpled pajamas allowed to come downstairs for a minute to gawp at the elegance and refinement of a fancy grown-up dinner party.

We don't belong here, Jamie told himself. *We're*

not ready. He couldn't help but think of Special Agent Trevor Wilcox III. He must have flown almost the identical approach, alone in the *Irene Adler*, having no idea what he was being asked to carry or why, facing the awesome sight below without the benefit of the steadying influence of someone like Hannah, who had seen it all, done it all—and survived it all.

But Trevor got through it. He didn't let himself get intimidated. Or if he did, he didn't let that paralyze him or keep him from doing his job. Whatever it was that killed him was caused by the people who could build all this. But he kept fighting to finish his job, even after he knew he was dying. He did better than go down fighting. He went down thinking. We can't—I can't—let him down. And there was one other thing he could think of to help stiffen his spine. In the end, Trevor had beaten them. Unless Hannah and he were misreading all the clues so far, Trevor had stopped the people who had killed him from getting what they wanted.

The *Sholto* fired her attitude thrusters to halt their forward motion. They were over their assigned landing spot. The overhead thrusters fired once, very gently, to propel them downward onto the field.

Suddenly Jamie's stomach did an all-too-familiar backflip. "Hey!" he cried out. "Our gravity field just cut out! We're in zero gee!"

"Not for long," Hannah said. "Standard safety

procedure. Unpleasant things can happen when one artificial gee field is inside another. Hang on. Our landing gear is just about one meter off the field now, so . . ."

They landed with a sudden, unceremonious bump.

"And we're down," said Hannah, checking her displays rather than the view out the window. Suddenly the whole ship shuddered for a moment, and there was a sound like the wind moaning past the hull.

"What was *that*?" Jamie asked. "We didn't lose pressure or something, did we?"

"Mmphmm. No. Just the opposite, in fact."

"*What?*"

"As of ten seconds ago, we have breathable air out there. Very close to a pressure match and gas composition with the surface of Metran. Cute. Very, very cute."

"They can't possibly be pressurizing this whole structure!" Jamie protested.

"Probably not," Hannah agreed. "But I wouldn't put it completely past them. When they decide to, the Elder Races can do practically anything. The show-offs. But my guess is that they use some sort of confinement field to create bubbles of pressurization where they need them. They just formed one around our landing point. Ain't that a neat trick?"

"Yeah. Really neat."

"Glad you enjoyed it. Don't feel even more intimidated or anything. Okay. I'm going to need about five or ten minutes to power us down and safe the ship's systems. Once we have that out of the way, we can work the really important problems. The big decisions."

"Okay, fine. I'll play the straight man. What big decisions?"

"What are we going to wear?"

* * *

It was a joke, of course. Except that it wasn't. Metrannans took dress very seriously. There were documented cases of humans getting themselves killed as a result of committing the deadly insult of meeting with a Metrannan in inappropriate garb. Supposedly, it was just as dangerous to show up dressed to the nines for the local equivalent of a picnic as it was to show up in rumpled work clothes to a formal reception.

The Metrannans imposed a more stringent rule on themselves when visiting human worlds, or at least indulged their love of dressing up, and often wore adapted versions of human-style outfits, with results that were often disconcerting or hilarious. Humans who dealt with Metrannans had to know how to keep poker-faced.

Supposedly, the human section of the Metrannan clothing database was larger—and more filled with errors—than that of any other species. To Jamie, that merely suggested that humans were the species second-most obsessed with clothing.

Fortunately, the dreadful mix-ups and errors of the early days had been resolved, and there was no danger of the database dictating that Jamie show up to a state dinner in a muu-muu and carrying a surfboard—an unfortunate occurrence from about sixty years back that would have been dismissed as urban legend if not for the photographs.

The dress requirements as stated for "generalized official business interaction activity" were far more sensible, and had them both in very conservative dark business suits. Jamie's charcoal-grey suit and blue shirt were of a cut and style and color that was not much changed since the later days of the nineteenth century, and Hannah's black jacket and knee-length skirt over a white blouse were almost as ancient a uniform.

Jamie didn't care for his fire-engine-red tie, and Hannah made it clear she had never been a fan of gathered lace at the collar, but both of them felt they had gotten off easy. Even if nearly all the bugs had been squeezed out of the Metrannan dress database, no BSI agent ever checked the database without worrying that it would require a tiara and roller skates.

"You look pretty good," Hannah told Jamie, straightening his tie. "Maybe it's time you thought about wearing something besides flight coveralls and flak jackets on missions."

"I'm wearing a flak jacket right now, underneath this getup," Jamie said, pulling his jacket closed. "It itches."

"Deal with it," Hannah said. "Come on. Let's get going."

They collected their duffel bags. Each of them also had a huge rolling suitcase—more like an old stone-age steamer trunk—full of clothes suitable for all occasions. They tried to wedge themselves and their luggage into the *Sholto*'s lower-deck air lock, but the big cases simply wouldn't fit with two people. They would have to do it in two passes—both of them going out together with the duffels, then Hannah waiting outside while Jamie went back for the larger cases. The pressure difference with the outside air was relatively small, and the lock cycled fast. The outer door swung open, and they looked out on a broad, strange, and oddly featureless milk-white plain.

Directly ahead of them was Free Orbit Level Station Nexus, the focal point of activity for Free Orbit Level Station, and, for that matter, the entire Grand Elevator. The wide silvery bulk of the cable cluster sprouted up out of the top of the Nexus, drawing the eye irresistibly upward into the black, star-spangled sky, up and up and up until the cable itself narrowed and vanished in the distance, and still up again—to the sight of Metran, directly and exactly overhead. The planet was in half phase, the terminator knife-sharp through the exact centerline of the world, sunset at the Groundside Station.

That, of course, put the local sun directly on the western horizon of the Main Landing Field as well, a reddish ball exactly bisected by the horizon. It should have been murderously, blindingly bright, but there was plainly some sort of dimming field in use that reduced the intensity of the light.

But if the sun was made a weakened shadow of itself, the planet directly overhead was a gaudy thing of blue-white-green beauty, seas and clouds and lands gleaming in the darkness, easily thirty times the size of the moon as seen from Earth.

As they looked upward, a lozenge-shaped elevator car, at first a barely visible glint of motion almost lost in the terminator, swelled up into visibility as it made its final approach to Free Orbit Station, riding its strand of cable straight through the roof of Station Nexus, even as another car launched itself upward toward the planet down below. *Up toward the planet down below,* Jamie thought in wry astonishment. The description was entirely accurate, but peculiar even so.

But the most startling, even daunting, part of the scene before them was the blackness of space all around. Viewports and portholes and windows in human-built spacecraft and spaceside facilities were *small,* for good reasons. They were expensive to build, and far more fragile in use than hull material. But there was also a psychological reason. Space-traveling humans were used to being sealed away from the vast and terrifying emptiness of it all.

But on the Main Landing Field of Free Orbit Station, things were quite the opposite. They were out in the open, exposed, the *Sholto* pinned to the surface of a vast and empty field, staring up—or was it down—at a terrestrial planet so big and bright it looked as if it was about to fall on them—unless they were about to fall on it.

"Okay," Jamie said. "Now it's official. I'm intimidated."

"And it's officially time to keep anyone from noticing," said Hannah. "Company's coming."

Three vehicles were headed toward them from Nexus. One was a robotic ship-servicer, of a type in common use in the spaceports of many worlds—including Center. It had, no doubt, already had a series of discussions with the *Sholto*, asking the ship what she needed in terms of power and supplies, negotiating amount and means of payment, and arranging the technical details, down to what sort of plugs and sockets and nozzles would be required to top up the ship's systems.

The second vehicle was basically a ramp on wheels. It drove straight up to the *Sholto*'s air lock, automatically adjusting itself to bring its top end level with the bottom of the air lock hatch, thus providing an easy way to descend from the ship.

"Thank the stars for that," said Hannah as the ramp eased itself into position. "I thought we were going to have to deploy the hull ladder. I wasn't looking forward to climbing down in this skirt and heels in gravity that's twenty percent above normal."

"And I wasn't looking forward to getting the luggage down the ladder."

There were two cubical cartons on the lower end of the ramp. As soon as the ramp had stopped, its seemingly solid upper surface began moving upward, in the manner of a conveyor belt.

"Whoah!" Jamie said. "I was about to start walking down that thing. Any idea what's in the cartons?"

"Use your startling skill as a detective," said Hannah drily. "Or you could just try reading the labels on the top of the boxes. Restocking supplies for the ship."

Sure enough, printed there in Greater Trade Writing and, unexpectedly enough, in somewhat stilted English as well, was a packing list of human-digestible foods and other consumables, along with a list of repair supplies. A flashing panel on the upper left corner of the label was requesting verbal approval and authentication.

Feeling odd about speaking to a packing crate, Jamie cleared his throat and read the indicated words in Lesser Trade Speech. "I am James Mendez of the human United Government Vessel BSI-3369 *Bartholomew Sholto*. I am authorized to approve and accept these supplies. I hereby approve and accept delivery of the supplies listed on this container, and authorize payment for them out of human United Government accounts." The label stopped blinking and turned a cheerful shade of orange. He then had to go through the whole speech again with the other box. Hannah waited outside while Jamie wrestled the boxes into the *Sholto* and the heavy luggage back out. Once he was done, Hannah went through the slightly involved process of closing, sealing, and locking the outer air lock hatch—and arming the self-destruct system.

It was a small item, but it was the almost instant delivery of human-digestible foods that, as much or perhaps even more than anything, made Jamie feel as if he had been put in his place.

If a Metrannan ship had arrived at Earth with only two days' notice, expecting a stay of short but uncertain duration, it would have been considered a miracle of organization to provide reprovisioning supplies in less than a week. Specialists would have been rousted out of bed in the middle of the night. Chemists would have been called in to test and retest everything for fear of poisoning the visitors. It would have required a full-court press in order to get the order delivered before the ship was scheduled to depart—and if the job were done successfully, everyone would breathe a sigh of relief and congratulate each other for not humiliating the human race.

Here, even though humans rarely visited—it was not unlikely Trevor Wilcox had been the last human here—human-suitable food was delivered by robots before the *Sholto*'s thrusters had time to cool.

"Sealed and armed," Hannah said. "If you happen to be the one who opens up when we get back, try not to get the combinations wrong—or else the *Sholto* might leave a ding in their nice shiny landing field when she blows up." That wasn't exactly true. It was considered bad manners to rig a spacecraft to explode violently at someone else's spaceport. Hannah had rigged the groundside destruct system. It would simply melt or burn most of the ship's interior if anyone set it off, just enough destruction to render the whole vehicle inoperative.

"I'll bear that in mind. Let's get moving."

The two of them moved carefully down the ramp, not quite sure if it was about to turn its rigid surface back into a conveyor belt, and also not quite adapted to the slightly higher local gravity. It was easy to overbalance a trifle while rolling their heavy trunks.

The third vehicle that had pulled up to the *Sholto* was an open-frame personnel transporter—or at least that's what Jamie assumed it to be. It was unmarked, unlabeled, and didn't boast any sort of robotic voice telling them what to do. It was nothing but an open platform on wheels, with a ramp to allow entrance and exit on one side. Vertical supports held up guardrails at about human knee, waist, and shoulder height. The railing on the side with the ramp on it swung open to allow them in. They stepped aboard and got their luggage into the transporter. The gate swung shut and latched itself, then the ramp withdrew into the base of the vehicle. The transporter started moving, leaving Jamie and Hannah to hang on to the bars of their cage.

"What's this feel more like to you?" Hannah asked. "Riding in one of the rolling cages from an animal show, or riding the tumbrel to the guillotine?"

"You read too many old books," Jamie said. "Until you asked, I was just thinking it was like riding in a golf cart. Thanks for the more comfortable imagery."

The vehicle did have one notably high-tech feature. It seemed to carry its own bubble of atmosphere along with it, and there was a distinct shift in pressure as it separated from the air bubble around the *Sholto*. As they moved, Jamie could see a sort of faint shimmering effect in the air around and above them, formed into a hemisphere centered on the vehicle with a radius of about five meters. They were, in effect, pulling the air along behind them, causing it to blow at them in all sorts of turbulence patterns that made it seem as if the wind was hitting them from every direction at once.

They rolled along the strange and featureless artificial landscape toward the Nexus, both of them feeling their eyes drawn irresistibly toward the cable cluster and the mighty planet, directly overhead. It felt like the eye of God himself was staring unblinkingly at them.

Jamie couldn't help thinking He couldn't be overly impressed with the two beings He was glaring down at.

SIXTEEN

LATER THAN SOONER

The Nexus grew closer. To Hannah's eye, at least, it seemed a small and even anticlimactic center to a place of such grandiose scale, not far different from a hundred domed settlements scattered about in human-settled space. *Except, of course, for the cable cluster stabbing down through the top of the dome, and the Elevator cars hurtling back and forth every few minutes,* she told herself. *That's a little different.*

Their vehicle slowed as it approached an opening in the high cylindrical wall that supported the base of the dome. The pressure field around their vehicle seemed to merge with a similar shimmering field that stretched across the opening in the wall. There was a slight popping noise, and a rush and a whir as the air in their bubble merged with the air inside the Nexus.

Their odd little open-frame vehicle rolled slowly toward an area where a half dozen similar vehicles were lined up. Their vehicle drove up to the end of the queue, brought itself to a full stop, and shut itself down. The gate in the back of the vehicle opened and the ramp reextruded itself. It was quite clearly the end of the line.

They stepped off the transporter, hauled their luggage out, and looked around, feeling rather uncertain. They had been told they would be met at the Nexus, but were given virtually no other information. Other than staying where they were until someone collected them, there was little they could do except watch the passing scene.

The facility bore a strong family resemblance to most other public transportation transfer centers— wide-open floor plan and broad walkways, allowing broad and rapid flows of foot traffic, as might be found in any spaceport or urban rail center. There were access gates to and from the Elevator cars, and to the Main Landing Field beyond. There were checkpoints and waiting areas and vending areas. A steady stream of purposeful passersby moved about, heading to and fro. Hannah was mentally settling in for the waiting part of the eternal travel ritual of "hurry up and wait" when Jamie spoke up.

"Something's wrong," he announced in a quiet voice. He didn't look at her as he spoke, but instead continued watching the interior of the Nexus, his face expressionless.

Hannah was instantly alert. She had to stop her hand from twitching reflexively toward her hidden sidearm. "What? What do you mean? Something bad?"

"There's something wrong with *them*, with this place. This isn't the way it's supposed to be."

"How can you tell that? We've only been here thirty seconds!"

"Even so," said Jamie. "There's something *wrong*."

Hannah had enough respect for Jamie's powers of observation and his tactical instincts to take him seriously. Prompted by his reaction, she began to see it for herself. There were two nearby sections of newly repaired wall panel—but the repairs looked to have been done hurriedly and not particularly well. It looked as if there were residual scorch marks on the floor near one of them. A fire? An explosion?

There were more security guards around than she would have expected, more heavily armed and armored than they should have been. Nor did the guards look entirely comfortable with their bulky equipment. And there was more than one style of uniform in evidence—a major red flag for the clothes-conscious Metrannans. They wouldn't bring in guards with clashing outfits unless it was absolutely necessary.

And, if she was reading Metrannan expressions and body language properly, more than a few of the passersby were giving the two humans suspicious, even angry looks. Maybe humans were rare in these parts, but not aliens. Metrannans should take them in stride.

"I see the wall and floor damage that's been

fixed badly and the heavily armed amateurs pretending to be security pros and the paranoid civilians," she said. "What else have you got?"

"If I'm reading the info on the status and schedule boards right, it looks like they've been scrambling to get caught up after some sort of major stoppage or problem. The passersby look twitchy, and they're staring a bit too hard at us. Shouldn't they be used to aliens at their main spaceport? And we're the *only* off-planet sentients I've seen so far. Shouldn't there *be* aliens at their main spaceport? Why aren't there? Why is everyone else staying away? The cars coming up from the surface are packed and the lines to go down are very short. Plus I just spotted twelve, count 'em *twelve*, Xenoatrics boarding a transporter to take them out to the landing field—and that's where you go if you're *leaving* the planet."

"And unless our briefing books are all way off, Xenoatrics do *not* like to travel," Hannah said. "You're right. Something's wrong." She thought for a moment. "This have anything to do with that War-Starter designation? Has the war started, or almost started?"

"No idea, but let's keep on our toes. This could be tricky."

"That's one way to put it. You just trying to be careful that no one accuses you of overstating the case?"

"I'm just plain trying to be careful," Jamie said, keeping his eyes on the crowd. "We don't *know* that whatever happened has anything to do with the mystery message or our mission—but that'd be the way I'd bet."

"What the hell could be in that message that could set all this off?"

"If we're lucky, we'll get the chance to ask someone who could actually answer that question. For now, let's stay sharp."

"And let's keep our reflexes under control," said Hannah. "No itchy trigger fingers."

"You know my deal. I let them shoot first—but then I shoot last."

Hannah didn't answer that. The words sounded like hollow tough-guy rhetoric, out of character for Jamie. The problem was that there was too much truth in the trite phrase, but not in the way some people might think. Jamie was superb and sudden death with any sort of weapon. The trouble was there was also an odd streak of pacifism in his nature at odds with his hunter's instinct. If the situation required it in the line of duty and/or in self-defense, he would shoot to kill—and then likely suffer sleepless nights or guilt-wracked nightmares for weeks afterward.

Hannah could easily imagine a circumstance where Jamie would allow an assailant the first shot, just to keep his conscience clear. For the moment, however, it didn't matter. Whatever they were walking into, it was big, something that affected the whole planet. They weren't going to get out of it with guns blazing. All they could do for the moment was stand and wait. It was enough to make even Hannah long for some action.

* * *

They were stuck there, waiting, for about twenty minutes. Both of them saw enough to confirm all their worries. There was an unmistakable air of fretfulness and fear in the Nexus Center, strong enough to be noticeable even across the species barrier.

Jamie noticed one other peculiarity. There seemed to be a clear hostility toward the Xenoatrics, the beings the Metrannans called the Unseen Race. From all that he had read and learned, the Metrannans' normal attitude toward the Xenoatrics was one of enormous respect, verging on the worshipful. It took no effort at all to catch the Metrannans scowling at Xenoatrics—or, for that matter, at the two well-dressed human loiterers. If the Xenoatrics weren't entirely welcome, then humans certainly weren't welcome at all.

The Xenoatrics—or more accurately, the artificial carapaces that supposedly contained the Xenoatrics—Jamie could not read at all. There no doubt were ways to interpret the mood of one of the Unseen by the twitching of the multiple arms and mandibles or the exact angle of tilt of the metallic head that was halfway between an ant and lobster, or the way the two long ostrichlike legs were held, but Jamie didn't know them.

But he did know that their escort hadn't shown

up. "Look," he said, glancing toward Hannah, "we can't stand around here forever."

"No," said Hannah, who very clearly and deliberately did not return his gaze. "But we can stand here for a good long time. Hours at least."

"We're already starting to look suspicious. I'm pretty sure I spotted some citizen reporting us to a guard."

She nodded absently but continued to scan the crowd, her face expressionless. "Did the guard come over? Did he arrest us? Are we in fact doing anything suspicious or illegal?"

"No."

"And what would you do if the guard *did* come over?"

"Um, probably show him my credentials and tell him that we had been instructed to stay where we were and await our local contact."

"My guess is that would satisfy him, at least for a while. And it has the advantage of being completely accurate."

"Well, yes."

"Now look at the other side of it. Think a move or two ahead. When our local contact, this Learned Searcher Taranarak, *does* show up, given what you know of Metrannan culture and psychology, what sort of state is she likely to be in?"

Suddenly the light went on. "Ah," said Jamie. "Flustered. Apologetic. Worried about losing face."

"And with any luck, that will make her more

eager to be helpful, to make amends. I'd be more than willing to trade tired feet and an hour or two of boredom in exchange for a well-informed local who feels under some sort of obligation to us."

"Oh. Okay. I guess that makes sense."

"Think of it as being on a stakeout, watching for a high-value suspect."

"I never much liked stakeout duty either."

"Patience is a job skill, Jamie. Patience is a job skill." She spotted something, turned her head to one side, and then spoke again. "And I think it's about to be rewarded. Five gets you eight that's our contact."

"No bet," said Jamie as he spotted the worried-looking female Metrannan who was plainly rushing toward them.

"Smart man," she said. "Now, we're going to be extra, extra, extra polite and incredibly gracious because we're just such nice people—and because with a little luck it'll pay off big-time later."

*   *   *

Taranarak spotted two humans, one male and one female—as best she was able to judge such matters—and huffed a sigh of relief as she trotted toward them as fast as she could in her long, flowing, muted brown robes of semi-hemi-formal greeting and welcome.

She opened her rearward eyes, just for a moment, and scanned the area behind her. No sign of being followed or observed, but it was a safe assumption—indeed, very close to a certainty—that she was being tracked in some manner.

She came within about a hundred short paces of the aliens and worked to compose herself. She slowed her pace to a dignified walk and forced a calm expression to her face. Things were happening too quickly. Her release from house arrest— her conditional release—and her reinstatement at the Geriatrics Institute had only just happened the day before. And now, here she was, greeting the human investigators, playing her part in the effort to pretend that everything was fine, all was in order.

She knew she was merely a game piece, being moved around as part of some strategy or other of Tigmin's. But she had no idea what the game was. Did they want the treatment recovered—or want it lost, destroyed, perhaps forever? Did they even know for sure themselves? Did they want the humans to help them find it—or would they instead do whatever it took to ensure it was never found again?

She herself did not know what choice to make. Was it better for Metrannan society as a whole to leave things as they were—or, more accurately, strive to put them back the way they had been before the riots had started? Or would it be wiser to accept inevitable change?

Too much, Taranarak told herself. Too much to worry about and not enough time to think it all through. *You can decide later.* With a start, she realized she was no better than the Bureaucrats. It was, no doubt, part of the fear of change bred into all of them. Put it off, push it away, choose later. Maybe the need to choose would go away. But some things could not be put off. There were the humans, not thirty short paces in front of her.

Learned Searcher Taranarak came to a smooth halt before the two humans and gestured, all four hands extended, palms up, before them. She spoke in Lesser Trade Speech. "You are Special Agents Hannah of geneline Wolfson and James of geneline Mendez. I am Taranarak of geneline Lucyrn. I offer you welcome to this world." Not the most poetic sort of greeting, but that was to be expected. Lesser Trade Speech was essentially the spoken form of Great Trade Writing, which had been invented for the primary purpose of setting down clear and unambiguous business contracts. It wasn't well suited to flowery phrasings.

The two humans imitated her gesture as best they could with only two hands each, then offered her a slight and careful bow.

"I am Wolfson," said the slightly smaller of the two, the one Taranarak judged to be female. Odd that they preferred their geneline name for formal individual identification. How many geneline names would be required to prevent that being confusing?

"I am Mendez," said the other.

Yes, that one must be the male. He was more similar to Wilcox than the other one, his voice was lower, and his upper body shape was less rounded. Taranarak lowered her hands, indicating that the formal greeting was completed. "Please," she said, "come this way." She gestured for them to follow her. As they started walking, she noted with surprise that they both had to carry some of their luggage and pull the rest on its own built-in wheels, rather than having the bags follow their owners under their own power. Should she have brought some sort of luggage carrier? Well, too late now, and that was far from the worst of her errors. "There is much for us to say," she said, "but the concourse is loud and far from secluded. Let us move toward a waiting area, which will be more quiet and private."

The two humans looked toward each other, and she had no need of her rush training in reading human expressions and gestures to know they were interested, perhaps even intrigued. "Agreed," said Wolfson.

* * *

A brief time later, they were in the number four Ranking Persons waiting area for the downward Elevator service. It seemed unlikely to her that even the Order Bureaucracy would have dared attach listening devices there—but it was, nonetheless, possible. She would have to take the risk—but carefully. She saw to it that her guests were comfortably seated in what she hoped was a fair simulation of human-style chairs, and began.

"Let me begin by apologizing for my tardiness," she said in Lesser Trade. "There have been a number of dislocations and schedule changes of late, and my Elevator car was significantly delayed. The problem was beyond my control."

"It is of no consequence," said the female agent, Wolfson, replying in the same language. "We had noticed various indications of recent difficulties here on the Free Orbit Level, and we fully accept that you were not at fault."

Taranarak cringed internally at the use of the word "fault." Wolfson was either quite skilled in her use of Lesser Trade Speech or being unwittingly brutal. Merely to use the word was to imply that there *was* in fact fault to be found, that it was not mere chance or ill fortune or uncontrollable events that had produced the problems, but incompetence or worse. Wolfson was agreeing that she, Taranarak, was not to blame—but was also telling her that Metrannans as a group, as a whole, were in some way inept.

Given the evidence they had apparently already seen, and given what they would inevitably witness on the surface, there was no point in pretending there wasn't something seriously wrong. "I apologize on behalf of those responsible for my tardiness, and for those who have caused the difficulties that you have noted. I assure you that every effort is being made to resolve the problems."

"To make assurances that an effort will be made is not an assurance that the problems will be solved," said Agent Wolfson. The words were harsh, but there was a note of sympathy in her voice. "That you cannot make such assurances suggests that much indeed is amiss. I sympathize with your circumstances, being forced to accept responsibilities for items you do not control, while those who caused the flaws do not lose face."

"I thank you for that," said Taranarak.

"A question," Mendez said. "Our initial communication requested that we speak with one named Hallaben. We have received no communication in return from him, and we meet with you instead of him. Have we committed some slight, or error, that he refuses to speak with us?"

Taranarak lowered her head for a moment. "Hallaben is dead," she said. "I was his assistant, and his friend, and am now his successor."

"We regret his death," said Mendez. "Agent Wolfson and I know full well the sorrow of losing a close colleague."

"I thank you for those words as well," Taranarak replied. "They are soothing to me." She checked a schedule board and saw she had even less time than she had hoped. "But there is much to say, and it may be this is the last chance for the three of us to speak freely. Much is observed, and listened to, these days."

The humans once again traded glances with each other. "'These days'?" echoed Mendez. "We were under the impression that even the other

Elder Races saw your world as an admirably stable society that suffered few alterations."

"I fear that our reputation does not reflect current circumstances," she said. " 'These days' are truly different—unpleasantly so—from days as they were."

"But why?" asked Agent Wolfson.

And so we come to the center, the focus. Taranarak needed desperately to know what the humans did and did not know. Were they—and therefore, presumably, their colleagues and superiors—aware of what the encrypted message contained? This was the moment where she might learn. She watched eagerly for the reaction to her reply. "I will tell you things you will quickly learn in any event from studying our news reports, or by speaking with any person you might meet. The story is known to all. A rumor became current. It was claimed that a major discovery, one that would vastly extend Metrannan life spans, had been made—then suppressed. It was suggested that certain organs of power, perhaps including the Order Bureaucracy, were withholding this treatment."

The human agents did *not* exchange glances with each other, or indeed reveal any particular reaction at all that she could observe. Instead they retained their expressions of puzzled interest. She knew precisely how much of an amateur she was, how many subtleties she might be missing. A twitch, a tremor, a shift in breathing patterns, might reveal all—but if so, she had missed the clue.

But even so, she would be willing to stake all— indeed she was *going* to stake all—that they did not know what was in the message Wilcox had carried. Except, of course, assuming they were even moderately intelligent creatures, and they took more than a few moments to think about it, she had just as good as *told* them what was in the message.

She was about to speak further, to warn them about what they were about to face, when a chime sounded and the status board in the waiting area flashed an alert.

"Ah," she said. "Your transportation—and accommodation—have arrived. I wish you a pleasant voyage to the surface. I will rejoin you there. I shall walk with you to the departure section."

The two humans stood. "I don't understand," Mendez said. "You traveled all this way to welcome us. Will you not accompany us to the surface so that we may speak more on the way?"

"I had hoped to have far more time to meet with you here, but I was delayed. Sadly, it is not in the least advisable for me to travel with you. The Elevator car that is about to arrive has been specially modified for your use during your time here on Metran. You will not merely ride it down to the surface. Its living quarters are a detachable module that will be automatically shunted to the rail link that connects the Elevator to our city. The living module will then be transported to a convenient central location in the city. The interior of the car is appointed for human use—including your lower gravity. That is why I may not travel with you to the surface."

"We are aware that low-gee and zero-gee conditions are unhealthy for Metrannans," said Mendez, "but surely the slight difference between your surface acceleration and ours cannot be enough to cause harm."

"Metrannans can and do adapt to mild shifts in gravity—in time," said Taranarak. "But until such adaptation, the sensation is most unpleasant. I believe it is equivalent to the maladaption to zero gravity some members of your species suffer. I believe it is called 'spacesickness.' Is that the correct term?"

Mendez frowned, and his color suddenly darkened by several shades. For whatever reason, Wolfson's demeanor changed as well. If Taranarak was reading her expression properly, something had suddenly amused her.

"I beg your pardon," said Taranarak. "Have I said something to offend?"

"No, no, not at all," said Wolfson. Mendez's expression suggested that he did not entirely agree. "We certainly would not wish to cause you discomfort. We will see you again in the city."

"Very well," said Taranarak. "Then please come this way."

She led them through the departure formalities

into the boarding area and toward their waiting Elevator car. In a few minutes they were gone, and Taranarak left to find her own car down, feeling vaguely worried and depressed—and a trifle dishonest. She could defend herself, to a certain extent. After all, she had not deliberately misled them—and if she had not warned them sufficiently, it could at least be argued that it was because there had not been enough time. But those thoughts were not enough to set her mind completely at ease.

They would indeed see her again in the city. But she doubted very much that they realized just how much else they would see down there.

SEVENTEEN

SIDEWAYS REALTIME DOWN

Hannah followed Jamie down the access ramp. It moved in a straight line for a while, but then led through a doorway and into a section where what the eye saw and the body felt were two very different things. It *looked* as if they were walking uphill on an extremely steep ramp, but no matter how far Hannah walked forward, down was always directly beneath her feet, with the way ahead always looking as if it was sloping upward. The local gravitational axis was shifting step by step. She looked ahead at one point and saw the top of Jamie's head as he walked along what appeared, from her point of view, to be a section of wall.

It was disconcerting, but not surprising, given the Metrannan susceptibility to changes in gravity. The artificial gravity field aboard the Free Orbit Level Station was oriented with "up" being toward the planet below—in other words, upside down as seen from anyone looking up at the Elevator from the surface of the planet. Obviously, at some point in the process of traveling aboard the Elevator between the ground and Free Orbit

Level, there had to be some method of transition-
ing between one orientation and the other.

As best Hannah could judge, the engineers had
decided to make that transition by having passengers walk along a spiral path designed to rotate the
gravity field gradually to the orientation used
aboard the Elevator car without forcing the walker
to move through any area that was not under full
and normal Metrannan gravity.

They reached the Elevator car itself and stepped
through a hatch and into its dimly lit interior.
Jamie staggered a bit as he went through, and
Hannah stumbled herself, almost crashing into
him. Gravity had shifted from Metrannan standard to Earth standard right at the entrance. It
didn't help matters that the lighting inside the car
amounted to nothing but a dim red glow.

The hatch automatically closed and sealed itself
behind Hannah. A moment or two later the room
suddenly brightened as light burst in through massive overhead windows, dazzling her. Only after
her eyes had adjusted to the sudden shift in light
could she see where they were.

The size and opulence of their elevator "car"
was startling—and so was its physical orientation.
Hannah had expected something like a large and
comfortable standard elevator car, and had been
wondering exactly how anything like that could
serve as their quarters while on the planet.

What they had instead was something like an
elongated hotel room, built lengthwise into a

cylindrical structure about four meters in diameter and twelve meters in length. Hannah took in a general impression of appointments similar to a human-style hotel room—two beds, a table, chairs, a small bathroom—but all that was trivial, minor stuff, compared to the breathtaking and disconcerting view out the *top* side of the cylinder. The endcaps of the cylinder were solid, and so was the floor under their feet—but the entire top half of the cylinder was transparent and provided a startling view.

At first she could not even understand what she was seeing, until she realized that *down* hadn't rotated through the expected one hundred eighty degrees, but instead, somehow, only through ninety. The trip through the access tunnel must have been even more disorienting than she had thought. *Down,* she decided after a moment, was now toward the cable cluster. To look up was to look *outward* from the cables, toward the local sun shining down on them, its fearsome light attenuated in some way that also allowed the full glory of the stars to be seen.

She almost had it worked out. They had entered through a hatch in the rear endcap of the Elevator car. Looking straight ahead was to look at their former "up"—toward the planet itself, though Metran was hidden behind the forward endcap of their Elevator car. Hannah looked behind her, expecting to see the Free Orbit Level Station, and let out a gasp of astonishment.

The Station was there, all right—but it was already many kilometers away and receding into the distance even as she watched. That bloom of light must have been the moment they moved out of the Station itself and into the sunlight. They had already started moving, and moving *fast*. They were still accelerating, diving straight for the planet. She had to give the Metrannan engineers credit for their acceleration compensators. There had not been the slightest tremor, the tiniest vibration, that could hint at any motion at all. The car had to be moving at well over a thousand kilometers an hour already, but its interior felt so solid and motionless that it might as well have been bolted to a granite foundation.

"Maybe it will keep us from going crazy too quickly if we think of this as riding a train with a glass roof headed toward the planet," said Jamie, sounding as dazed as she felt.

"Yeah," Hannah said woodenly. "That does sound a little better than diving straight *down* toward the planet at thousands of kilometers an hour."

"Um, how long does this ride take?" Jamie asked, sitting down heavily at the table.

"I don't know," Hannah said, still staring up at the fast-receding Free Orbit Station. "We never really got the chance to ask the question. Is there some sort of status display or something?"

"What I'd like to find is some sort of control to make the roof of this thing turn opaque."

"I'm with you," said Hannah. "But I bet there isn't one—or a status display either. The Metrannan do things differently than we do, and things that bother us don't bother them so much."

"And vice versa," said Jamie. "They sure go to extremes to avoid experiencing a shift in gravity."

"But they sure don't seem to have much in the way of a fear of open spaces. Go figure." She sat down next to Jamie and managed to position her chair so she had a view of the receding station. "But in the meantime," she said, "we have other fish to fry," deliberately picking an idiom that would make no sense to any Metrannans who might be listening. "You up for pro chat, or do you need a moment?"

"I'm okay. I guess."

Hannah laughed. "That's about where I am. I guess. So—what do you think? It's not even presumed surv now—our tour guide pretty much nailed it down as declared."

"I'll sign off on that," said Jamie with a nod. "Mike is visiting—probably his friend Cam as well."

"How do we treat it? Ignored, Realtime Safe, or AFS?"

"Given the designation that started the ride, I say we gotta go with AFS."

"Bingo. Right answer on the first try. Compact short plus signs?"

"I'll get the toys," said Jamie.

Hannah and Jamie might not have ever been in

a hotel-room-style Space Elevator car hurtling toward a planet at thousands of kilometers an hour before, but in another sense, they had been where they were many times: in a place utterly controlled by their xeno hosts and vulnerable to any number of eavesdropping techniques. They had developed a lot of practice in dealing with the problem—including how they *discussed* the problem of listening in. They managed by a combination of slang, jargon, and speaking elliptically. Fleshed out and made coherent to outsiders, their discussion would have been a bit different.

"*What do you think? It's not even presumed surveillance now—Taranarak pretty clearly signaled it was declared surveillance.*"

"*I agree. They are listening with microphones and probably watching us with cameras as well.*"

"*How do we deal with it? Do we just ignore it and let them listen and not care, or do we take steps that will keep what we say safe in realtime for now, and not worry if they can understand it later, or do we at least try to keep what we say secret forever by using Attempted Fully Secure procedures?*"

"*This case started with a War-Starter designation. I think we should just use AFS protocols.*"

"*I agree. I suggest we use a combination of written shorthand using BSI's Compact coding and modified American Sign Language gestural language.*"

"*Agreed. I will get the equipment we need.*"

The conversation itself was an attempt at real-time security. Probably whatever Metrannans were listening could manage to understand what was being said in time, if they played it back often enough, and worked with fluent English speakers and made the effort to track down the BSI jargon. But by then it wouldn't matter.

Attempted Fully Secure protocols were an effort to take secrecy up a notch to a point where there was at least a hope that the listeners could *never* understand—but it was called *Attempted* Fully Secure to remind agents that they could never be entirely *sure* the opposition wasn't able to listen and understand later on—or, worse still, immediately.

Hannah watched as Jamie reached for his bag and pulled out the tools of covert conversation: a stack of investigator's notebooks and a pocket destruct oven.

Writing in a pen-and-paper notebook was in and of itself a concealment method in a universe full of Elder Races that could detect virtually any manner of electronic signal. Any process that involved typing to or writing on or tapping on the screen of an electronic device produced some sort of signal that could potentially be recorded and played back to reproduce whatever was written. Not so with scribbling in a notebook. Of course, a camera could be used to read whatever was written on the page, but it was simple enough for agents to use their arms, hands, and bodies to block any outside view of the notebook, and to close the cover whenever the page wasn't being written to or read from.

Using shorthand was another part of the concealment process—and shorthand also made the writing faster. Even if the opposition took the trouble to learn to read printed English, and even handwritten English, getting from there to the hooks and pockmarks and slang of BSI shorthand would still be a major challenge. Jamie maintained that Hannah's handwriting was bad enough to represent a further barrier to understanding—including his. The destruct oven was the next stage in concealment. As soon as a page was filled, it was fed to the destruct oven's built-in shredder/burner. And that was just one-half of the process. Protocol called for one agent to write in shorthand, while the other read the writing and replied in sign language—and for them to swap roles every few minutes.

Someday, perhaps, the Kendari Inquiries Service would devote sufficient resources to learning the combination of hand-spelling, symbolic gestures, totally arbitrary gestures, visual representations of spoken puns, and even more esoteric elements that made up the BSI's version of sign language. It seemed unlikely any other species would put in the effort—and even the Kendari had yet to show any signs of trying. It seemed hugely unlikely that the Metrannans would do so.

"All right," said Hannah, "let's get started."

Jamie began. "do you knect the dots the way i do?" he wrote. "what tan sed sure made me think trev's msg was sumthing to do w/longlife treatment. formula 4 it? or maybe it's part of formula delib left out?"

Agreed, Hannah signed back. *The timing sure suggests it. Trevor collects a message from Geriatrics Institute. The message gets lost. Not long after a rumor starts spreading, saying longlife secret has gone missing. But why they would send it to us, to humans and UniGov, I don't understand.*

"+ formula *isn't* missing if they just give trev a copy. unless they give him *only* copy? crazy idea, but maybe poss. safekeeping? accident destroys all other copies & is no backup? can u think of other reason?"

I probably could, but there's no point in speculating. Hannah paused for a moment. *We must remember rumors are often very wrong. Just because the mob thinks it was a longlife treatment, that doesn't mean it wasn't a cure for Metrannan baldness. And just because we connect the dots that way and it makes a pretty picture, it doesn't make it the right picture. We could be making a wrong assumption—or Taranarak could be deliberately misleading us. And another big question: Why give the secret formula to lowly stupid Younger Race like humans? And why suppress cure for short lives? Many mysteries.*

"many many. like: where r we going? who will

we c? what clues could b on this world to tell us y trev offed, who did it, where key is?"

I was going to ask you all that.

"i kno. that's y i ask u 1st."

Thanks a lot, partner.

* * *

They ran through a notebook and a half's worth of paper, and swapped the jobs of shorthand writing and signing back and forth a half dozen times. They thought up a great many more questions, but didn't get much further forward with answers.

Finally they gave it up and decided to turn in for the night—if it could be called "night" with the full light of the local sun shining down on them. Fortunately, Jamie managed to find a status and control monitor, mounted and positioned and designed in a way that would seem totally counterintuitive to humans. The instructions for it appeared to be posted in six languages, one of which was Metrannan, four of which were completely unknown, and the last of which was very bad written-form Lesser Trade Speech. Jamie followed it well enough to opaquify the overhead half of their cylinder and dim the interior lighting.

They had brought along their own emergency rations, of course, but it was only common sense to leave those alone as long as possible. After a bit more digging and exploring, they found a cupboard full of ration packs marked as human-edible in several languages, including not only written-form Lesser Trade Speech and Greater Trade Writing, but even English. More or less. The lettering was a bit skewed somehow, and the spelling wasn't all it could be, but the package did say

Gud Four Humans to Be Eaten
(Safe Phude Fore Peeple frum Eerth)

As Jamie pointed out, that was open to interpretation, and might mean it was certified as safe for cannibals, but a quick check with their portable food testers gave the happy news that the Metrannans were better biochemists than linguists. The water tested as safe, even if it had an odd brackish aftertaste. The best that could be said of the flavors of any of the rations was that they were "interesting," but if patience was a BSI job skill, so was an iron stomach. They both got through what Jamie insisted on calling a "meal-like event" without incident.

Although the food—if one could call it food—was barely acceptable, the beds were beyond reproach, a vast improvement on the roll-up mats and sleeping-bag arrangements they had been using aboard the *Sholto*, and even better than the beds in their duty quarters back at BSI HQ.

It took a little doing, but Jamie finally did manage to decode the status display sufficiently to tell them how long it would be until they hit atmosphere and how long until they arrived on the ground. Neither of them wanted to miss either event, so Jamie set the alarm on his datapad to wake them a half hour before they hit air.

What Jamie hadn't counted on was the absolutely obvious idea that popped into his head the next morning, the moment the alarm went off and he swung out of bed. He hurried over to Hannah's bed to wake her and tell her about it—until he realized that not only was she no longer there, but that she had beaten him into the bathroom and the shower, leaving him with nothing to do but sit down and wait for her.

But Hannah managed to balance the sin of early rising with the good act of getting in and out of the bathroom quickly. The door soon opened, and she emerged, fully dressed in a slight variation of the business suit she had worn the day before. "Morning!" she said. "I *think* this thing can't run out of hot water, but I did my best to save you some, just in case. And the controls don't work exactly the way they do at home—to put it mildly. So watch it."

"But I—"

"Come on! Hurry up! We don't want to miss the show."

Jamie opened his mouth to protest—but then he stopped himself. It hadn't taken many missions for both Hannah and Jamie to realize that being in a split-gender field team in close quarters required a specialized etiquette.

For Jamie, one of the most important lessons

was knowing when to notice there was something he wasn't supposed to notice. Hannah might well be not quite as completely put-together as she looked. Some bit of feminine apparel might not be easy to do up in the tight confines of the bathroom. She might want him to get into the bathroom so that she could have a moment or two of privacy *outside* of it. "I'll be right out," he said.

* * *

Hannah breathed a sigh of relief as soon as Jamie was in the bathroom. There were a few adjustments to women's clothes that just weren't possible inside a cramped bathroom—and those adjustments were even trickier with all the concealed gear they both had to carry. Once she had a little more room to work in, it only took her a moment or two to get herself suitably pinned, buttoned, adjusted, and organized.

Jamie soon emerged, looking reasonably scrubbed and refreshed, but plainly a little put off. The sullen reddish lighting didn't make him look much happier. "So much for that theory," he said. "At least the easy part of it."

"What theory?" Hannah asked.

"Well, I got to thinking. The Metrannans can't possibly have many cars like this one—cars made up for humans, I mean. And this one doesn't look exactly brand-new. A few scuff marks here and there, lots of little signs that things have been used once or twice. So they probably didn't start from scratch and fire up some custom-built robotic lab to put all this together for us when we first signaled we had arrived in system."

"Right. Probably they have a whole fleet of these in storage somewhere, with cars modified for each species that might visit the planet. Vixa, Kendari, Pavlat, human, Stanlarr, whatever. More cars if the species comes here a lot, fewer if they don't come that often."

"Right. So connect the dots."

Hannah thought for a moment, then she got it. She shifted to sign language. *There are very good odds this is the same car Trevor rode in.*

Bingo, Jamie signed back, and reached for a notebook. He scribbled quickly, closed the book, and handed it to Hannah. "maybe he fig searcher wld travel same way he did. maybe he left backup copy or even *only* copy of key here in this car. that's y we nvr found it on *Adler.* it nvr got there."

Cute, Hannah signed. *But you're not fitting theory to data. You're using the absence of data as evidence your idea is right.*

"OK, so it's not ideal logic. it's at least idea we cn check. we cn search car. search n places and n ways metrannans not likely 2 look. i chckd bathroom jst now. fixtures etc dont fit metrs. i look for places hard 2 c in red light. c idea?"

I see it. Did the Metrannans? Do they have cameras in bathroom? If I were running things, I would.

"didnt think of tht."

But your idea is good. Yes, we should search—discreetly, so it doesn't look like we're looking. It's a long shot, but sometimes long shots come in. And if you do find it—keep your cool. Don't let them—or me—know you've got it until we're safe. Whenever that might be.

"The main thing is that I'm very, very glad the Metrannans did build an Elevator car custom-made for humans," Hannah said aloud, closing the topic by changing the subject. "But let's not miss the show! Go work the controls and get the opaquifier turned off. I want to see where we are."

"Right," said Jamie. It took him a minute or two, and he managed to kill the lights altogether and plunge them into total darkness twice, but then he got it right. The ceiling faded away and the sky bloomed into existence above them and before them.

They knew what to expect, but it was still a breathtaking sight.

The planet before them had grown until it took up half the field of view. Dawn was just breaking, off to the east, the terminator line sharp and clear. The lights of the planet's only city were a patchwork dazzle to the north, with a long and sinuous flickering of light marking the routes of transit lines threading down to the south, toward the Elevator's Groundside Station.

They had gotten close enough, and were still moving fast enough, that their movement toward the planet had become plainly noticeable. More than noticeable, it was frightening, with the ground leaping closer with every minute. The visual cues—and the sideways gravity under their feet—were utterly at odds with each other. It was impossible to decide if they were traveling on the flat and level, hurtling arrow-straight toward a destination directly ahead, or falling like a rock, dropping straight down. Hannah's internal perception of what she was seeing flipped back and forth every few moments.

The two of them stood, transfixed, as daylight flooded the land ahead and below, and the green and blue and white and lovely world of Metrannan moved ever closer.

"How high up are we now?" Hannah asked.

"Um. Hang on. Lemme convert," said Jamie. "Just over a hundred fifty kilometers. Our speed has been varying, but if I've got it right, our current speed is three thousand kilometers an hour. And I don't care what sort of aerodynamics or acceleration comp this thing has. I wouldn't want to hit the top of the atmosphere at this speed. We'd better start slowing down really soon or else—"

As if on cue, without a sound, without a shake or shudder, all motion came to a smooth and perfect halt. Or *almost* all motion. It took a moment to be sure, but then they could see their car was still moving, but at a far slower rate.

"Okay," said Jamie. "Good to know they do what I tell them to do. *Now* we're doing a leisurely, oh call it four hundred and fifty kilometers an hour."

"How soon until we hit significant atmosphere?"

"I have no idea of the pressure gradient for this atmosphere," Jamie said. "Could be ten seconds or ten minutes or maybe a hair longer. Not much more than that. About all we can do is sit back and watch the show."

And there was plenty to watch. There were few sights as endlessly fascinating as a living world from orbit, the constant change and interplay between light and dark, cloud and clear sky, land and sea.

A few minutes later, as they were passing through ninety kilometers altitude, their speed dropped again, to a steady two hundred and four kilometers an hour. Moments later, they could hear a low murmuring, a moaning and whistling, coming through the hull of their car as it shuddered and quivered through the thickening air. And, somehow, in some indefinable moment, they were suddenly not moving *toward* Metran, but there already, inside the atmosphere, part of the world, inside its realm and moving through it.

Whatever confusion Hannah might have felt about the direction of their travel was gone. The gravity in their car might be set at a ninety-degree angle to the ground, but that didn't matter anymore. They were moving *down*.

Perhaps they could have, should have, spent those precious minutes diligently and furtively searching the Elevator car as they had searched the *Adler*, dutifully looking for what was almost certainly not there, but it was inconceivable that either of them could have torn their eyes away from the spectacle before them.

Down they swept, toward what seemed an insignificant dot of cloud, a dot that swelled to truly massive size as they plunged toward it, then the cloud and the outside world vanished altogether in a cocoon of featureless grey, and then they were under it, through it, and looking straight down at the massive complex of sidings and access roads and marshaling yards and cargo sheds and vast facilities they could not identify at all—and in the center of them all, coming straight up at them, was Groundside Station.

They had arrived.

EIGHTEEN
IMPROPER DRESS
REQUIREMENT

Arrival, they quickly discovered, did not mean the end of travel. They had come to rest with their car's interior gravity rotated ninety degrees so their "forward" end pointed straight down. They could hear the clanking and banging of heavy-duty machinery. Suddenly, smoothly, their room was swung clear of the cable cluster, and they were free of the Elevator itself. It wasn't a car anymore. Hannah decided to think of it as a gondola.

They heard the grinding and clanking of heavy-duty motors powering up, and watched the world rotate through ninety degrees, coming about level with their own point of view.

It was a distinct relief to have the exterior universe right-way up—and also, somehow, it was reassuring to *see* the cable cluster that been hidden from their view for the whole ride down. They didn't get much more than a glimpse of it before their gondola was sliding toward one of dozens of round holes in the massive wall of the main Station chamber. As casually as a mail clerk of antique days might have popped a package into a sorting slot, they were dropped onto some sort of conveyor belt.

Hannah gave up all hope of keeping track of the shuntings and transfers and handoffs after that, and was not entirely clear about their surroundings until their gondola had been placed on a sort of flatbed rail car that was in turn being guided into position on what looked like an extremely advanced version of a magnetic-levitation rail link.

Moments later, they were under way again, hurtling along an elevated track, leaving Groundside Station behind. They watched as it receded from view. It reminded Hannah of the old medieval renderings of the Tower of Babel. Tall, squared-off, multileveled, with the cables of the Elevator sprouting from its roof, and an uncountable number of roads, rail links, conveyor belts, pipelines, and power feeds spanning out from it, like the main threads of a spiderweb, all designed to serve and feed the beast that sat at its center.

"Jeez," said Jamie, watching the monstrous Station recede behind them. "I sure hope we don't have to find our own way back through all that."

"I was just thinking the same thing," said Hannah. "Come on, let's eat what passes for breakfast before we get sidetracked by the next special-effects show."

* * *

Other than the utter lack of any sense of motion, there was a sense of luxury to their little train ride. They could look out the massive view windows at something like a normal landscape, dotted with vegetation that resembled short, stubby trees. They could see animals—eight-legged animals— grazing in the local red-tinged equivalent of grass. The lighting might be a trifle eerie, the animals might be strange, the "Safe Phude Fore Peeple frum Eerth" might have an odd flavor and consistency, but the horizon was where it ought to be, the coffee from their own stores was good, they were traveling rapidly toward their destination, their current accommodations were vastly more comfortable than the utilitarian metal-and-plastic fold-down interior of the *Bartholomew Sholto*, and they weren't being shown any huge or magnificent piece of engineering that could not help but make them feel utterly insignificant.

"I'm feeling lazy," said Jamie. "Do you mind if we talk about things we don't mind our friends hearing?"

"I'm with you," said Hannah. "My fingers are getting tired."

"Okay, then. Taranarak seemed to be in an awful hurry to bundle us into this thing," he said. "What do you think that was about?"

"I doubt it was anything more than keeping to a schedule," said Hannah. "From where *I* was sitting, it seemed as if she had a lot more she wanted to say to us, before we ran out of time. I'm no expert at reading Metrannan expressions, but I had her read as in a hurry to talk, and frustrated that we had to be put aboard so soon. She got to us late, after all."

"Well, the one piece of solid news she gave us wasn't exactly helpful."

"You mean Learned Searcher Hallaben being dead? Agreed. I was counting on him to be the most likely person to know something about Trevor Wilcox." Hannah frowned. It was a tricky game they were playing. Their cover mission of finding out about what happened to Wilcox was just too close to the real job of getting a lead on where the decrypt key might be. It would be all too easy to make a slip, and there was no doubt in her mind that the walls had very sensitive ears. "Maybe Taranarak will know something. I would like to talk to her again."

"It's probably all a fool's errand anyway," said Jamie. "Most likely what happened to Wilcox and the *Adler* was some fuel pump failed or some mechanic put a left-handed gravistran in backwards and the ship blew up out there somewhere."

All right, Jamie, you get eight bonus points for acting and misdirection. "Probably," Hannah agreed for the sake of the microphones, "but we have to cover all the bases. What I worry about is that too much time has passed, and the trail has gone cold. Hallaben's dying doesn't help matters. I don't know. Maybe we can get access to maintenance and servicing records of the *Adler* while she was landed—or docked, or whatever—to Free Orbit Station."

Of course, the *Adler* hadn't vanished, so those records couldn't help in solving that nonexistent mystery—but it was possible that the records *would* hold some sort of clue as to where or how Wilcox had hidden the decrypt key. After all, they had received their restocking supplies as soon as they landed. Say, for example, if Wilcox and the *Adler* had received similar service and then a second, last-minute restock. It might be that the items from the second restock were where the decrypt key was hidden.

All long shots, but they were down to long shots. Which reminded Hannah of another point. She worked it through as she poured herself more coffee and sipped it thoughtfully. If Wilcox had stashed the decrypt key aboard the gondola they were riding in, that would have been a high-risk, last-ditch sort of play. Wilcox couldn't know or expect that humans, let alone BSI agents, would be the next ones to ride in it—and he would have been just as aware of likely surveillance as Hannah and Jamie were. If the locals could see them *searching* for the key, they could have seen Wilcox *hiding* it.

But maybe there was somewhere else on the planet—some room he stayed in, some package he left with a trusted local, where he could have hidden the key. Except no, blast it, the whole idea made no sense. She had fallen into the habit of thinking of the decrypt key as a thing in itself, the actual goal of their mission, when in fact the whole point of the decrypt key was that it would unlock the message that had been recovered from the

Adler's secure computer file system. How could it be used to unlock the message if it was left back on Metran, light-years from the file itself? *Unless they kept a backup copy.* That made sense.

The *Adler's* secure file system was not merely built to be secure from infiltration or unauthorized access. It was robustly built, heavily armored, and shielded, designed to survive violent events—including the destruction of the *Adler* itself. Given that, so long as long as the ship was intact, the files in that system could be presumed safe from snooping or from destruction. But, whatever sort of recording device the key was on, it was almost certainly not as well protected as the message. A memory chip could be smashed or melted. Paper could be burned.

Wilcox could have trusted in the message's surviving aboard the *Adler*, but be much less confident in the decrypt key's survival. If there were a copy, it would have allowed Wilcox the luxury of destroying the original, secure in the knowledge that the message itself would be safe. In which case, in order to protect the message, all he would have had to do was to destroy the decrypt key. The moment the boarding party's ship docked with the *Adler*, Trevor could have simply destroyed the key. Maybe they hadn't been able to find it because it wasn't there.

There might well be a backup of the key somewhere, deliberately left behind. And that somewhere would either be someplace Trevor Wilcox had been on this planet, or *with* someone he trusted. Which meant, maybe, that Hallaben's death wasn't *such* bad news. Taranarak hadn't given the impression that Learned Searcher Hallaben had died suddenly or unexpectedly. He likely would have had time to entrust the backup key to someone. Or even if he had received the local equivalent of a safe dropped on his head, surely he would have had the common sense to protect his own life's work by putting it in something like a safe-deposit box.

"*You* went quiet all of a sudden," Jamie said. "Plus your coffee's gotten cold. I think I've figured out the flash heater. Want me to warm it up?"

"Hmmm? Yeah, thanks." Hannah grabbed a notebook, and quickly scribbled down a shorthand version of her thinking. Jamie finished heating the coffee and returned to the table. He stood there, watching silently, as she wrote. When she was done, she closed the cover on the notebook and handed it to him. He opened it, read her notes, tore the pages out, folded them, and shoved them into the destruct oven's shredder feed. He nodded, and then signed to her.

Cute. Might even be right. But if so, then why did Trevor do the clean-out? Why prep the ship to help us search for something that wasn't there? He did the clean-out AFTER the boarding party came aboard. Unless we have something wrong, that has to mean that there was still something worth searching for when he did it. It was his last effort, after all. I think he was knowingly using up his last reserves of physical strength and endurance before he died. He wouldn't have worked that hard, sacrificed so much, just to play games.

Hannah sighed. "You're right," she said out loud. "I forgot that part. And I think you're right about another thing. We've missed something. We *do* have something wrong."

"We're not the only ones," said Jamie. "Look out there."

Hannah hadn't been paying much attention to the passing scenery. They had arrived at the outskirts of Metran's one and nameless city. Ahead of them were proud and gleaming towers, a graceful and orderly skyline. She looked to where Jamie was pointing, and saw they were passing through what appeared to be a warehouse district.

A burned-out, still-smoldering warehouse district. Roofs had caved in. Goods of all sorts were spilled out on the ground, and they could see Metrannans moving through the wreckage. Looters? Scavengers? Repair personnel? Guards protecting the wreckage or the crime scene? They were past in a flash, and it was impossible to know more.

They were slowing down as they approached the center of the city. It was impossible to miss the other damage. Broken windows as obvious as punched-out missing teeth, blackened buildings, piles of wreckage shoved to one side of the street. "They surely do have something wrong," Hannah half whispered, shocked by what she saw. If they had read Taranarak's hints properly, all of the ruin they were seeing was directly linked to the loss of the message Trevor Wilcox had been carrying. It was more than enough to scare her. It wasn't hard to imagine someone needing someone to blame, wanting to shoot the messenger—and settling for the chance to shoot the messenger's friend.

She was starting to get a real idea of what that War-Starter designation really meant.

"We're going to have to be very, very, very careful," said Jamie. "The people out there aren't likely to be very calm or relaxed."

Hannah shook her head. "No," she agreed. "And neither are we."

* * *

Their gondola was shifted off the rail line and transferred to the back of a robotic flatbed truck. Hannah shook her head as she watched the passing scene, pristine and perfect streets and parks interspersed with scenes of ruin and wreckage.

At last they came to a halt on a quiet road on a hill that overlooked the city spread out far below. Lining the streets were widely spaced structures that were clearly no relation to any Earthly architecture. They were short and squat, and the windows were oddly spaced and the doors were in the wrong places, but they were still plainly places for people to live.

One house, the one at the end of the road,

seemed to have been singled out for some reason. The yard looked as if it had been chewed up by some sort of heavy machinery, and then hurriedly tidied up. There were large ugly dents and dings and gouges in the house itself, around the doors and windows.

Very official-looking vehicles were parked everywhere, and Metrannans in combat uniforms stood around with serious expressions on their faces and serious weapons carried in their primary lifting arms.

As soon as the vehicle carrying their gondola came to a halt, a squad of security guards dragged a heavy portable barrier across the road, sealing off the house—and their gondola—from all the other houses.

Hannah knew enough about how things went wrong, and had enough practice as a detective, for her to make a very well-educated guess at what had happened. Someone had been under very strict house arrest, to the point of the doors and windows being boarded up in some way, and lots of heavy traffic outside. Then they had taken down the boards and shutters, dressing the set, perhaps in hopes of pretending everything was fine in front of strangers.

Trouble was, at a guess, the damage to the house and grounds was too severe to be cleaned up in a hurry, especially with the security forces as overstretched as they presumably were. Perhaps there had been violent demonstrations in the area, and the security forces hadn't been able to keep the low profile they had been hoping for.

And then, somewhere in the middle of the botched plans and improvising, once it was clear they wouldn't be able to pretend things were normal anyway, it would seem that someone had had the bright idea of putting the aliens in the same compound and saving on guards that way.

Almost before the barrier was erected, the hatch on the endcap of the gondola swung open to reveal a beefy-looking guard brandishing a particularly nasty-looking weapon. "You two beings," he said in crude, heavily accented Lesser Trade Speech. "Get ready. We go in three standard short social time intervals." He turned and pushed a button to close the hatch again and was already walking away, down an access ramp, before the hatch could seal.

"Ouch," said Jamie. "I thought Metrannans were hyperconcerned about proper behavior and correct manners."

"They are," said Hannah. "Either they've got the local equivalent of a Neanderthal guarding us, or that was a deliberate insult. Don't ask me *why* they'd want to insult us."

"Okay, I'll ask you something else," said Jamie. "Three shorts. What's that? About five minutes?"

"About," said Hannah, not really paying attention.

"We'll get ready for what? To go where?"

"I don't know," she said. She thought for a moment. "I've been in a lot of situations where the locals tried to put pressure on me, one way or the other. But this is the first time I've ever been stuck in a mobile goldfish bowl without explanation or consultation. If they're trying to control our movements, I suppose it's working. But they'd better not count on it making us more cooperative."

"I take it you don't mind if our hosts hear you make that little comment," Jamie said.

"No, I don't," said Hannah. "We're the representatives of a friendly government, come to inquire after our colleague who vanished while trying to do a service for these people. Maybe they need to hear that humans, at least, don't think this is the way to treat one's friends."

"For all you know, this is the standard way they handle every alien who comes in on the Elevator."

"If so, then maybe I can tell them why they don't get more visitors," Hannah growled. "But I can't believe it. Especially those last little grace notes. Dragging a steel barrier across the road? Sealing us in? Ordering us around as if we were prisoners? No one is that ham-handed, except on purpose. It's a deliberate attempt to intimidate us. Let's make sure they know it isn't working."

"With any luck, if they are listening in, you just told them."

"Did I? Well, I'm about to do it again, if I can. Can you get that hatch open? Or are we locked in here?"

Jamie went over and studied the control panel.

"I should be able to," he said. "Unless it's been gimmicked from the outside, or welded shut or something. But if I do get it open, the folks on the other side probably won't be too happy."

"Good," said Hannah. "If they're mad, what are they going to do? Shoot us?"

"Could be."

"No," she said. "We've been under their complete control since we landed. If they wanted us dead, we'd be dead by now. They want us—or maybe just need us—alive. Open the door."

Jamie did as he was told, and Hannah stepped out the door and onto the top end of the ramp that had been positioned outside it. "You!" she called out to the guard, who'd taken up a position at the bottom of the ramp. "Tell your officer we will not be treated this way," she thundered, in the best and clearest Lesser Trade Speech she could muster. "The lowest criminals are permitted the right of proper dress! We will *not* risk humiliation for ourselves or on behalf of our race. We will *not* depart until we are clearly informed as to the nature of our destination, and until we are properly dressed for the time, location, and event in question! Is that clear?"

The astonished guard could only open and shut his mouth and let his closework arms twitch feebly.

"Is that clear?" Hannah demanded again. "Answer me!"

"Ah. Yes. Yes it is. My officer will be informed."

"See that he is—and promptly!" Hannah snapped, then went back inside and signaled for Jamie to shut the hatch. "Let's see if *that* got their attention," she said.

She resisted the temptation to let out a sigh or rub her forehead or show any other sign of emotion besides anger. After all, if the locals hadn't been watching them before, they almost certainly were after that tirade. She didn't dare end the performance she had just started.

"I'm sure you got their attention," Jamie said doubtfully. "But I'm just not sure we're going to be that much happier because of it."

"We will not be happier," Hannah said, speaking in Lesser Trade Speech to address the air. "But we will be more respected. I speak now in a language that those listening will not need to have translated. We came here in search of a lost comrade who vanished while performing a service for your people. We have seen many signs of fear and destruction since our arrival. We did not cause your problems. We did not set off the disturbances. We can make guesses, but we have been told nothing and know nothing of what has gone wrong. By human custom, and by that of your own people, our comrade's presumed death in your service places you in our debt. We need your help to learn his fate. If you need our help for your own purposes—as I suspect you do—then it is time to deal with us properly. Tell us where we are being taken and why!"

The interior of the gondola was silent. Hannah sat down, battling to control her emotions. It was a dangerous game, self-righteousness, especially when you were stretching and twisting the truth in the middle of it. Wilcox hadn't vanished, and there was nothing presumed about his death. But the game had to be played.

Moments later, both of their datapads beeped simultaneously. "I think that did it," Jamie said as he pulled his pad out of an inside pocket. "And it's got to be a good sign that they replied that fast." He looked at the screen, and then swore under his breath. "I just wish I liked the answer better."

Hannah checked her own datapad, determined not to reveal anything, no matter what it said. The Metrannans had responded all right—with a sequence of clothing database codings that did in fact report precisely what they should wear.

The calculation of appropriateness at the bottom reported the selected garments were ninety-six-point-three percent likely to be suitable for the event in question. That was the good news.

The bad news was the event-culture-equivalency estimate. According to its comparator algorithm, the human-style event most like what they were about to take part in was a trial at law.

With Hannah and Jamie as the defendants.

NINETEEN

ANSWERS TO QUESTIONS

"I think I liked the other outfits better," Jamie said as he and Hannah were bundled into the waiting aircar. After a brief and unsatisfying consultation with the databases, Jamie found himself in a white shirt with knit maroon tie, thick brown jacket, black slacks with oversized cuffs, and clunky brown shoes. All he needed was a pocket protector and old-fashioned spectacles held together with adhesive tape and he would have been ready to go to a costume party dressed as an archetypal ancient nerd of centuries back, from all the cartoons and jokes, as familiar a pop culture icon as the knight in shining armor or the caveman dressed in animal skins. Hannah's clothes were similarly drab, archaic, and awkward-looking: a dowdy brown wool skirt, a beige blouse, and black flat-heeled shoes. It took some doing to make Hannah look frumpy, but the outfit selected by the database had managed it.

The guard on duty sealed the aircar door from the outside and signaled for the driver to take off. But the law of inexplicable delays held true, and the aircar stayed where it was, even though it seemed as if they were ready to go. Not that Jamie was in any hurry. He didn't think it was going to be all that fun a trip.

"I'm not crazy about my clothes either," said Hannah. "But at least we've forced the locals to acknowledge that their traditions extended to us."

"Let's hope those traditions don't include trial by ordeal or single combat or anything fun like that," Jamie replied. "What I don't understand is what in dark space we could possibly be on trial *for*. We just got here, and for all intents and purposes, we've been locked up since arrival."

"I don't know," said Hannah. "But bear in mind that the only thing telling us what's happening is a low-grade artificial intelligence that's been programmed to simulate a fashion consultant. It might have gotten it wrong."

"Or it might not," said Jamie. "Maybe it's a trial—but we're just the witnesses. Look over there."

There was some activity by the house on their side of the barrier. An aircar landed in front of it. The main door of the house opened—and Learned Searcher Taranarak came out, dressed in formal robes of dark color and severe cut. A guard escorted her every step of the five meters or so to the aircar, and she got in.

"I guess they wanted us to fly in formation," Jamie said. Their vehicle and Taranarak's lifted off simultaneously, rising vertically to about two hundred meters or so before heading toward the center of town.

"Is *she* the one on trial?" Jamie asked. "For what?"

"Who knows? Maybe we're all codefendants in some kind of show trial, and we'll all be hanged together—or whatever they do instead of hanging around here. Metrannans don't exactly have necks."

"I thought you had it all figured out that we're still alive because they need us!" Jamie protested.

"Maybe. And maybe what they need us for is the show trial and the executions afterward. We'll just have to see what happens."

Jamie grunted. "And who it happens to."

* * *

Taranarak was bundled out of her aircar first and hustled inside to follow the route she had traveled so many times before. She strained to study everything as if she had seen none of it before. It was what changed that told her what was important. The trio of Order Bureaucrats had come to be called the Three, and that by itself meant something. They were, for all intents and purposes, the leaders of the planet, and a certain degree of myth, an aura of power, was starting to build around them.

The greatest change, of course, was merely that the Three were of any importance at all. Yalananav, Tigmin, and Fallogon not only shared power—they had more power among them than anyone ever had before in thousands of years.

For countless generations, Metrannan government had been so weak, so small, as to be almost undetectable. What need of government when all was stable, all was safe, all was unchanging? Change was Wrong, according to Bulwark of Constancy. Perhaps, after all, Constancy had been right, if change forced government—especially government like this—upon a society.

But that assumed that change was optional, something that could be rejected if it proved inconvenient. The truth was that change could at best be held off for a time, but that the longer it was forestalled, the faster, the harder, the crueler it would be when it at last broke free. Her people had slept through endless, all but changeless generations—but now they were paying the price in the form of a most rude and unpleasant awakening.

Her main concerns were to figure out the internal dynamics of the Three and get some idea of what they intended to do with her. It was hard to judge what changes were truly significant, and which were trivial happenstance. She could note who spoke first, who sat where, how far back she herself was required to stand, how long they made her wait before calling for her to enter the chamber. But what all that could usefully tell her, she had no idea.

The elevator opened, and the guards ushered her out. She turned automatically to the left—but the guards pointed her the other way. She realized that, this time, she was indeed being led toward the Great Room—or at least toward a smaller holding room just outside it. The guards hustled her inside and stayed there with her. There was no place to sit, nothing at all in the room. Taranarak resisted the urge to find meaning in that and settled herself until the Three were ready for her.

There was not long for her to wait. At some signal that was unseen to her, the guards roused themselves, opened the inner door, and led her into the round-walled confines of the Great Room. It was easily three times the size of the chamber in which she had been interviewed before. The Great Room could be used for many sorts of events, and had been designed as a sort of blank backdrop that could be dressed and decorated with whatever sort of set and theater might be desired for a particular occasion. It had been left utterly, even aggressively, undecorated. Its walls, ceiling, and floor were a steely grey, unrelieved by any sort of painting or design or pattern.

Taranarak was not in the least surprised to see a metal table and two human-style chairs set in the geometric center of the room. It took no complex or elaborate interpretation to understand for whom those places were meant.

The Three were seated at a table on a raised platform in front of the humans—but were they in fact Three anymore? Fascinated by what was before her, Taranarak barely noticed as the guards guided her to her own chair at a table next to the one for the humans. Things had changed indeed. Now Tigmin had the center chair, with Yalananav close by him on his right side. But Fallogon, near-silent Fallogon, was seated at the far left, as distant from Tigmin, and from Yalananav, as he could possibly be while remaining at the same table. Bulwark of Constancy was at the right of Yalananav, standing closer to him than he was to Tigmin.

It all had to mean something—but what?

* * *

Hannah and Jamie followed their guards into the huge, all-but-empty room, and were conducted to their places at the central table. They saw Taranarak seated off to one side, and three other Metrannans and a Xenoatric seated at a large table, facing them. The three other Metrannans were dressed in gleaming black tunics with elaborate silver decorations that made Taranarak's garb seem drab and ordinary.

"You are Special Agents Mendez and Wolfson," said the Metrannan on the right, speaking in Lesser Trade Speech. "Learned Searcher Taranarak is known to you. She is observing, but may not participate at this time, though it is possible she will be called upon later. I am Yalananav of the Order Bureaucracy. To my left is my colleague, Tigmin, and to his left, our mutual colleague, Fallogon. To my right, and also observing, Bulwark of Constancy of the Unseen Race." Yalananav turned to Tigmin. "The formalities of introduction are now complete," he said.

"Then let us begin," said Tigmin.

"Begin what?" Hannah asked. "Why are we here? What is the purpose of this meeting?"

"Your question is noted and will be answered in time," Tigmin said evenly. "At the moment, it is for us to ask the questions of you. You are required to answer."

"Under what authority?"

"Under *our* authority," Tigmin replied. "As I understand from the signals your vessel sent while you were approaching the planet, you are requesting the cooperation of local law enforcement in the investigation of the loss of your colleague. We are local law enforcement—and *we* require *your* cooperation."

"There were two discrepancies noted in the supplies you had placed aboard your vehicle after landing at our orbital station," said Yalananav. "We require an explanation of both these items."

"I beg your pardon?" Hannah said.

Yalananav rolled on smoothly, as if Hannah had said nothing at all. "According to our records, it was Agent Mendez who actually approved the deliveries. You requested and were supplied with a quantity of electro-setting repair compound."

"Yes, we were," said Hannah.

"It would be our preference that Agent Mendez speak to this matter, as he was the one who approved the delivery."

"It would be our preference to know what all this is about," Hannah said testily. "One does not always get what one wants. I am the senior agent present, and I choose to speak for my partner in this matter. If cooperating with you is a precondition of your cooperating with us—then it will be on our terms."

"Very well," said Yalananav. "If you wish to implicate yourself, that is of no consequence to us. You admit that you requested and received the repair compound."

"Yes. What of it? It is a perfectly standard repair supply and was a perfectly routine request."

"Why did you need it?"

Because that stuff sets like reinforced concrete and it will provide additional sealing and structural reinforcement to the damage on the patched windshield on the Adler. *I don't want to try a transit-jump with just our spit-and-chewing-gum repair holding it all together. But I'm not going to tell you that, you interfering old buzzard.* "Our craft, the *Bartholomew Sholto,* experienced some minor hull damage just before departure. A hold-down cable attached to another vehicle snapped and banged into our craft. The broken cable was not discovered for some time, and we were not made aware of the incident or the damage until we were well under way. There is no immediate danger, but we felt it prudent to take precautions. We plan to make temporary repairs to our hull before we depart."

"Our experts tell us that the damage to your hull would only be significant during an atmospheric entry. Do you plan to make such a maneuver? To land on our world, perhaps?"

"We have no such plans. When we have done our work here, we are expected to fly directly back to our base, which is in vacuum and in free orbit. Still, we deemed it wise to take precautions. Surely you would agree that it is only prudent to keep one's vehicle fully capable?"

"We will ask the questions here," Yalananav said. "You ordered and received a far larger quantity of the material than would be required to repair the observed damage to your ship."

You people certainly have been snooping, thought Hannah. *Checking our manifests, doing an external exam of the* Sholto. *What else have you been checking out?*

"As I said, we were not made aware of the damage until we were well under way. We used the ship's onboard cameras, but we couldn't be sure of the extent of the damage. Better to order too much repair material than too little."

"You did not even examine the damage to your ship upon arrival."

And you watched as we disembarked. Why are we so interesting? "As you said, the damage would only be of consequence during an atmospheric entry. The matter was not urgent—and we were eager to enjoy your splendid hospitality." Lesser Trade Speech did not lend itself to sarcasm, and she very much doubted that Yalananav had a sense of humor, but if a snide remark served to deflect his attention, that would suit Hannah. And why the devil were they interested in the repair compound?

"There was another, and stranger, discrepancy," Yalananav went on. "You accepted delivery of a twenty-four-day supply of Metrannan-digestible emergency rations. What possible use did you have for them?"

"I know nothing of such rations," said Hannah, quite truthfully.

"I do," said Jamie. "Though I know very little. It seemed such a minor point at the time, I did not bother mentioning it to my colleague. The packing lists for the two containers we accepted were printed in Metrannan Script, Greater Trade Writing, and written English—rather poor written English, with several mistakes. However, we were in a hurry, and as it was the language most familiar to me, I read over the English listing. There was one item with a garbled description. It was something like 'Made for/by Metrannan Meals Twenty-four Daily.' I took it to mean there were twenty-four mealpacks made by Metrannans for us, for humans. I gather they are in fact meals for Metrannans, which were somehow mistakenly delivered to us."

"If you were uncertain of the meaning of the listing," Yalananav said, "you should have compared it against the other languages, or else opened the package and examined the contents directly."

Jamie frowned. "If what we got were rations that a Metrannan could eat, but not a human, I was not uncertain. I was mistaken. I failed to understand a garbled notation properly. I note that you did not say that we ordered the rations—just that we accepted them. Correct?"

"That is correct."

Good for you, Jamie, Hannah thought. *You got them to answer a question. A small start—but a start.*

"Then at worst I am guilty of misunderstanding a poor translation done by some automated system in your resupply service. There. I have confessed. Why don't you arrest me for that? Except—excuse me. Haven't you done that already?"

"I do not understand."

"Arrested. Are we arrested? Held against our will under suspicion of committing a crime?"

"You are not arrested."

Jamie stood up. "Then we are free to go?"

A guard stepped forward from the rear of the room. "You are not free to go. You must remain."

Jamie sat down. "Then I must insist that you clarify our situation."

Silence. Plainly they had no intention of clarifying anything.

Hannah used the quiet moment to try to think. Jamie had just done a good job of using his own anger to push back at this gang of bullies. And bullies they were—all sly threats and leaning on people weaker than they, and doing it because they were scared themselves.

What worried her was that scared and inexperienced leaders in a crisis often spent a lot of time looking for someone to blame. If she didn't know better, she would have guessed they were toying with the idea of choosing humans for the role. Never mind that it made no sense. Never mind that it was, in fact, completely irrational. There they were, picking at minor oddities in their packing list, looking for—even manufacturing—evidence of conspiracies.

She could almost see the gears in their heads turning. Jamie and she were only a few inferences away from being accused of a plot to land on the planet, and either kidnap someone, or else collect some fiendish Metrannan traitor who would fly off to conspire with his evil human allies. They had already scraped together just enough nothing to build into a nearly plausible story.

Hannah's gut instinct was that the Metrannans *couldn't* clarify the situation because they weren't sure of it themselves. This session was a fishing expedition, an attempt to rattle them. Jamie, in effect, had called their bluff. Good for him—but now it was time to defuse things just a bit. "Let us not argue over terms and definitions," she said. "I trust we have answered your questions satisfactorily. We have cooperated. Now we seek your cooperation."

"First one or two questions more, if you please," said the one on the end, speaking for the first time. Fallogon, that was his name. "Are you familiar with the term 'maneuver-masking'?"

"I believe I have heard it in passing," Hannah said, trying to sound casual. "I don't know what the precise definition might be." That was a flat-out lie, but her internal alarm bells were going off, and this didn't seem the moment to reveal knowledge of covert piloting techniques.

"I am surprised that a spacefaring police officer wouldn't know the term intimately. It refers to various techniques whereby one ship is interposed between a detection station and a second ship, in hopes that the energy field generated by the first ship's engines would conceal any maneuvers by the second ship. Ship two hides behind ship one so the detection station cannot see it."

"I understand," said Hannah.

"It is a matter of simple geometry to demonstrate that this trick would conceal nothing from a second detection station, if it were any significant radial distance from the first, as seen from the point of view of ship one."

"I quite see that, yes."

"Can you explain the intermittent detection of a ship under thrust on almost precisely your own heading but several billion long scientific units of linear measure behind your own ship during its arrival deceleration?"

"In a word, no," said Hannah, keeping her

voice as cool as she could. "There are a lot of ships out there. I have no control over them and can't be called to account for what they do."

"Just so. Thank you for your answer."

Hannah hoped that the Metrannans were no better at reading human expressions and reactions than she was at reading Metrannans—but it was obvious there was *something* going on among the four beings behind the table in front of her—if the Xenoatric, the Unseen One, was in fact there at all. She hadn't seen it move a millimeter since their arrival. It could be a statue of a Xenoatric, or an empty carapace, for all she could tell.

The Metrannans were another story. She was nowhere near being able to understand what was happening, but it was clear there was a complicated dynamic at work. But who was headed up? Who was heading down? Tigman and Yalananav were obviously in some degree of alliance against Fallogon. But for how long? And how were the lines drawn, and why? And it seemed as if Fallogon was the one asking the tough questions— but offering them up soft and easy, almost like a defense lawyer trying to lead his witness without getting caught by the judge. Any halfway-decent interrogator could have made a lot more out of the maneuver-making angle—for the very good reason that there was actually something there. Instead he made it seem like a loose end to tie up after the other two had finished with their paranoid fantasies.

Hannah glanced at Jamie, then spoke again. "Unless there is anything more," she said, "I would like very much to make a start on getting *your* help with *our* problem. Our colleague, Trevor Wilcox, boarded his ship, left your world— and vanished. We come in search of any clue to what might have happened."

"You come very belatedly," Fallogon said. "It was roughly half of one of our local years ago that he departed from our world."

"But he was not listed as officially overdue for some time after that," said Hannah. "As for the rest of the delay, we are a small service, stretched thin, dealing with investigations on many worlds. But honor requires that we search, once our other duties permit it."

"What do you know of his mission here?" Yalananav demanded.

"That Learned Searcher Hallaben requested a human courier for an—item—a message or document of some sort—to be transported to the human world Center to another agency of our government. Trevor Wilcox was sent. For the sake of security, he was not told what he was to carry before he departed, nor was any other person in our service. So far as I am aware, no one in our service even knows if *anyone* in our government knows what the item was to be. The plan was for Special Agent Wilcox to be briefed when he arrived. We do not know if that happened."

Hannah paused, giving the Metrannans a chance

to chime in, but none of them took the bait. "We do not know *anything* of what happened after his departure. We need your help to find out more."

"Your story is not plausible," said Tigmin. "Why would your service agree to act with so little information? There must have been a briefing."

"With respect, to the best of my information, there was not. Nor did our service—the Bureau of Special Investigations—have much choice. We were not asked to provide the courier. We were *ordered* to do so."

"You are saying that your people—your government—were willing to do this task without explanation?" Tigmin asked. "That *no* human ever learned what the, ah, 'item' that Special Agent Wilcox was asked to transport was? Or why it was being entrusted to humans?"

There was something oddly eager in Tigmin's tone and expression. It was almost as if he saw the message's being lost beyond hope of retrieval as good news. Hannah decided to feed him a bit more of the same, just to see what would happen. Tell him the truth, but tell it the way he wanted to hear it.

"The arrangement was that Wilcox was to be briefed on arrival," Hannah said again. "It is my understanding that no other human was ever fully briefed. I could be mistaken or even deceived in that. When the point is to limit knowledge, one must also limit knowledge of who *has* knowledge. However, it is my belief that no human alive knows what the 'item' was—other than that it was clearly very important. As to why we were asked to do this task, except for the very general purpose of keeping the item safe, I doubt any human knows—for knowing *why* would likely reveal the *what,* if you see what I mean."

Yalananav frowned and drummed the fingers of all four hands on the table. "Why would your—what do you call it—Unified Human Government—UniGov?"

"That is the short and informal term, yes. UniGov."

"Why would this UniGov agree to such a request?"

Hannah decided to tell them what they wanted to hear. "Because we are the younger of the two Younger Races, and we are small and weak, surrounded by a Galaxy full of Elder Races of great age and wisdom and effectively unlimited power. We need friends. We need acceptance. It is to our benefit to be useful, trusted, reliable."

Yes, we're just poor lonely little puppies with big brown eyes all alone in the big scary woods. The words she had spoken were all true enough, if more than a little exaggerated. But if pretending humans were weaker than they were made the Metrannans happier and more relaxed, maybe they would let their guard down and let something useful slip.

"What is it you want to know from us that

could help you in your search after your colleague?" Fallogon asked.

"Technical information," Jamie said.

"Such as?"

Jamie pulled out a notebook and started writing in longhand as he spoke. "The full maintenance records for his ship. Everything that was done to and for his ship while it was here. Complete tracking data for inbound and outbound flight. Recordings of all voice and data transmissions from his ship." He finished up his written list with a quick scribble of BSI shorthand. He gave Hannah the briefest of glances at it before dropping his hand over it. It read *let f. use that to keep t. & y. chasing own tails. make 'em happy. sumthing going on.* "Can you think of anything else, Agent Wolfson?" he asked out loud.

"No, I think you've been quite thorough, Agent Mendez. Well done." She was distinctly relieved to know Jamie had spotted the same odd dynamics at work that she had. "Except, of course, for one other point," she said. "Presumably, someone at *this* end knew what the 'item' was." All the Metrannans, even Taranarak, seated silently to one side of the room, froze up, as motionless as Bulwark of Constancy. *And what is a Xenoatric doing sitting in on this very high-level hush-hush meeting anyway?* But that was a puzzle for later.

"It is at least possible that there was something about the item itself that directly or indirectly caused or contributed to the disappearance of

Agent Wilcox and his ship," she said. "Can you perhaps tell us what the item was, or anything at all about it?"

Again, silence, lasting three, four, five, six heartbeats.

Hannah suddenly found herself thinking of the off-duty seven-card-stud poker games in the back room of the BSI Bullpen. Now and then you'd get dealt the last up-card and it would be something that would make everything else fall very obviously into place. If you got dealt the fourth card to the straight flush, it would make your hand almost unbeatable—*if* you had the fifth card to fill the flush in your down cards. But either you had the right card or you didn't.

If you did, you would know instantly and know how to bet at once. If you *didn't* have it, but were ready with your bluff when the bet got to you, ready to pretend, that could be just as good. Make the other players believe you had the straight flush, and you'd rake in the pot on the strength of the cards you were *acting* like you had.

But if you hesitated, if you had to pause, compute, calculate, for a split second longer than it would have taken you to make the obvious choice of how to bet the real thing, then it was all over. No bluff would be believable after that. There was nothing that could help you recover from that brief-but-fatal hesitation.

"I am sorry," Tigmin said at last, after a quiet that lasted far too long to be believed. "But that knowledge died with Hallaben. We were not in our present positions of authority at that time."

And Hannah knew from one look at the expressions on all the Metrannan faces in the room, knew beyond all possible doubt, that Tigmin was lying.

Hannah struggled to repress a smile and hold her own poker face in place. *Maybe, just maybe, Jamie and I can win this hand after all.*

TWENTY

REVEALED IN DARKNESS

After two hours spent slogging through all the pointless technical information they could possibly have needed for their cover story, if they had actually cared about their cover story, Fallogon agreed to take mercy on them all and declare the session at an end.

Jamie and Hannah rode back in their aircar, stumbled back into their gondola, were sincerely grateful to watch the hatch close shut behind them, and even happy to see the guard posted outside. For a time, at least, until Tigmin, Yalananav, and Fallogon decided what to do next, they would be left to themselves. Hannah found herself understanding why the circus lions in the old stories were glad to get safely locked back into their old familiar cages.

"Man, oh man, oh man," Jamie said, dropping into a chair. "Getting back into one standard gee feels very good indeed. Why didn't that blasted database just tell us to put on black-and-white stripes or orange jumpsuits with numbers on the back? And you said it might not be *us* on trial."

"I'm still not sure it was," said Hannah. "It's

just possible that the whole show was about Taranarak. Otherwise, what was she doing there?"

"I don't know. Playing along to distract us? We only had about ten minutes to talk with her back on Free Orbit Station," he said. "Not exactly enough to judge her character and motives or knowledge."

"How do you think they felt about it when we told them we didn't know what was in the message?"

Jamie glanced around the room, tapped a finger to his eye and ear, and looked quizzically at Hannah.

She shrugged. "What use can it be to them, knowing that we're wondering about their reactions? Do they think we *won't* be trying to figure out what all that was about? Besides, I'm too worn-out to play charades."

"Okay by me," Jamie said. "They can't be expecting us to have a real high opinion of them by now."

"So? How do you think they felt?"

"Relief. Very, very obvious relief. Those three seemed glad to know their secret was safe."

"Three?" Hannah wasn't so sure Fallogon was happy about it.

Jamie cocked his head at Hannah. "Hey, I'm not *that* tired. I'm not going to start analyzing who's-on-first and who's dating whom and who's just broken up in plain English. And I hope that was cryptic enough for realtime purposes."

"I think it was. Anyway, *I* barely followed it. Let's talk history instead."

"Huh?"

"You had the same training courses I did. Same theory. Human history can offer insights and parallels to what goes on with the xenos. So what do you think? More like the French Revolution or the Russian?"

"What? *That* crowd? The Three? Hmmph. Early phase of the French Revolution, I'd say. Pre–Committee of Public Safety. Not the Jacobins, and definitely not the commissars."

"Yeah, that's what I thought. But why?"

Jamie frowned and thought it over. "Power vacuum," he said at last. "If I'm reading this right, the crisis was caused by a power vacuum. Not ideology, not a violent overthrow. They're just the guys who happen to be standing around in the right place when everything falls apart. The weird part here is that, as best I can see, the power vacuum was caused by the fact that the absence of government didn't matter for a long, long time. Then there was a sudden need for security, control— for *government*—after a zillion years of nothing changing and therefore no need for central control of anything. Then, *pow!*, a crisis hits and they *need* government all of a sudden. These guys get the job of putting things back together, and find out they like being in charge. They don't want things the way they were, or maybe they realize or at least believe it's not possible to put things back the way they were, but they'd like to stabilize things the way they are *now,* since they're in charge."

"Good luck with that one, with the French Rev as a model," Hannah said with a yawn. "But I think you're right. They've just about got things settled back down. They've established the new order. They want to keep it that way, and they don't want to take a chance on anything that might upset the very delicate balance. *Especially* since the new order has *them* in charge, as fate, or destiny, or the will of the people, or God himself, clearly intended."

"God in this case being the tin-plated potted palm?"

"Hmm. Maybe. I was just talking in general terms. The guys in charge *always* find a way to convince themselves that they got the job by divine right. But what *was* a Xenoatric doing there?"

"Maybe they just like having them around," said Jamie. "Or at least Tom and Dick did. I'm not so sure about Harry."

In other words, Jamie was circling back around to speculating on what Fallogon was up to. So was Hannah—but she needed to take a break first. "Agreed, once again. But that skates us right back onto thin ice. Later we can play charades and scribbles all you want. After lunch."

"Do you think they're going to drag us back for another session of twenty questions?" Jamie asked.

"You know as much as I do about what happens next. We ought to rest up in the meantime. I'm going to shut my eyes for a little while before we eat. You ought to take a break as well."

"Yeah, but I'm too keyed up. Trying to think about what comes next—and trying *not* to think about it."

"I know exactly what you mean," said Hannah. "But I'm going to try not thinking about it with my eyes shut." She stood up, kicked her clunky, sensible shoes off, hung her jacket on the back of her chair, and went over to her bed.

She slipped between the covers, closed her eyes, and let her worries run through her mind. Problem one: They had not yet been on-planet a full day, but already the cover story was taking over all of their time and attention. It was something she had dreaded from the outset but had never been able to find a way around. How would they string along the needless investigation into how the *Irene Adler* had disappeared and still find time and ways to track down any existing clues to where the decrypt key was hidden—and to how, exactly, Trevor Wilcox had died?

No. Not how he died. How he was murdered. Trevor Wilcox, after all, had died of old age in his early twenties. *Something* had triggered that—and triggered it shortly after he met with this Hallaben character, the head of research into the causes of old age. *And* that something had to have come from a world currently obsessed over the question of life extension, and what might well be the deliberate suppression of a life-extension treatment.

Hannah felt there was a very strong possibility that the message they were trying to decrypt was in fact connected to that treatment—or maybe was the treatment itself. It was hard not to wonder if Trip Wilcox had been killed in order to keep the treatment quiet. It was all murky, all circumstantial, but everything pointed toward the same conclusion: Wilcox had been murdered.

And that meant finding a murderer. The good news was that was something she was good at. Something she had done before. Something she would very much like to do again.

It gave her something to look forward to. And somehow, that was enough to help her drift off to sleep.

* * *

Jamie sat at the table, watching Hannah doze off. If patience was a job skill for a BSI agent, so was the ability to catch forty winks at a moment's notice. Usually, he was much better at it than Hannah. There had been plenty of times he had managed to sleep, only to awake and find her deeply annoyed at him for being able to drop off anywhere, anytime. This time, the shoe was on the other foot.

He knew why, too. Put very simply, he called the dead man "Trevor" and Hannah called him "Wilcox." He was taking it all personally—

probably too personally. There were endless ways that could wind up causing problems. Excessive identification with the victim could make an investigator squeamish about medical evidence, make him too eager for vengeance, cause him to idealize the victim to the point where the investigator could not or would not be able to recognize a character flaw that might have a bearing on the case.

But Jamie couldn't help himself. It was too easy to look into the mirror and see someone very much like Trevor Wilcox. A shift in the transit schedule, some little hiccup that might have gotten Jamie into an earlier training class, and Trevor Wilcox into a later one, and it might well have been Special Agents Wilcox and Wolfson investigating the mysterious death of Jamie Mendez.

It wasn't a far jump from there to the question of how well he, Jamie, would have dealt with the situation. Faced with the crisis that had confronted Trevor Wilcox, would he have done so well? Would he have kept his eye on his mission, his duty, to anywhere near the same degree?

He would like to believe so, but there was no way to know—and Jamie was honest enough with himself to have doubts. The best Jamie could do was to make use of Trevor's efforts, and work with the clues, the tools, the leads that he had left behind. But while that might be the best he could do, it certainly didn't seem good enough.

He sighed and pulled out his investigator's notebook. Standard security rules said he had to destroy the page he had written in the trial room, the one with the list of items they'd want, because it also contained his comments to Hannah in BSI shorthand. First, though, he had to check the page and make sure there wasn't anything else on it that he might actually need.

He paused before he opened the notebook and studied it for a moment. There had been a niggling detail worrying at the back of his mind, and it chose that moment to make its way to his conscious attention. There was something not quite right about the notebooks they had been using. Something subtle, something fleeting and odd. And it was only the *new* notebooks that seemed a bit off. Once he had used one for a while, it seemed all right. But once the last pages of it had been used, and he reached for a new one, he got that same feeling again.

He flipped open the notebook. Just one or two items that might be marginally useful. He quickly copied them to another page, then folded over the page with the shorthand on it, and tore it out of the book.

He reached for the mini-destruct oven, and was about to feed the page to it, when he remembered that he had seen the CHAMBER FULL light blinking earlier, meaning that he would have to empty it before using it again. But the CHAMBER FULL light was no longer on. The oven felt significantly lighter, and there were tiny wisps of ash stuck to it on the outside. Obviously, Hannah had already emptied it. He fed the folded page to it, and leaned back in his chair, wondering what to do next, what he could do that would be quiet enough to let Hannah sleep.

But then he stopped and frowned. There was suddenly something else at the back of his mind, another hint, another clue, that wasn't merely niggling at his consciousness. It was practically shouting at him. Something big and important. Something, he sensed, just at the edge of revealing itself to him. He froze, stock-still, afraid to move, afraid to breathe, even afraid to *think* for fear of scaring away whatever it was that his subconsciousness had spotted.

It was close. As close as the table in front of him, and the notebook and the chair with Hannah's jacket draped over it, close as the dead man whose last mission they were trying to complete.

Close as—

BLAAAT!

Jamie jumped twenty centimeters in the air. Hannah sat bolt upright. "What in the hell was *that*?" she demanded. "An alert? An alarm?"

Jamie cursed silently to himself and stood up. The clue was gone, whatever it was, suddenly far off, as far off as the slumbering *Irene Adler*, waiting for them in the dark and distant reaches of the Metran star system. "It was the doorbell," he said grimly. "Or at least the Metrannan equivalent. Apparently they're not merely half-blind in the blue end of the spectrum. They must be half-deaf as well."

He stood up and went to the hatch. He didn't need to bother opening it himself. It came open, and their old friend the guard was there. He thrust a datacard forward toward Jamie and spoke in his extremely limited Lesser Trade Speech. "Here. You take. Clothing rules are there. We collect you at time shown. Take you there, back. Is all."

"Now what?" Hannah asked, getting up out of the bed and rubbing her face. "And what do we have to wear? Tennis outfits? Clown suits?"

It took Jamie a moment to navigate his way through the information on the datacard. It seemed to be phrased in language that was halfway between a formal invitation and a legal summons, even more so than most documents written in Greater Trade Writing. "You were close on that last guess," he said.

"*What?* How many costumes do they think we can pack?"

"Well, take it as good news or bad news, but we *did* pack these costumes. It's a formal dinner. Black tie. Everyone from this morning in attendance, plus about forty more. No one we've ever heard of."

"You're kidding, right?"

"I wish I was," he said, handing her the datacard. "I hate wearing a tuxedo. It makes me feel like a funeral director or a wedding usher."

"Technically, I don't think black tie means tuxedo, exactly."

"Be that as it may, this says that a tuxedo is what I'm supposed to wear. An evening gown for you."

"Great. I always wanted to play intergalactic dress-up." She studied the card further. " 'A formal and public dinner.' I *think* that means it's for public consumption, for people to watch, not that the public is invited. Propaganda."

"What propaganda value do *we* have? We're a couple of cops from a no-account Younger Race."

"Agreed. Next to zero value. But it's what they've got. And we don't know what other rumors are flying out there. If something about Trevor or his mission got out—for example, that he was murdered—maybe they figure that showing two *more* human cops will send some sort of signal, prove the story false. We wouldn't be there for all to see, having a swell time at their splendid dinner party, if we had the slightest fear that our hosts had him killed."

"Suppose we *did* have the slightest fear of just that? Or maybe a bit more than that much fear?"

"Watch what you say, Jamie," Hannah said, pointing to her eyes and ears.

"Let 'em hear it," he growled. "With the paranoia we saw on display this morning, they'd *have* to realize that we'd wonder about that possibility."

"That may be," said Hannah. "But it doesn't mean they'll appreciate hearing it."

"What I don't understand is the big turnaround. This morning they were practically accusing us of fiendish plots against the state—and tonight we're the guests of honor."

"Sounds to me like we've been cleared of all suspicion," Hannah said, casually reaching across the table for Jamie's notebook. "Whatever that business with the repair compound and the Metrannan rations was supposed to be, they decided it wasn't true." She scribbled a quick line or two in the notebook, handed it to him, and watched him read it.

"once they decided 2 b-leve we didn't no wht msg ws—& tht msg was truly lost 4 good—then we wr no threat."

Jamie signed back. *How could the message be a threat to them?*

"r u kidding? they hv jst barely regained stability. all is delic8. Moe, Larry + Curly cn't feel secure. anything tht czs change s threat. longer lives change everything + they just got big dose of how much fun change can b."

"Okay," said Jamie out loud, "so there's a reason I didn't go into politics."

"Actually, you did," said Hannah. "That's the other reason we're going to this dinner, no matter what we think."

" 'Other' reason? What's the *first* reason?"

"The gun to our heads," she said. "We have to do what they say. We're prisoners, to all intents and purposes—but we're prisoners with a mission to accomplish. The 'other' reason is that we need to remember we're not just cops—we're an odd breed of diplomat as well. We're out here to protect and improve the standing of the human race. And sometimes that means getting what we need comes ahead of doing what we want. For example that means having dinner with people who aren't our best friends—while pretending that they are."

"Okay. Point taken. But I still wish I could skip the tuxedo."

"Come on," she said. "Let's crack open the suitcases. It's going to take us forever to get dressed and ready for this one."

* * *

By the time she had his tie straightened and his cummerbund adjusted, Hannah had to admit that Jamie cleaned up even better than she had thought. "Very sharp," she said. "Very stylish."

"Very stiff and uncomfortable," Jamie growled, pulling at his collar. "And very hard to pack all the portable gizmos and gear in the jacket, no matter how many pockets the BSI tailor put in."

"You've got it easy," Hannah reminded him, gesturing toward her full-length burgundy-colored evening gown. "See any pockets on this little number?"

"You've got your handbag. And isn't there a jacket that goes with that gown?"

"A jacket I'm supposed to remove as soon as I arrive."

"The Metrannans might not know that."

"Or they might," Hannah said, "and be so hugely insulted by it they decide to hold another little show trial. It doesn't make much sense to jump in and out of these little outfits all day long because our hosts take clothes so seriously—*then* start hoping they won't notice when we don't wear them properly. Besides, the jacket that goes with this gown wouldn't do much to conceal a shoulder holster. Which leaves me with the handbag to carry everything, and it doesn't even have a shoulder strap, which means I only have one hand free in an emergency."

"Okay, when it comes to performing our professional duties, your clothes are worse than mine. But you look very nice. The gown suits you."

Hannah smiled. "Well, it took you long enough. But when you did come out with a compliment, it was actually coherent, polite, and even sounded sincere. We'll get you trained for polite society yet. Maybe the next nice girl you meet won't flee in terror."

"You're not going to start trying to set me up again when we get back—if we get back—to HQ, are you?"

"No comment," Hannah said, in a very motherly tone of voice that spoke volumes. She watched as Jamie stepped to the table and started tucking his weapons and comm gear and other compact field equipment into the pockets of his tux. Maybe they weren't being watched as closely as they had thought. They hadn't spotted any cameras yet, though given how small even human spycams could be, that meant nothing at all.

"Something else I noticed about this crowd. Have you noticed they haven't once checked to see if we were packing heat?" Hannah asked. Neither of them had spoken the words "gun" or "weapon" since arriving on-planet and Hannah saw no reason to start.

"That's the fun thing about talking for realtime security," said Jamie. "I get to hear you use all that tough-guy slang. But yeah. I did notice that. I assumed we'd have to check it all at the door as soon as we arrived at Free Orbit Station. But they never even asked. No scanners that I've noticed either. Any theories?"

"Maybe they're all very new at this police state business, and not all that good at it yet. Maybe their snoopers can't spot our toys because they're so crude and primitive. Maybe they're short of personnel. Maybe they've already disabled or counteracted everything we've got in some weird Elder Race way that we won't even know about until it's too late. I could probably think of about a dozen other reasons—but I wouldn't want to get *too* specific while they're listening in. Let's just enjoy the good times while they last."

"These are the good times?" Jamie shifted to sign language. *New topic: We urgently need to find a way to chat with Taranarak in private. She knows a lot, and she's eager to talk. I don't think we're going to get anywhere at all unless we manage that.*

Hannah signed back. *I agree. One hundred percent. But unless you've got some bright idea, we'll just have to watch for our chances. Taranarak is no fool. She knows the situation better than we do, and has had more time to think it through. She's probably already figured out she's going to have to be the one to make it happen.*

"Or are the good times just about to start?" Jamie asked, resuming the spoken conversation and pretending that the signed exchange hadn't happened. He peered through the transparent top of their gondola and gestured toward the house Taranarak had emerged from earlier. "I think it's party time."

Even in the gloomy, red-tinged light of an evening on Metran, they could see that Taranarak was dressed in spectacular fashion, in a garment somewhere in form between a cloak and a gown in colors as iridescent as a peacock in full display, with a matching headdress of elaborate design. She moved with silent dignity between the guard that preceded her and the one that followed, needing nothing but her pride and bearing to turn them into a guard of honor, rather than a prisoner's escort.

"*That's* a slightly different look than she had on this morning," said Jamie. "I think it's a fair guess she's going to the same party we are."

"Sooner or later," said Hannah, "this might all

make sense, but so far I can't see it. Just looking at how chewed up the land is around her house, and the obvious damage to her house itself, it looks as if she was in some sort of really heavy-duty house arrest. My guess is that they've just eased up on her a lot—maybe because we showed up. But the ease-up *can't* be to make her look good in front of us, because they left so much evidence around that they *were* hard on her, plus they've still got goons all over the place and the end of the street sealed off—*then* they plunk us down right next to her so we *have* to see it all. And then they wheel her in to sit like the prisoner in the dock this morning—but tonight she's off to a public ball. Do *you* have a theory that covers all the known facts, Agent Mendez? Because I sure don't."

Jamie shook his head. "How about 'xenos are really weird'?"

"Well, that covers the facts, all right, but I was hoping for something with a bit more detail."

"Maybe we'll get that something soon," said Jamie, pointing toward a guard heading toward the entrance of their gondola. "It looks like they're coming for us."

* * *

Learned Searcher Taranarak of geneline Lucyrn allowed herself to be led to the center of the muddy, poorly maintained Order Patrol compound that had once been her sunward garden, moving carefully to stay on the paths, lifting the hem of her garment to avoid soiling it. At last her escort got her as far as the aircar landing pad. The lead guard stopped there, and only then seemed to notice an obvious fact. "The aircar has failed to arrive," he announced. He turned to the other guard, his subordinate. "Walk back out to the depot, advise them that no aircar has arrived, and have them send a replacement vehicle suitable for transporting one subject. And don't just pass the message. Stay there, and stay on them, until they confirm that an aircar has been dispatched."

"Wouldn't it be simpler to send the request by commlink signal?"

"Simpler, but less secure," the first guard growled. "This is to be a high-security event. Let's not start the evening by broadcasting our every move to the rebels. Now go."

"Yes, sir." The subordinate moved off toward the road, and the lead guard stayed where he was, very pointedly not looking toward Taranarak or acknowledging her in any way.

A moment or two later, the hatch on the human's mobile living quarters opened, and their guard led them down the ramp toward the aircar landing pad.

"Transport ops fouled up again," Taranarak's guard announced in a grimly cheerful voice. "No aircar for my charge. I just sent Zelphanot up the road to the depot to request a new one. It looks like no car for your friends, either."

"But sir, they're all to travel in one larger aircar

tonight, and it isn't due for another twelve short-duration units. I was wondering why you sent me early to get these two."

"What? Something's off-center. No one can decide what to do or how to do it. They sent 'em off in *two* cars this morning, but it's all friends in one big car this evening? And I just sent Zelphanot legging off to the depot for a small car. Stars and blackness, you can bet whatever you like that they'll cancel the big car and just send the little one. We'd never fit 'em all in, and they'd get there late, and there'd be trouble enough for everybody. You'd better head off after Zelphanot and countermand, make sure they just send the big car as per schedule."

"But that'll leave you alone guarding all three of them."

"An old lady and two alien two-leggers dressed in their best. What are they going to do? Rush me, then run for the Elevator in their fancy-dinner clothes and hope they blend in with the crowd?"

"Well—I guess it will be all right."

"Get moving. If they get the aircar order wrong, and our friends here aren't there to look happy for the cameras, *we* won't be here at all in the morning. Go."

The newly arrived guard needed no more urging. He turned and headed off in the same direction Zelphanot had taken.

The lead guard watched him depart impassively, then turned very deliberately so that his back was to the three prisoners. "It is a very pleasant night," he announced to no one in particular, shifting from the local language to Lesser Trade Speech. "I will take a walk around the perimeter, so that I might enjoy the evening while patrolling for intruders. It will be a very brief walk." And with that he set off, still without looking at Taranarak or the humans.

Taranarak waited until he was fully out of earshot before she spoke. She did not dare look at the humans. They had already met her high expectations by not responding in any way. No shouts of surprise or nervous laughter. Perhaps these two were formed in the same mold as Trevor of geneline Wilcox. If so, it would be a great good fortune. "Do not look toward me. Do not gesture or show any particular reaction. We are a little bored, a little annoyed, and a little mystified as to what has happened to our transportation, and also annoyed at the ineptitude of our guards. That is all. Do you understand?"

"We do," said the senior of the two, the female, Wolfson. "Speak to us."

"I shall do so. It required a huge bribe to buy these few short-duration units out from under the watchers and the listeners. I will not waste them. Tigmin lied this morning. All of us there in the chamber knew what was in the message. It was, of course, the longlife treatment."

"But why entrust it to humans?" Mendez asked, his voice as casual as his words were urgent. "Why send the only copy of the information off-planet?"

"There is no time to explain all that now. Later, if we survive, you will know all. We must stick to essentials."

"Then before we go further, you must answer *our* essential questions," said Wolfson, making no effort to hide the steel in *her* voice. "What was the purpose of this morning's interview? Why were you there? Was it our trial? Yours? Why was the Xenoatric—the Unseen One—there? What made us criminals this morning but honored guests tonight?"

Taranarak cringed inwardly. There was so little time! But the humans might well need answers to those questions if they were to survive—and Taranarak would most definitely need them alive if her own plans were going to work. "The Three— Yalananav, Fallogon, and Tigmin—play intricate and deadly games together, each maneuvering for advantage, each seeking supremacy. I believe that the Unseen Being, Bulwark of Constancy, is, somehow, financing or otherwise backing Tigmin—or else is seeming to do so in an indirect move in support of Yalananav. I believe, but cannot know for sure, that I was there to witness that the Three had power over *you*. However, I have come to think that there is no one clear reason for any event that involves the Three. I think it is possible that I was also part of some complex maneuver of Fallogon's in opposition to the other two.

"As to why *you* were there—this morning was an audition, a clearance procedure, for tonight.

The answers you gave were satisfactory and made it plain you were not a threat to the newly established Bureaucratic Order. Therefore, you can be presented tonight for propaganda purposes.

"You have propaganda value because the rumor had gotten about that a human being was somehow involved in the search for the lost longlife treatment and killed during the search. When you appear tonight, the mere sight of humans—especially humans who work for the same service as Trevor Wilcox—will suggest that the search goes on, that the authorities are in fact working to recover the lost formulae, and that the rebel claim that the treatment has been deliberately suppressed is a fiction. It will send the message that those who wish for the formulae to be recovered should support the Bureaucratic Order, and the work of the Three.

"I can expand on all these points later, but time is *short*! We have only a few moments before the aircar arrives, and all we say in the car, and for the rest of the evening, will be listened to, I can assure you."

"Very well," said Wolfson. "We will count ourselves satisfied—for the moment. Speak to the essentials you mentioned earlier."

Taranarak took a deep breath and spoke rapidly. "It was I who arranged for the emergency Metrannan-edible rations to be delivered to your ship. If, somehow, you are permitted to leave this madhouse planet—*you must take me with you*. If it can be done legally, normally, through proper channels, all the better. If I must be smuggled aboard somehow, then so be it. The rations are there to allow us that option. I do not request this favor of you—I demand it. And I do not demand it to save my own life—although it likely will. I demand it as the only means available to save my culture and my people."

The stunned silence from the humans would likely not have lasted long, even if their guard hadn't chosen that moment to reappear, and the aircar hadn't started its landing approach. But in a strange way, Taranarak was glad of the timing. She could think of many questions the humans would want to ask right away.

But none that she would not prefer to answer later.

Much, much later.

TWENTY-ONE
CHANGING FOR DINNER

The ride in the aircar provided a spectacular view of the city at sunset and flew them over parts of town they had not seen before. However, Jamie was far too distracted to take much of it in. The car they had flown in that morning had been converted to bench seating for the benefit of human visitors. Jamie had not really appreciated that detail until now. This vehicle had not been so modified and retained the hard, narrow saddles that the four-legged Metrannans preferred. They were excruciatingly uncomfortable for humans to sit on even in the straddle position, and of course that pose was utterly impossible for Hannah in an evening gown. They were both reduced to wedging themselves in sidesaddle, which was massively uncomfortable. Nor was the higher gravity much of a help.

Meanwhile, of course, Taranarak, possessed of both a body and a gown suited to the saddles, sat placidly and silently, watching their contortions and doing a far better job than the two humans of pretending that nothing at all had happened at the landing pad.

And as soon as the relaxing car ride was over,

they would have to wade through the horrors of, not only a formal dinner, not only an Elder Race formal dinner, but a *multispecies* Elder Race formal dinner. Jamie remembered reading somewhere that a human logician had computed that, given the mutually exclusive mores and rules of etiquette of the various Elder Race species, and the physiological limitations of the human body, with anything over six species in attendance, it became something close to a mathematical impossibility to get through the evening without committing a perhaps literally fatal social error.

On the bright side, so far as Jamie was aware, there would only be three species present at the meal: human, Metrannan, and Xenoatric. On the downside, two of the species there were among the most dangerous of all known species when offended or annoyed: Metrannan and Xenoatric. Jamie glanced over at Hannah, wedged in between two saddles, the expression on her face a veritable catalog of discomfort and negative emotions, and decided it might just be that humans belonged on the second list as well.

They were coming for a landing. Jamie breathed a sigh of relief. The ride was about to come to an end. Unfortunately that meant the meal was about to begin.

* * *

Hannah bolted a smile onto her face as she pried herself out of the car. Jamie offered her his arm, and she made no pretense at all about the fact that she needed it to keep upright, just at first. She had nearly regained feeling in both legs by the time they were ushered inside.

The Xenoatrics seemed to have polished and burnished their metal carapaces, and they literally glittered in colors of gold and silver and hard-edged steel. But even they receded into the background compared to the Metrannans. Taranarak's iridescent gown turned out to be downright dowdy compared to most of the outfits. Bright colors, designs with complex geometric patterns and elaborate decoration, and madly complex headdresses were the order of the evening. Perhaps the overall effect was less jarring to the Metrannans' red-adapted optic nerves, but it came close to making Hannah's Earth-evolved eyes water.

Hannah almost felt embarrassed by the stark simplicity of her own gown and the comparative drabness of its color. But perhaps the understated style of her clothes and Jamie's was distinction enough. It was to her eye, at least. She thought Jamie looked very much the poised, cosmopolitan, elegant gentleman. The gaudy, overwrought clothes of the other guests merely served as a backdrop to Jamie's crisp, simple tuxedo. What he wore was a welcome spot of refined quiet in the midst of clamor. But then, she was biased.

The drill seemed to be that the guests were all held backstage by a gaggle of minders and sorted out into a precisely calculated pecking order, moving from least to most important. It did not escape Hannah's notice that Jamie and she were posted quite near the head of the line, or that Taranarak was positioned only a place or two behind them. What she found more amusing was that the minders flatly refused to let her go in on Jamie's arm. She was, after all, senior to him. Therefore, he had to go first, and alone. It didn't really matter, anyway, as they were to be seated at separate tables.

The five or so Xenoatrics were assembled at the most senior end of the line—with Bulwark of Constancy last of all. One other thing struck her: Constancy was motionless, aloof, inert, for long periods of time—but the other Xenoatrics were engaged in animated conversation, among themselves and with the senior Metrannans near them in the line.

Once the guests were in order, they were required to wait where they were, in the order they were in, for no clearly explained reason, until it was somehow determined it was time to begin the Procession of Entrance and the door to the dining room was opened.

Guards of the Order Patrol, resplendent in formal red uniforms with green-and-purple piping, came to stand beside each guest. Then, one by one, the guests were escorted to their starting positions around their initial feeding vats, while complex, atonal—and dreadfully unpleasant—music played. Somehow the whole process resembled a bizarre variation on musical chairs.

Hannah allowed herself to be led to her own table, and tried not to be alarmed by the dining saddle set behind her place. She was the first one to her table. She quickly saw why—the seating at each table was also in order of seniority, counterclockwise around the round table. She remained standing as each diner was escorted in, in part because everyone else did, and in part because between her gown and the saddle, she simply had no other options. She located Jamie going through the same ritual at the far side of the room.

At last the Order Guards ran out of Metrannans and started working through the Xenoatrics. One of them—thankfully, not Bulwark of Constancy—was led to Hannah's table and took the last open place, to Hannah's right.

Once the Xenoatrics, the Unseen Beings, were delivered to their places, it was time for the guests of honor—or, more accurately, the hosts of the event—to be brought out from some separate holding room. Yalananav, Fallogon, and Tigmin did not so much enter the room as appear in it, stepping abruptly, three abreast, from a shadowy corner into the bright dazzle of a sudden spotlight, as music that sounded even more like a cat fight blared out.

The Three stepped forward together, carefully avoiding any pose or positioning that might indicate anything other than exact and precise equality among the three of them. The Metrannans in the room thumped their forefeet on the floor and their closework hands on the tables. Even the Xenoatrics offered their version of applause—a sort of low-throated trilling that sounded like something halfway between a birdsong and a synthesounder.

Hannah had expected the Three to sit separate from the others at some sort of special table where they could remain a little bit apart, a little bit exalted, a little bit better than their followers—but apparently this particular New Order hadn't reached that stage yet.

Instead, the Three took their places at three different tables, each taking the seat for the most senior person, but otherwise without any particular special treatment. Once the Three were at their places, the Metrannans sat down, while the Xenoatrics contracted themselves somehow and refolded their carapaces a bit to bring them in closer to the tables.

Hannah was relieved to discover that her escort Guard had produced a more or less human-style chair from somewhere while she was distracted. He set it in position and whisked away the Metrannan saddle at her place. She could see Jamie getting the same treatment on the other side of the room.

The briefing materials Hannah and Jamie had read while inbound to Metran had covered the procedure and etiquette of a formal meal on Metran, but somehow the dry words of the report didn't quite convey the feel of the event itself. In a sense, it was the opposite of a human dinner party, where the diners remained in place and the food was brought to them. On Metran, it was the diners that did the moving around.

There were six formal dining saddles set around the edge of each table—if "table" was the right word. Probably "feeding vat" would be a more accurate description. Each vat contained a particular dish, and the diners would assemble at their assigned spot for each course, eat whatever particular item was on offer at that table, converse with their neighbors, then, when a chime sounded, follow their escort to their next assigned seating at another table for the next course.

Perhaps by use of some hideously complex algorithm, the diners were in effect shuffled and redealt to a fresh grouping for each course, so that each diner encountered five new dinner partners with each change.

Hannah rather liked that feature of Metrannan dinner etiquette. She could almost imagine trying to introduce it at her next dinner party—or would have, if she ever gave dinner parties. But then she considered the difficulty of getting six or seven tables of six into her duty quarters, and the chaos that would ensue every time it was time to swap tables, and decided to drop the idea.

What she did not care for was the food itself or the way it was served. Things got off to a difficult start at her first table. Set into the center of the table was a large shallow metal container that resembled a wok or a frying pan. In the pan were small, eight-legged creatures scuttling around its interior. They more or less resembled a cross between a bald mouse and a crayfish. Their bodies were covered with a chitinous material, except for brownish-red strips of fur that ran along the topsides of their bodies.

The Metrannan diners would snatch one of the scuttlers out of the pan using their heavy-duty outside pair of hands, then use their smaller close-work hands to take the little creature apart. They used the fur strips more or less as zippers, pulling back on them to peel the animals right out of their shells before popping them, still wriggling, into their mouths. The fur strip, it would appear, added a little roughage.

As a matter of justice and logic, Hannah knew there was no real difference between what the Metrannans were eating—and how they were eating it—and eating a fresh lobster that had just been boiled alive. Even so, she was just as glad that her hosts didn't expect her to try a scuttler for herself. Sometimes, having an incompatible biochemistry was a good thing.

Instead, she noted that a small bowl of what appeared to be yogurt or porridge and a plastic spoon had been set at her place. Somehow, she couldn't work up much of an appetite for that, either. She noticed the servers didn't bring anything at all to the Xenoatrics. She had no idea what they ate, if anything. Maybe they simply plugged themselves into recharging receptacles.

The Metrannans at her table seemed intent on ignoring her, and instead conversed among themselves in Metrannan. Based on the nervous glances they directed at Tigmin, who was seated at a nearby table, her guess was that they were waiting for some sort of cue from the powers-that-be before they risked dealing with an alien, especially one from a disreputable Younger Race species.

The Xenoatric to her right, however, was quite another story. "I am Maintainer of Calm," it announced in mechanically accented Lesser Trade Speech. "You are either the human Wolfson or the human Mendez."

"I am Wolfson," said Hannah, a trifle startled. Should she have spoken first? Introduced herself? "Forgive me if my actions do not suit the required etiquette. This is all quite new to me."

"Your apology is needless. The general rule is for the senior party to speak first, and the junior party not to speak until addressed."

So all the Metrannans around the table are the ones violating etiquette. Interesting. "I thank you for clarifying that point." It occurred to Hannah that it was possible this Unseen One could provide her with some useful information. "I have almost no experience of your people. Bulwark of Constancy was present at a—ah—ceremony—I attended this morning, and Bulwark of Constancy is here tonight, but I have not noted that being speaking to anyone at all. I had started to wonder if that was the way of all the Unseen." She glanced across the room to the table that held Bulwark of Constancy and saw Bulwark was still motionless.

"Ah, yes, the well-named Bulwark of Constancy. But what does such a Bulwark do when the landscape itself shifts and changes around oneself? It is not unknown for those of our kind to behave in the manner of Bulwark of Constancy when under great stress."

"And perhaps the recent changes in how the Metrannans govern themselves have been stressful enough to cause Bulwark of Constancy's behavior?"

"Perhaps," Maintainer of Calm said doubtfully. "But while I have found the pace of change unpleasant, you will observe that I have not become excessively withdrawn, and neither have any of the other Unseen present here this evening. I would suggest there must be some other, additional cause for Bulwark's behavior, though I could not say what it might be. But I wish to learn more about your own mission here. There are many conflicting stories. Are you in fact here to avenge your fallen colleague?"

Hannah hadn't heard that idea before. "Ah, no. We are here seeking the cause of his disappearance. So far we have not found anything to suggest that it was anything more than an accident." Hannah felt a twinge of guilt for lying to the kindly Xenoatric. It was, after all, the first being she had met on this world who didn't want anything from her or suspect her of crimes.

"Indeed? You surprise me. But perhaps you are in possession of facts you have not yet integrated."

It was the most polite way anyone had ever told Hannah that it was obvious she was lying. "You are very kind," she said.

"In any event, there are many, Unseen and Metrannan alike, who would be most interested in your missing colleague's mission. It is said in many versions of the tale that he was somehow involved in an attempt to recover the lost longlife treatment."

"But why would that be of so much interest to the Unseen?" Hannah asked.

"Because we are few, and the Metrannans are many. Our Enclave in the city is smaller than it once was, and in fact has grown smaller and smaller across the centuries. If the Metrannans suddenly were longer-lived, there would no doubt be many more of them. There would be still greater pressure on the Enclave—and what would become of us?"

You could always move somewhere else. Hannah thought the words, but was not foolish enough to speak them. The idea might seem obvious to her, but she was from a species whose entire recorded history wasn't long enough to be a rounding error in the annals of the Unseen Beings. She could not even imagine how much remaining in a particular place could affect a culture that had lived in that same spot for millions of years.

There were other populations of the Unseen on other worlds—but that was far from saying that the Unseen of Metran would be welcome there. Then Hannah thought of the Xenoatrics she had seen headed for departing spacecraft at Free Orbit Station. Perhaps there were some Xenoatrics desperate enough to migrate—but that was no solution for the Enclave as a whole. Every Xenoatric who left was making the problem of the remaining group's survival more difficult. "I thank you for speaking openly with a stranger about such difficult questions."

Maintainer of Calm made a dismissive gesture. "The difficulty is in living with the questions. Speaking of them is not difficult at all."

Hannah could not help but look again at Bulwark of Constancy, still motionless, semicatatonic. Speaking of them was hard enough for some.

At that moment a chime sounded. Hannah blinked, and looked down at the feeding vat to see that all the scuttlers were gone. Time to change tables—preferably before she had to watch the servers bring in fresh supplies of the critters.

She said her sincere and grateful farewells to Maintainer of Calm and allowed her escort to guide her to the next table.

* * *

Jamie glared down at his third bowl of yogurtlike pap and sighed in resignation. " 'Safe Phude Fore

Peeple frum Eerth,'" he muttered to himself. If someone could have given some sort of assurance that eating a bland but human-digestible paste while wearing a black-and-white monkey suit and being ignored by a succession of tablesful of snooty aliens was going to be the official low point of his BSI career, that would have been of some help—but right at that moment, he was fully prepared to believe that it was all going to be downhill from there on in. It was only a minor consolation that Hannah hadn't had any better luck than his on her last two tables, after she had managed to draw what appeared to be a talkative Xenoatric the first time out.

His attention had wandered a bit, and it was only after the senior member of the table had arrived that he suddenly realized that his luck had changed—but he couldn't be sure if it was for better or worse. He found himself sitting next to Fallogon of the Three. The being who had interrogated him that morning.

"We are known to each other, and may dispense with introduction ritual," Fallogon said in Lesser Trade Speech the moment he sat down.

As Jamie sat, he noticed out of the corner of his eyes that the four other Metrannans at the table, and indeed most of the other Metrannans in the room, were watching in what looked rather like astonishment, and even outright envy. Who was this pap-eating Younger Race alien to be addressed by one of the Three? "Yes," he agreed meaninglessly, "we are known to each other."

"It is a pity that your biochemistry is incompatible with ours," Fallogon said. "I am told that this thatchberry soup is superb." With that, he lifted a long metal tube from the table, stuck it into fluid in the large bowl-shaped depression in front of him, and used it as an oversized drinking straw. The other Metrannans around the table did the same, and Jamie reflected on the differences in etiquette and sanitary practices from one species and culture to the next. "The soup is excellent," said Fallogon, "and I was most careful to arrange matters so that I would sit next to you at a table otherwise occupied by complete blockheads who did not speak a word of any language other than their own. And I have taken other precautions that need not concern you to ensure that, in spite of speaking in the center of a large and crowded room, we may converse in perfect privacy."

And you probably picked me to speak to instead of Hannah because she asserted her seniority. You're hoping I'll be easier to intimidate. You might even be right. He decided that the best way to keep from being pushed around would be to do some pushing of his own to start. "I see," he said. "Plainly you have arranged matters so that you might tell me something. Might I ask what?" *And ain't that a respectful way to address a planetary leader who could make you vanish even more completely than Trevor anytime he wanted?*

"You are not entirely correct," said Fallogon, staring intently at him. "I have arranged matters so that I could ask you a question. The question is as follows: Would you like to know the exact coordinates of the *Irene Adler*?"

Jamie forced down his shock and surprise as fast as he could and spoke before he had a chance to think, because he didn't dare take the *time* to think. "Yes, of course," he said. "That is what we came here to find out. If we can find the *Adler*, we stand a very good chance of knowing what happened to Agent Wilcox."

"Nonsense," said Fallogon, in a gruff, unflappable tone of voice. "Your present ship, the *Bartholomew Sholto*, arrived in our star system docked to the *Adler*. The damage to the *Sholto* is consistent with a cable under tension snapping loose. The other end of that cable was attached to the *Adler*. You did your best to mask the *Adler*'s maneuvers behind the *Sholto*'s braking burn, but you were tracked by an off-axis station that had a clear view. The *Adler* is in a distant orbit, waiting for your return."

"Your off-axis tracker must have spotted some other spacecraft in the same general volume of space. Why would we go through all that elaborate effort?" Jamie asked, in what he hoped was a calm and unworried tone. "Or more accurately, what in space made you *think* we'd go through all that effort?"

"There are two of you. The BSI has craft designed to carry two people. The *Sholto* is too cramped and small to be a suitable two-person craft. According to your statements, you were dispatched here because things were quiet enough so that your service felt you two could be spared. That makes it highly unlikely that there was a shortage of available two-person craft. Therefore, you flew here aboard the *Sholto* for some particular reason. The *Sholto* is the same type and class of ship as the *Irene Adler*. The use of identical objects when that use is odd or inconvenient always suggests an effort at deception to an intelligence professional. It does not require much imagination to come up with possible scenarios where it would be useful to have one ship masquerade as the other.

"Furthermore, if there is cable damage to the *Sholto*, there is likely similar damage, perhaps more damage, to whatever it was docked to when the cable snapped. You requested far more repair compound than would be needed by the *Sholto*. If the damage occurred back at base, you would not need additional repair compound—but you would if the cable was attached to another vehicle, and it snapped while you were traveling to Metran, and the other vehicle was damaged as well. Do I need to go on?"

"No," said Jamie, his heart pounding, his palms sweating. "You are obviously much practiced at interpreting data—and, with respect, perhaps at overinterpreting it. Why would we bring the *Adler* with us? What point would there be to our mission in the first place if we had already recovered the *Adler*?"

"Frankly, I don't know," Fallogon said. "I have been puzzling over the matter since the moment your vehicles were detected. Is Trevor Wilcox alive? Did he deliver the message? Did he complete his mission? If so, why are you here? The only reason I can think of for bringing the *Adler* along would be to have it available quickly for some reason—and yet you have left it at the edge of the star system, where it will take several days to reach it."

Fallogon was not even bothering to see if Jamie would answer the questions he asked, as if he were assuming Jamie would deny everything and simply didn't wish to bother playing out the charade.

"At last I came up with a theory that more or less fit the facts. Wilcox died or was badly incapacitated on the flight home. The *Adler* was recovered only recently. The message itself was recovered from the ship—but the decryption key was not. Or perhaps it was the key that was located, but the message that was lost. Your agency—correctly—determined that the message contained information of paramount importance, and decided—perhaps incorrectly—on the high-risk plan of sending the *Adler* along on your mission in hopes of recovering the sense of the message as rapidly as possible.

"Your desire to find out how Wilcox was killed or injured is no doubt sincerely felt, but finding that out is merely your cover story. Your true mission is to search here on Metran for any clues to where the decryption key or the message was hidden aboard the *Adler*, or else to recover a backup copy of the missing part."

"If you believe these remarkable theories to be true," said Jamie, "then why are we here? Why aren't you continuing the interrogation from this morning instead?"

"Because, contrary to what my two colleagues in the Three seem to believe, you can do us no harm," Fallogon said calmly. "They saw much the same evidence that I did and invented plots and conspiracies, plans to land the *Sholto* on the planet and kidnap—well, let us say that the list of possible victims was quite extensive and required you to have some remarkably complex motives for your actions."

Jamie wondered if he should be worried that Fallogon was willing to tell a no-account Younger Race xeno that he thought Tigmin and Yalananav were paranoid fools. *Dead men tell no tales, so tell the dead whatever you please.* "I am glad to learn that you do not fear us," he said.

"If I regarded you as a threat, you would no longer exist," Fallogon said bluntly. "If you were a mere inconvenience and offered no potential benefit to me, or to the Three, or to the peoples of Metran, you would no longer exist. However, you represent a chance—a very slim chance, at this point—for great benefit to all. I will ask you no questions at this time. Instead I call upon you to reflect and consider. But time is very short, and we do not have the leisure to play games. Therefore, I will give you these facts, with no further effort to lie or mislead on my part.

"The message carried by Wilcox contained vital data concerning the longlife treatment. Data that we have not been able to reconstruct, and likely will not be able to reconstruct anytime soon. In my estimation—not shared by my colleagues—our new Bureaucratic Order can only hold things together for a brief time. After the inevitable collapse, there will be no hope at all of reconstructing the data.

"We have a copy of the message itself—but not the decryption key. If what you call my 'remarkable theories' are in fact correct, and you are here in search of the decryption key, I can tell you flatly that it is not on this planet—or if it is here, it is hidden in such a way that an all-out search by hundreds of agents with intimate knowledge of local culture, custom, technology, and geography, working day and night with unlimited resources for months on end did not locate it.

"Every locale, every object, every vehicle even remotely connected to Hallaben, or Agent Wilcox, or anyone else associated with the case has been searched and searched and searched again. It is difficult to prove a negative. For that reason, and that reason alone, I cannot say with absolute certainty that the decryption key is not on Metran. But the odds of you and your partner locating it after we have failed are, at best, astronomical."

Jamie tried his best to give nothing away. "Is there any chance of the message being decrypted without the key?"

"Our scientists estimate that a range of ten to twenty Metran years—say, eight to sixteen of your years—as the earliest time they could have any hope of decrypting the message manually. It might take—will almost certainly take—much longer, perhaps twelve twelve-years. That is unfortunate, as I very much doubt we have even a single twelve-year left."

"But you imply that the longlife formula could save you, somehow. Wouldn't it upend things again, destabilize your society even more than it has been?"

"For all of our history, we have seen the other Elder Races with double, triple, twelve times our life span, some of them far longer than that. We learned to accept the brevity of our lives because we had to. The uprising happened not because our people had been given hope for longer lives but because that hope had been offered, and then snatched away. The Bureaucratic Order has not changed that fact—it has only imposed sufficient repression to subdue the violence—for a time. It cannot keep our people from dreaming of what they could do with lives that were twice as long— or of looking for someone to blame because that dream has been denied.

"For endless years our civilization was stable, as stable as that flat plate before you on the table. Now it is as if that same fragile plate were balanced precisely on a knifepoint. My colleagues call that 'stability.' I do not."

"But I say again, the longlife formula would simply inject a massive new instability into the situation. How could that help?"

"Because the people will be able to look forward to what they might have, what they *will* have, rather than backwards to what was stolen from them. They will have hope. The change in life span will alter many things—but, unless you care for armed guards everywhere, blackened buildings, and three old fools issuing orders for more and more security that will only end when everyone is locked up, I would suggest that things *need* alteration. Do you agree, or do you have another view?"

"I am not suicidal; therefore, I will not answer that question."

"Well put. But allow me to finish my statement, that you may reflect on it fully. If it is the case that you have the decryption key, but not the message, then there could be nothing easier than giving you another copy of the message. You may return home with it, match it with the decrypt key in the presence of our representatives, and all will be well."

"Why would you trust us with such vital information?"

"First, because I think it has been demonstrated that it is not safe or prudent to do such research here. Second, because we will *not* be trusting you. The message is held within two layers of encryption. The key sent with Wilcox merely unbuttons the first layer. There is a second-level key, held by a Metrannan diplomat on Center. A mixed team of human and Metrannan researchers will use the message to develop the actual treatments while working on Center."

Information had been so compartmentalized on the UniGov end that Jamie had not even known about the second-level key. At a guess, neither had Commander Kelly. But here he was, being briefed by the local head of the secret police. "I do not understand," Jamie said. "Why would you want or need human scientists to be involved in a vital program?"

"You are a young member of a very Young race, but you have skill in questioning," said Fallogon. "The reason is simple—and it is also the reason that the underlying data and research cannot be replicated here."

For the first time, Fallogon looked uncomfortable, even embarrassed. He shifted in his saddle-chair, and fiddled with his drinking tube. "The reason—the reason is this. Your biochemistry is different enough from mine that you do not dare try this excellent thatchberry soup. However, human and Metrannan biochemistry is in fact quite similar. Similar enough that Hallaben had no need to do much in the way of original research. He simply read a number of your scientific journals and based his work on what he found there."

Jamie had gotten a fair number of shocks already, but that one had to rate as one of the biggest. An Elder Race using *human* scientific research as the basis for a breakthrough treatment? It seemed inconceivable. His first thought was that it would be a huge propaganda win for the human race—but then he realized how much of a humiliation it would be for the Metrannans—especially on the subject of geriatrics and life extension. And would UniGov really *want* all the Elder Races suddenly realizing that humans could teach at least some of them a thing or two about biochemistry, and, perhaps, about other topics?

The human race was far too weak to dare appear as a threat to anyone. Jamie had been starting to think that the War-Starter designation had been hung on the case because of the near civil-war disturbances on Metran, or perhaps because the potential disruption caused by life extension might be as bad as a war. But maybe BSI-DLO had been more worried, and rightly so, about the dangers of humiliating Elder Races. *They wouldn't like it if they thought we were getting uppity,* he told himself.

It might well be wiser, far wiser, to continue to be underestimated while making forward progress that no one noticed. And on the other side of the coin, keeping quiet about the whole affair, providing low-profile assistance to the Metrannans, could be a very useful way to gain some leverage, to do some horse trading, to gain a useful ally.

"That is interesting information," Jamie said, in one of the great understatements of his life. "But why couldn't his successors simply return to the journals and find the information again?"

"Because all of his work notes, including the journal articles, were destroyed by those who feared change. Much good it did them. What, exactly, he studied, how he applied it, and how far different his final results were from the reading that inspired them is impossible to say. I know it sounds absurd, but one of the items our people are most eager to recover is the bibliography, the citations of what papers Hallaben read. That data, all by itself, might provide signposts enough to reconstruct the work. Without those clues, it might not be possible to replicate his work in any reasonable time, or to do it at all, based on just the few surviving reports on the results of his work. But if it *could* be done, it would require workers intimately familiar with the subject area—that is to say, human workers."

Fallogon was silent for a time. "But all this is for nothing unless we have the message and the first-level key," he said at last. "We have the message. If *you* have the key, then all is well."

Jamie knew that he was far out of his depth, so far out at sea that he couldn't even touch the bottom or see the far-off shore. "As you suggested, respected senior, I think it would be best if I reflect and consider."

"I expected no other answer," Fallogon said. "But come. I believe it is time for the next course."

Jamie looked up to see that the soup tureen in the center of the table was empty, and the other diners at the table seemed to be very pointedly not noticing that he and Fallogon were deep in conversation. Fallogon made an imperceptible gesture, and the chime sounded, signaling the end of the course. The entire room had been waiting for them—or, more accurately, for Fallogon. It would seem that this one of the Three cared not at all if everyone knew he was talking at length to a Younger Race xeno—so long as no one knew what they were saying.

Jamie pushed back his chair and stood as rapidly as he could, before Fallogon could get up, and the rest of the table did the same—one or two of them leveling undisguised glares of annoyance at Jamie. Maybe they did not care to be kept waiting between courses—or perhaps they were jealous of the attention one of the Three had lavished on him when Fallogon should have been making conversation with them.

Fallogon bowed very slightly to the others at the table, then turned once again to Jamie. "I've enjoyed our conversation," he said. "Reflect well. We shall talk again, sooner than you think."

Jamie watched as Fallogon allowed himself to be guided to his next table. "There's no hurry," Jamie said as his own escort materialized at his elbow. "No hurry at all."

TWENTY-TWO
HIDING THE LOST

The dance of the diners went on and on, from table to table, leaving Hannah feeling more and more distracted with every move, a pawn moved around too many times in too many directions. Jamie's prolonged conversation with Fallogon had been agony for her. What had that been all about? Jamie had kept up a devil of a good poker face throughout— but not good enough to fool Hannah. Something had happened. Something big.

Adding to the irritation was that Fallogon talking to Jamie was seen as some sort of signal that humans were acceptable dinner companions, even fashionable. Stony silence turned to endless condescending chitchat from every Metrannan who spoke Lesser Trade, all of whom seemed suddenly eager to tell her how clever it was of humans to have survived as long as they had, and how they were sure to get some scraps of good-quality technology, and, better still, advice, from the wise and good Metrannans—perhaps even from the Unseen Beings.

It took all of Hannah's training, along with every drop of patience she could muster, to be civil in the face of it all, even as she faced two more courses for her hosts that looked no more appetizing than the first one, while she received yet another bowl of yogurt-substitute at every table. It left her very little chance to think things through.

But the next time the chime sounded, she found herself in luck, at least of a sort. Taranarak was seated next to her. But on second thought, Hannah could not believe there was any luck or chance involved in the fact that she was not only at the same table as Learned Searcher Taranarak, but at a table wherein Taranarak was the most senior, thus placing her right next to Hannah. The only real luck that Hannah could see was that the dish being served at her new table was a salad. It was not moving and did not appear to be alive. But even so, she was going to stick with her yogurt-substitute.

It had to be that they had been deliberately placed together. But by whom, and for what reason? She had to assume Fallogon had manipulated things at least insofar as seating himself next to Jamie—but that did not mean he was the only one manipulating the game of musical chairs. For the moment, it didn't matter. What she had to decide was what to do about it.

"We are known to each other, and thus may dispense with rituals of introduction," Taranarak announced to Hannah.

"Yes, we know each other," Hannah agreed. What a strange and rigid world this was, where announcing that one could forgo a ritual had become a ritual in and of itself. But Taranarak was not "known" to Hannah in any meaningful way. Hannah had only learned her name while en route to the mission, had only met her the day before, and by the most generous calculation, they had spent only a couple of hours in each other's presence.

Even so, Taranarak was as close to an ally, a partner, in this case as Hannah was likely to get. And Taranarak was willing, even eager, to talk. However, that was of limited value, given their fellow diners and their surroundings, and the near certainty that their conversation was being monitored. But Hannah's own ignorance was so profound that her gut feeling was that she had to grab any chance to question her.

Obviously, anything discussed during their little chat on the aircar landing pad had to be off-limits. But there *had* to be something worth asking that could be spoken of here. Hannah remembered something Taranarak had said either a lifetime ago or the day before. *"I will tell you things you will quickly learn in any event from studying our news reports, or by speaking with any person you might meet."* That was the key. What was common and everyday knowledge to everyone in the room who wasn't human?

A thought came to her. Learned Searcher Hallaben. He was at the center of the case. In a sense, he had set everything in motion—then vanished from the stage. Hannah leaned toward Taranarak and spoke in low tones, trusting to the noise and bustle in the room to keep the others at the table from hearing—and hoping none of them would try and intrude on the conversation. She had to assume there were listening devices directed at her, but why should she care if she kept to topics that were common knowledge? "I wish to know about the death of Hallaben," she said without preliminaries. "I am not even clear as to when, exactly, it happened."

"Hallaben died two days after Special Agent Wilcox departed," Taranarak said, seeming puzzled that Hannah would bother asking about such a minor matter.

"That seems a particularly inconvenient moment for him to depart life."

"Is there ever a convenient time for death?" Taranarak asked, nibbling thoughtfully on a stalk of something celery-like she had fished out of the salad. "And, for example, it would have been far more inconvenient if he had died two days *before* Special Agent Wilcox departed."

Which is another way of saying that he died as soon as he was no longer useful, Hannah said to herself. She didn't see anything to be gained in sharing that thought with Taranarak. "What, precisely, was the cause of death?" she asked.

Taranarak gestured dismissively. "Old age," she said. "He was found in his quarters the next morning. As I recall, the postmortem reported that he had died about eight to twelve hours before he was found, of sudden-onset-aging syndrome, if you want the technical term."

"Sudden onset?" An alarm bell started to go off in the back of Hannah's mind. Someone else had died of what might well be termed sudden-onset-aging syndrome.

"It's a perfectly ordinary way to die," Taranarak said, "even for a geriatrics researcher. Hallaben was a trifle young to die that way, but not remarkably so. In fact, the syndrome is more or less a side effect of living a healthy life. It's the death we hope for."

"I do not understand."

"We Metrannans often say farewell to our friends by saying 'May you live long and die quickly.' As I am sure you are aware by now, we have made only very limited progress in extending our life span." Taranarak grimaced in the Metrannan version of an ironic smile.

"Yes, I am aware of that," Hannah said, playing along. *Except for a certain longlife treatment we won't mention in public or near microphones.*

"However, we have made great strides in delaying the onset of the *symptoms* of old age. Instead of spending the last few years of life in gradual decline, generally speaking, Metrannans enjoy vigorous good health—until the very end stages of life. At some point, the body stops responding to the various medications that prevent physical decline, and the subject experiences rapid, sometimes sudden, even abrupt, deterioration.

"We have learned to hold off the decline for years, but then it comes all at once. That is an oversimplification, but it is close enough. A Metrannan of advanced years will awaken one day, perfectly capable, active, and alert. By evening she might be muddleheaded, tired, and confused. That night, or the next, one organ will fail, releasing toxins that cause another to shut down, releasing another wave of toxins, and so on. Once it is set in motion, the cascade effect can proceed very quickly, normally in a day or two—sometimes much faster, half a day or so."

"From what you say, the whole process, from onset to death, takes something like three to five days. Was Hallaben exhibiting symptoms by the time Wilcox departed?" Hannah asked, trying for a tone of voice that would suggest that she offered the question for no other reason than force of habit and reflex, because investigators thought in terms of witnesses, sequences, evidence. Not because she was starting to see it, to understand.

Taranarak frowned. "No. But that in and of itself doesn't mean anything. The process doesn't take place on a rigid schedule. I was speaking in generalities. But there is at least a theory that onset can actually be triggered by the release of tension. One finishes a job, or a worry goes away, and one allows oneself to relax, to breathe easy again— and, so goes the theory, that in and of itself can trigger sudden-onset-aging syndrome if the subject is already susceptible."

"So, just to play it safe, a Metrannan should never finish all his or her work."

If Taranarak recognized that as a joke, she showed no sign of thinking it funny. "Perhaps not," she said, a touch of frost in her voice.

Hannah frowned and turned her attention to her yogurt-substitute, spooning the tasteless stuff into her mouth. Was she reaching, trying too hard, bashing together puzzle pieces that didn't really fit each other? It all *sounded* perfectly routine and ordinary—but on the other hand, Taranarak had just described a Metrannan who died of something he was too young to die of, died of it faster than usual without any of the normal early symptoms, died of it just after the discovery he had made had been successfully suppressed by sending it off-planet, and died of it alone.

Add to all that the fact that Hallaben was the most important scientist on the planet, that the Order Bureaucracy was run by a pack of borderline paranoids, and that, nonetheless, his death was apparently met with no interest all, and the alarm buzzers in Hannah's head were sounding twice as loud. There was an old rule of thumb in internal investigations: If there's a serious crime that a corrupt police official hasn't looked into, assume he is a suspect.

"Agent Wolfson, it is time to shift to our next tables."

"Huh? What? Oh!" Hannah looked up to see everyone else getting up from the table.

"I had to call to you twice," Taranarak said with a smile. "You seemed to be enjoying your food quite intently."

"Oh, yes. Absolutely," said Hannah, scanning the room to see what table Jamie was headed to this time. As far as she understood at least, this was to be the final course. All they had to do was get through it, and they would be all right. But then she saw that whoever it was pushing the pieces around the game board was not quite done with them yet.

Jamie was being seated next to Bulwark of Constancy.

* * *

From any distance away, Jamie reflected as he sat down, a being encased in a carapace that resembled a metallic lobster on ostrich legs merely looked ridiculous. From a distance of roughly eighty centimeters, the same being was absolutely terrifying. Jamie found himself understanding exactly what a jack-lighted deer felt like.

But Bulwark of Constancy declined the opportunity to lunge at Jamie, pin him to the table, and tear out his vital organs. Instead it stalked to the table, folded its legs, and remained utterly stationary. The four Metrannans at the table were obviously just as nervous as Jamie was. Having seen the behavior of the other Metrannans and Xenoatrics during the meal, it didn't take much to deduce it was Bulwark of Constancy that worried them and not Unseen Beings in general. That knowledge did nothing to comfort Jamie.

Jamie decided that the best reaction was no re-action at all. He reached for his inevitable bowl of pap and began to eat it as slowly and carefully as possible, trying to make it last as long as he could, doing his best to look straight ahead and at nothing else at all.

"We are known to each other," said a loud booming voice in his ear. Jamie jumped half out of his chair and nearly threw his bowl of flavor-free paste across the room. "We may dispense with rituals of introduction."

Jamie turned and saw that Bulwark of Constancy had shifted its body around and bent its head—if it was a head—down to be exactly level with Jamie's face, no more than ten centimeters away. "Good," said Jamie. "Yes. Right. I agree."

Bulwark of Constancy studied Jamie's face for an uncomfortably long time and spoke again. "You should be killed," Bulwark of Constancy announced, then pulled its head back and up to the vertical position and resumed its previous motionless state.

"Right," Jamie muttered in English. He realized he was gripping his bowl and his spoon almost hard enough to snap them to pieces. He relaxed his hands and tried to calm himself. "Got it," he went on, half-babbling. "Thanks for the information. And just by the way, if you're wondering why you don't get invited to more parties, I think I have a theory."

But right at that moment, it would have suited Jamie right down to the ground if *he* was never invited to another dinner party, ever again.

* * *

At long last it was over. Hannah collected her jacket and rushed to find Jamie. It wasn't hard to do, as he was searching for her. "We have to talk," she said. "Now, and fast. I found out more than I wanted to know."

"I sure hope you didn't find out more than I did, or else we're in real trouble," said Jamie, his face pale and his expression grim. "Scratch that. We're in real trouble no matter what. Let's get outside, where there's at least a chance no one will be listening."

"No argument from me," said Hannah. She grabbed him by the forearm and half dragged him outside to the area around the aircar landing pad. The night was dark, and though the landing pad itself was well lit, there was only spotty illumination around its edges. The other dinner attendees were there as well, of course, chatting among themselves and waiting for their transportation. There wasn't enough light for signing or shorthand, but that didn't matter. Between the darkness, the out-door setting, and the ambient noise of other conversation and the aircars coming and going, they ought to be private enough. And if not, then so be it. They had to talk no matter what the risk. Keeping their voices low and using English would have to be sufficient security.

But it was obvious they both had news. Who should go first? Hannah decided that as the senior agent present, she had more of a need to know everything soonest. "All right," she said. "You get the first slot. What have you got?"

"Fallogon knows everything," said Jamie. "Or more accurately, he's *deduced* just about everything. Practically everything about our mission, down to the *Adler* taking damage when the *Sholto* did. He knows we're after either the message or the decrypt key. He was hoping *we* had the key, because they have another copy of the message. I did my damnedest to keep from confirming it all, but he barely bothered to ask me if he had figured it all out correctly. There's more, but that's a start. Oh, plus here's a real shocker. Whenever Bulwark of Constancy takes time out from being catatonic, he or she or it or whatever is certifiably, homicidally, insane—and not much of a conversationalist. What have you got?"

But Hannah didn't get the chance to answer. "You both here. Good. Both you come," said a deep-throated voice behind her, speaking in thickly accented Lesser Trade Speech. "Fallogon want you both."

Hannah resisted the temptation to curse in every language she knew. "What I've got is plenty—maybe," she said. "It might be nothing at all. But obviously it's going to have to wait." She turned to face the guard who had found them. " 'Lay on, Macduff,' " she said to the guard, " 'and damn'd be him that first cries, "Hold, enough!" ' " It seemed unlikely that the guard's English was any better than his Lesser Trade Speech, but it did no harm to quote the classics.

* * *

Five minutes later Hannah was standing alongside Jamie, Fallogon, and Taranarak, watching the aircar that was supposed to get them back home lifting off into the sky. At least it would serve to take their guards back to base. Fallogon had announced to the guards that he would be flying the humans home, and, needless to say, no one argued with him.

Once they were aboard Fallogon's aircar, even Hannah and Jamie were willing to accept the arrangement. Two of the saddle-seats had been pulled out, and a basic but comfortable rear-facing bench seat wide enough for two humans had been installed instead. They both sat down on it gratefully.

Their host gestured with his left strongwork arm and the car took off. Hannah craned her neck around to peek into the forward driver's compartment. The guard/pilot was sitting there, watching the aircar's automatic systems do the flying for him.

"The flight is short," said Fallogon, "and there is much to discuss. For what it is worth, I can assure you that there are no listening devices or recording systems in this vehicle. Our talk will remain among the four of us."

"Forgive me, sir," said Jamie, "but that assurance is not worth a great deal precisely because *you* are one of the four—and also one of the Three, if you can forgive a very small joke."

"I can forgive it," Fallogon replied evenly. "But we all seek the same thing."

"An explanation for the loss of the *Adler* and the death of Special Agent Trevor Wilcox III?" Hannah asked sharply.

Fallogon made a small gesture of dismissal with his closework hands. "We need not concern ourselves with cover stories," he said.

"If there has ever been a law enforcement service in this galaxy that did not concern itself with the murder of its own officers or agents by a foreign power, then that service cannot have survived for long," said Hannah. Out of the corner of her eye, she saw Jamie looking at her in shock and surprise, but she paid him no mind. She had to stay focused on Fallogon.

"You come very close to implying that I ordered

the death of Trevor Wilcox," Fallogon said in a low and dangerous voice.

"No, sir. I imply no such thing. You would have no motive for such an act. You did not do it. But it is quite obvious that there are competing centers of power on this world and that they work at cross-purposes."

"What evidence do you have that he was murdered?"

"None that I wish to discuss at this time," said Hannah.

"Which I take it to mean in this company," said Fallogon. "But you also claim the loss of the *Adler*. I dispute that claim. My people tracked a vehicle with a thrust signature that was quite similar to that of the *Sholto* and precisely the same as the recently recorded thrust signature of the *Adler*, flying well aft of the *Sholto* in a manner that was obviously an attempt at maneuver-masking."

Hannah hadn't expected them to be able to get good enough data to get a thrust signature. And maybe they hadn't. It could easily be a bluff. But what did that matter? What good did it do to pretend any longer? But still, she could not quite bring herself to come straight out and agree that he was right. "That which has been lost can sometimes be found again," she said. "If the brief summing-up I got from Special Agent Mendez is accurate—then you are very much hoping that is true not just for ships, but for documents that have gone astray."

"Are you all talking about the message sent

with Wilcox?" Taranarak asked. She looked at Fallogon. "*Has* it been found?" she asked.

"Be silent for now," Fallogon said to her. "We are not dealing with your area of expertise." He turned back to Hannah. "Things are near the breaking point," he said. "We are past the point of playing games and scoring points with clever gambits. This planet is like a sealed and pressurized container that is exposed to heat. Such a vessel might be very near its failure point and show no outward sign of trouble. Only in the moment that it bursts open are the stresses revealed, and only then are the contents of the vessel released. As I explained to young Mendez, the sense of order and control on this world is illusory. If we can restart the research into the longlife treatment, the stress and pressure will be vastly reduced. We will be able to hold together long enough to restore and revive our society. Therefore, I must ask you the same question Learned Searcher Taranarak just asked of me. Has it been found? Do you have the decryption key?"

That question was clear and limited enough that Hannah was willing to take the risk of answering it. "No," she said. "We do not have it or know where it is, or even know if it still exists."

"Have you no leads? No clues?"

Hannah was about to say no to that as well, but she didn't get the chance. "Our investigations continue, sir," Jamie said. "We do not wish to go further than that."

That signal was clear enough. Jamie didn't want her to answer. Either Jamie *hadn't* had the chance to tell her everything he had learned over dinner, or he had spotted some other clue that she had missed—or else he was playing some other sort of game. But Jamie Mendez had learned the hard way some time before about saying too much too early. It didn't matter. Her partner was trying to keep her from saying "no." So she didn't.

Fallogon seemed annoyed. He stared at Jamie while addressing Hannah. "I must say, Special Agent Wolfson, that your junior partner is not afraid to speak back to his betters. Is it wise to work with someone quite so given to rashness?"

"There is a human saying, sir, that one should not judge a book by its cover. And I have had many occasions to learn that I should trust Agent Mendez's judgment."

She glanced toward Jamie, and was startled by the expression on his face. She had expected something like a slight nod of thanks or a calm neutrality. Instead what she saw was distracted surprise. Jamie had just thought of something, realized something.

Fallogon did not notice. "Very well," he said. He glanced out the window. "We are approaching our destination. It has been a long day for all of us. We will continue this tomorrow, after you have had a chance to discuss matters among yourselves. And I should advise you to include Learned Searcher Taranarak in your conversations as much as possible—for I have no doubt you *will* be dealing quite a bit with her area of expertise. I will arrange for you to have free access between your portable quarters and her home."

"That will be most helpful, sir," said Hannah, glad for a reason to be courteous and appreciative. She wasn't comfortable rubbing Fallogon the wrong way for as long as they just had. "We thank you for it."

Fallogon shrugged. "I assure you, it is for my bene—"

There was a sudden flash of light, then another, and finally a third. Then, a heartbeat behind, as the slower-traveling sound reached them, a roaring blast, then another, then a third, smaller, sharper, harder explosion. Hannah looked down to their gondola, and to Taranarak's house—or rather, to the pillars of fire where they had once been.

Their own car lurched sideways and slewed around to a new heading before boosting out of the area on full power, thrusting almost hard enough to knock Jamie and Hannah into the Metrannans' laps. "It's an attack!" Fallogon shouted.

Hannah kept her attention on the ground. She could see that a third and smaller pillar of fire was all that remained of the aircar that had been meant to carry their party. It looked as if it had been hit in midair by some sort of missile and then crashed. The guards inside it must surely be dead.

And if Taranarak, Jamie, and she had been in

that aircar, the one they were supposed to be in, they would have been dead too.

The driver of their own vehicle boosted to a higher altitude and took off, headed due south, away from the flaming ruins of their quarters, their transport, and Taranarak's home.

TWENTY-THREE

GAMBLE BLUFF GAMBIT

Jamie gritted his teeth and hung on for dear life as the aircar bounced and jounced along the sky. It didn't have the same glass-smooth acceleration compensators as their gondola—and their nice comfortable bench seat didn't come with seat belts. But then the ride steadied down as the driver guard took over from the automatics.

Fallogon was the first to regain his composure. "Agent Wolfson, I have an important question," he said in a calm but urgent voice. "Your ship—the *Sholto*—does it have a self-destruct system?"

"What? Ah, yes. Of course." Any ship that might carry sensitive data or information did. Jamie was surprised Fallogon had even bothered to ask.

"Powerful enough to do damage to surrounding structures? I think it likely that your ship might be a target of the same attackers that just struck. I am concerned about the safety of the Free Orbit Station."

Hannah hesitated before she answered. "Yes. At least it's possible. The standard spaceside destruct system was replaced with a far more powerful unit just before we left. We, of course, switched to the groundside destruct system when we disembarked, and it is active now. It *should* just melt or wreck sensitive gear. It shouldn't be possible to activate the spaceside destruct—but the wiring and mods were done in a terrible hurry. It is possible they were cross-connected—or that the groundside destruct could touch it off."

That sounded incredibly unlikely to Jamie. He knew Hannah well enough to have a sense of when she was bluffing. Gunther's team wouldn't have and couldn't have cross-connected the two systems. Most likely Hannah was just thinking fast and had something else on her mind. Quite possibly it was nothing more than the fact that, even if just the groundside destruct system were activated, it would render the *Sholto* permanently inoperable. Probably Hannah just didn't want to be stranded.

For his part, Jamie had just learned some things that very much made him want to get back to the *Adler* as quickly as possible. Maybe Hannah had as well, and saw no reason to stop Fallogon from helping that happen quickly. "Do you truly believe that such an attack is possible?" Jamie asked. "And if so, why worry about our self-destruct system when we've just seen a bomb attack? Why wouldn't they try to hit our ship the same way? After an explosion as big as the ones we just saw, it won't really matter so much if the ship's self-destruct system blows."

"We would be foolish indeed to assume that whoever blew up your mobile quarters, Taranarak's house, and that aircar won't strike again. However, I doubt anyone is lunatic enough to risk using a bomb on a spacecraft docked at Free Orbit Level Station. They will assume you three are dead. They will have no need to attack your ship. But they may wish to *search* it. And if they do that, and attempt to open the hatches—well, you see the problem."

Fallogon thought again. "We have the advantage of their believing you three are now dead—but virtually all the other advantages are with the attacker. And whoever it is clearly has access and resources. We are going to have to think very carefully—and very fast."

"Sir, if all you say is true, and it certainly seems to be, then it is essential that we return to our ship at once and protect it," Jamie said. *If for no other reason than we don't want to be stranded here waiting for your civil war to start up again.*

"You must do more than merely return to your ship," said Fallogon. "You must leave the planet— and it should now be obvious that it will be very difficult for us to protect you, let alone for you to protect your ship."

"Why?" Taranarak said, finding her voice for the first time since she witnessed the destruction of her home. "What is the reason for all this? Why kill us and blow up our homes?"

"Because someone apparently still believes you

have a chance of producing the longlife treatment and does not want you to succeed." Fallogon thought for a moment, then touched a stud on a small panel by his chair and spoke in Metrannan. "I have told the driver to use full emergency speed and detection avoidance and to get us to the Groundside Station liftpod center as soon as possible, and to arrange for a habitable liftpod to be prepped and ready when we get there."

"What's a liftpod?" Jamie asked.

"It is a small wholly automated reactionless-thrust spacecraft customized for the fastest possible transit between Groundside and Free Orbit Station. Liftpods are used for emergency medical evacuations, movement of urgent cargo, and similar things. They are far more expensive to operate than the Elevator cars—but using one of them now will be much less expensive than having a hole blasted through Free Orbit Level Station."

"You mean that's it?" Jamie asked. "We're leaving now? We've been on-planet less than a day."

"And in that time you have, in effect, been put on trial for your lives and been the target of a violent assassination attempt committed by someone who didn't worry about killing my guards in the process. I will see to it that they *learn* to worry about that in the near future. But I think you have had demonstration enough that this is a dangerous place. Beyond those points, I can assure you, with near-absolute certainty, that the decryption key is not on this planet. There is no sense in offering yourselves as targets—and endangering those around you—while you waste time searching for what is not here."

And no sense in your keeping a destabilizing influence around one heartbeat longer than you have to, thought Jamie. "I see the force of your arguments," he said. It seemed quite likely to him that what was really going on was that Fallogon had invented the whole theory of the bad guys— whoever they were—poking around the *Sholto.* Probably the real story was that Fallogon had concluded that they didn't have the decrypt key. Therefore, they could be of no help to him. Very shortly after reaching that conclusion he had been handed a most compelling reason, or perhaps excuse, for getting the two troublesome humans out of his hair and on their way home.

He turned to Hannah and spoke again, still in Lesser Trade. "It looks as if we have wasted the trip," he said. "All of it for nothing." It was an odd sort of bluff. He was certain—well, almost certain, or at least reasonably sure—that he had found something big. Very big. But until he had a chance to think and to talk things out with Hannah, he saw no reason to tell Fallogon anything at all.

For all Jamie knew, Fallogon himself could have ordered the bombing attack. Jamie had no doubt that Fallogon was capable of it. The only real question was whether he would kill his own people. Perhaps he faked the death of the guards in the other aircar—or perhaps he sacrificed them for the sake of making it all that much more convincing.

"If you have gained nothing," said Taranarak, "then I have lost everything. My home has been destroyed! They sought to kill me as well."

Fallogon looked at her evenly. "Yes, they did," he said. "Or at least so it appears. But as you have been scheming and conspiring to depart for Center with these humans since the moment you learned they were inbound toward our planet, I wonder if appearances could be deceiving. Perhaps Tigmin and Yalananav were thrown off the scent by the manner in which those emergency rations got aboard the *Sholto*. I was not. But I would suggest that anyone willing to climb aboard a spaceship with a pair of alien security agents is not likely to be overly sentimental about her home. They will depart aboard their ship. You will travel with them. None of you will be permitted to return and incite further trouble. I will not be fool enough to throw away the chance to be rid of you all when it is offered to me."

It was Taranarak's turn to be shocked and afraid. She gasped. Her eyes widened, her outer arms gripped the handrails of her saddle-seat, and her closework hands clasped themselves together. "I—protest!" she managed to say at last.

"Your protest is noted. Your protest will have no effect whatsoever on my decision. Now, if you will all excuse me, I am the head of security, and there has just been a major attack on the city. I have a great deal of work to do." And with that, he unfolded a portable desk from beside his seat, activated a display screen, put on a commset headphone, switched on a hush field, and set out to ignore his passengers altogether for the remainder of the flight.

Jamie stared at him in bewilderment. It was an astonishingly rapid change of attitude. Exactly how many parts had he seen Fallogon play that day? And what, exactly, was the game he was playing? And on which side—or sides—was he playing? Then he realized there was far more consistency than he had seen at first. All he had to do was see everything through the lens of *whatever would get the longlife treatment back.*

If that meant misdirecting the questioning to protect the humans in the morning, but feeding them information in the evening, so be it. If it meant dismissing them altogether the moment they were not of use, arranging their departure, then saddling them with a Metrannan troublemaker more determined than he was to get the formula, that was not a problem. A skilled chess player might go to all lengths to defend a particular piece—then sacrifice it in a heartbeat if doing so would ensure a win. It was a perfectly acceptable and proper gambit, and it would never occur to anyone to object to it.

Unless, of course, one was the chess piece in question.

* * *

The liftpod was a thirty-meter-long needle-nosed silver bullet lying on its side. It had a forward nose skid, two aft skids for landing gear, and a personnel hatch up toward the bow, but was otherwise featureless. The hatch was hinged at the bottom, so as to open out into an access ramp.

A harried tech was rattling off a hurried explanation of what was going to happen, and Taranarak—who was scarcely less flustered—was doing her best to translate what he was saying into Lesser Trade. It was not going well.

Eighty meters away, Fallogon's aircar was already buttoning up again. It lifted off almost at once, abandoning Jamie, Hannah, and Taranarak to their fate—and, probably more importantly, getting Fallogon away fast. If he wasn't there long, it increased the chances that he could get away with claiming he had never been there at all. In the snake pit of Metrannan politics, there could be any number of reasons he might need to deny it.

Only a few hundred meters away was Groundside Station, somehow looking even more like the Tower of Babel in the dimness of the predawn hours.

"You—that is, ah, we—will be sealed into the passenger cabin," Taranarak was saying, echoing what the tech was saying. "It will be small, a tight fit, but you—we—should all fit. Air content and pressure and gravity will all be normal throughout the journey. There are no viewports and only one small status board. This is a vehicle for rapid emergency transport, not for tourists to look at the passing scenery. As soon as the hatch is sealed and they have run the last checks, the vehicle will go into, ah, horizontal hover, and lift to about—let's see, it would be about fifty of your meters, if I have that right. The landing skids will retract.

"The liftpod will rotate until the nose points directly down—no! forgive me! until the nose points exactly *up*. The liftpod will accelerate to about, oh, in human measures, about eight hundred kilometers an hour very quickly and hold that speed for the first few minutes, until it is clear of the lower atmosphere. The liftpod will then accelerate at, let's see, let me convert, about thirty-eight of your acceleration units—yes, thirty-eight gravities. It will shut down its engines and coast for a brief period while it rotates to put its engines forward.

"It will decelerate at the same rate and come to rest a few twelves of meters above the target point on Free Orbit Station.

"It will make a landing in the same horizontal attitude, about eighty-four meters from the *Sholto*. The hatch will open automatically, and an air tunnel will form between our landing point and the *Sholto*. There will be air pressure so that we may walk from the liftpod to the *Sholto*. All is completely automatic."

"How long?" Jamie asked. He was thinking of the tactical situation and doing his best to squeeze out every bit of information possible. Any minor detail might be the one that saved their lives. "How long will it take us to get there?"

"Hmmm? What? Didn't I say? Forgive me. Let me figure the conversion. About one and a twelfth of your hours, if I have that right."

"Which do you think would be scarier to calculate," asked Hannah. "Our maximum velocity or our average velocity?"

"Both, when you consider we're going to do the whole run about a hundred meters away from the cable cluster," said Jamie. "Wouldn't it be fun if we hit it? Thanks, Taranarak."

They walked a few paces away from the Metrannans and looked up at the vehicle and the cable cluster. "Well, here we are," Jamie said, "with all our clothes, equipment, and food blown up, and we ourselves presumably presumed dead. All we've got is the clothes we're standing up in, plus whatever we have in my pockets and your handbag, which means there's me in my tuxedo and you in your very lovely evening gown, along with a Metrannan in fancy dress who's halfway to being in shock and has no supplies of her own at all—besides the supply of emergency rations she had smuggled onto our ship. We're about to be loaded into a giant lawn dart, then fired into space so we can get to our own ship before a set of possibly ruthless and/or imaginary bad guys can try to break into it and maybe set off the self-destruct system and strand us here on this lovely planet. And if we get past all *that,* we have to shoehorn all three of us into a ship meant for one person, boost as fast as we can for the outer system, then figure out what we do from there. It seems to me we're in trouble. Again."

"Thanks for the summing up," said Hannah. "Don't ever volunteer to be the morale officer."

Taranarak was halfway across the tarmac to the liftpod's hatch. She gestured and called to them to hurry up. "You try hurrying in a gravity field that's an extra twenty-one percent," Jamie growled. "That's one bright spot about leaving sooner than we thought," he said to Hannah. "Maybe my feet will stop hurting." Then Jamie remembered there were problems going the other way, and he upped his pace, to get to Taranarak sooner. "Taranarak!" he called out. "Gravity aboard our ships is only about four-fifths of what you're used to—and we sure don't have any meds on our ship that could help you."

Taranarak had been looking spooked and disoriented to start with. Hours before she had been at a fashionable dinner party hosted by the rulers of the planet. Since then her home had been destroyed before her eyes in an attempt on her life and she had been ordered into exile. Jamie's words seemed to take a minute to penetrate into her brain. "What? Oh! Yes!" She turned to the technician and spoke with him. He spoke into a pocket comm unit, listened, then spoke to her again.

"Very good. My thanks for thinking of that.

They have a small stock of a palliative drug that should at least see me through the first few days."

"Good. I *think* we can adjust the onboard gravity to help you, but I don't know the ship's systems that well. Ah, you might also ask if they could provide you with some clothes suitable for wear on the ship—and any other small necessities. We won't have *anything* suitable for use by a Metrannan." They might even have trouble scrounging up supplies for her once they got back to Center—if they made it that far—but there was no point in worrying that far ahead.

"Excellent, excellent suggestions." She turned to the tech again, who seemed to be starting to feel harassed himself. He gave another positive reply, though not as cheerful a one. Taranarak turned back to Jamie. "They will grab whatever they can off their supply shelves in the next two short-duration units, throw it all in a container, and put it aboard the liftpod with us. But we must board *now*."

"No argument from me," said Jamie. "They've already tried to blow us up once. Let's go."

* * *

The interior of the liftpod's passenger section was an almost featureless cylinder, completely covered in a sort of yellowish-white padding material, just spongy enough to be a little bit hard to walk on. There were thick woven loops set at regular intervals into the floor, the side panels and the overhead panels to serve either as handholds or as strap-down points for cargo.

By the hatch there was a combination door-control and status panel set at eye level for a Metrannan, and the interior of the hatch was padded with the same material as the rest of the compartment. That was it. Obviously the idea was to leave the interior wide open, to leave as much space as possible for whatever might be needed in a rush at Free Orbit Level Station. From Hannah's point of view, no seats at all was a major improvement over Metrannan-style saddle-seats. The moment the hatch was shut, she kicked over her shoes and lay down with her feet on the floor, her head propped up a bit on the padded side of the interior. "Wake me up when we get there," she said, "and I'm almost not kidding."

Jamie loosened his tie, pulled off his own shoes, and sat down next to her. "Um, don't you think that maybe we should talk about a few things?"

"No," said Hannah. "I think we should rest. Once that hatch opens on the station, we've got to get outside, deal with whatever the situation is, get aboard the *Sholto*, and get away. There's nothing I know about that we have to discuss that will matter between now and when we boost off the station. After we get *that* done, we'll have lots of time to talk, and enough to talk about to keep us busy until we match course with the *Adler*. And we'll have a lot more chance to talk privately. For all we know, Fallogon set this whole thing up from start to finish to get us aboard this hypersonic padded cell so he could listen in on all the hidden mikes, and Taranarak is in on it with him, and *she's* wired for sound and had an intensive course in English before we got to the planet."

"You *are* paranoid. Maybe with reason, I grant, but even so." Jamie glanced over at Taranarak. She was squatted down on the deck and digging through the small box of odds and ends that were going to be all the Metrannan goods she would have for a while. Maybe for the rest of her life. "Right about now she looks more like someone almost catatonic with shock and not so much like a secret agent."

"Yeah, well, later on I'll tell you about my slightly more realistic theory that says Hallaben's unfortunate death was no accident. The point is that if we get killed before we get aboard the *Sholto* and out of here, none of it matters—and once we're aboard the *Sholto*, it won't matter if Taranarak is a plant. How could she report back? Plus it'll be a lot easier to speak privately in any event. We can hide in the *Sholto*'s air lock and pull the hatch shut if we want."

"*I* won't want," said Jamie. "I was locked in that air lock for long enough."

"Whatever. But for now, the best we can do for ourselves is rest up as best we can, check whatever gear we actually have, and think about what it might take to get us back to the *Sholto*."

There was a faint hum and a low whistling

sound from the outside of the ship. "Were those takeoff noises?" Hannah asked.

Jamie stood up and went over to the status display. "No," he said in a strained, mock-calm sort of voice. "We missed the takeoff. If I'm doing *my* conversions right, we are already at about two thousand meters and climbing—and if you want to stay sane, don't think about what the gravity orientation is on this thing relative to the ground."

"Good advice," she said. "Now check your gear."

TWENTY-FOUR

DOWN AND OUT

When the Metrannans made a system automatic, they went all the way. According to the information placard attached to the status display board, not only would the hatch open automatically when the liftpod landed itself, but there was no way to override the mechanism and do it on manual. A sensible arrangement if the beings aboard were totally untrained and/or incapacitated or if the liftpod was carrying cargo only, but not so great for a lightly armed and jumpy pair of Special Agents who would prefer to go out the door when *they* were ready, and not when the door was ready.

They had both gone over the weapons and gear they carried a dozen times and were as sure as they could be that everything was all ready. The main item in the armory concealed in Jamie's dinner jacket consisted of a lightweight all-plastic slug-throwing gun, designed as much to get past detectors as it was to fire bullets. The rounds it fired were a special high-density shatterproof plastic, but even so they packed a lot less stopping power or penetration ability than a conventional gun. He also had a pocket laser cutter that could serve as a low-power laser pistol in a pinch, a single baby stun grenade, an even tinier smoke grenade, a set of night-vision goggles, an encrypted pocket comm, and a Swiss Army knife.

Hannah's equipment was even sparser, thanks to the limitations imposed by a lady's evening bag. She had an identical plastic slug-thrower, but not the laser cutter or grenades or goggles or knife. She did have a pocket comm matched to Jamie's and a small spool that held fifty meters of superthin, superstrong tapeline strong enough to hoist a piano, plus a pair of lethal little throwing knives, a tube of eyeliner, a lipstick, and a compact with a mirror.

Taranarak, needless to say, was carrying no weapons or useful gadgets of any sort, and her carton full of supplies didn't seem to contain anything that might prove helpful.

"All right, Jamie," Hannah said, speaking in Lesser Trade for Taranarak's benefit. "You're our tactical genius. How do we play this?"

"We have no idea at all what we're up against out there," said Jamie, "so it's a little hard to say. If it's sixty Order Guards in full battle gear, we don't have a chance, of course. But what we've got going for us is that it's probably a small conspiratorial group— and they probably think we're dead already. However, unless they're completely blind and deaf, they're going to notice this liftpod coming in for a landing, so we can't count much on surprise."

"Or we might get lucky and we might beat them there—or they might not be coming at all."

"Maybe. But tactics and optimism don't mix too well. So here's what we're going to do. I'm going out first, because I'm the junior team member and because I'm better with weapons—but mostly because I can move better in trousers than you can in that outfit. You and Taranarak stay put in the liftpod—and you stay as far from the door as you can until I say otherwise, just in case someone out there decides to take a few potshots at it or throw in a grenade.

"Hannah, you stand by, ready to move out when I tell you. You carry your gun in one hand, wear your pocket comm as a headphone, and carry everything else in the purse. I'm going to run like hell as soon as the door opens, find some cover, then see what I can see. I'm going to want to get to some sort of spot where I can provide covering fire for you, Hannah, when you come out. Taranarak, you're going to stay put in the liftpod until we know what's going on. Hannah and I are used to working together. My apologies for that. We don't have a weapon or a comm unit for you and you don't have the training."

Plus we really don't know if we can trust you, thought Hannah. "That all seems clear enough," said Hannah. "Come on, Taranarak, let's get to the forward end, away from the hatch."

Jamie stood by the hatch, watching the status display. "The acceleration compensators are just *too* good on this planet," he said. "I would feel a lot better if there was some vibration or sense of speed or *something*." He watched the display. "We're about two minutes out," he said. "Taranarak, again, my apologies but I'm going to switch to English now, just to make it harder if anyone's listening in."

Jamie pulled out his comm unit and unfolded it into headset mode, put the receiver in his ear, and positioned the mike in front of his mouth. Hannah did the same.

"Comm check, comm check," Jamie said in a low voice. "And what we do if the comm units don't work I have no idea."

"I hear you loud and clear, partner," said Hannah. "How do you hear me?"

"The same. Good. One less worry. We're about one minute out. Stand by."

There was a trio of low clunks and thuds. "Landing skids just came out," Jamie said in a near whisper. There was a squeak and a groan, but no shake or thud or sense of motion. "And we're down. Stand by. I think if I'm reading this right, the automatic systems are growing an atmosphere-zone around us."

"I don't know if it's possible to run through those pressure-containment fields or not," said Hannah. "Careful you don't go try the experiment when you start moving around."

"Right. Okay. Good safety tip. The status display says we've got pressure out there now. I think the hatch is about to open. Here we go."

The hatch swung out and down to serve as an

access ramp. Jamie was through it almost before it was finished opening.

Hannah tightened her grip on her pistol and swallowed hard.

* * *

Jamie resisted the temptation to do anything fancy like a tuck-and-roll dive. Not in a tuxedo without much give in it, or in a gravity field that was twenty-one percent too high. Instead he settled for a quick trot down the access ramp, then a quick turn to the aft end of the bullet-shaped vehicle, in hopes of getting himself away from the obvious target of the hatch. He got himself in under the lift-pod between the aft landing skids. There was no other piece of cover anywhere nearby on the giant bowl-shaped landing field. He went to a kneel-down to make himself a smaller target and made a rapid sweep of the horizon.

It took a moment to get his bearings. He spotted Nexus Center, almost dead ahead as he faced in the direction that the ramp faced. But where was the *Sholto*? She seemed to be nowhere in sight. Maybe the bad guys had gotten there first, used their superduper Elder Race technology to defeat the locks and the self-destruct system, and launched her away.

But then Jamie turned around to look behind himself. There! Not a hundred meters away. "The *Sholto* is still there and intact," he whispered into his headphone mike.

"Any sign of company?"

"Not sure. The lighting's not so good." They had landed just before "dawn," as measured by Groundside Station, but as seen from the vantage point of a location tens of thousands of kilometers above that point on the ground, the sun was well up in the sky—directly behind the *Sholto* as seen from where Jamie was. Whatever trickery the Metrannans used to filter the red-tinted sunlight was working just fine, but it was tough seeing much of anything with the *Sholto* more or less in rose-colored silhouette. "Hold it. Yes! Movement for sure. But I can't see more than that." Jamie thought of the night-vision goggles, but decided against trying them out. More than likely they'd be just as dazzled by the full-in-the-face bright sunlight as his naked eyeballs. Better not to lose time getting them out and fumbling around to get them on and maybe knocking off his comm headset or dropping his gun.

"Can you at least tell how many?" Hannah asked.

"One that I can see for sure," Jamie said, "and I can't really see more than jerky movement in front of the main air lock. But the light's tricky as hell, and there could be twenty more of them around the back. The crazy thing is that whoever it is isn't paying any attention to the liftpod that just landed behind him."

"So what do we do?"

"Move now, before whoever that is gets his act

together. Come out of the hatch and move to your left, toward the nose. Cover me from there. I'll move in and try and angle around enough to get the *Sholto* out of silhouette and see who's there before I start shooting. Come in behind me, but stay back far enough to give cover."

"Understood. Don't be shy about shooting at the ship. The plastic rounds won't penetrate the hull."

"What worries me is they won't penetrate anything else, either. Let me know when you're in position."

"Right," said Hannah.

Jamie kept his eye on the *Sholto* as he reached into his jacket pocket for his one and only stun grenade. He flipped the safety off by feel and glanced down at it to make sure it was primed and ready to go. He heard a flutter of movement off to his left, but didn't turn his head.

"Okay," said Hannah's whispered voice in the headphones. "Ready."

"I'm going on three," Jamie whispered back, trying not to notice his stomach tightening up. "One. Two. *Three!*"

Jamie straightened up and started jogging toward a point slightly to the right of the *Sholto*, pistol at the high-ready position in his right hand, grenade in the left, his eyes fixed on the ship as his movement made the lighting angle shift. Another few steps and the sun would be out of his eyes, and he'd be able to see.

A glint, a shimmer of fluid, metallic movement. Something or someone tall and thin was standing on a mobile ramp that was pushed up against the side of the *Sholto*. Then he understood what he was seeing. A Xenoatric, an Unseen Being, working intently with some sort of electronic control box that had leads attached to a ship access panel on the side of the *Sholto*.

Bulwark of Constancy.

Whatever, whoever, he had expected to see, that wasn't it.

Jamie leveled his gun at Bulwark of Constancy and moved in, uncertain what to do. There didn't seem to be anyone else around. Constancy was alone. And he wasn't the least bit sure a plastic bullet would do anything more to Constancy's carapace than it would to the ship. Maybe— maybe—he could end this without finding out.

"Get away from the ship!" he shouted out in Lesser Trade, in the loudest, most belligerent and authoritative voice he could muster. "Move all your limbs away from the ship and come down the ramp NOW!"

Constancy jerked upright, apparently aware of him for the first time. It swiveled toward him, and Jamie remembered the words it had spoken to him. *You should be killed.* "Down the ramp NOW!" he shouted again. "Let's go!"

Constancy lifted its legs, one after another, and moved its wicked, metal-taloned feet. It moved, slowly, carefully, down the ramp. It had something in one of its manipulator mandibles. It raised the mandible, and pointed the object at Jamie.

He was half a heartbeat away from firing at Constancy when he saw what it was, or at least what it appeared to be.

A spray gun. It looked like the sort of thing a gardener might use as a plant mister. He lowered his weapon just a trifle—and suddenly Constancy was moving faster than he thought it could down that ramp, raising the sprayer toward him, aiming it at his face.

BLAM! BLAM BLAM BLAM! Hannah was firing, emptying her four-shot gun at Constancy. At least three of the rounds struck it, smashing and shattering on its carapace, rocking Constancy back, nearly toppling the Xenoatric. But it regained its balance and started moving again, if more slowly. "Shoot!" she shouted at him. "Stay back from it, do *not* hit the spray gun, but *shoot!*"

Jamie raised his own gun and fired four times, BLAM BLAM BLAM BLAM, as fast as he could, straight at Constancy's head. Its sensory cluster jerked backwards with each shot, stunning it a little bit more each time, but still it kept on coming. It was at the base of the ramp, turning toward him, shifting into a running stance—

He backpedaled to keep away from the nightmare creature as he threw the stun grenade at its feet.

There was a boom and a thudding echo off the surrounding force field that held in the atmosphere, and the air was full of smoke—and Bulwark of

Constancy was down, twitching and shaking, the spray gun falling out of its mandible.

"Don't touch that spray gun!" Hannah shouted as she ran up. "Let it roll clear! Don't even breathe near it!"

She came up to Jamie, dug in her purse and pulled out the spool of tapeline. She tossed it to Jamie. "I'd like to kill Constancy where it lies," she said, "but not only is it against the rules, I don't think we've got anything that could crack through that carapace and do the job for sure, anyway. So tie Constancy up with this. I've got to get the *Sholto* open fast and pull out the Hazmat handling kit. I want to use long tongs to get that spray gun in a hermetically sealed evidence bag—then seal that bag up in two or three more bags. And it would be very, very helpful to get it done before Taranarak gets tired of waiting in the liftpod and wanders out. If we can get away with it, I don't want her to know the first thing about that spray gun. Now or ever. We spotted Constancy trying to get into the ship. It moved as if to attack us. We knocked it out and tied it up. End of story. No spray gun."

"What—what is the spray gun? What's in it?"

"Death," said Hannah. "Old age. The antidote to the longlife treatment. I'm guessing—but I'm right. I'd bet a year's pay that was what Constancy used to kill Hallaben. And I'd bet *ten* years' pay that spray gun was the murder weapon used to kill BSI Special Agent Trevor Wilcox III."

"*That's* what killed Trevor?"

"That's my very confident guess," said Hannah. "And if we play this smart, and fast, and careful— we can keep the Metrannans from ever knowing it works on humans, too." She stood next to Jamie and looked down at the Xenoatric. "But I have this figured right. Bulwark of Constancy used it on Wilcox—but was never able to confirm that it had any effect on him. Maybe we can even keep Bulwark of Constancy from knowing for sure that it works on humans. Don't you think *that* would be a good idea?"

TWENTY-FIVE
OUT AND AWAY

The next hour or so was a blur for Jamie. If, if, if, he had inhaled so much as a microdroplet of that stuff, then it might already be working. He might already be doomed to suffer the same fate as Trevor. But Constancy had never gotten close enough to fire, and barring some freak combination of an infinitesimal leak and just the right air current, it just plain hadn't happened.

Hannah wasn't wasting time worrying about such nonsense. Inside of four minutes after the gunfight, she had the ship unlocked, the hatch open, and was burrowing through the evidence-bag supplies and hazardous material equipment. Inside of another five minutes she had the spray gun sealed inside four layers of containment, any one of which should have been protection enough. She got the spray gun hidden aboard ship where Taranarak wouldn't be likely to find it, then set to work prepping for departure before the local authorities could stir themselves to investigate the odd goings-on.

Jamie used a length of tapeline to strap Bulwark's still-twitching legs together, and then did his best to tie her various manipulators and mandibles together, but even he knew he couldn't do much of a job. Once Hannah was satisfied that she had concealed any sign of the spray gun full of age-inducer, Jamie went to fetch Taranarak. She was openly contemptuous of Jamie's attempt to restrain the Unseen One.

"Bulwark of Constancy will be able to slice through all that in less than three short-social-duration periods," she said. "It will barely slow it up. The only question is how long it will be until it revives."

"Any idea of how long that might be?"

"No," she said. "It might awaken in any period of time you care to mention. It might happen right now, or tomorrow."

"How about never?" Jamie asked sourly. "I'd choose never."

"Fine. But suppose it's now?" Hannah said from the *Sholto*'s air lock. "I don't want to be here when Constancy does wake up. The sooner we get out of here, the better. We've got clearance. Let's lift before they revoke it."

Jamie followed Taranarak up the ramp and into the air lock. Taranarak looked down one last time at Bulwark of Constancy. "Your reactionless thrust system," she said. "It will not harm Bulwark of Constancy to use it so close to where the Unseen lies?"

"No," said Jamie, looking down. "No, it won't, worse luck." He paused a moment, then looked at

Taranarak quizzically. "You do understand that it's as near a certainty as anything can be that Bulwark of Constancy blew up your house and tried to kill you and me and Agent Wolfson a few hours ago? And that it is entirely possible it was behind many of the other efforts against you? You told us you thought Constancy was manipulating Tigmin and Yalananav."

"I understand all that. But Bulwark of Constancy is of the Unseen People, one of the Eldest Races. I would not wish any of them harm. The Unseen are venerated throughout the Galaxy."

"Not in my neighborhood, they're not," Jamie growled. "Now let's get this ship buttoned up and get out of here."

* * *

Departure was spookily routine, given that there had just been a firefight on the landing field.

But Fallogon himself had issued the order for the *Bartholomew Sholto* to be given priority departure clearance, and, however, exactly, Bulwark of Constancy had gotten there ahead of them, Constancy had done it covertly. Probably no one at Free Orbit Level Station was even aware the Unseen Being was on-station, let alone that it had been caught trying to tamper with the *Sholto*.

And besides, the whole system was automatic anyway. Jamie was keeping Taranarak company on the lower deck while Hannah sat in the pilot's chair on the flight deck, but Hannah wasn't doing much in the way of flying. The Grand Elevator's Traffic Control Center took over direct control of the *Sholto*, commanding her to boost to an altitude of about twenty meters, then begin moving outward toward the rim of the massive station.

"Ah, Hannah, Taranarak's just turned a really weird shade of pinkish green down here," Jamie called up.

"What? Oh!" Hannah, watching her controls as intently as she could, hadn't even noticed when they drifted clear of the Station's artificial gravity field and flipped to zero gee. Hannah hastily powered up the *Sholto*'s one-gravity field and looked down below in time to see Taranarak hastily swallowing a little vial of liquid—presumably a dose of the antinausea medicine the liftpod techs had given her. "We'll see about increasing our gravity field as soon as we're secured from departure," Hannah said. "Can you hold out for a while at reduced gravity?"

"Um—urgh—ah—yes. Yes, I think so," Taranarak replied, her speech a little slurred. "I think the medication is already helping a bit."

"I'm very glad to hear it," Hannah said with absolute sincerity. Dealing with a spacesick Metrannan couldn't be a pleasant prospect.

But then, most of what was coming next was certainly not pleasant.

* * *

There were a thousand things to do, and a thousand decisions to make—starting with deciding what to do first. As soon as they were secured from initial maneuvers and in the groove for their constant-acceleration departure trajectory, Hannah and Jamie allowed themselves a brief time-out in order to change from their much-bedraggled formal clothes and into shipboard coveralls—which were, after all, clothes that even Metrannans would agree were more appropriate to shipboard life. Then Hannah wrote up an urgent signal to Fallogon, reporting the encounter with Bulwark of Constancy, but leaving out all mention of the spray gun. It described Bulwark of Constancy as a prime suspect in the bomb attack and requested that the Xenoatric be detained.

Hannah showed it to Taranarak to see if there were any points where she might suggest changing, but Taranarak seemed distinctly underwhelmed by the entire idea. "You can send it if you want, I suppose," she said. "But I doubt it would do any good. Detaining an Unseen being is something close to blasphemy. Even if there are good reasons for taking such a step—and obviously there are in the present case—there will be such massive resistance to the very idea that no one will act on it in the first place. *I* am resistant, and, as you said, it tried to kill me. Even to me, the idea of arresting one of the Unseen sounds unseemly and improper."

"But surely there must be some way of dealing with an Unseen being who causes trouble," Jamie protested.

"Oh yes, of course. The normal procedure would be to petition the Council of the Unseen Race to restrain their erring compatriot. However, you will not be surprised to learn that is a lengthy, even ponderous, process. And, let us not forget that Bulwark of Constancy is no average Unseen being. It would be closer to say Bulwark of Constancy is the Fourth of the Three. Constancy has developed an expansive network of power and influence among those who resist change."

"Which is just about everyone on the planet," said Jamie. "Very well. We'll send the signal, and it won't do any good. What will happen next? What will Constancy do—assuming Constancy wakes up and recovers?"

"Constancy will recover, I assure you, and will need only a few moments to free itself from the restraints you put around it. Then, I would assume, it would simply stand up, walk to Nexus Station, and requisition one of the Unseen ships that are on the field at Free Orbit Station. Constancy will then pursue us and kill us."

Hard to miss the confidence in that prediction, Hannah thought. Taranarak didn't say "try to kill us" or "make an attempt to kill us."

"They'll just permit her to walk in and take a ship?"

"Of course. Why not?"

Hannah resisted the urge to answer that question. It was obvious that that way lay madness.

"Would she be able to get a fast ship? An armed ship?"

"Oh yes, absolutely. The Unseen would not bother with anything less."

"No, of course they wouldn't," said Hannah. "All right, then. I'm going to go through the motions, and send the message—and then, Jamie, you and I need to talk flight plans."

"You won't be needing me for that, will you?" asked Taranarak. "I do feel in need of a rest."

"So do we," said Hannah with perfect truthfulness, "but we'll let you get started first. Jamie, rustle up some coffee for both of us, and then come on up to the flight deck."

* * *

It took some doing, but somehow Jamie managed to get up the rope ladder while carrying two cups of blessedly hot strong coffee. Hannah accepted her cup gratefully and eased back in the pilot's chair while Jamie leaned against a bulkhead.

"At least we don't have to hide in the air lock for privacy," Jamie said, speaking in English in a voice that wasn't much above a whisper. He glanced down to the lower deck, where Taranarak was settling herself down into a sort of a nest of whatever soft and padded material they had been able to scrounge up. "One look at her face—and her anatomy—and I knew she wasn't going to try the rope ladder if she didn't have to. My guess is that, given the choice, she'll stay off the flight deck for the whole trip."

Hannah blew on her too-hot coffee, smiled, and spoke one word. "But."

"But," Jamie agreed, "even if it's a zillion-to-one shot that she's a plant, she *might* be a plant. And if there are multiple copies of the message floating around, that means there are potentially many Metrannans who might want to get their hands on the decrypt key. I believe Taranarak is what she appears to be—but Fallogon—or one of the other members of the Three—or for that matter, Bulwark of Constancy—might have set her up for us. She *might* be packing forty-seven different tracking and listening devices inside that headdress, and she *might* speak English better than us, and she *might* be waiting around for us to say something we shouldn't. I don't believe it, but it might be true. And the stakes are too high for us to take chances. So I say we don't say or do anything that might tell her something until we're safely back home in Center's star system and can holler for help from BSI HQ. That more or less covers your 'but,' if you'll forgive an unintended pun?"

"Gee, you blush easy sometimes. Yeah, pretty much. But there are some decisions we need to make *now*. We've accomplished very little of value so far—but we do have a lot more current information about conditions on Metran, we know what the message was about and what it was for, and we've got ourselves a refugee passenger who happens to be the greatest living expert on what the message was about. Plus we've got that kill-juice that Bulwark of Constancy was about to try out on you. We need human scientists to analyze that stuff, understand it, and maybe find a way to counteract it."

"You think the stuff is that dangerous?"

"You remember how Doc Vogel said that when there have been wars between two species, lots of times one of the two went extinct? I think there's a good chance that that stuff could make *us* extinct, if it's what I think it is."

"Okay, so what do you think it is?"

"The existing standard geriatric treatment for Metrannans is to delay decline until the last possible moment, so the patient is still vigorous until just before death, so that he falls apart all at once. That's how Hallaben died, though he wasn't at risk for the syndrome. And that's how Trevor died.

"I think that Hallaben found out how to keep those cellular failures from ever happening, or at least from happening for decades. And if you find out how to keep a set of switches turned *on*, you've also learned how to switch them *off*. Maybe taking the longlife treatment required deactivating some part of the existing geriatric treatment, and that's what this stuff was. Or it was some other byproduct of the research. Something to *cause* old age so you test to see if it could be counteracted. Bulwark of Constancy was involved in the longlife project, in a sort of negative sense—

trying to get it shut down. I think Constancy got hold of the stuff and exposed Hallaben and Trevor to it—fed it to them, made them inhale it, whatever—just before Trevor departed. Hallaben died as expected, probably while Trevor was still en route up the Grand Elevator to the *Adler*—but Trevor stayed alive. Bulwark of Constancy decides to let the old-age-in-a-spray-gun have longer to work. Constancy chases Trevor's ship, hoping to find him safely dead. Except he's not."

"I get it," said Jamie. "Trevor cons the Metrannans that Constancy sends aboard the *Adler* into docking through the nose hatch. Bulwark doesn't want to be seen—and has got to be even worse on a rope ladder than a Metrannan. So Constancy sends a bunch of Metrannan flunkies aboard to search for the decryption key. They don't know much about humans, and Bulwark of Constancy wouldn't have been crazy enough to order them to check for signs of premature aging. They come back without having found the decryption key and reporting Trevor as being in good health—which he is, more or less. He's aging rapidly, but still holding together well enough to fool a bunch of xenos."

"Constancy can't destroy the *Adler*—not with a shipful of Metrannan witnesses. It concludes that the aging treatment doesn't work on humans and maybe the biochemistry isn't all *that* similar—but then Trevor never arrives. Months pass with no word, no decryption key, and no joint human-Metrannan lab busily working away on the longlife treatment. Does that mean Trevor did die, and his ship was lost forever? Maybe Constancy figures out that the treatment *did* work—just not so fast on humans."

"But wait a second," Jamie objected. "Something that kills over the course of a couple of weeks isn't much use against someone with a gun. Why did Constancy pull that spray gun on us?"

Hannah counted off on her fingers. "One—it was the only weapon Constancy had. And/or two—it wasn't expecting *us*. It thought we were safely dead. It was expecting it might have to spritz a couple of Metrannan cops. Then it'd just have to stall long enough, requiring proper and respectful treatment, until they keeled over. It took Hallaben a couple of days to die—but he might well have been incapacitated long before he died. Three—you told me yourself that Constancy had gotten to the point of borderline deranged—and maybe it's crossed the border. Four, if you hadn't had the stun grenade, it would have just shaken off the bullets and kept coming. It almost *did* manage to spray you as it was. We just barely *did* have a defense. And five, maybe it was just very, very eager to have a guinea pig. It sprays us down, abducts us, locks you up for a couple of weeks, waits to see what happens—and knows for sure whether the stuff works on humans. I've run out of fingers, but I could probably come up with more motives if you gave me a chance."

Jamie shivered. "No, I think that's a good enough list. But I've got another question. What, exactly, was Constancy doing there? What did Bulwark of Constancy hope to accomplish by breaking into the *Bartholomew Sholto*?"

"Not a thing in the world," Hannah said. "My guess is that Constancy thought it was breaking into the *Irene Adler* to search for the decrypt key. It figured out that we had disguised one ship as the other—but got it backwards. At the very least, it needed to make sure the *Sholto* wasn't the *Adler*. Maybe it was going to steal the ship and take it somewhere private where it could spend years searching it, if need be."

"But it wanted the decrypt key destroyed! Why not just blow up the ship and be done with it?"

"If you want, I can stack a few more guesses on top of each other. It wanted to find the key, hold it in its manipulators, know that it controlled it as a matter of positive fact. It'd never know that for sure if it simply destroyed the spacecraft. Or maybe it figured that, someday, it would be to Constancy's advantage to have the key in its possession as a bargaining chip for use with this faction or that. Say, someone interested in using the data in the message to create bioweapons instead of a longlife treatment."

"You've just convinced me that part was perfectly possible. Constancy *used* that spray gun like a weapon. It tried to aim and fire it at an opponent. And if it was expecting a few droplets of it on my skin, or my inhaling just a trace of it, was going to be enough to kill me—then the amount in that spray gun in the lockup is probably enough to kill half of Center City."

"Yeah. Unless it's just distilled water and Hallaben died of natural causes and since we've been gone Doc Vogel has figured out that Trevor died of some rare disease with a long incubation that he contracted three missions ago."

"I don't believe that any more than you do. What you're saying is that all you have right now is circumstantial evidence and some logic that holds together fairly well. But they've got Trevor's body still in the morgue, and we've got that spray gun full of something to be analyzed. I'd bet whatever you like Forensics is able to make a connection."

"No bet," said Hannah. "I agree. We can't nail it down until we get that stuff back to the lab, but I feel quite certain we now know how Trevor was killed and who did it."

"Great," Jamie said sourly. "Mission accomplished."

"No," said Hannah. "Not until *Trevor*'s mission is accomplished. Which brings me to our next decision, and it's a nice complicated one. If Taranarak is correct, we can expect pursuit by a faster and more powerful ship, and that ship could launch any minute. We might not have much of a head start. We've got the spray gun and the new information with us. Do we risk losing all that—and ourselves—by taking on the delay and confusion of linking up with the *Adler*—or do we give up on finding the decrypt key aboard her, use the remote-destruct system to blow her up as we go past, and just go home with what we've got?"

"I say we don't write off the *Adler*," Jamie said. "We can't. I don't want to say a single syllable about why." He gestured toward Taranarak. "Not until we have *her* safely back in Center System. All I'll say is this: We've been led around by our noses and chivvied around since the moment we landed at Free Orbit Level Station. It's time that we call the shots and decide where to go and what to do. I don't feel like playing it safe or being chased away from finishing our job."

"I'm with you," said Hannah. "But I felt I had to at least bring up the other option."

"Fine. But just deciding to bring back both ships is step one. There are about forty-seven different scenarios for how to do it. I don't think there's any point in getting fancy about maneuver-masking or trying to pretend the *Adler* isn't there. We'll *have* to light her engines by remote command long before we're anywhere near her if the two ships are going to match velocities. If there is a fast ship chasing us, it will get close enough to see the energy output no matter what games we try to play. We might as well just run as fast as we can without wasting time and thrust reserves trying to fool someone who won't be fooled." Jamie thought for a minute. "There are a lot of variables to play with."

"I think my tactical officer just requested time in the chair I'm in so he could start working out possibilities."

"He did indeed," Jamie said. "*After* I bed down somewhere for a while. I'm too tired to think straight. But with Taranarak's nest taking up half the deck, I'm not sure where. Maybe if I leave the air lock door open, I could sleep in there for a while."

"Leaving me to doze off in this glorified dentist's chair?" Hannah asked. "Gee, thanks. We'll need to work out better sleeping arrangements and so on, but it's going to have to wait." She yawned hugely. "I'll rig some alarms on the detector system so it'll start howling if it spots a ship on our tail."

"Okay," said Jamie. "But I wouldn't say no if you shifted to, ah, boost pattern seven-b before you turn in. It's optimized to give near-max boost, minimum time, and makes no effort at detection avoidance. Speed is going to be our best defense, I think."

"Agreed," said Hannah. "Go climb over Taranarak, use the washroom, and turn in. I'll go after you."

"That order I'll obey without argument, cap'n. Good night."

Hannah watched him head down the ladder,

then ordered the nav system to shift over to pattern seven-b. Jamie was right. Speed was likely to be their best protection.

What worried her was that sometimes, even the best was none too good.

TWENTY-SIX

EDGE OF CENTER

The days that followed were difficult in the extreme for Taranarak. She had often fantasized about escaping from Metran—but that was a far different thing than the harsh reality of being cast out, left homeless, dependent on the kindness of barely civilized aliens for her own survival. It was hard not to dwell on all she had lost. In all likelihood, she would never again set foot on her home planet.

That was, far and away, the deepest wound and the widest. But it was far from being the only one. Life aboard the exceedingly cramped quarters of the *Bartholomew Sholto* made her life in house arrest seem the apex of luxury. There was scarcely room enough to turn around without bumping into one of the humans or the other. Privacy was virtually nonexistent, and using the human-style sanitary facilities was an exercise in humiliation.

It was likewise most disturbing that she was forced to watch the two humans constantly scrambling up and down that dreadful flexible ladder arrangement. She grew somewhat more used to the sight in time, but the mere sight of it never failed to make her feel just a trifle queasy. Needless to say, she flatly refused to use the ladder or visit the flight deck herself.

All she had in the way of clothing was two sets of maintenance worker's coveralls supplied at the last minute by the liftpod station crew, and the only food she had, aside from the emergency rations she had herself arranged to have aboard, were a few unappetizing long-store rations and lower-class leisure snacks scooped up by the liftpod crew.

But all that was as nothing compared to the attitude of the two human agents. They were polite, yes, even courteous and respectful—but it was clear that they did not trust her in the least. They frequently shifted to their own tongue in order to exclude her from conversation on anything remotely technical or confidential. They spoke in low voices. They concealed datascreens and even hid their antique paper notebooks from her view. They seemed to work on the assumption that any or all of her possessions contained recording devices.

She could not really blame them for the precautions. After all, an attempt had been made on their lives as well. Bulwark of Constancy had been attempting to break into their ship. And in their very brief stay on her world, they had spent nearly every moment entangled in murky plots and schemes.

But understanding their motives did not wipe

away the sense of humiliation—and of uselessness. She had nothing at all to do, while the humans were both constantly bustling about, making plans, making lists, discussing scenarios, working out contingencies.

Toward the evening of their first day out, Taranarak at last felt she had actually contributed something, that she was something more than an encumbrance. Even so, it was not a happy moment. It happened when an alert started to sound on the main control board. Agent Mendez had been spending most of his time working on what he called "tactical options," whatever exactly that meant, and he was the first to see what the alert meant. "Ship launch from Free Orbit Station," he announced, doing her the courtesy of speaking in Lesser Trade Speech. He studied the displays as Agent Wolfson scrambled up the rope ladder to see for herself. "There have been plenty of those since we left, of course—but our nav plot projects this one on a near-intercept with us."

"And the ship-thrust pattern signature matches what we have on file for a particular class of ships flown by the Unseen Race," Agent Wolfson said. "We're getting data from the ship's transponder. Definite Unseen Race ship. Massing about twenty times what we do. Even getting a ship name: the *Stability*. That's got to be our friend Constancy. Looks like you got it right, Taranarak," she said, calling down to the lower deck.

"I sincerely wish I had it wrong," Taranarak

replied sadly. "Bulwark of Constancy took a lot longer to get moving than I expected. I was beginning to hope that it wouldn't pursue."

"Can we be sure that it *is* Constancy?"

"If it is a ship of the Unseen People, yes. The controls on those ships are configured so that no Metrannan could operate them. And I cannot think of any other of the Unseen with any reason to pursue us."

"Is Constancy going to catch us?" Mendez asked.

"Yes," said Wolfson, quite calmly, as she studied the displays. "Assuming everything continues as it is. But our job is to make sure things *don't* stay the same."

"If I understand the plan," said Taranarak, "we are to boost toward your other ship, brake to a halt next to her, transfer to that ship, then fly on to transit-jump range. Is that correct?"

"No," said Wolfson. "But that's the profile we're flying right now. That's what we want Bulwark to *think* the plan is. I'll take the slight risk of telling you that much and a bit more."

And you allowed me to believe the same thing up until now, just in case I was somehow relaying information back to Metran. But there was no point in taking offense when her hosts were fighting to save all their lives.

"We don't have enough stored boost energy to fly that profile," said Agent Mendez. "Human ships aren't as efficient as Elder Race ships. A ship this small can't afford to speed up, slow down for a rendezvous, then speed up again. Besides, if we're being pursued by a ship as fast as the *Stability*, we don't dare to slow down for a heartbeat. So the *Adler* will have to light her own engines and accelerate enough to match speeds with us. We configured her for remotely controlled operation before we left her behind."

Wolfson studied the plots a moment or two longer. "Once Bulwark of Constancy sees two vehicles under boost and moving toward mutual intercept, it will know it's seeing the real situation. Let's confuse her a bit more before we do anything else. We'll let her build up some velocity in a slightly wrong direction. *Then* we'll shift our course and increase our thrust to a matched-velocity intercept and rendezvous with the *Adler*—but we won't activate the *Adler* or light her engines until we're well under way on our new course. Let Constancy see it all in stages, and perhaps be deceived or confused by each one in turn."

"If so, Constancy will not be the only one deceived or confused," said Taranarak.

"Our apologies for that," said Agent Wolfson. "I acknowledge that we have not been entirely forthcoming. We believe you to be our friend and ally—but we are playing for such high stakes that we dare not trust our own personal feelings. And it is possible that you could be an unwitting spy. Transmitters or other devices could have been inserted into your clothes or other belongings without your knowledge. Surely you would rather be a living friend whose feelings had been slightly hurt, rather than all of us getting killed—and the longlife treatment lost, perhaps forever—because we extended our trust too far."

"I accept your apologies and explanations, and appreciate the situation," said Taranarak. But that didn't mean she had to like it. It also crossed her mind that if the *Stability* changed her heading to match the *Sholto*'s final intended course before the *Sholto* made her own move, the humans would know—or at least assume—that Taranarak was the source. They were giving her a test. And if she failed it, they weren't likely to stop to ask if it was accidental or deliberate before they responded.

* * *

"Well," said Jamie, hours later, "I've heard the phrase 'a long stern chase' before, but I never thought I'd be in one."

"Let's hope we get out of it," said Hannah. "What's the current projection?" They had shifted their burn profile ninety minutes before and seen the pursuing vehicle alter her own course to a new intercept point.

"The short form is that we got a big head start, and the *Stability* didn't start pursuit anywhere near as soon as we expected. However, her ship has much higher acceleration than we do, and will catch up with us. If all the projections about how our ship and Constancy's ship will perform are correct, we'll beat her to the transfer-jump point by a hair under two hours—*if* everything goes perfectly. That projection is still trending downward a little bit."

"A little bit? You were projecting it at two and a half hours a while back. I'm starting to get really twitchy. I think it's time to wake up the *Adler*."

"Once we do that, we'll have all our cards on the table," Jamie cautioned. "The *Adler* could still match with us if she lit an hour from now—if we cranked her engines up to max boost, full throttle the whole way."

"And if she held together under the stress, and if she hasn't been leaking thrust power at more than the projected rate since we left her, and if about six other things. We've *got* to allow for some margin of error. That ship—and this ship—have both been through too much to crank them up to max *anything* and expect them to function properly. And there is one other card we could play, if need be. If the *Stability* suddenly cranks her acceleration past where we *think* she can go, and we project interception before we can make our transit-jump—then we can still escape. We light the *Adler*'s engines, fly both ships toward our intended matched-velocity rendezvous—then skip the rendezvous and docking. If we abandon the *Adler*, we won't have to cut the *Sholto*'s engines and fiddle about with the docking and transfer and so on. That will save us a couple of hours right there.

"Plus we can detonate the *Adler* remotely and

use the explosion to mask the exact parameters of our jump from Constancy. That'll make us a lot harder to track if Bulwark pursues us into Center System—and I think we have to assume it will, if it doesn't manage to finish us off here. Abandoning the *Adler* might be the difference between life and death."

"We cannot abandon the *Adler*," said Jamie. "I am not going to say one word about why until we're safely aboard her and through the transit-jump—but we can't."

Hannah was quiet for a moment before she spoke again. "Jamie," she said in a low and gentle voice, "if this was just about risking our lives, I wouldn't mind so much. That's our job. But if we're right, and that stuff in the spray gun is what killed Trevor, we need to get it back to Center and analyzed, give them a chance to find countermeasures, before Bulwark of Constancy decides all humans are degenerate troublemaking Younger Race scum and figures it can solve the problem by dropping a thousand liters of the stuff into Center City's water supply. It could wipe out the city. Or maybe it wouldn't take even that much. Maybe a thousand liters would be enough to wipe out the entire population of Earth."

"I know," said Jamie. "I understand that. But Bulwark of Constancy could launch an attack like that right now, if it wanted to. It could beat us to transit-jump range, jump to Center System or the Solar System, and get there long before we did.

And even if we managed to get that spray gun back to Center, who knows how long finding a counter-measure might take? Maybe there *isn't* a counter-measure. But *if* we can get that message cracked, the odds are very good that there will be information inside it that would save the labs weeks or months or years in counteracting it."

Is that the reason, or the excuse? Jamie's argu-ment was sound—but was it his real motive? What *wouldn't* he talk himself into if it would help him complete Trevor's mission? "All right," she said. "It's just barely possible we're gambling with the survival of the human race—but all right. I trust your judgment. We won't abandon the *Adler.*"

* * *

Just under an hour later, the *Adler* lit her engines. Not long after, Constancy's ship made a slight course correction as well. They were down to an hour and fifty minutes between when they would reach the *Adler* and when Constancy would inter-cept. Slowly, far too slowly, that number started to rebound very slightly over the next several hours. Careful study of the nav plot showed that Constancy was reducing her rate of acceleration very slightly. Maybe it was fearful of overstressing its own engines. Maybe it had miscalculated some-thing—or they had. Maybe Constancy's engines were detuning a trifle, and it was unaware of it. Maybe a lot of things.

Two more days passed, but other than all three

ships crawling along their projected flight paths, very little seemed to change. Midway through the second day, the *Stability* adjusted her thrust upward again and stopped her very gradual loss of relative position—but she did not seem to make any effort to make up lost ground.

"My reading is that she's not even trying to catch us on this side of the transit-jump anymore," said Jamie as they checked the plot projections for the thousandth time. "Or else Constancy is about to pull some all-mighty rabbit out of its hat, do some stunt we're not expecting at all, and pounce on us at the last minute."

"That's always possible," said Hannah, "but I think you're right. Constancy's running that ship flat out as it is. Push it any harder, and it might risk wrecking the whole propulsion system. It's decided to close in for the kill on the other side of the jump. Constancy's figured out that we're all going to make the transit-jump at about the same velocity—which is another way of saying we'll have pretty much lost all the advantage of our head start by then. Once we're in Center System, we'll be at more or less zero relative velocity, and the advantage will be with the *Stability*, because it can accelerate faster and has greater power reserves, and probably better detection systems. If she can finish us off before we can call for help, or even just before help arrives, that will suit her just fine."

"And you say *I'd* make a lousy morale officer," said Jamie.

"I never said I'd be good at the job," Hannah replied. "Besides, we've got few surprises for Constancy."

"Let's just hope it doesn't have any surprises for *us*. Come on, let's get back to prepping for the transfer. The faster we can switch gear from one ship to the other, the happier I'll be."

The plotting points moved closer together. The *Adler* drew closer to the *Sholto*, and the two ships matched velocities as well, both of them moving at virtually the same terrifyingly high speed. After what seemed like endless hours of everything happening very slowly, suddenly everything seemed to happen at once as the nav plot computer flashed the status reports on the main display.

Range to target ten thousand kilometers. Five thousand. A thousand. A hundred. Fifty. Ten kilometers, and the *Adler* was actually visible, her visual-acquisition lights blinking blue and green in the darkness. Main engine stop on both ships. Final maneuvers on attitude thrusters. Five kilometers. Three kilometers. Commence auto-rendezvous and dock sequence. One kilometer. Half a klick. Three hundred meters. *Adler* holding steady attitude. *Sholto* in active docking mode, coming about to stern-first attitude. Ships nose to nose. Docking alignment confirmed. One hundred meters. Fifty. Twenty. Stand by for soft dock.

A bump, a thud.

Soft dock confirmed.

A series of hard, rattling bangs as the capture latches slammed into place.

Hard dock confirmed.

Hannah was already at the nose hatch, checking the pressure seal, getting it open, entering the tunnel between the ships.

"Display confirms good power, pressure, and temps aboard the *Adler*," she shouted. "I'm opening the hatch to the *Adler* now."

"Okay," said Jamie.

"Right!" a slightly muffled voice replied. "I'm in! Stand by a second." Silence for a little bit, and then Hannah's head popped through the *Sholto*'s nose hatch. "It looks like the *Adler*'s held together just fine." she announced. "No sign of any leakage from our repairs. Let's get the transfer done and get back under power before Constancy flies up our rear end." She reached out her arms. "Hand me that first bundle."

* * *

Taranarak had to admit that the humans' endless planning and rehearsal were paying off. In a stunningly short time, all the gear they had packed and prepped, all the bundles stacked in the flight deck, all the supplies that might help keep them alive in the days ahead, had been moved from one ship to the other. Their sense of urgency was infectious, and she stood on the *Sholto*'s lower deck, eagerly watching the seemingly impossible gyrations of the humans. It was clear that they were not descended from tree dwellers—they *were* tree dwellers. No sensible being, descended from sensible creatures that lived their lives on good safe flat ground, could ever have tolerated such movements.

She might get used to the sight of them climbing, but seeing them move through the zero-gee tunnel between the ships, seeing Wolfson flitting around in the weightlessness of the *Adler*, directly over Taranarak's head, was something else again. It was of very little comfort to see that Mendez appeared to be slightly distressed by his much more limited work in the zero-gee ship. Weightlessness might be a very useful thing for cargo handlers, but it would never be suitable for any sort of refined person.

But then, at last, they powered up the gravity system aboard the *Adler*, and it was time for the last bulky, awkward, inconveniently shaped object to be moved from one ship to the other. Taranarak took a double dose of her fast-dwindling stock of motion-sickness suppressant, and set out to do what she had, short days ago, promised never to do.

She grabbed hold of the *Sholto*'s rope ladder with her outer arm pair, awkwardly lifted her left forward foot onto the first rung, and started climbing. The sensation was terrifying. The humans made encouraging noises, and urged her on, rung after rung, but it was a nightmare all the same.

And then came the horrors of the docking tunnel. She knew what she had to do, knew the danger was really quite small, but even so, it was terribly hard. To move deliberately into a zero-gee zone, to scramble along on the netting hung along its sides, to flip over in midair—then to emerge back into blessed gravity, but moving down the rope ladder, moving blind, the humans still humiliatingly comforting, mortifyingly helpful, until she was past the flight deck, then down on the lower deck, and safe.

Safe for the moment, at any rate. The worst was yet to come. Because this was a human ship. And they were already rushing to make their jump. And human ships shut down their gravity systems for transit-jumps.

"There we are," Mendez said, as soon as she was down. "Close the hatch at will, Hannah. Undock, get us clear, and let's get under boost again."

* * *

Twenty minutes later, the *Adler* was back under boost, with the *Sholto* a few hundred kilometers behind and matching course.

It felt surprisingly good to be back aboard the *Adler*, Hannah decided. It might be cramped—more so with three of them aboard—and it might be in worse shape than the *Sholto*, but it was where they were supposed to be. She realized that she had been suffering an unconscious itch the whole time they were away from the *Adler*, a sense that she was not doing her proper work, almost that she was shirking her duty, because she wasn't aboard the *Adler*, searching for the decrypt key. The problem was, of course, that she still wasn't doing that job.

Other things had to come first. Hannah braced herself in the space where the pilot's seat used to be and slathered the last of the electroset compound over her improvised patch-up job on the wrecked side viewport. She smoothed the material down as best she could, shrugged, shook her head, and shoved the two power leads into the stuff. She flipped off the safety on the powersetter and pushed the button. Low-voltage currents moved through the claylike substance and induced a state change. Within seconds, the compound was hard as steel-reinforced concrete—and about as transparent. They had lost even more of their view out, but there was at least a fighting chance that their ship would hold pressure as they went through the transit-jump.

"Hannah! I'm ready for you now," Jamie called out. "And let's not forget we're on the clock."

"Who could forget, with you around? I'm coming."

She went down the ladder to the lower deck and helped Jamie wrestle the second acceleration chair, the one that Gunther had attached on the lower deck, back up the ladder and onto the flight deck. Even Jamie had to agree that during the transit the pilot would need a pilot's seat more than a passenger would. The original pilot's chair was still stuffed into the *Adler*'s air lock to keep it out of the way. They had briefly discussed dumping it into the *Sholto* before undocking the two ships, but that would have cost them extra time and effort they did not have to spend.

Speaking of time, they were coming up on a mere fifteen minutes until transit-jump. Hannah hurried to get the chair where it needed to be and bolted down to the deck. In a way, it was a good thing they were so rushed just before the jump. It kept them from becoming worried and distracted over what was going to come next.

Or maybe it didn't. She glanced up at Jamie's face as he worked to tighten down the final bolt. He was eager, enthused, even excited. Whatever it was that he swore not to talk about until they were through the jump was clearly on his mind.

"Set!" Jamie said. "Okay. I'm going to go get Taranarak strapped down, then do the best I can for myself." There weren't any good places besides the pilot's chair for riding out a transit-jump. Jamie and Taranarak had to throw blankets and padding down on the deck and strap themselves in with cargo hold-down belts.

"I'll go down with you and talk to her one more time," said Hannah. She went down to the lower deck and knelt on the floor next to where Taranarak was already strapped in, already as dosed up against zero gee as they dared—and already scared out of her mind. "All you have to do is remain calm and in control," Hannah said in

Lesser Trade, feeling as if she were a medic tending to some hard-luck roadside-injury victim. "We'll only have the grav system off for about thirty seconds before the jump, and I'll power it up as soon as we're through. It'll be uncomfortable for you, but that's nowhere near enough time for it to get dangerous." *Unless, of course, something goes wrong or the passage through the jump takes an unusually long period of subjective time.* But no sense pointing all that out to Taranarak. She knew it all already, without being reminded of it.

"Thank you," said Taranarak. "Your concern is appreciated—but now you must return to your post. I will feel far more secure seeing you at the controls."

"Ten minutes, Hannah," said Jamie in English as he floundered around a bit with his improvised restraint system.

"Okay," she said. "I'm on it. Thanks for the use of the chair."

She scrambled back up to the flight deck and made herself ready. The autosequencer was the one flying the ship now, but Hannah was there as the all-purpose backup system, with at least some hope of dealing with the unexpected—as if there hadn't been enough of that already. She glanced up at the lumpen mass of electroset compound and muttered a prayer to whoever might be listening that it would hold.

She checked her status boards and switches once again. What had Jamie come up with that she had missed? It had to be that he had figured out some clue to where the decrypt key was. He had as much as said so, for all of his refusing to speak at all. Had he really found something? Or was he wrong? Had he miscalculated, or found some way to kid himself, fend off the guilt he felt over failing Trevor, failing to complete the mission?

Three minutes to go.

The sequencer was setting to work in earnest, powering down unneeded systems, shifting everything into safe mode. It occurred to Hannah that they were asking a lot of the poor old *Adler*, moving her from dormant mode to remote ops to crewed status and then a transit-jump in rapid succession, after all she had been through already. And what about the *Sholto*? She was scheduled for an automatic transit-jump ten minutes after the *Adler*. The plan was for her to position herself to do one last bit of maneuver-masking, putting herself and her thrust plume's energy field directly between the *Adler* and Constancy's ship. Constancy would know that the *Adler* had jumped, of course, but not knowing precisely when or where would make it a lot harder for Constancy to find her on the other side.

Main engines throttling down. Life support shutdown. Cabin lighting off. This time it ought to be a nice, smooth, well-calibrated jump, without any overstressed jump generators or off-center loads or support cables taking too much dynamic load. Ought to be. Didn't mean it would be.

"Grav systems off in five—four—three—two—one—zero!" Hannah realized a split second too late that she had done the callout in English. Never mind. Taranarak no doubt had noticed the change all by herself. She shifted to Lesser Trade Speech and spoke again. "Transit-jump in twenty human brief-duration units." She wasn't even going to *try* to do conversions to Elder Race units on the fly in her head. "In fifteen! In ten! Nine. Eight. Seven. Six. Five. Four. Three. Two. One. TRANSIT!"

Something grabbed hold of the ship and shook it once, twice, hard. Outside the surviving viewports, she could see fat green blobs of glowing, sparking light. There was a low humming sound, almost like a slightly off-key choir singing. A soundless flash of pure blinding white light lit up the interior of the *Adler*—and they were through.

The friendly and familiar sight of the stars as seen from the Center System bloomed into being all around them. The *Adler*'s nav system came back on and instantly acquired one, two, three positioning beacon signals. Hannah overrode the sequencer to bring up the grav system sooner, and felt one point two one gees of gravity pressing her down.

"Jamie?" Hannah called over her shoulder, still working her board. "How did you like the ride?"

"That was it? We're clear? Jump complete?"

"I think we've earned an easy one, don't you? You okay? And how's our passenger—or patient, or whatever?"

"Pinkish-green again, and gurgling, but I think she's recovering already."

"Maybe she's getting used to it," said Hannah. "Keep an eye on her while I phone home and whistle up the booster."

The moment the rest of the ship's systems came on, Hannah brought the ship around to aim her nose—and her directional antenna—squarely at Center. Because they weren't under boost, and therefore didn't have their main engines pointed directly at the inner systems, in effect serving as a powerful jamming system, their communications range was much better than it would normally be, and Hannah was confident their signal would be heard.

She double-checked her celestial-navigation aim against the positioning beacons and got a satisfyingly close agreement. She powered up the *Adler*'s main radio transmitter, routed its signal through the directional antenna, and transmitted thirty seconds of Mayday calls. It would take hours for the calls to cross the endless kilometers between their position and the planet, and days for help to arrive, even under the best of circumstances. But that was not the only reason to send the Mayday at once.

They were going to have to power down everything possible and rig for silent running before Constancy showed up. Hannah took a little time right then and there to shut down systems they weren't going to need for a while. Every little power output she killed would increase their chances of staying hidden. She dearly wished that she could have killed the grav system, but there was no hope of that, unless she were willing to kill Taranarak as well.

As soon as the Mayday calls were completed, Hannah spun the ship at random and fired the main engines for thirty seconds, just so as to shift their position and velocity away from where it had been at transit-jump arrival. With any luck, that would make it harder for Constancy to track them. As soon as the burn ended, she switched over to the broadcast antenna and sent the wake-up code for the booster stage that had gotten them through the first part of their journey. It almost wasn't necessary. The *Adler*'s nav system already had a fix on the *Adler*'s own position, and got a location lock on the booster at almost the same moment the booster woke up and answered.

"Okay," Hannah said to the booster. "We're here and you're there. Good." She cued up the next message for the booster and sent it. Then she told the nav system to zero out their velocity relative to the booster and handed ship control to the automatic systems. The nav system flipped the *Adler* around to another new heading and fired the main engine very briefly, and then gave a few little love taps to the attitude jets.

Hannah was very pleased to see that the maneuver had used up very little propulsion power because they barely *had* any propulsion power left.

They certainly didn't have enough juice left even to make a start on braking maneuvers. They were utterly dependent on BSI HQ sending a rescue vessel. They had made a conscious and deliberate decision not to take the time required for transferring power from the *Sholto*, on the theory that the other ship would need it more for the job it would have to do. *This plan had better work.*

She had a clear board and no duties for a few minutes, until the *Sholto* was due to arrive. The plan Jamie had cooked up relied on both the booster and the *Sholto* playing their parts. It would be vastly inconvenient if the *Sholto* failed to put in an appearance—but she could put that worry off for a few minutes.

"Jamie!" she called out as she released herself from her seat restraints. "Get on up here and—"

But Jamie was already at her side. He didn't speak, or even look at her. Instead he reached for the stack of notepads that Trevor had left behind. "We're here, Jamie," she said, but he paid her no mind. He was flipping rapidly through the first notebook and muttering to himself. Hannah found herself wondering if maybe Jamie wasn't quite all there. Maybe he *had* caught a whiff of the aging drug. Maybe he was just a little more disoriented from the transit-jump than she realized. "James," she said in a louder voice. "We're here. Even if every thread in Taranarak's dress is a high-power transmitter, Constancy is light-years away. Taranarak is too punchy to understand anything and no one can hear us. So talk. What was it you found, or figured out?"

Jamie paid her no mind, but instead finished flipping through the pages of the book. He shoved it at her, and grabbed for the next one in the stack. "Count!" he said. "Count the pages in that one. Double-check me while I do the next one."

"*What?*"

"Count the pages. It's simple enough. Just do it."

But she didn't do it. Instead she stared at him, a cold feeling of fear in the pit of her stomach. She had just decided on a risky course of action that still had plenty of chances to get them killed while exposing every human on Center, maybe every human everywhere, to grave danger. And she had done it on the basis of trusting the judgment of a young man who obviously thought that, in spite of their situation, counting the pages in notebooks was the most important thing he had to do.

The good people of Center, and Earth, and every human world, might be in more trouble than she had thought.

TWENTY-SEVEN

ACROSS AND DOWN

Hannah stared at her partner for a very long time. "James," she said at last, speaking very slowly. "James, I think you need to lie down for a while." *Maybe a long while. With ropes tied around you.*

"Count them! Forty-eight!" he announced triumphantly. "Sixteen pages in each section! In all four books! I was right!"

"*That's* the big clue you didn't want to talk about until we got here? Agent Mendez, in case you've forgotten, we've got a xeno spacecraft, piloted by a psychotic who killed Wilcox, about to complete a transit-jump right into our laps so it can continue trying to hunt us down and kill us. We've got a certain spray gun that I'd really like to get back to the boys in the lab. I've got a semiconscious xeno on the next deck down who is either a spy for one of about four factions on Metran, some of whom would like to kill us, or else a refugee who might have vital information—and I've got *you* counting notebook pages. I am seriously starting to think about forcibly sedating you. What in the hell are you *talking* about?"

"On Metran. All the notebooks felt wrong," he

said. "All our investigator's notebooks felt too fat when they were new. They felt right after I had used them for a while. I thought at first it was just the higher gravity. But then I figured out the real reason—and just now I got the chance to confirm it. And I was right!"

"*What?*"

Jamie flipped the book shut, and pointed to the cover. "*You* gave me the idea, the connection, when you told Fallogon not to judge a book by its cover. It says right there. *Sixty sheets. Twenty lined, twenty graph, twenty blank.* But it's not true! All four of the surviving books on this ship have forty-eight sheets each—exactly sixteen each of lined, graph, and blank paper."

"So what? You've lost it, Jamie. And you've lost me. You've got about thirty seconds left to convince me that you are not completely out of your mind."

Jamie pointed at the spiral wiring binding that held the notebook's pages together. "Look there! Not a single, microscopic bit of scrap or paper fluff. Not a sign at all that any of the pages had even been there. Not on any of them. They've all been very carefully removed."

"So what?"

"So the Metrannans count in fours and sixteens and sometimes by twelves, and four books, each with four sets of sixteen sheets making up forty-eight total sheets would be a very nice, neat, round number to them—and they *like* things nice and neat and even, if you hadn't noticed. And I really doubt that the Metrannans sent into this ship by Bulwark of Constancy could read English or Arabic numbers. If they wanted to see if any pages had been used and torn out, *they would have counted the physical pages.* Trevor figured that out too, after he was searched—but he had some reason to use one or more pages of the notebooks, and he didn't want to leave any clue behind that he had done so, in case there was another search."

Hannah started to see it. Just a glimmer, but she started to see it. "But if they *had* counted the pages on the first search, then checked again on a second search, they'd spot the anomaly. He'd have drawn attention to the thing he was trying to hide."

"Maybe. Maybe not. If the first searchers *didn't* count the pages, or if they *didn't* take relentlessly detailed notes, or the second searchers didn't *read* the detailed notes, then Trevor could have gotten away with it. And if there was a second search, they might not think to count the pages again. But what this tells me is that Trevor removed at least one page from at least one of these notebooks, then figured out that he needed to hide the fact that there were missing pages. So he tore out enough sheets from *all* the notebooks to make them come out even. And the only reason it would be worth doing all that is if he had written something very, very important on a notebook page and didn't want the bad guys to notice."

"But what happened to the leftover sheets?"

"I think he burned them."

"Hold it. You had me going for a second there," said Hannah. "But you just jumped the tracks. Burned them where?"

Jamie grabbed at one of the notebooks and flipped it open to the last page of the graph-paper section. "There," he said. "The only thing written in any of the surviving notebooks. *Where we protect our treasures/unless we must destroy them.* That's the reason he left four books behind. We wondered about that, too, remember? Three as window dressing, and the fourth to hold that message. It's not a doodle. It's not a joke. It's a message to us. To you and me."

Hannah looked at the logo over the motto. "BSI. *Burn Stash Immediately.* The destruct oven?"

"Except the joke logo is a message too," Jamie said. "The *B* for Burn and the *S* for Stash are finished, and very elaborately decorated. But not the *I*. It's not finished. The *I* for Immediately isn't done. Burn Stash—but not immediately."

"But the destruct oven was filled to bursting!" Hannah objected.

"Right! And it *shouldn't* have been. A stranger, a xeno, would have no way of knowing that—but Trevor was assuming we'd know BSI procedures and regulations and how the oven was supposed to be used, so we'd be smart enough to figure it out, but we weren't. There's no *way* Trevor had enough classified material on board the ship to fill that oven so completely. Besides, we know he jettisoned a large amount of stuff. Why burn things needlessly when he could have just dumped it all overboard? Either the oven should have been totally empty, or it should have held a small amount of unburned material, ready to be destroyed if need be, or else we should have found the ashes or burn residue of whatever single datastore device held the decryption key. And if the destruct key *was* burned, it must have been just before the boarding party came onto the ship. In that case, what point would there be in doing the clear-out he did *after* the search? A full oven makes no sense."

"So why *was* it full to bursting?"

"Because he stuffed it full of whatever paper he could find, along with anything else that might hold data that he hadn't thrown overboard already, and I can tell you why he did that, too. If you were a xeno from a species that tended to be very concerned with clothing and appearance, and you managed to pry open a concealed chamber and get a choking faceful of ashes, maybe you wouldn't search that spot too carefully. And there's one other thing—"

An alert buzzer went off. Hannah checked her board. "It's the *Sholto*," she said. "Right on schedule. Hold on. I've got to make sure she gets herself into position and we've got all the communications working right."

"Right," Jamie said distractedly. "Go ahead."

Hannah worked her boards while Jamie struggled

to keep from fidgeting like an eight-year-old impatient to open his birthday presents.

Hannah refused to be hurried. If they wanted to live through the next few hours, they had to be sure the *Sholto* was ready to play her part. "All right," she said. "That's done. *Sholto* linked in, and she will make her matching burn in a couple of minutes. I can monitor from here. You were saying there was something else?"

"Yes!" Jamie said. "Something both of us missed. I almost had it once on the planet, but it got chased out of my mind until Fallogon started pontificating at us. He said something like a sealed vessel under pressure wouldn't change the way it looked."

"Yeah, so?"

"So the oven is sealed for use. When we first popped open the cover *over* the destruct oven door, *it kicked ash into the air*. There was ash outside the oven door. That couldn't happen unless the oven was opened after it was used to burn something."

Hannah thought about that for a second, then got an eager look in her eye. "Okay. Let me see if I can put this together. You're saying that Trevor burned a bunch of junk, probably including the missing notebooks, in the destruct oven—then *opened it up again*. He did that because he wanted to hide something in the oven, and he wanted the ashes to discourage a thorough examination of the oven, in case the bad guys found it during a later longer search. Which suggests that there was something unburned in there that he wanted to stay hidden. And we can both guess what that might be."

"Right. Perfect. Exactly."

"It's going to be a messy job," she said.

Jamie grinned. "I've figured out how to do it," he said. "And I'm volunteering."

The nav system lit up, showing the *Sholto* coming about and making her velocity-matching burn. Seconds later, the *Adler*, the *Sholto*, and the booster were all flying in formation, in a rough equilateral triangle that measured approximately ten thousand kilometers on a side. Hannah barely noticed. She was too busy thinking about the destruct oven.

* * *

Jamie's first idea for keeping the ash under control had been to use the *Adler*'s emergency pressure suit. But that was too much, too complicated. Instead he went with the same breathing mask he had used while waiting out the repairs in the air lock, plus a pair of rubber gloves. That and a cup to scoop the ashes out and a few large evidence bags to hold them were all he really needed.

They had to move a recuperating but still wretchedly unhappy Taranarak up out of her pile of padding and blanket so as to get at the entrance of the refresher compartment.

Jamie went in, wearing the mask and gloves,

and closed the door behind him to keep the ash out of the main cabin. He knelt down, popped up the deckplate, and watched happily as a few motes of ash jumped into the air. He checked his datapad for the combination, keyed it in, and opened the destruct oven's door, slowly and carefully.

Only a tiny bit of ash jumped into the air. Jamie set to work at once, slowly and carefully scooping out the powdered ash and melted scraps of plastic. It was with something akin to both grim satisfaction and glee that he pulled out a blackened length of spiral wire, of the type used in BSI notebooks, and then another, and another, and another. The wires were the remains of the complete notebooks that had been burned, along with the surplus pages from the four books that had survived.

He started to worry when he realized that he had almost cleared out the entire oven chamber, one slow scoop of material at a time, without finding anything. The air in the refresher chamber was thick with dust and floating ash, and a residue of the stuff was adhering to every available surface. His knees were aching. But he wasn't finding anything at all.

Could he have missed it? Were they going to have to sift through all those bags full of ash, looking for some blob of material that only *looked* burned and melted that held the decrypt key? Or had all his lovely logic been wrong, from beginning to end? Maybe Trevor had been using the notebooks to keep an endlessly detailed personal diary and simply decided to get rid of them after the gear jettison, maybe when he was already too weakened by the aging illness to go through the effort of dumping all the notebooks out the air lock.

Jamie had the oven almost completely empty, and was down to the very bottom of the chamber, before he brushed his gloved fingers on it. He pulled his arm out of the chamber and peered down into its dusty interior.

There, at the very back, carefully taped to the rear wall of the chamber, was a neatly folded square of what appeared to be official BSI investigator's notebook lined paper.

Jamie resisted the urge to hurry. Better to cross the t's and dot all the i's. He cleared out the rest of the ash, then wiped down the interior of the oven chamber with a cloth. He checked as much of the chamber as he could visually, and then stuck his hand back in and ran it around every square centimeter of the surface to confirm there wasn't anything else in there. He sealed up all his bags of ash and debris, wiped himself off as best he could, and put on a fresh set of gloves. Then and only then did he allow himself to reach in and oh-so-carefully peel the square of paper off the back of the oven's burn chamber. He made one last check, both by hand and by eye, to confirm that nothing else had been taped down under the square of paper.

And if all that slow and careful work also allowed him a little time to savor his triumph, he was not going to feel too guilty about that. He could have made up a pretty good list of reasons for why he had earned that moment.

Jamie carefully dropped the square of paper into a small transparent evidence bag, stood up, dusted himself off just a trifle more, and made an oddly triumphant exit from the refresher compartment.

* * *

Hannah was there waiting when Jamie came out. He peeled the breathing mask off with one hand and used the other to give the square of paper to Hannah.

Even Taranarak took an interest, forgetting her motion sickness enough to stand up on her four legs and stare at the paper. "Is that it?" Taranarak asked eagerly. "Is that the decrypt key?"

"Let's open it and find out," said Hannah. "Nice work, Jamie. Very, very, very nice work. I promise to give you an extremely large benefit of the doubt the next time I think you've completely lost your mind. Where was it, exactly?"

"Taped to the bottom of the burn chamber. Trevor must have burned a bunch of notebooks and other junk, scooped it all out, taped that paper in place, then dumped the ashes and burn debris back in on top of it. Go on," he said. "Open it up."

Hannah didn't argue. She reached over to a wall panel and pulled out a fold-out worktable, and the little bench seat that went with it. She sat down. Jamie grabbed one of the packing cases of gear from the *Sholto* and sat down on it opposite her, while Taranarak moved to stand between them. Hannah opened the evidence bag, slipped the paper square out, and examined it carefully. "It's taped shut," she said. "I don't want to tear it. Scissors?"

Jamie handed her a pair out of his evidence kit almost before she was finished asking. She carefully snipped the transparent tape apart, handed the scissors back, and unfolded the square. Inside was another square of paper. The outer piece was blank on both sides. It was obviously nothing more than an improvised envelope. Nonetheless, Hannah put it carefully back in the evidence bag. This was a time to be thorough, not a time to rush.

She unfolded the inner sheet. It was blank on one side. There was writing on the other, obviously written with great care.

She read it over—her heart sank as she did so. She handed it to Jamie. "I think we're in very big trouble," she said. The writing on the inner sheet of paper read this way:

> To good old, Hallaben to see back half of insult twice. Wen Her mutt cited know more grant of bank officer. Ungreen leaks hate this conic section. Blank the town Red. Good sunset vision might mean a being gets the blanks with other end of Newton's glass. Climbing Jacob's leads to heavens door held open. A killing

lightness weighs them down. Edgar's
mantel, like Vogel's Eagle Name Source.

"Okay," said Jamie as he put the paper down. "Does that stuff about the benefit of the doubt apply to Trevor?" he asked. "Because maybe Trevor was pretty far gone by the time he wrote those words."

"Is the news good? You are neither of you acting happy," said Taranarak in Lesser Trade.

"What?" said Jamie. "Oh, of course. Sorry." He shifted to Lesser Trade himself. "Forgive us. The note is in English—sort of—and force of habit made Hannah and me both drop into speaking English after reading it."

"I can already see that the note cannot be the decrypt key," said Taranarak in Lesser Trade. "It should be in Greater Trade Writing symbols. Hallaben would never have encoded anything using human writing. What does it say, anyway?"

"It's nonsense. Gibberish."

"Microdot?" Hannah asked. "Maybe the writing is meant to camouflage some sort of microdot or microwriting?"

"We've been through that," said Jamie. "Trevor didn't have the equipment." He shook his head and looked up at Hannah. "I really don't want to believe he was crazy," he said. "And I *can't* believe it. Everything else was so clear, so purposeful. Maybe it's not gibberish. Maybe it's code."

"No," said Hannah, staring at the words, and

starting to feel just a trifle better. "Not code. *Clues.*"

"What?"

"Clues. Puzzle clues. But done up to hide them in plain sight from people without the background to spot what's wrong or odd. It *looks* like plain old English prose. If you were an alien who didn't speak or read English, you'd never know from how the words looked that it wasn't a farewell note to his mother or something. And if you were an alien who *did* read English fairly well, you'd want to tear your heart out. You wouldn't be able to make heads or tails out of this—because the text *reads* like crossword puzzle clues. Not exactly like them, but close. Puns. Jokes. Word play."

Jamie's face lit up. "Yes!" he said. "You're right. It's a puzzle. He left a puzzle for us to solve. And the answer will lead us to the—"

An alert tone went off, squawking at them from the flight deck. "Oh, for the love of God!" Hannah jumped half out of her seat at the noise. "That scared me half to death. You're right, Jamie. He left us a puzzle—and we picked a hell of a time to finally get around to finding it."

She stood up and made her way up the ladder and looked at the main display and shut off the alert. "It's the *Stability*, all right," she announced, raising her voice a bit to be heard on the lower deck, and speaking in Lesser Trade. "She's here a lot sooner than we expected, way ahead of schedule, and she's at a lot closer range than we figured.

We're fine for the moment, but we've got to get busy pretty quick."

Jamie looked up to Hannah and tapped his finger on the note from Trevor. "Hannah, we have to deal with this. *Now.*"

"I agree. But we're going to have to find time for both problems," she said, trying to sound a lot calmer than she really was. Probably Jamie was doing the same. "Hang on, I'm coming down." She climbed down the ladder again and sat back down at the table, doing her best to seem calm, dispassionate, and professional. She doubted she was fooling anybody.

Hannah turned to Jamie and spoke in English. "We're on the clock, but there's something we have to decide before we go any further. We have to decide what to do about Taranarak. Do we trust her or not? I think the odds against her being a plant have just kept getting longer—and I don't think it much matters anymore. If there's something in her clothes or gear or whatever that can give Constancy a directional fix, we can't do anything about it anyway—and I think it's too late for anything we say to do Constancy any good even if it is listening somehow—and I very much doubt that our Unseen friend is listening. I think we might as well brief Taranarak now."

"I agree," said Jamie.

"What is going on?" Taranarak asked in Lesser Trade, her voice betraying her fear.

"A lot of things," said Hannah. "Constancy's

ship, the *Stability*, is out there. We can track her because we saw her transit-jump entry, and because she's just lit her engines and we can detect her thrust plume. Our nav system is doing that now. And our nav system ought to be able to keep a pretty fair track on her by dead reckoning between burns, but we *won't* be able to see her directly unless her main thrusters are lit.

"Our nav system knows where *we* are, and knows where the *Sholto* is and where the booster is, and we've all matched velocities. It's very unlikely that the *Stability* has spotted any of our vehicles yet, even though she has better detectors than we do. We're pretty sure that she can't detect our ships unless they light their engines or transmit a signal. But the second any of our vehicles do any of those things, Constancy will be able to track them and shoot at them and kill them. We're going to play it as safe as we can by keeping all our systems powered down as much as possible so as to give Constancy less chance to detect us."

"So we just sit here and hide until we run out of food, or air?" Taranarak asked.

"No," said Hannah. "Jamie has worked out a plan that involves the booster and the *Sholto*. It ought to at least give us a fighting chance of escaping. The risks are high, but we're doing our best to reduce them."

"But our primary mission is to get the decrypt key back to Center," Jamie said. "Surviving would be very nice, and we'd very much like to do it—but sending the key by laser or radio signal would do just as well as physically delivering an object that has the key on it. We intend to keep searching for the key. If we find it, making sure the key code gets back to Center is going to take priority over our own survival."

"And finding this"—Hannah tapped at the handwritten message—"makes our job even more difficult. It seems very likely that it contains puzzles and jokes that serve as clues that will tell us where the key is. So we have to play two very serious games at the same time—hiding from Constancy while trying to lure it into a trap, and at the same time trying to solve this charming little puzzle. And if we do find what we're looking for, and it's a choice between survival and BSI HQ on Center getting the decryption key—well, you understand."

"I understand, and I completely agree. But I doubt I can help with either problem," Taranarak said unhappily.

"I think you're wrong about that," said Hannah. "This note was hidden in a way that made it easier for humans to find than Metrannans—but even so, we just barely managed to find it. If the decrypt key is still hidden on this ship, it's hidden so as to make it harder for Metrannans to spot it than for humans. You might be a big help with that." She turned and looked to Jamie. "But right now, this second, I need *you* to come look at the tactical plot."

"We're going to be up and down this ladder all day long," Jamie grumbled, following after her.

"Well, you'd better get used to it," said Hannah.

Jamie dropped into the pilot's seat and pulled up the navigation plot display. "Well, it could be a lot worse," he said, after studying it for a moment. "Our three ships are deployed pretty well. It would be better if they were farther apart, or *not* flying in formation with each other, just to make things harder on Constancy, but stuff like that would make things too much harder for us, too. We just don't have the tools to manage a tactical situation that complicated. The *Stability* is more or less in the center of our triangle, closest to the booster.

"The *Stability hasn't* matched velocities with our ships, of course, because Constancy doesn't know where they are, but she's moving in more or less the same direction but somewhat faster. She's going to pass through our formation, approximately at its center, in about an hour. The *Stability*'s going to be between us and Center from there on in, which means that Constancy would almost certainly intercept any signals sent between BSI HQ and us— so we'd better not send any signals."

"We weren't planning on it anyway," said Hannah. "That's why we sent our call for help when we did. So what happens now?"

"Well, we've made our move by *not* moving," said Jamie. "We didn't do the normal post-transit-jump thing and immediately start our braking maneuvers. If Constancy was counting on tracking us on braking thrust, it's out of luck. It's got two choices. Constancy can search the entire volume of space we might be in, or it can leave the ship's engines off and wait, and call our bluff, force us to light *our* engines.

"We're moving at a helluva fast clip, and we're going to *have* to start braking sooner or later, or else we're going to blow right through the system and never come back. If we don't light our engines soon, we won't be able to stop in time. But the *Stability*'s got more powerful engines, and more stored power. She can wait longer—and for that matter, she could blow through one side of the Center System and out the other and Constancy wouldn't care—it's not trying to get to Center. What all that boils down to is that it can wait us out.

"*Except* we're on our turf now. It has to know we might have called for help already. And in fact we're not planning to do a braking run. We're counting on getting rescued. And Constancy ought to have seen that possibility. For all it knows, there could be a pair of heavy cruisers headed this way right now. They could blow the *Stability* out of space and rescue us with no fuss or bother. On the other hand, it also might be aware that one or both of our ships is awfully short of stored propulsion power. It doesn't know about the booster, and it can't know for sure which of the two ships it knows about we're on—and it can't rule out that we might have crews on both ships."

"Okay, now that you've got my head swimming, what happens next? Is Constancy going to just sit there and wait for us to blink first and fire our engines?"

"What I'm hoping is that *Constancy's* head is swimming. My guess is that it launched after us with no better plan than squashing us like bugs when it caught us. Now it's in over its head. I doubt Constancy realizes how difficult a thorough search of a volume of space this big can be—and as time goes by, and the possible trajectories we *might* be on expand, the search volume is only going to get bigger. The *Stability* will have to fly through a volume of space, scanning as she goes, and then stop, move over, and scan the next sector. And on top of everything else, of course, even if Constancy manages to kill us, it has to think about making its escape afterward, and that creates a whole *new* set of complications."

"Any chance it might just decide to give up and go home?" Hannah asked.

"If you had sat next to Constancy at that dinner, you wouldn't bother to ask that question," Jamie said with a shudder.

"Well, it sounds to me as if just sitting tight and waiting for us to blink first and start our braking run would be the more rational strategy for Constancy to follow."

"Maybe," said Jamie. "But it was mad enough to be spitting rivets before we left, and it's had a lot of time to get more frustrated since. My guess is that it goes for the active search." He stood up and punched a series of commands into his datapad so its main display would show a lower-resolution repeater display of the nav status screen. "For now, all we can do is sit tight. So we might as well go back down to the lower deck, keep Taranarak company, and start staring at Trevor's crossword puzzle clues."

* * *

Twenty minutes later, Jamie had learned very little from the clues, other than that he didn't like crossword puzzles very much. "Maybe it's something else *disguised* as puzzle clues," he said. "Maybe we're supposed to read the first letters of each sentence, or the last letters, or the capitalized letters, or something."

"Or maybe we should do what I suggested a while ago just to be polite and to keep Taranarak happy," Hannah said. "Maybe we should ask her about a few things in this." She shifted over to Lesser Trade. "Taranarak—it would be utterly hopeless to try and translate this message as it stands. But there is something I have just noticed in it. In my dealing with the Elder Races, I have often encountered beings who tell me how young I am, or how young the human race is. They do this when they wish to be insulting, or intimidating. However, that is not true of Metrannans, is it?"

"I do not understand."

"Would it be rude to tell a Metrannan he or she

was, or seemed, young?"

"Not in the least," she said.

"But it would be terribly insulting to make any mention of a Metrannan being or seeming old, would it not?"

"Oh, far worse than insulting. It would be dreadfully rude—especially coming from a being from another race who was of about the same age but could expect to live twice as long."

"That is as much as I thought," said Hannah, and shifted back to English. "Okay, that's a start. That first sentence—'To good old, Hallaben to see back half of insult twice.' If your idea was right, and we were supposed to read one element of it, like capitalized letters, then all the other elements would be meaningless, and you'd just toss them in anywhere to make the message look like real prose. But if this is supposed to be like a crossword clue, then *everything* in a clue is supposed to mean something—including the punctuation and commas. Since calling a Metrannan 'good old This-or-that' is about as deadly as an insult gets, that made me think 'for good old' followed by a comma is supposed to stand by itself, a separate phrase inside the clue-sentence. But what does the phrase mean?"

"Wait a sec," said Jamie. "Suppose 'To good old' means 'to *get to* good aging'—long life? To achieve it? But what's the 'back half of an insult'?"

"No, no," said Hannah excitedly. "Think crosswords. Not 'an insult'—the *word* 'insult.' Letter by letter, the back half is 'ult.' Syllable by syllable, it's 'sult.' Twice?"

"Sult-sult?" Jamie frowned. "No! Sult repeated! Sult and *result*. So it means 'To cause good aging—long life—show the results to Hallaben.' "

"And it's got to mean the results of the message itself. It's *got* to. Unless it leads to another puzzle that leads to a puzzle that leads to a puzzle that leads to the decrypt key. In which case I'll start a research project to bring Trevor Wilcox III back to life just so I can strangle him."

"No. I want in. You can hold him down and I'll beat him with a shovel. But I don't think Trevor would dare get that cute. 'To age well, show the thing this helps you find to Hallaben.' Translation: This message will tell you where the decrypt key is."

"Good," said Hannah. "Good! But I think it's also saying in a sort of sideways way that the clues point to each other. There's going to be layers to this."

Taranarak spoke in Lesser Trade. "Excuse me," she said, "but your datapad seems to be indicating something."

Jamie snatched it up and looked at it. "That's for sure," he said. He looked to Hannah. "I think the party is about to start," he said. "Constancy is on the move."

TWENTY-EIGHT
SEEK AND HIDE

Taranarak watched as the two humans scrambled back up that infuriating ladder to the flight deck. It was not only disconcerting to see them move that way, it was becoming downright mortifying. There were plainly any number of things that humans—crude, half-civilized, oh-so-Younger-Race humans—could do far more easily than Metrannans. Things that went far beyond climbing ladders or dealing with shifting gravity fields. Things like being able to stand up to the Unseen Race, and, indeed, all the Elder and Eldest Races. Improvising, taking risks, trying things that had not been done before.

Nor was it that they were unafraid. Even across the gulf between her race's gestural signaling and that of humans, it was easy to see just how scared Mendez and Wolfson were. And yet they pressed on.

It struck her that she was, in that very moment, witnessing a battle between the Youngest and one of the Eldest known surviving sentient races in the Galaxy. Age versus youth. It was inspiring, in a way. But, regardless of who won this confrontation, the *way* they were fighting it told her volumes. Perhaps the Elder Races might have a lot more to be worried about than they realized.

* * *

"I was beginning to think Constancy had decided to go for the sit-and-wait strategy," Jamie admitted as he studied the nav plot. "That would be a nice play-it-safe way to go. Custom-made for an Elder Race attitude. But the *Stability* has lit her engines. She's *definitely* moving into position for an active pattern search. And pow! The *Stability*'s active detection system just lit up. Big, bright, and powerful, that's for sure. Better than I thought she'd have. But it's like Constancy just switched on a really powerful searchlight. If it manages to get close enough and point it directly at us, it'll see us for sure. But exactly because it's so powerful, *we* can see the *Stability* from way far away, no matter which direction the detector is pointed."

"So we can see Constancy better, but it'll be able to search faster than we figured," said Hannah.

"Right. And, sooner or later, depending on what search pattern it chooses and how that pattern interacts with dumb luck, it'll find the booster, the *Sholto*—and us. Maybe not in that order. We might have to play our next card a little sooner than I thought."

"Anything more you can do? Anything more you need to see?"

"Not right now. It's going to be a while before

the *Stability* shifts course into the next leg of her search pattern. That'll tell us a lot."

"Then let's get back to the puzzle."

* * *

" '*Wen Her mutt cited know Moor grant of bank officer.*' " Hannah read out loud. "There's an inspiring quote to live by."

"Wait a second," Jamie said. "Read it aloud again."

" '*Wen Her mutt cited know Moor grant of bank officer.*' What are you hearing?"

"Different words than I see when I read it on paper," said Jamie. studying the paper. "At least in the first part of the sentence, every word is a pun and a misspelling of some other word. 'Wen Her mutt cited know Moor.' Hmmm. Lemme see."

He scrawled out the nonsense phrase, then wrote another version directly under it.

" 'When Her mutt sighted no more'? No. Wait a second. 'When *hermit* sighted no more!' Something happens when you can't see a hermit anymore?"

"Not exactly," said Hannah. "Keep on misspelling and punning. "Bank officers don't give grants—they make loans. 'Grant of bank officer' is a loan—but make that *alone*. 'When a Hermit is sighted, the hermit is no longer alone.' And maybe—maybe—the capitalization of 'Her' makes it seem likely that the hermit is special or important and/or female."

"Or else 'Her mutt' might mean 'her dog,' or it might even be a pun inside a pun—Hermit's her-mutt. The female hermit's dog, or the hermit's fe-male dog," Jamie said. "This is starting to make my brain hurt. Maybe it's 'When the female hermit sights her dog, she is no longer alone.' That actu-ally almost makes sense."

"Wait a second!" Hannah said. "I think I can make the *next* part make absolute sense. 'Ungreen leeks hate this conic section.' More puns and mis-spelling. The kind of leek that isn't green is a leak, l-e-a-k. And if I were an ambitious leak that wanted to accomplish something, what I would hate would be the thing that stops me—a patch."

"And we found out the hard way that the leak patches used aboard the *Sherlock*-class are round—they're circles."

"Perfectly valid conic section there. Good! And let's not forget one of the patches was missing."

"I think we're getting warm," said Jamie enthu-siastically.

"What have you found?" said Taranarak in Lesser Trade. "Your voices and faces seem to show happiness and excitement. What have you found?"

Jamie opened his mouth to tell her, then shut it again. "I regret to say that, when you look at it all together, we haven't found much at all. Translated to Lesser Trade Speech, what we have so far would be something like 'Show the results of this riddle to Hallaben if you want long life. If a female person who lives alone is seen by her pet, she is no longer alone. Leaks do not like round patches.' "

Taranarak was silent for a moment. "I am starting to wonder if perhaps you are all insane," she said.

"In a way, that's the idea, Taranarak," said Hannah with a weary smile. "Trevor's ship, this ship, had just been searched by xenos, and he was very much afraid that it would be boarded again after he died. He wanted *us* to be able to find the decrypt key, but not *you,* if you see what I mean. So he worked out a way of setting down clues that would be impossible for an outsider to understand—and just barely possible for one of us."

"I'm going to take a break from crosswords and check on the deranged alien who's trying to kill us all," said Jamie. "The *Stability* should have dropped into her search pattern by now."

* * *

Jamie climbed the ladder once again and sat in the pilot's chair. He was more worried than he let on. He was starting to wonder if maybe Taranarak was right. Maybe Trevor *had* gone crazy. Maybe Hannah and he weren't too far behind. Playing word games seemed an insane way to spend their time when Bulwark of Constancy was out there, trying to track them down.

He rubbed his eyes and studied the plot, expecting to see that not much had changed.

That was not what he saw. What he saw instead

was not good. Not good at all. "Hannah!" he cried out. "I need you! *Now.*"

She was up the ladder and at his side almost at once. "What's happened?"

"My mistake. My big, fat mistake that might get us all killed. I assumed that the *Stability* was going to drop into her search pattern in a nice, efficient logical way, by boxing in the forward end of the volume first. I forgot Constancy's new to all this. It's doing what looks like a helical outward leg that doesn't make any sense at all. Except—"

"Yeah," said Hannah. "I can see it."

"It's pretty hard to miss," said Jamie. "And we will be too. Beginner's luck for Constancy, I guess." The pattern Bulwark of Constancy was flying was more or less parallel to the triangle defined by the positions of the *Sholto*, the *Adler*, and the booster. And in about half an hour, the *Adler* would sweep directly through its path.

"It's time to create a diversion," said Hannah. "I think we have to give her the booster. Squirt a signal and command it to light its engine and run. Do it so it's at least plausible that the booster was running away to avoid being spotted before the search pattern can catch it."

"Suppose Constancy doesn't take the bait?" asked Jamie.

"Then *we* light our engine and run before *we* get spotted."

"I'll do my best, but the pattern's not going to get anywhere near the booster."

"Yeah, but the *Sholto*'s even farther out of position. We *might* be able to make the booster's run look like it was being flushed out—but not the *Sholto*," said Hannah. "If the *Sholto* ran, it would look like what it was—a diversion."

"Okay then. We fire the booster—and try to make it convincing. I'll have to use a low-power tight-beam radio signal. I'll do as tight and short a squirt as I can and wait until Constancy's ship is as far off-angle as it's going to get. I doubt her ship is even equipped to detect radio—but Constancy still *might* pick it up."

"Understood," said Hannah. "Make the risk as small as you can, but send the commands. And hurry. We've got other work to do."

"Huh?"

Hannah sighed. "The odds of our not living through this just went way up," she said. "We've got to solve that damned fool puzzle fast and hope it actually leads us to the decrypt key. If Constancy is going to kill us all, I'd just as soon we send the message first."

"It'll take me a little while to get this set up," he said. "I'll see you down there."

* * *

Hannah allowed herself a moment on the ladder. She stopped, rested her head on a rung, and let out her breath with a long and weary sigh. How had they come to this? Trying to wade through a morass of puns and riddles in order to save not just a way of making a whole species of beings live longer, but also to suppress a weapon that might be able to wipe out humanity. And *that* was the vital work! Dodging the homicidal Xenoatric who was trying to get another crack at them had to be treated as no more than a distraction.

Never mind. Press on. Keep going. She moved the step or two back to the table and slumped down in her chair.

"Is everything all right?" Taranarak asked.

Hannah laughed sadly. "No," she said. "Do you want the details?"

"I am not sure that I do."

"You don't." Hannah picked up Trevor's message from the other side of death and read the next line or two out loud in English. "Blank the town Red. Good sunset vision might mean a being gets the blanks with other end of Newton's glass."

That part was almost too easy. *Paint* the town red, and a being gets the *blues*. But this thing had layers to it. Good sunset vision? Red. Hannah thought of the strong red cast to all the lights on Metran. And Newton's glass? A telescope, maybe?

Jamie came back down and sat on his box. He set his datapad down on the folding table. "As the angles shift around and so forth, we'll get our lowest chance of Constancy detecting our squirt signal in about fifteen minutes," he said. "I've programmed things to send the message then. I can monitor well enough from here until then. I don't *think* Constancy's ship will be able to detect the squirt signal—but I've got to tell you—if she does, it's all over. The *Stability*'s going to be on us *fast*. You're going to have to be in the pilot's station, ready for action."

"Thanks for the cheery thought," Hannah replied. "Meanwhile, back in the message—any idea what Newton's glass might be?"

"What classes did *you* sleep through? A prism, of course. He used a prism to split white light into the colors of the spectrum."

"That makes more sense here than telescope."

"You're thinking of Galileo."

"Whatever. I think I have the next part of the message. 'Paint the town red.' "

"Gee, I thought I would have to use my secret decoder ring to crack that part."

"So there was one easy section. The next bit is something like 'the ability to see well in red light might mean a being gets the blues with—has trouble with—the other end of the spectrum.' "

"Not much of a shocker there, either," said Jamie. "A species able to see well in the red end of the spectrum generally can't see well in the blue end of the spectrum." He turned to Taranarak and spoke in Lesser Trade Speech. "There is something in the puzzle-message that seems to be about differences in how your people and mine see color. The lighting in this ship. Is it comfortable for you?" As he spoke, he worked his datapad, holding it so neither Hannah or Taranarak could see what he was doing.

"Not particularly. It is a bit harsh, and bright. It makes things seem cold and washed-out."

"If we live through this, I will see what I can do to adjust it," Jamie said. He turned the datapad over and showed the display to Hannah and Taranarak. "What color or colors do you see? Taranarak, you go first," he asked. To Hannah's eye, the display showed five thick stripes in varying shades of blue.

Taranarak peered carefully at the screen. "There are two—no, three variations of blue," she said.

"I see five different shades," said Hannah.

"Actually, according to my datapad's painting program, there are eight—but I can only distinguish six myself," said Jamie. "Thank you, Taranarak. That was extremely useful." He switched back to English. "So we've got a lot about red and blue, and something about paint," he said.

"There were cans of touch-up paint in that locker behind you. One of them was slightly used."

Jamie jumped up and opened the locker and pulled out the cans of paint. He set them on the table. "Red. Black. And blue-grey. The blue-grey is the one that's been opened. And it's the one that matches the ship's general interior."

He looked at Hannah, and she looked at him. "I think we're getting close," she said quietly.

"So do I," said Jamie. He checked the time.

"But right now we need you in the pilot's seat again. This is where we blow our cover."

"Grab the message and some notepaper," said Hannah. "We're going to work the rest of this from the flight deck. Taranarak—wish us luck."

TWENTY-NINE

ALL FOR ONE

Hannah buckled herself into the pilot's chair as Jamie watched the countdown on his datapad. "Okay," he said. "The *Adler*'s sending her command signal to the booster in five, four, three, two, one—now."

Hannah's throat was dry, and the palms of her hands were sweaty. She stared at the nav display, eyes locked on the dot that represented Constancy's ship. Any change there, any sudden movement, meant the signal had leaked and Constancy had seen it—and gotten a lock on the *Adler*. If that happened, they wouldn't have a prayer of outrunning the bigger ship—but they would have to try.

Nothing. No response. Not that it meant anything. Constancy could be a little slow off the mark or just taking its time getting the *Stability*'s weapons hot.

"How long until the booster makes its move?" Hannah asked. "And for that matter, what is it going to do, exactly?"

"The engines should light three minutes from *now*. It'll boost directly away from Constancy's ship at maximum thrust until it runs out of power," said Jamie, watching the display as intently as Hannah. "Not subtle, but I didn't have much time for finesse. And I really wish we weren't throwing away one of the only two cards we have to play."

Hannah chose not to remind him they had *three* cards to play, *three* ships to sacrifice. " 'Climbing Jacob's leads to heavens door held open,' " she quoted. "Gotten anywhere with that?"

"Jacob's ladder, obviously," said Jamie.

"Ah, but it wasn't a ladder," said Hannah. "There's a fun fact for you. That's a mistranslation. It was a staircase, or a stile, or something."

"Thanks for clearing that up. I'm sure Trevor was working from the original Greek."

"Aramaic, I think."

"Whatever. I don't think Constancy detected our message to the booster. It would have responded by now."

"Let's hope the booster gets its attention."

"Bible trivia to one side," said Jamie, still watching the displays, "if we assume that all the mistakes in Trevor's message were deliberate, it might mean something that Jacob's whatever doesn't lead to Heaven's door—capitalized singular possessive. It leads to the lowercase-plural heavens door. It leads to the heavens—the sky and stars, not to paradise."

"Kind of the way that ladder behind you leads to a hatch that opens to the heavens."

"Kind of like that, yeah. Exactly like it, in fact. But what's the part about 'held open' mean?"

"Hold it," Hannah said. "Coming up on the booster firing. We've got to watch this."

The booster lit its engines, and even at the small scale of the nav display, it started to move, and move fast.

But it did not move for long. The *Stability* responded with astonishing speed. The glowing dot that represented the *Stability* accelerated violently, straight for the booster. It was another stern chase, but it was not a long one. Jamie and Hannah watched in silence as the xeno ship moved in on their decoy—but neither of them expected the end to come as soon as it did.

The two ships were still separated by thousands of kilometers when the booster flared up, flashed over into nothing, and then vanished from the nav plot as if it had never existed.

"My God!" said Hannah. "What did it use to destroy it at that kind of range?"

"I don't know," said Jamie. "Maybe some kind of heavy particle beam. But that ship's got weapons I wasn't expecting."

"But maybe—maybe—that's bought us a little time," said Hannah. "Constancy's going to have to put on the brakes, slow down again, reverse course, and resume the search pattern." The thought wasn't much comfort, seeing how fast that ship could attack. How long would they last when their time came?

Maybe not long at all. They would have to be ready by then, all their duties complete. "No more leaving the flight deck," she said. "Things might happen fast. I'm going to have to be close to the controls from now on. But even so—back to work," she said, not bothering with false heartiness or bravado. She looked Jamie straight in the eye. "We couldn't be much closer. We almost have it. I'm sure of it."

It seemed to take Jamie a moment to come back to himself. The effortless, casual suddenness of the booster's destruction had thrown him as well. "Ah, yeah," he said. "Yeah."

" 'Held open,' " said Hannah. " 'Climbing Jacob's leads to heavens door held open.' What's that supposed to mean?"

"I don't know."

Hannah stood up, grabbed on to the rope ladder, and climbed upward a rung or two. Suddenly she had it. "I know," she said. "At least I think I do. It doesn't seem like much. The top of the ladder is on those little rails that slide back and forth. You have to push the top of the ladder one way to line the ladder up with the hatch lip, but you have to shove it back the other way to close the hatch properly. 'Climbing Jacob's leads to heavens door held open' translates to mean 'You can climb the rope ladder through the nose hatch when it's open.' "

"Yeah, but so what?" asked Jamie.

Hannah climbed back down and shook her

head. "I have no idea." She glanced at the nav plot. "There's good news. It looks like Bulwark of Constancy has decided to examine the wreckage or some bloody fool thing. The *Stability*'s matching velocities with the debris cloud from the booster."

"If it exploded violently enough for our little nav plot display to come close to overloading, there probably aren't any fragments larger than five centimeters across."

"Yeah, but apparently Constancy doesn't know that," said Hannah. *And we get to live a little bit longer while it discovers that.* But there was no point in saying *that* out loud. "What's next on our little list of riddles?" she asked.

"I copied it into my datapad," he said. "Lemme see. 'A killing lightness weighs them down.'" Hannah looked down—and saw Taranarak, sitting on the lower deck because she couldn't bear heights, and was just barely fully recovered from her brush with death, caused by a few seconds' exposure to zero gee during the transit jump. "Metrannans," said Hannah. "'A killing lightness weighs them down.'"

"Of course!" said Jamie. "One more left," he said. "'Edgar's mantel, like Vogel's Eagle Name Source.'"

"Vogel. I hadn't really focused on that before. That's got to be Doc Vogel, back at base. It's an in-joke reference that would only make sense to a BSI agent who'd served at HQ since Vogel started there."

"Okay, so what? What's Vogel's Eagle?"

"Hold it. Hold it. Your datapad. Link into the ship's database and pull up a German-English dictionary. Get me the German word for 'eagle.'"

Jamie's eyes went wide. "I don't have to," he said. "I know that one. I just didn't put it together. The German for eagle is 'Adler.'"

"So, so that becomes—the name source for the *Irene Adler*. The Sherlock Holmes story. 'A Scandal in Bohemia.' Is there an Edgar in that story?"

"No! But there's an Edgar who wrote stories!" Jamie said. "Edgar Allan Poe. And he had a story, a detective story, a famous one, where there was a mantel that played a big part in the plot."

"*That* class I didn't sleep through," said Hannah. "'The Purloined Letter,' by Edgar Allan Poe. The whole point of it was that the letter was hidden in plain sight, on the mantel, but disguised to look like something else."

"And that links back to the earlier clue, with 'Her' capitalized," said Jamie. "Name Source is capitalized. The other 'Her' refers to the same thing—Irene Adler."

"Not the character in the story. The ship. *This* ship."

Jamie rubbed his head and groaned. "All right," he said. "If—if—we've got all this right, and if Trevor's mind hadn't aged into senile dementia before he wrote this down, then what the hell does it all mean?"

Hannah glanced at the nav plot again. Bulwark of Constancy was just coming up to the volume of space where the booster had been when it blew. Maybe—maybe—it could find some debris there that might tell it that the wreckage wasn't the *Sholto* or the *Adler*, but Hannah doubted it. The main thing was that the search would keep Constancy busy for a few more minutes. It might just be long enough. "Let me go over it again." She took the datapad from Jamie, read the original message, and translated it into what they thought the answers were.

" 'If you want longevity, show the results of reading this to Hallaben. When a female hermit sights her dog, she is no longer alone,' or maybe the dog isn't in there. It *might* mean something can be seen only when the hermit is alone—or maybe only when the hermit *isn't* alone. 'Blank the town Red' brings 'paint' to our minds—and some paint has been used. Leaks hate patches—and the fact that there's one gone is called to our attention. The Metrannans get the blues when they try to see blue—and it's blue paint that has been used. And pardon the expression, but maybe the mentions of red are just red herrings. Climbing the ladder leads to the hatch—when it is open. Metrannans have to have gravity. In 'The Purloined Letter' the object of interest was hidden in plain sight."

"Let's leave the dog out. I think the dog is the

real red herring, if you know what I mean," said Jamie. "We're reading in one or two layers too many. I think 'Her mutt' just means 'hermit.' But anyway, probably a patch has been painted blue, and slapped over something in plain sight, and that's where the decrypt key is hidden. And it's been done in such a way that it would be harder for Metrannans to find, because of their bad blue-end vision and need for gravity."

"There's a lot about sight and seeing in all the clues," Hannah observed.

"Yeah," said Jamie. "Trevor's telling us that we can see it from where we are, right now, inside the ship's cabin."

"But you can only see it when the *Adler* is or isn't alone, or on the ladder, or with the hatch open, or when—"

Jamie looked up sharply at Hannah. "We never closed the upper hatch at all while the two ships were together—except from the other side, from the *Sholto*. But there's no outer nose hatch to give us an air lock, so when the *Adler*'s away from other ships, when she's alone—"

"The hatch is shut. It has to be. And if the Metrannans entered through the upper hatch, they would have to have the gravity system on, and they'd have to pull the ladder into position over the hatch lip to get up and down. The hatch would have to have stayed open the whole time they were here!"

"But wait a second. Trevor didn't rehide the key

until *after* that search was over. If there's anything we've worked out with a great deal of confidence, that's it. He didn't hide the key until after the search. So why would the hatch position matter? It would only matter if he knew they'd *never* use the lower-deck air lock hatch."

Hannah shifted to Lesser Trade Speech, and called down to the lower deck. "Taranarak! You were telling me about the day you were arrested, when you went to meet with Bulwark of Constancy and they picked you up on the way home."

"Yes. That was the day it all started to fall apart, so far as I was concerned."

"Tell Jamie. Tell him what Bulwark's main argument was, the reason you couldn't let everyone on the planet, and all the Metrannans in the Galaxy, live twice as long."

"Because, Bulwark of Constancy said, 'Change is Wrong.'"

Hannah turned toward Jamie and grinned. "*That's* why," she said. "That's why the hatch position mattered. Trevor was worried about a second search. And he knew Bulwark was sure that Change is Wrong. If they had come in through the nose hatch the first time, then they would do it that way the second time, and the third, and the fourth, and forever. Because the other side of that rule is 'Do Everything the Same Way.' They would *always* come through the nose hatch, and the nose hatch would always have to stay open the whole time they were on board."

"That's a stretch," Jamie said. "Sooner or later they would have to work out that the lower-deck hatch would be easier for them—but yeah, I understand the logic." Jamie looked up at the docking hatch—the door to the heavens—with a gleam in his eye. "But the *Irene Adler* is alone right now, and the hatch is closed, and that's the best time to see—who knows what?"

At that moment, another audio alert sounded. Hannah and Jamie both checked the nav plot—and both of them saw what had caused the alert.

Bulwark of Constancy's ship had changed course yet again.

It was headed straight for them, straight as an arrow for a bull's-eye.

"How?" Hannah demanded, her blood running cold. "How did it lock in on us? What could the booster debris have told it?"

"Nothing," said Jamie. "It's just a little slow on the uptake. My guess is that her detectors *did* pick up our radio command—but Constancy didn't pay it any attention or understand what it meant at first. It just got really smart just a little late in the game and triangulated back from the direction of the radio signal source and the booster's start position." Jamie stared at the nav plot for a moment. "I've got an idea," he said. "It's going to take some timing and luck, but I've got an idea. You go take a look at that hatch."

"But—"

"Do it," Jamie said. "If you find it fast, we might still have a chance to radio in the key sequence before Constancy gets in range. I think I can keep us alive at least that much longer."

Hannah looked at her partner and saw that there was no time or reason to argue. If she was going to trust his judgment, this was when to do it. "All right," she said.

She reached for the ladder again and scrambled up to the hatch. Hannah knew in an instant that whatever Trevor had done, he had done in zero gee. She remembered what Jamie had spotted in the logs. The *Adler*'s gravity had been kept at three-quarters of a gee—except for a two-hour period when it was cut to zero. She had just figured out what those two hours had been for.

With the stanchion pushed back on the rails away from the hatch lip, there was a hell of an overhang between the top of the ladder and the hatch proper. In zero gee, inspecting the closed hatch would be an utterly simple task. But with the gravity system cranked up to one-point-two-one gees for the benefit of Taranarak's delicate stomach, it bordered on the impossible.

"I beg of you, be careful!" Taranarak called out as Hannah leaned out from the ladder to grab on to an awkwardly positioned handhold on the side of the hatch.

"Calm yourself, Taranarak," said Hannah in Lesser Trade. "Or, better still, don't watch." But

Taranarak's fright did serve to remind Hannah that there was a long straight drop to the lower deck if she let her hand slip. And breaking her neck would be every bit as fatal as a dose of Bulwark of Constancy's long-range weapon.

Hannah found a spot to keep her right foot on the ladder's top rung while wedging her left foot on top of a cable conduit and keeping a grip on the handhold. It wasn't exactly comfortable, and it was going to turn intensely painful if she stayed in that position too long, but it got her face up close to the inside cover of the nose hatch and left her with one hand free.

Even with her eyes no more than thirty centimeters from the hatch, even knowing that she was looking for a circular hull patch twenty centimeters in diameter, painted to match the grey-blue of the ship's interior, it took her a while to find it. At last she spotted it—aligned exactly over the hatch's centerpoint, painted to a smooth and perfect finish.

She reached up with her free hand and got the edge of a fingernail under it. Obviously, the patch hadn't been stuck down with the normal adhesive, or else she wouldn't have been able to get it free with a crowbar. She worried her fingernail under it a bit more and got enough of it clear to poke her fingertip under it and give it a gentle tug. A moment later, she was peeling the whole patch off. She got it free, managed to roll it up one-handed, then tucked it into the breast pocket of her coveralls. She needed both hands to get herself back over to the ladder before she lost all feeling in the foot that was wedged into the conduit.

She was down the ladder and back on the flight deck in a matter of moments. "Got it!" she cried out. "I've got it."

Jamie looked up at her, grim and worried. "We might not get to keep it long. Constancy's headed our way fast."

Hannah pulled it from her pocket and unrolled it again. There was a whole sheet of paper from an investigator's notebook stuck to the back of the patch, and every square centimeter of the paper was covered with Greater Trade Writing symbols in what appeared to be an entirely random sequence.

"So there it is," said Jamie. "The key that will unlock it all."

"I'll grab a camera from the evidence kit and photograph it," said Hannah. "You get ready to transmit the image file to Center."

"Right. I'm as ready to deal with Constancy as I'm ever going to be. I figure we've got about eight or ten minutes."

"That's not long," said Hannah.

"It's long enough to win," said Jamie with a tired, defiant smile. "Time enough to force Bulwark of Constancy to face some changes. Go take that picture."

Hannah went down to the lower deck—and saw Learned Searcher Taranarak. "We have it," said Hannah in Lesser Trade. "We have it. Here it is." She laid the patch with the sheet of paper still attached to it on the table and allowed Taranarak time to look upon it, to touch it, to understand that her goal, that the future of her people, was in reach.

Hannah grabbed the evidence camera and took the picture. She took multiple shots of it, then, working very carefully, she peeled back the paper from the patch itself, and confirmed that other side of the sheet was blank. After all they had been through, she had no interest in transmitting only half the decrypt key.

She rushed up the ladder and handed Jamie the camera. He dropped it into the proper slot on the control panel. "We're set to transmit," he said. "But I'm going to hold off just a little bit. Sending the decrypt key this way won't be exactly secure, after all—and maybe the stunt I've set up will actually work."

"Don't cut it too close, Jamie." She stood just behind where her partner sat, slightly hunched over the control panel. She checked the displays and watched him work the controls.

"I won't," he said, and glanced at the nav plot clock display. "Here we go," he said, in a tired, tired voice. "It's been a pleasure to serve with you, Agent Wolfson."

"Very much likewise, Agent Mendez," she said, putting her hand on his shoulder. She was glad that at least the two of them were going to go out together, in the moment when it was all about to end. Hannah suddenly realized that she had absolutely no idea what Jamie had cooked up. "What's going to happen?" she asked. "Are you going to use the *Sholto* to try and decoy Constancy away from the *Adler*?"

"What? No. Just the opposite," he said. "The *Adler* is going to decoy Constancy away from the *Sholto*."

She had just time enough to look at him in horror when the *Adler* lit her engines. "*What?*"

"We're going to blow right past the *Stability*," Jamie said. "Don't worry, we'll be out of range of her particle beam. I think. But the main thing is to get her turning in pursuit of us and away from the *Sholto*."

"Jamie! We only have about twenty minutes of boost power left on this bird—and Constancy's ship outguns us."

"One way or the other, twenty minutes will be enough," he said, watching the nav plot. "And I worked the vectors pretty carefully. The *Stability*'s going to have to sacrifice about sixty percent of her effective thrust just making the turn and coming about to the right course heading. She won't gain on us. Or the *Sholto*. There!" he pointed to the nav plot. "The *Sholto*'s going into her suicide run. Right up the *Stability*'s thrust plume. The *Stability*'s own energy wake will blank out her aft sensors—if Constancy's even bothering to keep watch. It didn't know we had three ships."

Hannah watched in astonishment. She could see it. She could absolutely see it. He had put the *Adler* on a course vector that forced Bulwark of Constancy to put on the brakes, hard, before she was able to come about to fly in pursuit—and the same course put the *Sholto* directly behind Constancy, where Constancy could not possibly see it—and *Sholto* was boosting fast.

And Gunther's crew had put a very big and powerful new self-destruct system aboard the *Sholto* just before mission departure. Hannah watched as the *Sholto* entered Bulwark of Constancy's energy wake. Another stern chase, but this one would be mercifully short. The *Sholto* closed the distance even as Constancy was actually drifting slowly away from the *Adler*.

"I configured it for detonation at a range of one kilometer," said Jamie quietly. The fear and anxiety had drained from his face. He could see it was going to work. "That ought to be close enough."

"Yeah," said Hannah. "It ought to be." She looked at her young partner and was glad for what she saw in his calm face. This was the moment when he would pay the debt, balance the books. The Unseen being who had killed Special Agent Trevor Wilcox III was about to die—but it would not be revenge, or bloodlust, or an eye for an eye. It would be self-defense, a law officer using deadly force to protect himself and others from harm. Whatever shadows the necessity of killing might cast on Jamie's soul, they would not be the far darker and crueler shadows made by taking pleasure in killing. Bulwark of Constancy had put Trevor Wilcox under sentence of death with a squirt from a bottle. Constancy had killed Hallaben, and put the whole Metrannan race under sentence of premature, useless death. But that sentence, at least, was about to be overturned.

The United Human Government Ship BSI 3369 *Bartholomew Sholto* crept, unseen, closer and closer to her target, until she was seen no more, altogether lost to the view from the *Irene Adler*'s instruments.

Until, in a brilliant flash of light, the *Sholto* flared up into view for one moment—in the act of bringing final and permanent change to Bulwark of Constancy.

" 'Out out, brief candle,' " Jamie whispered.

And the light faded out. Constancy had lost its Bulwark.

Commander Kelly had kept her word. There was in fact a rescue ship on standby, and relatively close—but the *Irene Adler* wasn't exactly on a standard approach vector by the time the recovery ship made radio contact. It was going to be a while before the pickup got made.

That was almost all right with Hannah, Jamie, and Taranarak. Somehow, without the fear of pursuit, with the decrypt key safely in hand, with the knowledge that they were going to live through the flight, the idea of the three of them being cooped up for another thirty-seven hours on a one-person ship seemed a lot more endurable. They read. They ate. They slept.

And they talked. Pickup was only a few hours away when Jamie remembered one thing he had been puzzling over. Maybe one of his fellow inmates would have an idea.

"What I can't understand is why Trevor felt he had to *re*hide the decryption key," said Jamie as the three of them sat around the table, dawdling after breakfast.

"What do you mean?" Taranarak asked.

"Well, obviously, Constancy's Metrannans didn't find it the first time they came aboard, so wherever the key was at that point had to be at least a fairly safe place to stash it. But then, unless we're reading the whole thing wrong, Trevor went through this huge and elaborate effort to rehide it *after* they were gone."

"That bothered me too," said Hannah. "Why fix what isn't broken? Why move it from a hiding place that worked?"

"Ah! I see. You have a wrong assumption there," said Taranarak. "He did *not* need to hide it for the first search. Hallaben did not give him a physical object to conceal. Hallaben gave Wilcox a sequence of Greater Written Trade characters to memorize. The key was hidden inside his head. Just incidentally, my research has led me to believe that Hallaben *did* create a backup of the decrypt key. Based on various hints I found among Hallaben's papers, I am morally certain that he asked a trusted associate with a superb memory to remember the same character sequence.

"Plainly, once Agent Wilcox realized he was dying, he felt the need to transcribe the decrypt key before he died, or before his memory started to fail—and, as you say, he hid it and set out clues for finding it that would greatly increase the chances that a human, and especially a BSI agent, would find it, while greatly reducing the odds that a Metrannan would succeed."

"Wait a second," Hannah protested. "If you

knew about this trusted associate knowing the key, why didn't you speak up? Why didn't you just go to the trusted associate and ask for the character sequence?"

"Because I only reached that conclusion a day or so before your arrival—and because trust can be misplaced. Based on what you have told me of your work, it would seem that the trusted associate in question killed Hallaben almost immediately afterward, and probably deliberately purged the character sequence from its own memory store. Bulwark of Constancy was no pinnacle of trustworthiness."

"But why didn't you tell *us* about Trevor memorizing the key?"

Taranarak touched her inner closework hands to her outer strongwork hands, the Metrannan equivalent of a shrug. "We never did get much time to talk," she said. "Besides, you never asked."

* * *

Once they got back to base, Jamie learned another important truth. It turned out that saving the world involved an amazing amount of paperwork. Jamie was stuck in his cubicle in the BSI HQ Bullpen for most of his first morning back on duty, filling out the forms justifying the destruction of the booster and the *Bartholomew Sholto*. Once that was done, he had to file another report on the destruction of all their other hardware in the gondola explosion.

Hannah poked her head into Jamie's cubicle. "You still at it?" she asked.

"Almost done," he said. "Just filling out the last of it."

"Come on," said Hannah. "Hurry it up. Kelly's waiting to brief us. Rush assignment."

"All right, all right," Jamie said, moving fast to get things shut down and neatened up. "I just need a second." He signed the last of the forms and dropped them in his out-box. "You know, if we keep losing ships and hardware on these little missions of ours, Commander Kelly is going to start taking them out of our pay."

"Keep quiet about that," said Hannah. "I wouldn't want you to be giving her ideas."

Kelly's voice barked from both their pocket comms. "Agents Wolfson and Mendez. My office. *Now.*"

"Okay, okay," Jamie said, standing up. "Can't she cut us a little slack? I mean, doesn't it count with her at all that we probably saved the human race last week?"

Hannah grinned. "Yeah, we probably did," she said. "But that was *last* week. Let's go."

ABOUT THE AUTHOR

Roger MacBride Allen was born September 26, 1957, in Bridgeport, Connecticut. He is the author of twenty-one science fiction novels, a modest number of short stories, and two nonfiction books.

His wife, Eleanore Fox, is a member of the United States Foreign Service. After a long-distance courtship, they married in 1994, when Eleanore returned from London, England. They were posted to Brasilia, Brazil, from 1995 to 1997, and to Washington, D.C., from 1997 to 2002. Their first son, Matthew Thomas Allen, was born November 12, 1998. In September 2002 they began a three-year posting to Leipzig, Germany, where their second son, James Maury Allen, was born on April 27, 2004. They returned to the Washington area in the summer of 2005, and live in Takoma Park, Maryland.

Learn more about the author at www.rmallen.net, or visit www.bsi-starside.com for the latest on the BSI Starside series.

Don't miss the
next exciting mission!

BSISTARSIDE

Coming in 2008